CROWN OF ELLOVA

VOL.1

SIENNA HARLOW

Published by Sienna Harlow on October 29, 2024

Soulbond Romance

1st edition 2024

Ebook ISBN: 979-8-9916830-1-2

Paperback ISBN: 979-8-9916830-0-5

Cover designed and copyright by Maldo Designs

Edited by Ivy L. James, Kelly Andersen, and Sierra Cassidy

CONTENTS

What to Expect

Crown of Ellova is an adult book written for an 18+audience.

- Violence and strong language in a fantasy setting
- Sexual harassment (NOT by the love interest)
- Threats of violence (NOT by the love interest)
- Menstruation
- Parental death (not on page)
- Alcohol consumption
- Brief mention of pregnancy (not the main characters)
- Perceived infidelity (heroine is NOT married but love interest briefly believes she is)
- *Graphic* sexual scenes with enthusiastic consent

On a lighter note, readers will also find...

- Strong female friendships
- Swoon-worthy heroes
- The use of a strawberry in a sexual scene
- Minimal action scenes and very little political intrigue
- Character-driven plots that include many, many chapters filled with romance, angst, pining, and long conversations about feelings

NOTE: This author and the medical community at large strongly advise against putting fruit on or near your sexy, fun parts. This is a work of magical fiction, and no attempt at recreation should be pursued.

Izadella: Iz-ah-dell-ah
Leon: Lee-on
Nueena: New-ee-nah
Tavien: Tay-vee-en
Viella: Vie-elle-ah
Lillian: Lil-ee-an
Jedrick: Jed-ricc
Grayden: Grey-din
Zilas: Z-eye-lis
Lyrora: La-roar-ah
Erenia: Ee-re-nee-uh
Hiliyah: Hi-lee-ah
Alachite: Al-luh-kite
Nyvenah: Nye-ven-nah
Camarra: Ka-marr-ah
Kole: Kohl
Everett: Ever-ret
Cyanna: Sigh-anna
Lazalai: Laz-ah-lie
Vaylin: Vay-lynn
Kaylena: Kay-lee-na
Zarella: Zaa-rell-ah
Alvina: Al-vee-nah
Drystan: Dry-stan

Ellova: Ello-vaa
Adreania: Ah-dree-knee-ah
Versairen: Ver-sair-renn
Kalvorn: Cal-vorn
Venneem Mountains: Ven-nee-m
Altinia Mountains: Al-ti-niaa
Bardhana: Bard-ha-na
Lavencia: La-ven-sia
Elbasan Sea: El-bass-ce-nn

Zemra: Zem-rah
Navlue: Nah-vloo
Shyrell: Shai-rell
Lochkiss: Lock-kiss
Vedesdron: Ve-dez-d-ron
Ellovians: Ell-oh-vee-ans

<u>*The High Court of Ellova*</u>
The high fae court
Guardian: Nyvenah, Realm Keeper
Court Color: Purple Capital City: Lavencia
Governs, guides, and oversees all six courts to ensure the safety, wellbeing, and happiness of all Ellovians.
<u>**The Gem Court**</u>
The fae court of artisans
Guardian: Lazalai, Artistry Keeper
Court Color: Yellow Capital City: Quartzridge
Artist, jewelers, perfumers, beaders, leatherworkers, metalwork, painters, potters, carpenters, and sculptors.
<u>**The Ink Court**</u>
The fae court of knowledge
Guardian: Reyna, Scroll Keeper
Court Color: Black Capital City: Bardhana Library
Educators, scholars, healers, scribes, writers, poets, and temple workers.
<u>**Court of Shells**</u>
The fae court of the sea
Guardian: Koray, Wave Keeper
Court Color: Blue Capital City: Meridia Cove
Sea crews, dock workers, fishers, shipowners, sea sentinels, and water guards.
<u>**Court of Green**</u>
The fae court of provisions
Guardian: Camarra, Seed Keeper
Court Color: Green Capital City: Calantha Meadows
Farm keepers, livestock guardians, garden tenders, bakers, chefs, cloudkeepers, and provisions providers.
<u>**Court of Swords**</u>
The fae court of protection
Guardian: Bria, Sword Keeper
Court Color: Red Capital City: Larissian Fortress
Guards, sentinels, blacksmiths, and sentries.

<u>*Glossary*</u>

Fae: A magical being with powerful qualities. They look similar to mortals but tend to be taller with pointed ears. All fae possess magic and have a lifespan of a thousand years or more, but with enough magic, they can be nearly immortal. How powerful a fae is depends on their bloodline; magic is passed down through birth. Iron will burn to the touch and can kill them.

Mortal: Mortals (also known as humans) possess no magic and have a lifespan of 70–80 years.

Dewling: In Ellova, fae children are considered dewlings until they are 50 years old. A 50-year-old fae would look the same age as a 25-year-old mortal.

Mates: The term used for a committed fae relationship and meant to be a permanent union. A title of respect and claiming, couples must be together for decades before one can state someone is their mate. Matehood doesn't always last forever because fae lives are long, but it's mourned when it ends.

Zemras: Soulbonded mates. This merging of souls exists solely to connect two fae souls on an eternally deeper level for paramount emotional, spiritual, and physical intimacy. Zemras share pain, pleasure, and power.

Zemra Stones: A magic crystal set that can only be found in the Zemra Temple. The physical symbol of their soulbonded matehood, each crystal holds a small part of each other's magic. Through the connection they share with the stones, they can sense each other's emotions and needs. The Zemra magic connects them by soul, magic, and mind.

Zemra Temple: A hidden temple. Veiled in secrecy, but if mates truly believe that they are Zemras, they will attempt to enter the temple. Zemra guides are required to find the temple, and acceptance into the temple is followed by a Zemra ceremony with friends and family. It has age restrictions and laws regarding a visit. Consequences are harsh for even attempting to find it without the blessings of the faes' court Guardians. Unsanctioned visits to the temple resulting in a bond are punished with complete separation for one month.

Zemra Temple Rejection: A fae only has one chance to attempt to access the temple with their mate. If their mate is not their Zemra, the temple will not allow them to enter. A temple rejection is mourned and typically the couple's relationship will end due to the emotional pain of choosing wrong and never being able to find their Zemra.

The Divide: The invisible barrier between the mortal and fae realms, where the Merawood Forest ends and the kingdom of Adreania begins. The Divide was created to stop the stolen fae crown from siphoning all the magic in Ellova.

Merawood Forest: An enchanted forest that protects Ellova. The forest stands between Ellova in the east and the mortal kingdoms to the west.

The Verge: Protective enchantments between the Merawood Forest and Ellova. A vow of no harm to Ellova is needed to enter. It is the only way it will allow anyone to pass through. If a traveler is lying, the Verge rejects their oath.

Realm Keeper: Governs, guides, and oversees all six courts to ensure the safety, well-being, and happiness of all Ellovians. Only the fae with the most power will be accepted by the Ellovian throne.

Lochkiss: If eaten, it grants the ability to speak and hear underwater. It has a gummy texture but no taste. The lochkiss turns water into air. It also gives the ability to control buoyancy. The effects last for weeks.

An enervation death: A fae death by a broken heart. If a fae experiences great heartache like the loss of a child, mate, or Zemra, it can result in shattered magic, which leads to death. Bright white scars spread out over the skin as their magic slowly seeps out of them. There is no healing or recovering from a broken heart. How long the death takes depends on age and how much magic they were born with.

Anafaea flower: Fae flora. The anafaea flower has not been seen in centuries. In the fae history scrolls, it is said it could cure almost anything and force even death to yield to it.

Anafaea Elixir: A healing mixture containing water blutells, anafaea flowers, the salvidah herb, and healing water from the Airvell River as well as other ingredients.

Shyrell: Resting during bloodline bleeding. Magic is passed down through birth. Since any fae bleeding typically displays the possibility of fertility to carry on the magical bloodline, it is a sacred tradition for the heads of the family to bring tea and sweets. The suffering one experiences to one day continue the family's magic is met with gratitude. Bleeding is treated with great care and rest. Fae bloodline bleeding happens once a year.

Jewelsmith: A fae who can manipulate metals.

Sharing shades: A type of claiming through fashion at public events. One way to show others that the couple is spoken for. Formalwear is cut from the same fabrics so the couple will match.

<u>Family Bloodlines</u>

<u>*Zarella Verrelia's Family Line*</u>
Great-Great-Grandmother: **Zarella, First Realm Keeper of Ellova**
Great-Grandmother: **Lilac**
Grandmother: **Rose**
Mother: **Nyvenah** - *Mated* - Father: **Alachite**
Daughter: **Nueena** - *Zemra*: **Tavien Delwinn**

<u>*Alvina Vanabalt's Family Line*</u>
Great-Great-Grandmother: **Alvina Vanabalt, the Forger**
Great-Grandmother: **Naewyn**
Grandmother: **Voelle**
Mother: **Ambra** - Father: **Nolan Aranelle**
Daughter: **Izadella Aranelle**

<u>*Fae Queen Inara's Family Line*</u>
Mother: **Inara, queen of the mortal realm**
Married - **Drystan Fasaile**
Daughter: **Arelia**

<u>*The Broken Royal Mortal Line*</u>
Brother to the King: **Kalden Fasaile**
Past King: **Drystan Fasaile** - *Married* - **Unknown Queen**

Current King of Adreania: **King Jedrick**
4 deceased sons
Son: **Prince Grayden** - *Married* - Daughter-in-Law: **Princess Erenia**
Daughter: **Princess Lyrora**

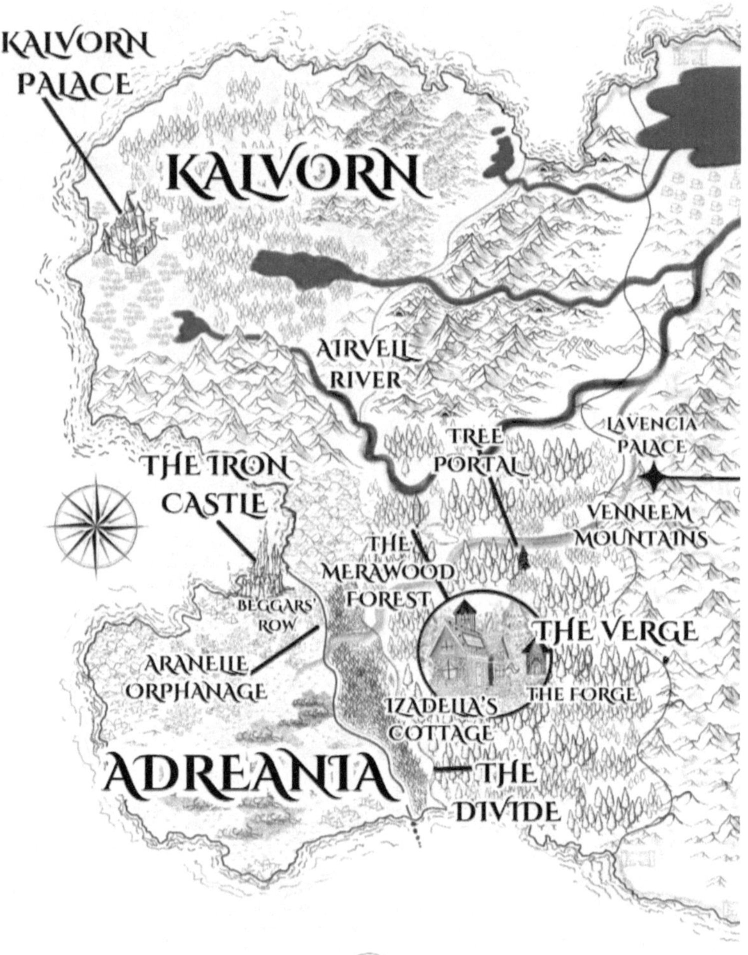
THE MORTAL REALM
KALVORN PALACE
KALVORN
AIRVELL RIVER
LAVENCIA PALACE
THE IRON CASTLE
TREE PORTAL
VENNEEM MOUNTAINS
THE MERAWOOD FOREST
BEGGARS' ROW
THE VERGE
ARANELLE ORPHANAGE
IZADELLA'S COTTAGE
THE FORGE
ADREANIA
THE DIVIDE
ELBASAN SEA

THE FAE REALM

MAP ICONS

THE INK COURT

THE GEM COURT

COURT OF SHELLS

AIRVELL SPRING

AIRVELL LAKE

THE GEM COURT

ALTINIA MOUNTAINS

QUARTZRIDGE

ELLOVA

THE INK COURT

BARDHANA LIBRARY

LAVENCIA

THE HIGH COURT OF ELLOVA

MERIDIA COVE

COURT OF SWORDS

LARISSIAN FORTRESS

CALANTHA MEADOWS

COURT OF SHELLS

COURT OF GREEN

COURT OF GREEN

COURT OF SWORDS

NUEENA'S SHIP

To Nicole, for a magical friendship.

CHAPTER 1

I'm a fool to have fallen for a mortal, no matter how kind and handsome the healer is.

Even if everything I've ever told him has been nothing more than half-truths and gilded lies, excitement still twists in my chest at the thought of seeing him tonight. All we have is one night a month, and though our interactions are tragically brief, I long for each stolen, precious moment.

I try to shove the thoughts of the healer, Leon, out of my head and focus on the crown in my hand, the cerulean light of the forge's flames glinting off it.

When sunlight streams through the stained-glass windows of my workshop, as it does now, it paints the room with iridescent reds and yellows, pinks, and blues. The glimmering glass above me creates an image of flames with bursting stars coming out of the fire.

"Della? That wouldn't be for me, would it?" Nueena asks playfully from behind me.

"Fuck!" I fumble with the crown as I launch to my feet, whipping it behind my back and turning to block it from her view. The desk rattles with the movement, and the freshly cut flowers from my garden sway in their crystal vase. A few loose pearls I was working with roll away into the gem-encrusted forge beside my desk, but most fall to the floor with soft clinks, scattering around the stone floor.

Nueena's tall, graceful form leans against the aged doorframe of my workshop, a mischievous smile on her full lips and a shining gold tiara on her head, nestled in her tight curls. Her black hair cascades down her back, and the last of the sunlight behind her haloes her deep brown skin and brings out its golden undertones.

Once I've recovered from her sudden appearance, I grin back at her. "Of course not. It's for someone who knows to *knock* when I'm working on my court's coronation gift to them. Turn around, please. I have a few more details to add before I leave."

She laughs and turns slowly. "Fine. I won't peek."

I whirl back around, not needing to check if she keeps her word as I stick my hand into the lit forge to retrieve the dispersed pearls. It is not the warmth of the enchanted forge's pale blue flames that I feel first; it's the magic's welcoming pulse. Never burning me, the soft flickering of the fire is a tender caress on my skin.

The gift of my jewelsmith's magic.

I pick the crown back up. Gold flowers surround the large amethyst nestled in the center. Vines and leaves are carved around the side of the headpiece with small diamonds scattered like stars around the golden flora.

"You're here early. Is everything all right?" I turn her crown over in my hands, examining what may be missing from her headpiece. Every aspect needs to be perfect.

She sighs deeply. "All is well. I just couldn't have another conversation with my parents on the endless trivial details of my coronation."

Nueena is about to be crowned the youngest Realm Keeper in all of Ellova's history. She will rule over the Ellovian High Court and the five faerie courts of Ellova. Her magic will soon surpass her mother's, the current Realm Keeper, and it will be time for Nueena to take her place.

The entire realm has been preparing for Nueena's anticipated coronation for months. I've been assisting her when I can, but the tasks are endless. She's preparing to host the five court Guardians and their courtiers at the Ellovian Palace. Weeks of ceremonies, festivities, and revelry that I have been looking forward to for decades. All to celebrate Nueena in the way she truly deserves, leading up to her actual crowning day.

"What was today's detail?" I ask.

"My evening ended with a whole discussion about which plates we should use for breakfast with the Guardians. Breakfast plates! Can you think of anything more inconsequential?"

I rifle through the bowls of gemstones, precious metals, and loose jewelry that are strewn about my desk, searching for some gold to melt. "Which one did you like best?"

"I picked some lovely yellow ones but was told that might appear I was playing favorites for the Gem Court, so I had Tavien choose for me, and he distracted them while I snuck out. If they can't have my opinion, my Zemra's will have to do." There is a smile in her voice at the mention of her love.

Her Zemra.

Her soulbonded mate.

Ancient fae magic weaves their souls together for eternity, forging a powerful and irrevocable connection between Nueena and Tavien. They share a love I cannot even dare to dream about.

A Zemra's soulbond is out of reach for half-mortals like me.

I chuckle, grab a few spare coins, and return to her crown. As soon as I hold them, magic flows through me, drawn to the gold, which melts into a puddle within my cupped palm. The warm metal gleams, the last wilting piece fully submerged. I imagine the shape I want and command my magic to flow into the metal, and it shifts into its new floral form. Fluid petals rise until the transformation fades and a gold rose sits solidly in my hand.

My charcoal sketches of the crown are spread on my work desk, and I compare the golden flower with my artwork, pleased with how it has turned out.

I agonized over the final design and details to create the perfect crown for Nueena. Spent months in the artisan markets hand-selecting each flawless gemstone. My masterpiece will be presented to her by my court's Guardian at the Gem Court's crowning ceremony as part of a grand display of loyalty to her and the High Ellovian Court.

Holding the heavy crown in one hand and the newly formed rose in the other, I place the golden flower gently onto the surface near the purple gemstone that adorns its center. At my touch, the underside of the flower welds to the metal, adding to the other gilded floral elements. The magic within me is quick to create, sending vibrations through my fingertips, eager to mold and to make.

"Your crown is almost complete," I tell Nueena over my shoulder.

"Really?" Elation in her words. "I know I should love all the crown makers' gifts equally, but I already know your court's will be my favorite."

Our backs are still to each other, so she misses my triumphant smile.

I touch six evenly spaced spots surrounding the large amethyst with my finger. With my touch, a hollow dip forms in the gold, and I place an emerald in each crevice. Happy with the placement, I lightly tap each gemstone and the gold shimmers, moving like a wave around the emerald to secure it in place. I trace my finger around each stone and swirl etched into the crown; the liquid gold follows my finger's path and creates new whorls and grooves in the glittering metal.

Perfect.

On the inside of her crown, in tiny cursive letters, I write my initials into the gold with my fingertip, signaling its completion. *IA.* Izadella Aranelle.

I wrap the crown in silks and place it on a stuffed pillow in a small, bejeweled golden travel chest. With one touch, the lock fuses together.

"You can turn around now. Your gift is hidden away."

I gently place her crown on the floor under my desk next to Farren's fluffy bed, currently empty of the small black fox, before I grab my dagger off my workstation.

The forge's low flames wink off the golden weapon. Engraved on the blade's handle is Farren's little face. I gather up the dark fabric of my travel skirt to expose the top of my thigh and place one heeled boot on the work stool. Leather cords are sewn together to make a holder deserving of the beautiful weapon. Attaching the bronze buckles together, I strap the dagger to my right leg. The leather pulls tight on my skin, leaving an impression on my ample thigh.

The gown I've chosen to wear tonight is a deep emerald green, almost the exact shade of Leon's eyes, embroidered with gold thread in delicate swirls and leaves going up the curves of my thick waist. The neckline of my gown is jewel-encrusted and glimmers in the blue light. A streak of gold dust on my eyelids highlights my brown eyes.

One of the swords my father forged leans against the wall, and it is the last thing I grab.

"Is all your jewelry packed up for tonight?" Nueena asks. It's not safe for her to join me on my journey to the mortal realm, but she always keeps me company as far as she can. Unlike the dark clothing I must wear as part of my disguise into the mortal realm, she wears a fine riding gown of lilac.

Her Zemra necklace dangles around her neck; the small shard of amethyst is dull since Tavien's twin crystal is parted from it. As part of their soulbond, the stones hold a small piece of each other's magic.

Every full moon brings the familiar swirl of elation at seeing Leon, spending just a few moments with him, despite the fear of getting discovered. "Everything is ready to be sold at that wretched King's Bazaar." I take a step closer to her. "You know I appreciate you coming with me through the Merawood forest, but we may need to consider your safety more now that we're so close to your coronation. This has to be the last night you come with me. It may no longer be safe for you—"

Nueena waves her hand dismissively to cut me off. I know before I can even ask her to stay behind that she will refuse. "You've never come close to getting caught sneaking into Adreania in the decades you've been bringing provisions to the mortals." Her golden-brown eyes are tender, her smile reassuring, before she reaches up and affectionately flicks my nose. "Calm your worried heart, Del."

My attempt to swat her hand away is thwarted when she grabs mine in midair, pulling me out of the small stone workshop that houses my forge and into the yard of my cottage.

The evening sun pours through the tall trees that surround my home, its fading light flickering off the surface of the small lake and painting my dearest friend of over a century in a gentle, warm glow. Frogs splash in the cool waters, and flowers grow in patches, filling the space between the trees and around the pond, giving the crisp air a kiss of floral sweetness.

"Besides," she adds over her shoulder, "if we don't go, how would you see that handsome healer you are so *very* fond of?" She winks at me and my heart beats faster at the mention of Leon.

In a few hours I'll be in his presence. Just the thought of him spreads small flutters under my corset, my mouth going dry.

He is not *mine* of course, not really.

How could there be a future for us? Anyone in service to the mortal King Jedrick Fasaile lives a life fully devoted to him and the stolen fae crown he wears. Still, Leon claims my thoughts as I fall asleep each night.

I gently pull my hand from Nueena's, my thick golden cuffs clinking together as I attempt to convince her one last time. "The Divide between the mortal and fae realms can still be dangerous and I'm not the one being crowned Realm Keeper in a few weeks. The entire Kingdom of Ellova needs you to be safe! Tavien needs you safe; *I* need you safe." It's hopeless to argue with her, but it must be said. I'm sure she heard the same *be safe* speech from her Zemra before he helped sneak her out of the palace.

She ignores me and makes sweet humming noises to her horse, Citrine. "Della worries too much, doesn't she?"

I roll my eyes. Onyx, my horse, steps closer to me, dragging the wooden cart attached to him, and I give him an affectionate pat.

The large cart Nueena brought from the palace kitchens is filled with provisions for my mortal cousin, Cyanna, and the sweet children she cares for at her orphanage in the mortal realm. They are the reason I have left the protection of the fae realm every full moon for the past decade.

She is the last of my father's bloodline, too precious to me to abandon.

Lining the bottom of the cart are jars filled with purple rice, dried beans, and finely ground brown flour, with sacks of potatoes and grains resting atop them. The delicious-smelling chocolate rolls are wrapped in small blue handkerchiefs and nestled alongside cooking oils, spices, and fresh fruits and vegetables.

"Help me hide my ears?" I reach into my pocket and pull out two short gold chains. She moves to stand behind me, gathering up half of my hip-length, reddish-golden curls. While I am only half-mortal, my fae ears would give me away.

At the sharp tips of my ears are piercings adorned with small, thick hoops. I clip each chain to the hoops and pull the ends of the chains together behind my head. My jewelsmith magic fires up within me and the tips of my fingers heat, the metal obeying my desire to fuse the pieces. With the two chains forged together, it pulls my fae ears flat against the side of my scalp, hiding them completely. Nueena lets down my hair and it falls over my honeyed, golden skin.

From the front, I look fully mortal.

"Ready to go?" I ask her. Our horses, Citrine, named after her golden eyes, and Onyx, wait patiently for us. They nibble on the small pink flowers that grow around the tallest tree in this forest, their coats dark as night. I slip my foot into the silver stirrup and mount my horse, fanning out my skirts to avoid wrinkles. The large leather satchel tied to Onyx's saddle is brimming with the jewelry I've packed to be sold tonight at the King's Bazaar.

The sky fades into a dusky purple. Together, we make our way deeper into the Merawood Forest—the woods that protect the fae realm of Ellova and separate it from the mortal kingdom of Adreania.

Iron Realm.

Above us, a harmony of unfurling petals welcomes the future ruler of Ellova. The bright flowers that cover the ground all turn to face Nueena as sunflowers do to the sun, the forest life blooming in her presence to acknowledge her power. Any branches in our way are pulled back by unseen magic, and buds grow beneath her horse, living a beautiful, brief existence before the soil reclaims them as if they were never there once she passes. Only their saccharine scent lingers. Fireflies follow lazily behind us as lush stalks of hydrangeas rise gracefully from the dirt with the last hint of sunlight illuminating our path.

Ancient trees of the Merawood Forest are undisturbed by mortals and fae alike. The mortals on the other side of the Divide do not know Ellova still exists, and the fae have had no interest in venturing near the forest since the war.

A war the fae lost, and so they were never seen again by mortal eyes. Over the past few thousand years, we have become a myth to the mortals. With all the magic gone from their realm, and our existence hidden behind glamour and protective wards, we are nothing more than bedtime stories for small children.

We ride alongside a dreary, dry riverbed. Nueena frowns down at the smooth rocks.

Thousands of years ago it held the healing waters from Airvell River, the river of magic that the fae allowed to flow through the Merawood Forest and into the mortal realm. Now, it's nothing but an empty reminder that the fae gave the mortals healing and prosperity during the brief union of realms. That there was once peace before the mortals' betrayal.

A betrayal that Adreania is still being punished for.

We are only alone for a few moments before I hear a rustling in the trees above us. My heart leaps with joy at the ball of dark fur and bright blue eyes that peer down.

Farren, my beloved pet fox, sits waiting for us. His pointed nose tips up, smelling the air before he scampers to the lowest branch. He lets me pull him into my lap, careful of his sharp nails as he sticks his nose under my hand for attention, and I scratch his ears while we ride.

"When will you be back at the palace?" Nueena asks. "We still have some planning to do for the coronation ball. Perhaps the Gem Court has someone you would wish to take?" Nueena keeps her head straight, but her eyes slide to me in question. "Might be nice to have someone to dance with that evening."

My gaze is drawn up to the new stars that have joined the evening sky. "My court has plenty of worthy dance partners. Ellova has no shortage of males to entertain myself with, plenty of them happy to keep my bed warm too, but—" Any relationship built during my half-mortal life would end in heartbreak for the fae male who chose to be with me, condemning him to grieve for a lifetime far, far longer than mine. My words come out numbly. "—it simply isn't worth the risk. And Leon is…"

"The one you actually want to be with," she adds quietly, nodding with understanding. She's heard about Leon every full moon since I first met him two years ago tonight.

I force a laugh, the sound bitter on my lips. "Not that allowing myself to get attached to a mortal is a brilliant idea, either." Any relationship with a mortal like Leon was impossible. Where would we even go to be together?

Mortals are forbidden in Ellova.

I could not live in the mortal realm, where I would succumb to death without the magic to keep me alive and delay my aging. He couldn't reside in Ellova, where the magic drives mortals to madness.

It never stops my wishful thoughts, though.

Sharp black spires peek out from above the treetops. The Iron Castle of Adreania. Somewhere in that desolate castle, Leon is probably preparing for tonight.

I wonder if he's thinking of me too, or if the sensation of falling when I think of him is a blissful torture only I endure.

"What type of commission did Leon have you make this month?" Nueena's tone is light, calling me back from my dark thoughts.

"A sapphire tiara for Princess Lyrora."

"With how horrible of a king her father is on top of the horror of having Prince Grayden as a brother, she deserves a closet full of them," Nueena says with a scowl.

Farren hops down to chase the small, plump red mushrooms popping up from the ground. He lets out a frustrated huff when the fungus disappears before he gives up to chase mossy spirals winding up the thick trunks.

We ride in silence as more stars slowly appear, twinkling above us as we come to the Divide. Nueena is off her horse in a flash. New flowers burst around her feet the moment she touches the ground. She releases the dagger at her belt and bends down to slice the stems, gathering up the newly formed bouquet to press her nose into the petals. Nueena inhales as she rises to her full height and places them in the cart.

She returns the dagger I made for her hundredth birthday to her belt; the handle shaped like twisting leaves. "Ready?" she asks, staring up at me. The soft pulse of magic flowing gently follows Nueena; occasionally it swirls around her, moving her hair like a soft breeze.

I dismount from Onyx. "My love, time for you to keep Nueena company."

He looks back up at me, blinking his understanding, and dashes in circles at Nueena's feet.

The stillness grows as we walk towards the invisible barrier of the Divide, where the Merawood Forest ends and the mortal realm begins.

Just as the Verge protects us in the fae realm on the other side of the forest, the Divide holds in the mortal kingdom of Adreania in the south. Kalvorn is north of Ellova; Merawood Forest stands between the two kingdoms, keeping us in Ellova safe. A mountain range keeps Adreania and Kalvorn apart, with Versairen across the sea.

This is the worst part: the Divide is not meant to be crossed by those who hold magic within them as the fae do. It was constructed to keep us safe inside it after the war. No matter how many times I step into the mortal realm, the apprehension for the crossing sits like sharp rocks within me.

Like a scythe has sliced the realms in two, the faint shimmer of the barrier between realms is only visible from the right angle, but the presence of two different worlds is stark at our feet. The demarcation line is visible under the moonlight that illuminates our way. We stand on the soft green grass filled with small white flowers at the edge. Behind us is the rich green forest overflowing with life and magic; we face nothing but dirt and rocks, a blanket of death.

A sea of barren trees with branches more akin to bone than bark stand at odd angles, hanging listlessly. Small piles of snow that have yet to melt are scattered across the ground.

Nueena frowns down at dead grass that has started to creep under the Divide like black veins burning its way into the Merawood Forest. "The darkness is spreading." She kicks at the blackened soil. "The enchantments protecting the forest should not have allowed this. We need to tell my parents that the wards are failing, and the magic is being siphoned again. They should see the corruption for themselves before I secure the wards."

"Could it be something else?" I bend down to run my fingers over the inky veins that branch out from one another like a lightning strike.

"The stolen fae crown King Jedrick wears is the only magical item in the mortal realm, but I can think of no other reason this would be happening again. The wards have stood for thousands of years." Nueena's lip curls in disgust when the wind picks up, carrying the overwhelming smell of damp dirt and rotting wood from the broken branches that litter the forest floor in front of us.

Nueena's expression is solemn as I prepare to cross. Her scent of raspberry, vanilla, and lilies envelops me as we wrap our arms around each other. "Be safe," we say at the same time, sharing a small smile of reassurance when we pull apart.

I try one last time for her to return to the safety of the palace. "You don't need to wait for me. I'll be fine."

She scrunches up her nose and shakes her head. "Someone needs to know where you are and when you return." She pulls a blanket from her satchel and lays it over the bed of flowers at her feet.

"We will be right here." She sits, and Farren moves to follow me, but she gathers him up in her arms.

I nod, giving Farren one last chin scratch, and pull Onyx into the mortal realm.

CHAPTER 2

I step over the Divide and barely manage to stay upright, taking a shallow breath of the suddenly freezing air.

A cold sweat breaks out over me as I am drained of the magic that has coursed through my veins since birth; it dissolves within me, the sensation almost painful. My breathing is heavy as my fae essence vanishes temporarily.

Without that warmth in my veins, my body feels achingly empty.

My gasping breaths join the howling winds that greet me, and I lean on Onyx for support. Shivering, I grasp the soft fabric of my winter cloak, pulling it tighter around my body. The forest's icy grip digs into me; winter eternally resides here.

I roll my neck from side to side, trying to adjust to the familiar hollow feeling, and turn back to Nueena. She holds a struggling Farren, who whines in her arms, his blue eyes locked on me.

"I'm all right," I say to them and give a final wave.

Tucked inside the cart is a corked bottle. The cool liquid reaches my lips as I drink the sweet water greedily. Healing magic lingers in the crystal-clear waters of the Airvell Spring in Ellova, and a rush of energy returns to me, warming me from the inside.

I ride Onyx alongside the dusty riverbed. With no foliage on the ground, Onyx has nothing to distract him, so he continues at a lazy pace, seemingly unbothered by the change in scenery.

Slowly, the kingdom of Adreania's enormous black ironstone wall appears in the distance, standing nearly fifty feet tall. It wraps around the mortal kingdom of Adreania, once desperate to keep out any fae with its hideous iron fortress, but now mortals are more like prisoners.

The massive wall is an obsidian monument of hate.

Onyx and I ride to the densest part of the dying forest, where I let him rest for the night. My nails drag across Onyx's shining black coat; I scratch behind his ears and run my fingers down the side of his face. He twists his head to bump the side of my body playfully as I breathe in the ever-present scent of sweet hay on his mane and whisper, "Stay here."

In the distance, a few apathetic guards walk at an idle pace atop the wall, with nothing to do and no one to watch for. To their knowledge, the decrepit forest outside has been empty for centuries.

The only official opening is at the main gate on the other side of the kingdom, facing the Elbasan Sea. My secret entrance is concealed in plain sight between two thick trees that stand ten feet apart. At the base of each tree is a long wool cover, glued with dirt and brown leaves that hide the large wooden door. I slowly haul up the creaking door to reveal a tunnel just big enough for two with a sharp ramp. Once I am inside, I tug two levers; one closes the door, and one maneuvers the covers back into place.

The hidden tunnel, only known to my family, was built by my father and his brothers over a hundred and thirty years ago. The brothers built it to save their sister, who was exiled to the Merawood Forest for a crime she didn't commit. Later, it was the only way for my father to visit my mother and me at the cottage.

I run my fingers over the worn wood as I pass, a memorial to a mortal man who loved a fae woman and their half-fae child until the very end.

My fae eyesight helps me to navigate the cart easily in the dark that leads me to my cousin's back door. I hold my breath, unable to avoid the frigid water that drips on me while passing under the wall.

Leon wanders into my thoughts. Seeing him for only a few moments each month has never been enough time.

Ever since I stupidly fell for him the minute he walked up to me in that crowded ballroom two years ago, it was clear that knowing him was going to be as much of a blessing as it would be a curse. Leon is a wonderful man whom I will never be allowed to know in anything more than lingering glances and a few stolen moments.

Guilt pulls at me for every lie.

From my false name of Arra that I introduced myself as all those years ago, to my home, to my life, everything I have told him was part of a crafted false identity, a cloak of someone else I must wear to be here, no matter how briefly.

My journey is swift, and I silently send up a prayer of gratitude to the goddess when the faint light that frames the barn's entrance finally comes into view.

The door is made of iron, as nearly everything in Adreania is. Iron is the fae's only weakness, burning to the touch. It's never bothered me in the way it would a full fae, though. It's unpleasant but not the fiery burn most fae would experience. I take after my father in that way, but I still slip on my leather gloves.

I pause at Cyanna's door, listening for any sounds on the other side. I remove the sword my father made long ago that was kept hidden in the cart. My knock is as light as possible before taking a defensive stance with my blade pointed at the door. The likelihood that guards are awaiting me is low. Not a soul besides Cyanna knows this door even exists, but I take no chances, no matter how many uneventful nights I have stood here.

A small window slides open at the top of the door and a pair of large eyes stare back, widening with joy. The panel shuts, and the sound of locks opening echoes through the tunnel before the door is thrown open, a rush of the stable's warmth and the rich animal smell welcomes me out of the cold.

My cousin, who has been waiting for my arrival, ushers me inside with a wide, youthful smile. Her hair falls haphazardly from her bun, framing her round face, cheeks dusted with freckles, and what appears to be a streak of flour. Although I am a hundred and thirty-three, I pass for a mortal in my early thirties here, and she could be my older sister, having just turned forty. We share the same dark chocolate eyes and light copper curls.

"Hello, hello!" She practically sings her honeyed welcome as she helps to heave the cart the rest of the way in. "How was your journey?"

Cyanna takes time to tightly embrace me before we leave the stables and step into the covered yard at the back of her home, where her poor excuse for a garden sits. Near a small pond, wilted buds of cabbage are peppered among sagging potato stems.

Long ago, Adreania flourished under the Fae Queen Inara's rule. The harvests were bountiful, and the realm was in peace, but the once-prosperous farming communities are now nothing but dusty fields of broken hopes.

As the stolen fae crown King Jedrick wears absorbs more of the energy of Adreania, food is harder to grow, the harvest producing a little less each year. Unnoticed for centuries, the ground has been slowly dying, and animals and mortals alike are feeling the effects of the uncontrollable crown.

The crumbling stone walkway leads into a large kitchen, connecting the stables and a back door of the orphanage. A few teenagers who call this place home look up when we appear. They rush to help us unpack the cart on the doorstep in a flurry of greetings and helpful hands. The kitchen slowly fills with everything I have brought. The young residents of the Aranelle Orphanage put things in their places while a few items are left out for breakfast tomorrow. Leaving the young chefs to their kitchen duties, we head into the main living space.

A young blond boy passes me a sleeping infant so he can help the others unpack. I hum a fae lullaby while gently rocking the orphanage's newest charge. The sleeping babe has an angry purple rash peeking out under her collar, a sign the little one has caught faerie's revenge, the sickness that has plagued the mortal realm for centuries.

"How are the children?" I ask Cyanna.

"They get sicker with every passing month." An aching sadness returns to her soft face. "I wish you would take us with you to Ellova."

My heart breaks at that. "The madness the magic brings would be so much worse if I took you back to the fae realm." Oh, how I wish I could bring her and all the children to the safety of Ellova. I place the sleeping child in an empty crib.

It was probably foolish of me to tell her what I am, but she once begged me to bring her and the children back to my home. I couldn't let her think I would choose to leave her behind while I returned to my lush life at the palace, never wanting for anything, while she suffered.

Two dozen children of all ages are spaced out around the room, playing on the floor, sleeping, or reading. A constant noise of coughs followed by rough, rattling breaths. It takes a moment for the first child to notice me, but when she does, a joyous noise rings in the air. They wrap themselves tightly around my skirts. More follow along, demanding my attention and chatting merrily if they have the strength. Olive, who is around six, pulls a squirming frog from her pocket and gives it to me.

I laugh at the creature in my hand. "Oh, well, thank you!"

She smiles brightly, delighted at my response to her wriggling gift.

"What should we name it?"

She all but yells, "Hopkins!"

"I told you to leave the frogs in the pond!" Cyanna cries before she carefully takes the frazzled frog from me and returns it to the small girl. "My dear, please, leave the frogs alone."

My laughter is cut short by the clock that chimes somewhere in the distance, signaling my departure. Cyanna wipes her hands on her black dress before turning back to me with a mischievous smile. "Have fun tonight, *Arra*. Say hello to that healer of yours!"

My smile spreads with the heat on my cheeks at the mention of Leon. "He's not my anything." Just through her windows is the outline of the Iron Castle. Its ominous form in the distance towers over Adreania.

Cyanna's humor fades to furrowed eyebrows and pinched lips when she sees where my gaze is. "You need to leave. You don't have much time to set up for the bazaar. Be safe!"

I tighten the satchel around my shoulders. "I will."

She walks with me to the front door and checks to ensure the alley is empty. No one must ever know we are related; if I am discovered to be fae, it could be disastrous for her. When she trusts it is safe, we share a quick embrace, and she locks the door behind me. The scraping sound of metal on metal sends me off. Four separate locks slide into place. The bitter winds swirl around me as I step onto the dirt road.

Every minute that passes brings me closer to Leon, and that pushes me forward.

The full moon illuminates the small homes that line the streets, made of any leftover materials that could be found during construction. Flickering candles light their rooms, the broken windows poorly patched up attempting to keep out the night air. Crying infants and coughing can be heard from inside the homes.

The pathway leads out of Beggars' Row. The closer I get to the castle, the decrepit shacks masquerading as homes slowly give way to large, well-built houses with dark green ivy crawling up their walls, and wooden fences wrapped around their large yards. I glance through one window. An overworked maid runs after two chubby children while their mother reads by a roaring fire, her husband beside her. He will not be forced to rise with the sun like the workers whose labor paid for that fine house.

Finally, I reach King's Trove, where the shops dedicated to opulence and the greed of the wealthy line the streets. My shop sign, *Arra's Gems – Royal Jeweler*, swings in the wind.

I cut through an alley that takes me to the back door of my empty little shop and the small living quarters attached. My key slides into the lock and I enter a dark room. The only sound is the echoing clank of swords hitting thigh armor as the Trove's nightly guards patrol past my front door.

The shop was owned by my father's family and sat empty for years until I started to sell my jewelry out of it to earn coins for Cyanna. I had tried to sell anonymously, away from the castle's prying eyes, but ten years ago, King Jedrick heard that my jewelry shop was favored among the wealthy, and Arra, the mortal woman I pretended to be, was quickly given the title of Adreania's Royal Jeweler. My attendance has been required for each full moon bazaar ever since.

Those who seek my jewelry know it can now only be bought at the King's Bazaar.

I light a few candles, the fire-illuminated table set for an imaginary family. A few small jewelry tools lie around to give the illusion I work here if the shop is ever broken into, but the stone walls of the shop's living space are just as bare as the cabinets in the kitchen, the drawers in the bedroom empty of all evidence of life.

Three letters have been shoved under the door. The cream-colored envelopes bear just the name "Arra" in bold letters and the royal wax seal. My heart skips in my chest and I tear at the fine paper.

Lady Arra,

I hope this letter finds you and your family well. I would like to discuss something with you.

Is there a day that would suit you best? I can come by your shop, whenever you have a moment. Send a response with any kingdom guard and it will be delivered to me.

Yours,

Healer Leon

The first letter is dated almost a month ago, the day after we spoke at the last bazaar. I can think of nothing we would need to discuss, but my heart skips a few beats. Leon must think I have ignored him this whole time. The two other letters request the same meeting.

Our only communication for the last two years has been in fleeting moments when he commissions yet another jewelry piece, ensuring more opportunities for us to speak month after month.

The thought of seeing him here, away from that castle, just the two of us, is thrilling. Alone. Free of demanding courtiers and watchful guards. For a few minutes, I could pretend he lives in this house with me. A warm sensation spreads within me, and I savor it before pocketing the letters.

The sooner I can leave, the sooner Leon can explain what his letters are about.

CHAPTER 3

I take out the wooden boxes from my satchel. Once the jewelry I brought has been arranged, I look for more hidden in the shop. Pulling up the floorboards in the small kitchen, I find rings and necklaces that did not sell last full moon. In the dirt of a flowerpot, three necklaces are wrapped in cloth. Dozens of thin gold and silver bands jostle merrily as I remove them from the teapot on the stove.

All the trays slide into a small golden chest before being covered with purple velvet, ready to be taken to the Iron Castle. Stamped on each side is the crest of Adreania—a black circle that symbolizes the stolen fae crown with a sword going through it.

A familiar knock rattles the front door. I pull it open before Theodore has finished knocking. He manages to pull back his hand before it connects with my face, a smile on his. I gave him a pendant for his wife once and have long since earned his crooked smiles. His shaggy gray hair flops forward as he bows at the waist. His companion guard mirrors the respect offered.

"Hello, Theodore, Clive, how are you?" I ask, knowing a response will not be given. All the guards are instructed to remain silent while in the presence of courtiers or royal merchants. The Adreania royals have laws that have deemed the guards "lesser" than me, so I should not attempt to make small talk with either of them.

Clive turns his wide back to me, head on a swivel, looking for danger. Four more castle guards are on horseback, holding long iron spears next to the carriage.

I could have easily walked to the castle, but I have no illusions that the escort is for myself. The guards are here to ensure my jewelry is safe so the court can continue to drape themselves in gems and gold while they attend lavish parties on the backs of those who struggle most in the kingdom. My jewelry chest is loaded into the wide royal carriage with me, and we travel the main road leading to the castle.

Theodore and Clive sit in front of me on a wooden bench; outside we are surrounded by the other four guards on horseback, who ride around us in a diamond shape of protection.

Through the windows of the other passing carriages, curious eyes peer out at my carriage, shop owners returning from the coast or other merchants who found some sort of affluence in this broken city but not enough to be invited to the bazaar.

From deep within my bag, I retrieve a blue silk sash with the Adreania crest sewn on the front that marks me as one of the king's personal craftswomen and courtiers.

It's an honor not given to many and clashes with the green and gold of my gown. I despise that King Jedrick is even aware of my existence. As much as I long for a few moments with Leon, being in the presence of the stolen fae crown on Jedrick's head boils my blood.

Every few feet we pass tall, hollow glass pillars. Long branches of slow-burning wood are bright within them, smoke swirling into the night sky while the flames light the way up the entrance of the castle. Thousands of candles hang from the windows, illuminating the tall spikes of its peaks, shadows moving behind them. The guards at the gate part to let us through the dark archway into the gardens. Theodore and Clive carry my chest and continue with me through the servants' entrance leading to the courtyard.

The courtiers who have arrived stand near the gardens that

circle the open area while they sip wine out of golden goblets. When they hear the soft jingle of the jewelry chest, they clear a path, greedy eyes tracking its route to the castle's main entrance. The large wooden and iron doors remain closed for guests, but they open for me to stride in with my guards and shut again with a loud click.

A gust of wind follows us into the wide hall leading to the ballroom. We trail behind the somber servants carrying heavy trays, who walk swiftly past the gray walls lined with paintings of the royal family of Adreania.

The largest painting is that of King Jedrick's ancestor, King Drystan. Drystan is painted alone, the fae crown atop his head, his hands gloved in leather. The first king of Adreania and the first crown thief. No paintings remain of Queen Inara, the wife he killed, whose fae blood stained his hands until his death. Whichever artist had been tasked to bring his likeness to canvas captured the coldness in his gray eyes. The same gray eyes King Jedrick and Prince Grayden share.

When my great-great-grandmother forged the crown it glowed, alive with magic, delicate leaves overlapping each other to form the golden circlet, the ancient fae language carved into it.

A crown that cannot be removed until death.

Even if there were a painting of Queen Inara, it would have been a lie. King Drystan made his beautiful wife wear a glamour ring to hide her fae appearance. Much like every full moon, the urge to set Drystan's painting on fire persists in me as we walk to my vendor table.

Music plays softly around us; the ballroom warmed with the massive fireplaces on each side. On one side of the ballroom are the dais and stage, where the royal family will sit and the evening performances are held. Plenty of room for dancing and merriment in the middle, and on the other side the merchants and vendors are setting up.

Twenty other artisans and royal merchants from the King's Trove stand next to their luxury items, setting up for the rush of sales the beginning of the night brings. My small table stands nearest the main doors, the farthest corner from the dais. I am the last of the artisans to arrive and quickly lay out everything I have to sell. The most important piece I have with me is the delicate sapphire tiara I made for Princess Lyrora. She and I have rarely spoken for an extended period of time, but I know she will look divine in it.

A clock on the wall strikes, signaling the start of the King's Bazaar, just as the last of the jewelry is laid out on silk tablecloths. The doors burst open, bringing in the harsh winds and a steady stream of courtiers as they rush to the tables, eager to spend the copious coins they did not earn.

I take a deep breath and wait for Leon.

Excited women approach my table, loudly selecting their favorites. The wealthiest among them arrive wearing no jewelry but stop at my booth first to purchase the best pieces before continuing deeper into the ballroom to show off their new treasures. Well-kept hands grab for ruby rings with tiny diamonds swirling around a stone from the deepest mines in Ellova. Sapphire or emerald earrings atop golden star hooks are snatched up, and delicate necklaces strung with obsidian, garnet, topaz, or blue pearls fished from the Elbasan Sea are fought over before the buyers thanklessly toss me their coin bags. The more advantageous shoppers purchase multiple items.

After an hour or so, my table holds a diminishing supply, all the best pieces sold. I assist the last few women shopping, but my eyes move around the crowd, hoping Leon will appear.

Bells chime, the nobility abruptly halting their dancing to turn towards the dais at the back of the room to await their king, silence settling over the crowd.

Trumpets blast a moment later, signaling the arrival of the Fasaile royal family and with them the only man I've ever cared about. First to appear is Princess Lyrora, youngest of the royal siblings, both living and dead. She sits on her iron-wheeled throne, her head held high. Her handsome guard pushes her up a small ramp and brings her next to her father's empty and extravagant throne.

"The prince has returned!" A delighted voice carries around the room with it an echo of cheers.

I was unaware Prince Grayden had gone anywhere.

The quiet ballroom is once again filled with shouts and well wishes. A woman near me yells, "Welcome home!" as Grayden ascends the dais with his wife, walking slightly in front of her, never offering the Crown Princess Erenia assistance up the stairs or acknowledging her presence.

Princess Erenia wears the same bored expression she always does. Her long, midnight-black hair is twisted in intricate braids around the crown of her head. Her dark lipstick stands out against her pale skin, only highlighting her frozen frown.

In the ten years that I've sold jewelry in this room, I've never seen her smile. Given she's married to Prince Grayden, I imagine she has little here to bring her happiness.

He's lanky with thinning blond hair and a blond beard kept short. Cold gray eyes scanning the crowd do little to disguise his disdain for the evening. He takes his seat on a smaller throne next to his father's on the opposite side of his sister.

He ignores her too.

Flowers rarely grow here but the ones that do are being wasted as they are thrown onto the edge of the dais in preparation for their king.

King Jedrick hobbles in with Leon and my heart speeds up, overwhelmed with his strikingly beautiful features. Leon has an essence about him, something I could never quite put words to, this pull towards him. One night a month has never been enough; I leave here aching for a few more moments from him.

What started as a silly little crush two years ago has bloomed into a connection so intense it leaves me breathless.

My desire for a future with him taunts me, teases me. Pathetic hope and bitter yearning have become a constant shadow while I walk these castle halls.

Just seeing him soothes something deep within me.

Everything I want is trapped in a place I cannot stay, with a mortal I cannot keep.

Leon's attire is basic for his role here, black leather boots over black breeches. Going down his spine is a tightly laced vest showing off his broad shoulders. Half of his hair is tied at the back of his head. The rest brushes his lower neck, a few gray streaks throughout his black hair.

At King Jedrick Fasaile's arrival, the crowd bows immediately. He moves slowly, clutching a golden cane with a large gemstone for a handle as he stumbles to his throne, leaning most of his weight on Leon.

Leon gently helps King Jedrick to sit on the pile of cushions laid on the throne as he takes gasping breaths after such a short walk. The frail Adreanian king coughs loudly, covering his mouth with a white handkerchief, before he leans back into the chair to close his eyes. He was once blond like his children but now his hair is gray like his sallow skin.

My handsome healer glances towards the back of the ballroom where I am and we make brief eye contact before he returns to King Jedrick, the stolen fae crown stuck on his head.

Jedrick wearing it disgusts me, and I cannot stop the curl of my lip at the sight of the dark circlet on his unworthy head. His ancestor, Drystan Fasaile, was the reason for the war between the fae and the mortals, each side fighting for the crown Jedrick now wears. The crown my great-great-grandmother, Alvina, forged for a fae queen whom the mortals betrayed so long ago.

The mortal King Drystan murdered his fae wife, Queen Inara, the dearest friend of my great-great-grandmother, Alvina the Forger, and Nueena's ancestor Zarella, the first Realm Keeper of Ellova.

Concerned murmurs ripple through the crowd.

Two noblewomen drinking wine not far from me turn their heads to each other, lowering their voices. "Poor thing, King Jedrick. He won't last much longer."

"Any day now. Prince Grayden will make such a fine king," the woman near her continues gleefully with adoring eyes at the prince.

"Long live the Fasaile line!" another shouts.

Jedrick coughs violently again, but this time when he pulls the handkerchief away from his face, it is stained with blood. Princess Lyrora leans in to look after her father, gently placing her hand over his arm in comfort.

Leon replaces the king's bloody cloth with a new one, sympathetic eyes on the king.

Prince Grayden stands, not bothering to check on his father. The crowd is quiet and expectant, waiting for their prince to speak. Grayden is dressed in a fine black velvet shirt with a high collar that almost reaches his chin; it is heavily embroidered and falls to the tops of his slender thighs clad in black pants. The cost alone could have fed so many in Adreania, the neglect of his people sewn into every fiber.

"Noblemen," Grayden begins, "I come bearing sorrowful news of the kingdom to the north and Kalvorn's careless disregard for your lives and the lives of your children." Grayden takes a dramatic pause to rile up the crowd. "I met with King Zilas and his poor excuse for a queen! They are as *heartless* as we knew they were. Three days ago, we met in the middle of the Elbasan Sea, and I *pleaded* with King Zilas on behalf of our kingdom. Told him of our suffering, of the sickness, the barren land. How the children of Adreania go to bed hungry, our men have no work, the fields will all be but dust soon." He moves around the dais. "I beseeched him for aid, medicine, food, for access to his libraries to search for a cure for the sickness. He declared he would send ships of food, Kalvorn's best healers, but do you know what he wanted in return?" He half screams the last part.

The crowd shouts incoherently back at him.

Fear slithers like a snake coiling around my chest.

I know he is going to say Inara's crown. How could he not? It was once the most magical item ever created.

It's what Grayden wants, waiting for his father to die to claim it.

The Kalvornian king must know the legends of what that crown could once do, if on the right head, not the poor excuse for a king before me. How dare Grayden withhold something he has no right to claim at the suffering of his own people. A just ruler would have given Kalvorn what they wanted to ensure his kingdom's survival.

A servant passing by gives me an odd look and I soften my features to remove the disgust clearly written on my face.

Grayden's voice is filled with rage, face red as he paces the stage. "HE WANTED THE CROWN!"

My hands start to shake, and I slip them into my pockets.

"We will not be enslaved to the Kalvornian king! He claims all he wants to exchange to end our famine, heal our sick, is the crown. We will not give in! If they will not give us what we need most, then we will take it from them by force!" He lifts his arm in the air as the crowd's cheers start to die. His smile is cruel when he adds, "As if he could wield the power of Drystan's crown! Only men of the powerful Fasaile line can wear its glory!"

Grayden's lies spill so easily over his tongue, or perhaps he truly believes it. If it didn't mean an immediate execution, I would stand on my booth and ask Grayden why Inara, the original wearer, could wear the crown if it could only be worn by Fasaile male heirs when she was neither, but I keep the words to myself. Grayden's lack of knowledge on how the crown actually works is probably the only reason his sister is safe from him.

All four of Grayden's older brothers died mysteriously.

Princess Lyrora stares out at the crowd, appearing bored with her brother's shrieks, and ignores his malice. She should be the ruler of Adreania, not her vile sibling.

The courtiers rapidly speak among one another in hushed tones. They know that any war will impact their leisurely lives; a war will bring with it fewer parties and fewer resources for them to take for themselves. Some are looking at each other, hands over mouths, doubt creeping into their faces at the likelihood Adreania would lose. Only a few shout back at the perceived injustices of Grayden's venomous speech.

Surely to save his people, he could hand over the fae crown that sits upon his father's head.

Kalvorn is a prosperous kingdom, one without poverty and illness. Their king and queen are rumored to be kind and generous rulers. Only a small mountain range separates Adreania and Kalvorn, but they are almost two different worlds.

Jedrick looks down at the floor at his son's words; the once-golden circlet is flush on his head, gray and dull, devoid of the magic it held thousands of years ago when it sat upon Inara's curls when she was crowned queen of the mortal kingdom, the gold illuminated with the type of magic only a fae could harness.

Now the crown is only a symbol of power, of what once was.

Grayden's smile is vicious. "Do not worry, for I have found a way to bring back the magic! When I am king, Adreania will prosper again!"

The crowd goes silent, stunned expressions frozen on their faces.

"Once I restore the fae magic to the crown, we will have everything we need! You have never known such riches!"

Liar.

Such a fucking liar. The fae and their magic are just the subject of children's stories to him.

This is a new low for him and I fight the groan begging to be let loose at his absurd declaration. What he says is impossible. A ridiculous lie to receive support for this ill-fated war over a crown neither man can truly possess.

To promise the return of magic is utter nonsense.

CHAPTER 4

Grayden continues his hate-filled monologue. "Our spies have returned, and we now know Kalvorn is readying their armies to come for the crown. They are preparing to invade since we will not bow down to them and give them what they want. We will fight! So tonight, we celebrate, and tomorrow we plan. Once I am king, a new era will rise!"

He raises an arm in the direction of his wife. "Not only will we have magic, but we will also have your crown princess's mother kingdom of Versairen on our side. We will not lose!"

Princess Erenia's hands and jaw are so tightly clenched that I worry for the princess's teeth. Part of her marriage treaty to Grayden dictates if one kingdom goes to war, the other must fight with them. Cheers follow him as he walks past her without a glance and leaves the dais. The music starts up again.

The thought of him becoming king, wearing the stolen fae crown only to pollute the land with his cruelty, fills me with sorrow. The people of Adreania are already going hungrier every season. King Jedrick may not be evil like his son, but the soil struggles to produce a harvest. With each passing year, less and less grows. The land is dying, and its citizens suffer. Grayden will only bring more pain. He has no way to control magic; even if he could access all the magic that has been stored in the crown for thousands of years, it would destroy him.

That amount of magic would drive him to madness in mere moments. His mortal form is incapable of surviving it. He should be grateful the magic is dormant for now, needing a fae to release it, or his line would have ended long ago.

Passed down from power-hungry father to power-hungry son, the crown sits like a stone on Jedrick's head.

A woman with light brown hair who has been gossiping in the crowd close to my booth starts to gasp and cough, sending nearby courtiers into a frenzy to get away from her in fear she may have the sickness. A few others start to panic, looking around for the sound. I watch in horror as two guards go up to the coughing woman, ready to remove her.

"I just choked on my wine!" she gasps. "I'm not ill. Please don't. I'm fine, truly!" Her terrified expression with the deep wheeze to her words makes the statement unconvincing.

The guards don't seem to care whether it is an illness or an accident. Not stopping, they move towards her to force her outside.

I look frantically to the dais for Leon. What will the guards do to a woman they suspect to be ill? Relief rushes into my chest at the sight of him jumping off the dais to the ballroom floor, abandoning his king's side.

He takes long, powerful strides in our direction as guards roughly grab the woman. "Wait. WAIT!" The command in Leon's voice stops my heart for a moment.

Leon comes up behind the guards, who pause, looking at their king for clarification if the healer is to be obeyed. Jedrick gives a slow nod, and they fall back a few steps.

"Let me check on her," Leon demands. In a soft tone just for her, he says, "This way, please." He offers a gentle, reassuring smile.

She tearfully nods, quick to follow him further into the room, closer to me. I suspect she would have called the other women friends before this moment, but now they make a show of getting out of her way. Off to the side near my booth, Leon asks for permission to examine her, and she agrees, tears streaming down her face.

"Can you lift your hair for me and turn around?" He gives her a comforting look.

She does what he says, holding her breath, hands shaking. He checks her unblemished neck, which lacks the stark purple rash that would be spreading down the length of her spine were she afflicted.

"Nothing to worry about, no discoloration that I can see," he says loudly to the small crowd. To her, he adds, "All is well. Return to the celebration. Perhaps avoid the wine."

Her face crumples with relief before she throws her arms around him. Even whispers of the sickness would have caused her to lose her social standing. Undeserved jealousy burns bright within me for a moment, but the coughing woman quickly pulls away from him, her eyes wide, perhaps realizing hugging the king's personal healer is not something done in polite society.

"Thank you," she says with a hiccup, pink coloring her cheeks.

The feeling of jealousy fades slightly when his eyes slide to me for a moment before he gives her a kind, uncomfortable smile and sends her on her way back to her friends. No matter how improper it was to show gratitude in that way, she still got to embrace him, even if it was just for a moment.

To wrap her arms around him and feel his warmth.

A touch denied to me.

Following the departure of the royal siblings, actors line up on the dais that has been transformed into a stage, musicians readying their instruments, signaling that the performance of the night is about to begin. King Jedrick sits off to one side to watch the performance. A retelling of his life to honor him.

Again.

Every bazaar, some play portrays the lives of past kings or Jedrick's exaggerated greatness. It's all a pile of fresh horseshit.

Servants move the massive candelabras towards the front to light the stage while the crowd moves closer for a better view. One of the actors in a large fake crown has fallen to the ground in a theatrical death, and the actor portraying a young Jedrick grabs the crown off the dead king, quickly placing it on himself while the crowd cheers.

Leon faces the stage, watching the play for a moment, before slowly turning towards me, and our eyes lock.

The cool metal of a ruby necklace I'm holding slips through my fingers and hits the table, knocking over an earring display, much to the alarm of the noblewoman who is purchasing it. She has my apologies but not my attention as she drops a bag of coins on the table and leaves with a huff.

So quickly I almost miss it, he nods in the direction of the nearly empty wine table, and he casually heads that way.

I lay the purple velvet cloth over the last of the bright jewelry, and a few guards step closer to my abandoned table. The women still shopping make irritated noises but move on to other vendors.

Drawn to him as I am every night I slip into this miserable kingdom, I approach the wine table. It would be wise to wait for him to come to my booth, but the temptation for just a few extra moments with him is too alluring.

Leon stands with his back to me, inspecting the wine bottles laid out on decorative blue fabrics for the courtiers and a few of the chosen vendors.

He doesn't turn, only stands taller when he senses my presence. His head tilts slightly in my direction, and alarmingly green eyes gaze at me as he places an empty crystal wine glass in front of me.

Without breaking our eye contact, he sips on his freshly poured wine. I beam at him and for a moment we just stare, lost in each other.

A few lords and ladies linger at the end table to boast of their profits from the month while drinking bottles of the finest wine imported from Versairen, the kingdom across the Elbasan Sea, paying no attention to the handsome healer and me.

My heart beats wildly, and I am suddenly thankful mortals have such poor hearing. "Healer Leon, how are you this evening?" I keep my voice low, only for him.

"Quite well, Lady Arra. The bazaar is always my favorite night of the month." He smiles briefly, and it steals a little of the breath out of me. "It brings the best company." His deep voice melts some of the fear I carry as I tempt fate with my deceptions here.

"That it does," I whisper. The sensation of fluttering luna moths erupts in my stomach in his presence.

I pretend to look at the bottles, but Leon leans across me, his outstretched arm ever so slightly sliding up against my own. His shy smile widens at my sharp intake of breath. He selects a cerulean crystal bottle and pours the pale wine into my waiting glass.

"I asked the wine master this morning. It is the driest they have available tonight," he says, handing it to me.

We can only speak for a handful of minutes each month like this. I've told him so little about myself, and what I have revealed has been twisted with lies upon lies. The only truth he knows about me is my love for dry alcohol. As I take a small sip, the bitter taste of the oaked wine coats my mouth. Every month, for the first moments in his presence, I can barely focus on anything but him. I'm struck by his features; he's handsome in a way that brings a flutter to my stomach at having all of his attention. His sharp jaw is dusted with a shadow that has not seen a blade in days. His nose is prominent and perfectly straight.

The bustling ball around me seems to fade when he looks at me, every bit of my longing reflected back at me in those emerald eyes, pulling me in.

"Thank you." I keep my voice low. The delicious tartness of the wine draws me to drink more. He is quiet for a moment, watching the glass rise to my lips again. He clears his throat before speaking, finally looking up at me.

How can one mortal be this fucking handsome? A gray streak of hair slides from the leather strap that holds it back and falls in front of his eye. I envision my fingers gliding through his hair, roughly pulling him towards me. To sink into him with a burning kiss and peel off the layers he wears as he hastily removes my gown.

"I received your letters after I returned from my travels. I apologize for the delay in response." I hope he can hear the sincerity in my voice.

He nods; his answering smile is charitable. "I was beginning to believe you were avoiding me."

"No! Never!" His smile widens at how quickly the words rush out of me. "I've done some traveling this month, sourcing new materials. My journeys often take me away from my shop."

"May I call upon you tonight, then, after the bazaar? Or even tomorrow? I can return to your shop. I wish to speak with you privately." His easy grin has vanished, his eyebrows slightly together with an intensity he has never shown me before. "It is of the utmost importance."

I should tell him that would not be possible, as nothing he needed to tell me could possibly matter to me. Outside of Beggars' Row, Adreania holds no mortal affairs I need to trouble myself with, but looking at him, I find I cannot resist a few extra minutes with him tonight.

"I'm heading to the coast tomorrow. I hope to be back by the next bazaar, though my business there may keep me away for longer." Disappointment fills me from having to lie to him once again. I need to give him a reason not to show up again at my empty shop in the future or ask questions why the shop sits empty all month, devoid of the family I pretend to have.

His face pulls down slightly and I do not miss how his shoulders slump just a fraction, so I quickly add, "But you may escort me when I return to my shop tonight. I will not have much time, and the walk may be cold, but I'll be glad of your company this evening."

Relief paints his face. Small creases appear at the corners of his eyes when his smile returns. "Thank you."

"Of course."

His happiness at my words fades slightly and is replaced with a slight frown. "H-how is your family?"

The family crafted from my endless falsehoods. The one I spun when first arriving here to make my lie convincing after Grayden showed a bit too much interest in me years ago. The husband, a blacksmith, and three little ones, or was it two?

"They are fine." What did I say their names were again? *Oh, Ello-*

va's grave, don't ask more questions about them. One was definitely named Arra, so that was easy.

"Are your children happy to be out of school?"

"Oh, yes, very much so." I'm not entirely sure about school schedules, what mortal children learn, or why they wouldn't be continuing their education.

In Ellova, fae children are called dewlings; their education is integrated into everyday life if they are not at the Ink Court for lessons. Before I can change the topic, he leans in closer, a deep frown on the lips I've spent years fantasizing about. After glancing in both directions to see if anyone is paying us any attention, I lean forward, offering him my ear.

"It is best if you are getting away. Jedrick is terribly ill." His voice is a whisper, lips ever so slightly brushing my ear, sending a shiver down my back.

"I will light some candles for his recovery." Overwhelmed with his presence, I all but moan the lie.

"Lady Arra, if something happens and I am unable to meet you tonight, promise me something. When you get word that Jedrick has died, do not return here ever again, for any reason, no matter what anyone from the castle says or threatens. Do you understand me?"

The last part is not a suggestion, and his words pour ice into my veins, extinguishing any lust that was kindling within me.

"It will no longer be safe for anyone but especially for you once Jedrick passes. I overheard Grayden speaking about you." His eyes darken with anger. "You have caught his vile attention, so you must leave. No matter what you hear, when the royal death trumpets blast, stay far away from here." He pauses before adding in a tender voice, "I will be able to sleep knowing you are safe at the coast. If possible, stay away as long as you can."

Before I can ask why I suddenly have Grayden's attention again after years of being ignored by the prince, a group of drunk courtiers surround the table, attempting to take a few bottles of wine we stand in front of. Questions swirl, but whatever he is saying this for, it is not safe to discuss it here, so I only nod.

He lightly touches my elbow, guiding me away from the boisterous lords, but it's too late.

"Healer!" One of them lifts their glass, spilling some of his red wine down his arm, staining his sleeve. "Come give cheers to the king's health! The jewelry maker can join us!"

Under his breath, Leon mutters, "Fuck." He leans down to my ear. "Head back to your table and I will be there shortly."

Without a glance back, I stride towards my table to find a woman standing in front of it. It's not until I pass the vendors closest to me that I hear their whispers.

Princess.

CHAPTER 5

$\mathcal{P}$rincess Erenia's tall frame is covered in a loose gown in such a dark shade of blue it appears black so far away from the dais's lights. I rush behind my table and curtsy before I peel away the fabric, revealing my jewelry to her.

"Welcome to my table, Princess Erenia."

She is strikingly gorgeous, with sharp cheekbones and full lips painted with a dark berry stain. Her eyes are a startling, icy blue, and her gaze seems to pierce right through me. I fiddle with my hair, smoothing it down as if she could see my hidden ears. Her face holds no warmth, neither in her expression nor in the color on her cheeks. Leon has, over the years, commissioned jewelry for her birthdays or holidays, but she and I have never spoken. My only glimpses of her have been while she sat, miserable, on that dais next to her husband.

She looks me up and down with an assessing eye, though it's not a glance of judgment. "You must be Arra, the darling jewelry maker."

For a moment, I think she says it to mock me, but her small smile holds no cruelty. "I am a jewelry maker, but I do not claim to be darling."

She finally looks down at the gold before her and selects my smallest piece, a small ring with a delicate blue stone in the center. She smiles a little wider at that as she tries it on. "Oh, I think Leon would wholeheartedly disagree with you."

"I don't—"

She holds up her hand. The small ring is a perfect fit. "I'll take it." She hands over a large coin bag, with enough coins to buy twenty rings.

"This is far too much." Her generosity is too kind, but when I try to only take what the ring is worth out of the bag, she covers my hand with hers.

"Take it. Use it." Erenia pushes my hand towards me. "I wish you the best." She turns suddenly and strides away, leaving me with more questions. Why would she wish me the best?

A twinge of trepidation at her last words lingers. Does she know what Leon is about to tell me?

As if my thoughts have called to him, he appears again, staying near the edges of the crowd.

I should attempt to look busy or feign interest in the play in case someone is watching, but I cannot pretend to look away at his approach. He gives me a warm smile as he approaches me. "Hello again." His voice is low and smoother than honey when he stands before me.

"Hello." That damn pull towards him starts low within me, and I am lost in his presence.

"Lady Arra?"

Having stopped listening to whatever he was saying, I have no elegant response for him. "Huh?"

He chuckles and leans over, hands on the table, and I immediately mirror his motion. Our noses are too close together but neither of us moves just yet. I savor this nearness even if we cannot touch. His sweetly healing scent drifts over to me. Strawberry oil and the herbs he uses with his medicines.

"My birthday gift for the princess?" he asks. "She has been most helpful with my research."

Comprehending his question this time, I nod. "Yes, of course. It was finished to your specifications."

Two women walk up to the table, breaking our stolen moment. I lean back, already missing his closeness, and pull out the delicate tiara from the square piece of black silk it was wrapped in. When I hand it to him, our fingers brush and we both watch the movement, neither of us moving away. It is flawlessly designed, perfectly balanced, and exactly as he described to me.

Anyone in this crowded ballroom would agree it is stunning, but I want his words. Just for a moment to pretend his thoughts of the crown are what he thinks of me.

"Does it meet your expectations?" I wait impatiently for him to inspect my work, but he doesn't even glance down at it.

"It's truly beautiful." His eyes don't leave mine when he says it, his words so genuine in their softness. "Like all of your work."

The moths fluttering in my stomach turn into heat, warmth lighting me up from the inside at his praise. "Thank you." Drawn in again, we return to leaning towards each other to talk.

"You are incredibly talented, Lady Arra," he adds.

I laugh. "Many years of dedication and hard work. Talent is just the gilded first step." My fae ability to manipulate metal certainly helps, but better to change the subject. "How is your research into finding a cure going?"

"Not well, I'm afraid, but I did make an interesting discovery in the royal library recently. In a hidden tome, I found illustrations of what I believe may be the lost anafaea flower. The fae flora may no longer exist, but if that flower were found, I believe it would be a key ingredient to any cure, but that would mean traveling beyond the iron wall. I've sent word across the Elbasan Sea to Versairen to see if their libraries are home to any similar research. King Jedrick has promised a year's salary and a generous land transfer to anyone who can connect us with what I need to cure the sickness."

My eyebrows draw together. Why would the Adreanian library hold any information on the anafaea flower or the fae? Inara, the first queen of the mortal realm, was the only fae to ever live here. "Do you think some knowledge exists in Versairen for a cure?"

He looks disheartened by the thought. "No, I do not, and unfortunately, Grayden believes Kalvorn might already have a cure since they are not affected by this sickness. When I was studying medicine in Versairen's capital, healers would theorize about the fae flower, but none was ever found. I hope to find it one day but I'm afraid the anafaea might be truly lost to us."

That flower would cure the sickness that has fallen on the mortals. In the fae history scrolls it is said it could cure almost anything, force even death to yield to it, but that was a long time ago.

If it did bloom again, it would not do so in this heartless land, but if he wishes to try and find it, I will not crush his hope to save those who need him. "I am sorry." It is a risk, but I gently place my hand on his arm in a sympathetic touch. "If the flower is out there, I am sure you will find it."

He pauses for a moment, looking down at my hand, before he places his own on top of mine, the caress electrifying, and squeezes it before stepping back. "Fortunately, I have had much success with willow bark as a pain reliever, so my experiments are not for nothing." His expression turns wistful. "It would have been nice for you to have joined me for an afternoon to see my research. Jedrick rests after lunch, and I often try to sneak away for a few hours, midday, for my own pursuits."

I nod. "I would enjoy that."

His smile widens at my response as we stare at each other.

It's nearly painful, this longing for moments I can never have. It would have been lovely to listen to his voice while he shared his passions. To see his life's work, to know him just a little better than our current situation allows. To bask in his company for an afternoon together outside of this crowded ballroom.

He opens his mouth to speak again but closes it, leaning back to stand up straight. We both turn at the sound of the king coughing off to the side where he watches the horribly boring play of his life. "I have to return to King Jedrick now." Annoyance flashes across Leon's face, but it is gone just as fast. He rewraps the sapphire tiara and gives me a short bow, holding it to his chest.

"Since you will be gone, I will not request my monthly commission from you, but I hope—" He pauses for a moment, collecting his thoughts, and my heart aches to tell him the truth. "Never mind. Enjoy your evening, my lady. I will return at the end of the night to be your escort."

Neither of us moves. My heart skips a beat, hoping for one more word from him. He opens his mouth to say something else, but nothing comes out. He shakes his head ever so slightly before he downs the rest of his wine. He gives me a tight smile, but it doesn't reach his eyes, and he walks away towards the dais, where Jedrick's coughing worsens, not allowing me a moment to respond.

I plant my feet firmly, resisting the urge to race after him, demanding answers.

~

The night goes on slowly and leaves me with plenty of time to think of Leon, as I've sold most of the jewelry. The last few women shopping at my booth do not seem to notice my annoyance as I wait for this night to end. Noble men and women amble from vendor to vendor or dance in the center of the room when the play draws to a close for its final act. The courtiers' servants walk swiftly to carriages with their lords' and ladies' needless items.

With every purchase, I place a handful of the gold coins into many smaller leather bags. The satchel at my feet grows until it is almost full of the little bundles, each with just enough gold coins to support a family for a month.

I arrange the last few pieces I have left before I can leave this heartless place, so focused on my task I do not hear Princess Lyrora approach.

"Hello, Lady Arra, how are you this evening?"

Unlike in Ellova, the royals here expect formal greetings, and I drop myself into a deep curtsy.

The young royal looks up at me, pleased, from her wheeled throne pushed by her guard, her bored lady's maid standing just to her right. The previous week brought on Lyrora's twenty-second birthday, an age the royal healers who delivered her feared she wouldn't reach. She and I met years ago when I was commissioned by her father to add gold-painted flowers and decorative gems on her iron throne, and she has been kind to me in every meeting since.

She turns to her lady's maid. "That will be all for now, thank you." Her voice is kind when she speaks, a stark contrast to her brother's hateful tone. The maid bows and heads off, still close to the wall but out of earshot.

Her guard, however, does not move, his hand resting on the sword by his hip. He looks only a few years older than Lyrora. Dark auburn hair slicked back, he keeps an eye on the crowd, glaring at those who venture too near.

"Did Healer Leon already visit you?" Her friendly question takes me off guard.

"Er, yes, yes, he did. You've just missed him. I believe he went to check on your father."

She nods politely. "I will see him later, I'm sure."

I look down at the nearly barren table. "Your Highness, you have my apologies. Most of the jewelry has been sold. Had I known you wished to purchase some jewelry, I would have reserved my favorite pieces for you."

"That is all right. Leon has bought me some beautiful pieces from you." She reaches up to touch the pink diamond necklace he asked me to create for her two summers ago.

For the last two years, he has commissioned something from me each month. The night we met, he requested a locket, and the month following, a variety of cufflinks. Soon it became pastel gemstone bracelets for Lyrora and obsidian necklaces with black diamonds for Erenia. Occasionally, a few simple earrings for some other healers aiding him. Half of his requests seem to be made up on the spot and he is never very interested in the final results I present to him, so I suspect he simply wants to ensure my family's survival and support my fraudulent business.

Guilt and gratitude twist my already anxious stomach, knowing he spends so much of his coin every month so we can share a few heartbeats together.

"I am grateful to have more than enough," Lyrora continues. "I wanted to thank you for all the pieces you have created. I've enjoyed wearing them and I know they have brought Leon much joy commissioning them." She looks at me with a strange sorrow. "He speaks so highly of you. I wish you two could have been better..." She pauses before settling on "friends."

I'm at a loss for words. Why is she saying this and what does one say to that? Did Leon tell her of his plans to warn me from returning?

If Arra, a mortal jewelry maker who lives in Adreania, were real, what friendship could there have been between Leon and me? What paths would cross for a married artisan and a man who gave up his life to aid the crown, forsaking anything that distracts him from the care of his king? Has he ever seen a day of rest from Jedrick's constant needs in the years he's worked in that castle? Those who have sworn blood oaths to the crown live a life of endless service, a higher calling to the throne. One of the many, many reasons we would never have a life together. We could never be anything more than passing acquaintances in a dull life here.

I can only give her an honest answer. "That would have been nice." It would have been wonderful if we could have truly been friends.

Before our conversation can continue, her guard leans down, whispering in her ear.

Her shoulders stiffen, knuckles turning white on her throne's handles. Fear spreads over her features, her lips pressed together in distress. "I'm so sorry, Lady Arra. I must go, but I wish you well with everything. May the gods keep you safe." Before she can say more, she is swiftly pushed away by her guard, and suddenly I realize why.

Prince Grayden moves slowly through the crowd. The guests part, bowing along the way.

He stops only to speak with a few men, ignoring the women at their side, but he keeps his eyes on me before he walks over to my table. I pretend to fix a piece of jewelry for a woman trying on my last bracelet. When he is in front of me, I grind my teeth and bow deeply, holding my dress out to my sides. "Welcome back. How were your travels, Your Highness?"

"Fine, Lady Arra, just fine." He looks down his nose at me, wearing a smile that doesn't reach his eyes.

"I have some jewelry that would look lovely on your wife. Perhaps a sapphire necklace? To match her eyes?"

He ignores my reference to Princess Erenia. "I offer you a treat." He snaps his fingers, and a servant steps forward with a tray. Grayden holds out a plate of cut-up fruit, a rarity since nothing sweet grows here anymore, and my blood turns to ice, the breath trapped in my lungs.

The fruit on a silver platter is the size of my fist with a bright green rind and light purple pulp inside. It has been cut up wrong; it's meant to be peeled, but this was hastily cut down the sides, the juice spilling out over the dark purple twisted seed. I stare at him, and he looks pleased with my silence.

It's a rare and sacred fae food that only grows when a new heir is to be crowned and comes from the navlue tree. But that tree only grows in one place…

The throne room in Ellova.

Dread crashes into my chest.

Who in Ellova has betrayed us?

Panic rises so swiftly within me that the world sways. Does he know about Ellova?

If he does, who told him?

"Try it." His words are not a suggestion. "It is the sweetest thing you will ever taste. Like pure sugar."

The crushing panic makes it difficult to speak but I manage to choke out, "No, no thank you." This fruit is only to be eaten at Nueena's coronation. It's forbidden for anyone to touch it before the sacred ceremony crowning her Realm Keeper.

His eyes narrow on me. "What?"

I try to shrink my body, shoulders tightening in on myself. "I couldn't possibly. Such a fine gift should be yours and yours alone, Your Highness." I force myself to sound only slightly curious. "Wherever did you acquire such a fruit?"

"A new friend gave it to me." His tone is harsh, final. "And now I want you to try it." He holds out a slice impatiently for me to take.

He has moved behind my table now, my back going completely straight with fear as he nears me. Thunderous applause erupts in the room from something on the stage. Bright lights draw the crowd towards the front, their backs to us, leaving us in the unbearably hot darkness.

"Are you denying me?" His voice is full of venom this time, any false kindness fading at my refusal.

He attempts to stand in front of me, taking a step closer. I mirror him by taking a large step back, only for him to come forward again. There is no logical reason any true Adreanian would refuse his request; most would be thrilled at this opportunity to taste an exotic fruit. Even when he's denied something so small, his rage is boiling to the surface.

"You honor me, but—"

Taking the last two desperate steps I have behind me, I find myself with my back pressed against the stone wall as he closes the gap I was desperate to keep between us. Grayden presses his lips to my ear, and I stop breathing. Screaming for help would be futile. The iron guards watching will do nothing, the courtiers wouldn't care, and my fellow vendors wouldn't dare intervene.

His hand wraps around my throat, not squeezing but holding me in place. "You and I are going to be quite good friends soon."

"Oh, I don't think so." It slips out of me, and I curse myself as his hand tightens. My nails dig into the wall behind me to stop me from reaching for my dagger. It would be so easy to slide it from its holder and plunge it into his neck, but that would be to sign my own death warrant.

"My father ordered me to leave you alone, but he's on his way to greet death, and then I'll be king." He sharply taps my cheek, the sting emphasizing his words. "You want to be a good Royal Jeweler, don't you? I'll be needing you to make me some exceptionally special items for my impending coronation. The moment you hear the word of the old man's death, you are to report directly to the castle, alone. If you don't, I will have your little shop burned to the ground with your children in it. Do you understand?"

He says it with a smile as if it's something he bestows on me, an offer I should be grateful for instead of the vile threat that it is. Nausea rolls over me at his monstrous words that reek of liquor and smoke.

I try to nod but he grabs my hair and pulls my head back, exposing my throat, before he leans in closer to my ear.

"Good, and maybe one day after I'm king, I'll fuck you on that throne." And he shoves a piece of the navlue fruit into my mouth, rind and all. I nearly choke on it, and the overpowering sweetness makes me gag.

He releases me, leaving me coughing and rubbing my neck, gasping for breath as he walks into the crowd of courtiers, who still watch the play.

Fuck him and fuck this wretched kingdom.

I grab my satchel and throw the remaining pieces into it without care. It's heavy with the weight of the gold coins from the night's profit. As I turn to race out of the hall, the cheers of the crowd at the performers' final bow follow me out.

CHAPTER 6

Desperation to escape claws at me.

Off to one side of the bazaar is a stone archway leading to a long hallway only servants use. My heeled boots echo in my attempt to flee Grayden and his atrocious words. They are sinking into my skin and my stomach turns; my skin feels contaminated where I can still feel his foul grasp.

What if Grayden is following me? Frantically seeking somewhere to hide, I almost stumble, turning around, but the hallway is empty. If he decides to find me again, he will know I came through the castle's main entrance and will search for me there. I need to slip out through one of the back exits that wrap around to the front. It's impossible for me to leave now; I cannot risk anyone following me to Cyanna's door.

I race down the hall, music fading with every step. I almost miss the sliver of the night sky behind thick blue curtains not completely pulled together. I pause for a moment before taking a few steps back.

A balcony garden.

I push the heavy curtains out of my way and pull on the iron door handles. Thankfully, the large glass doors open with ease, letting in the icy air, and I slip inside.

Dark clouds promise a storm-filled night. The scents of roses and rain linger in the air, and I take deep, desperate breaths. Closing the door, I press my back to the chilled wall for a moment.

Unlike the chaos of Nueena's garden, this one is meticulously organized. Wooden planter boxes with a variety of plants and flowers take up most of the space. Vibrant pink flowers with glossy green points on their stems peek out next to a small patch of buds with dark leaves with red veins. Vedesdron, a powerful poison, and in the other corner, a small rose bush is nestled with geraniums.

Eyes closed, I try to relax, but at the sound of heavy steps approaching, fear fills me again, the knot in my stomach twisting painfully.

If Grayden has followed me and we are without an audience, I can fight him off; of that I am sure. The low likelihood of me getting safely out of Adreania if I fight him makes me hesitate. His guards are always close by, willing to turn a blind eye to his cruelty. My hand hovers over my leg, ready to pull out the dagger strapped to my thigh. The steps grow louder and stop at the door. The handle slowly turns as my fear digs into me.

Please don't be Grayden.

A tall shadow stretches across the balcony, the light from the hallway hiding their face.

"Arra?" Leon shuts the door behind him, head moving back and forth, searching for me. He holds a large lantern that illuminates the garden. The relief of Leon finding me has a soft noise escaping my lips, and he whips around to find me half-hidden in shadows.

Our eyes meet, and he takes broad steps. Suddenly, he's in front of me. I tilt my head up to see him, and my heart sputters. Leon frantically roams my face and arms looking for any sign of harm, brows pushed together above a heartbreaking frown.

"Arra, are you hurt? I saw you run from him." His tone is sharp with an undercurrent of unmistakable rage but softened with the genuine concern in his eyes. I get a little lost in them; they are a green hue, so rare in color. I wish a gemstone like it existed so I could make a necklace out of it and wear it forever. Not unlike an emerald but darker green, with more depth to the color.

Slowly nodding, I continue to stare at his handsome face. My throat tightens and my eyes start to water. This is surely the last time I will ever see him. I can never come back here, to this castle, to this kingdom.

I try to memorize his features as if I were a painter instead of a jewelsmith and could capture him forever in oiled paints and stretched canvas.

As tears form in my eyes, he takes a step closer to me and caresses my cheek, replacing Grayden's sting. He uses his thumb to wipe the lone tear making its way down my flushed face and I lean into his touch, closing my eyes. The ring he wears is cold against my skin. If I don't leave soon, I'm afraid of what I'll say to keep him close.

The secrets I'm willing to whisper, the truth on the tip of my tongue.

"Arra, did he do anything? Did he put his hands on you?"

Without the word *Lady*, it feels intimate to hear my false name on his lips. Even if it's not my real name, I love the way he says it. He says it like a prayer, and not for the first time, I wish he knew to call me Izadella.

To hear that would truly be a gift.

It would mean I could be honest with him, that he could truly know me.

When I do not respond immediately, he must fear the worst because concern leaves his face and is replaced wholly with anger at the implication the silence brings.

I shake my head and lie. "Just vulgar words and vague…threats." Threats, promises of whatever nightmare he has imagined for the cursed day he becomes king. "Did he follow me?"

He shakes his head. "No, the royal family retreated to their chambers for the evening. Arra, you need to leave," he whispers, his breath on my skin with the closeness of a lover.

I only have a moment to say goodbye, but the words are caught in my throat. How do I tell a man I barely know what light he brought to my life in such a short time? That even if my words were a falsehood, my feelings for him were forever true?

"Arra, do you hear me?" he asks over the sound of the rain that starts to fall, pelting the glass that surrounds us. I nod dreamily without comprehending his words. His hand still touching my face is all I can think about. I want his hands touching me everywhere. He closes the space between us, our chests touching now. What was he saying, for me to leave?

"I'll go home," I whisper, looking at his lips.

"No, not home anymore. Home isn't safe."

That pulls me out of my thoughts. I almost laugh at the thought of the Ellovian palace not being safe, but if Grayden has the coronation fruit, we might all be in danger. Then I realize he speaks of the false life I've built here in Adreania, a life built on outright lies and half-truths. The little apartment above an empty jewelry shop that never opened with three children whose names I can never remember.

"Tomorrow after sunset, take your family to the fisherman's cove. There you will find a tavern on the north side with a blue door, the Black Bell. In the darkest corner, find a grumpy fisherman named Oliver. He owns a boat called *Hanolis' Sun*. Give him this."

He removes his hand from my cheek, leaving it so cold it's tempting to grab his palm and put it back. Leon holds out a necklace I recognize. He had commissioned me to make it the night we first met, years ago. An *A* is etched on the oval gold locket. My hand shakes as I take it. The tangled chain is warm from his pocket.

I opened the little door to find a tightly folded note.

He covers it with his palm. "Do not open it yet. Only open it when you meet with him. It's his instructions to take you and your family away from here. You will leave and sail to safety. Grayden will destroy everything when he inherits the crown, and you need to be somewhere safe. Please, let me protect you."

He watches me slip the locket into my pocket before continuing.

"I have a small plot of land waiting. The house is old but has enough room for everyone. The local blacksmiths will help you start over. You will not need to worry about anything; that I can promise. You will be safe. Your...husband—" He stumbles over the word. "—will be given work and your children an education. You can start over somewhere you will be cared for." Pain and desire are etched in every line on his beautiful face.

Safe.

His mix of sweet herbs and tart strawberry burns through me, leaving in its wake a fever of longing, of agony.

My desire to scream that there are no little ones or husband, that this has never been my home. I want to tell him who I really am and beg him on my knees to forgive me for lying for all these years, how desperately the truth begged to be told every time he stood before me.

He's gone to such great lengths to ensure my safety, and it's breaking my soul into shattered pieces of desperation. He stands close to me, but I need him closer, and I can hold back no longer. I wrap my arms around his center and draw him against me, no space left between us, and still, he doesn't feel near enough. His arms are instantly around me, clinging like he never wants to let me go.

I rest my forehead on his broad chest, savoring him.

The last few minutes we have left to share in this lifetime are over and I try to memorize every heartbeat we share chest to chest. Mine is swift like the beat of hummingbird wings, while his mortal one is slow and rhythmic. A bitter reminder that in a few decades he will fade away, but as fae, I will live on for hundreds of years without him. Our brief moments spent together under each full moon will be the only remnant of him.

The last memory he existed at all in my life, a balm to soothe the ache his mortal death will one day bring.

I truly was a fool to fall for this mortal, but I can't bring myself to regret him.

He's never been this close before, always standing across the table from me when he bought my jewelry month after month. I want to get drunk on the smell of him, taste it on his skin. Run my tongue up his throat and…

"Healer Leon!" someone calls in the distance, and his arms tighten around me. The faint press of his lips in my hair breaks something within me and I close my eyes, relishing the touch, desperate to stay with him.

"You need to go, Arra." He whispers it in my ear, leaning down to press a soft, lingering kiss to my cheek. I nod, of course I do, but I still cling to him, not wishing to part from this man. The thought of doing so brings physical pain. He looks down at me with open longing, hunger in his eyes. "I will see you again, all right? Grayden will get what's coming to him. Men like him always do. Trust me." The last part he says through gritted teeth.

"Goodbye, Leon." I press my lips together to keep myself from laying bare my agonized soul and ripping apart the tapestry of lies woven to him in this place.

"Healer Leon?" The guard's voice shakes with uncertainty.

"WHAT?!" Leon bellows at the incoming guards through the door, his arms still around me.

"The…the king," he stammers, voice slightly muffled, "he isn't well."

Leon presses his forehead down to mine and mutters under his breath to me, "Obviously not. He's fucking ancient."

I cannot help but giggle at that.

He yells back to the guards, "I'll be there shortly."

Their footsteps fade away. We spend our final seconds together staring at each other, leaving so much unsaid.

Finally, we pull apart. I move deeper into the balcony shadows, and when Leon is certain I will not be seen, he opens the door but turns back for one last moment with me. "You look beautiful tonight," he says before walking back into the hall.

I take a few deep breaths and attempt to ignore the misery forging itself inside my chest before I walk through the side halls, desperate to leave Adreania and never return to this horrid castle.

The servants' hallway running parallel to the ballroom is crammed with castle staff working into the night. Almost at the end, I see Theodore and Clive, who are standing with a group of bored soldiers. They rise to attention when they see me. I'm too distracted to pay attention, and with the burning in my eyes clouding my vision, I collide with someone. The young woman's metal serving tray loudly meets the floor. Her hands fly to her mouth, eyes wide in horror when she sees my sash.

"I'm so sorry, my lady. I'm so terribly sorry. This is all my fault." She whimpers and now I am not the only one holding back tears.

She drops to the floor, head bent, her cheeks a bright red as she tries to clean up the spilled food. Kneeling to assist her only seems to fluster her more.

"No, no, my lady, let me." She shakes her head furiously, which loosens the twisted bun of the same reddish-gold hair color as mine, a rare shade here. She is shorter than I am, with a leanness to her figure that tells me that in a castle full of food, even the scraps are out of reach. More servants rush to help her, Theodore and Clive close behind. With the small army of servants who have appeared to help clean up, the overwhelming urge to return to Nueena overtakes the desire to offer my unwanted help.

"I wish to depart." Not bothering to wait for Theodore and Clive, I start walking towards the main gates, refusing to be delayed any longer for the carriage to be brought. They chase after me; their armor that has never seen battle clamors as they run to keep up. Once they reach me, they flank either side.

"My lady, the carriage will be brought around as soon as possible," Theodore pleads, breaking the rule not to speak with me. Guilt slips in; if anything happens to me, they will be held responsible.

"No need. I have nothing left to sell and no one would dare rob me. Let's go." They look at each other but follow me for the journey back. The streets are quiet, and finally, I reach the shop. Turning to face them, I give a fake smile. "Thank you for the escort. I bid you a good night." My tone is harsh, hoping it discourages any further conversation.

Clive nods at my dismissal, but Theodore looks concerned and continues to break the rule of not engaging me in conversation.

"Are you sure you are all right?" Theodore whispers.

"Yes, thank you, just tired from the excitement."

They both nod knowingly, looking convinced, and I fight not to roll my eyes at how quickly men assume the weakness of women.

I slam the door shut and turn around. Once the front door is locked, I lean my back against it so I do not collapse. The rush of panic slowly eases, leaving only a desperate need to lie down. My soul aches at leaving Leon. The only solace is the rising bittersweet relief that now I no longer need to live Arra's life but never seeing him again seems like too great a cost.

CHAPTER 7

$\mathcal{M}$y chest tightens and I try not to think of Leon as I change into a plain black dress with a black cloak behind the dressing partition. Stepping out of the green gown, I roll it up and hide the sash within it. The lone jewelry shop candle is gone in a breath, and I race out the back door after ensuring no one has followed me from the castle.

The moonlit walk back is quiet in the midnight hours, allowing me to move swiftly to Beggars' Row. I reach into my satchel and pull out the small bags of coins.

Making my way to the first house, I leave the provision coins on their window. Each bag is grabbed quickly, never there longer than a few seconds. The only sound is the slight echo of my heels and the chorus of whispered *thank yous* that follows me down to each shelter.

Home after home and family after family are given back the courtier's wealth. Halfway down the street, the smallest of the homes leans at an odd angle, its window broken, the icy air slithering in. An elderly woman stares out of it. Our eyes meet and I place two bags near the large, jagged crack in the glass.

"A little extra to repair your window," I say lowly so no others can hear.

Her pale hand, covered in age spots, reaches out for mine. She does not seek more coins, just a soft squeeze to my fingers in silent gratitude. Before I leave, I give her my gloves and cloak.

I'm shivering by the time all the coins have been passed out, save for Cyanna's full bag. Passing her broken fence leading into the desolate yard brings a shred of relief. The moment my knuckles rake against the rotted wood on the last of the three knocks, the signal to declare who I am, the door swings open and Cyanna shoots like an arrow into my arms. She pulls back just enough to look down at me before pulling us together again. "Why are you late?" she demands, her eyes red-rimmed.

"I'm sorry. I got caught up at the castle."

She shuts the door behind us, locking out the cold. Her home is quiet; all of the children are sleeping peacefully, most sprawled out in the living room. I hand her the few pieces of jewelry I have left and the rest of the coins I've saved for her.

"What happened?" Cyanna's caring voice is low as she thrusts a cup into my shaking hands. "Are you all right?"

The broth is rich with herbs, and I inhale the earthy scent before I drink deeply, welcoming its warmth.

"No, but I will be." The answer is honest, and the rest pours out, weariness woven into each word as I tell her everything that has happened. "If Grayden expects to see me again, he is a fool. He can demand the moon fall into the Elbasan Sea, but even kings do not get all that they wish. If he sends guards to the shop, he will find it empty and no records that Lady Arra ever existed, nor did her out-of-work blacksmith husband and her four children—"

"Three," Cyanna adds helpfully, checking on the other sleeping children in their cribs.

Despite the dark conversation at hand, a smile spreads over my lips. "—three children who never existed. Arra will be a ghost. The shop is registered under a false name."

"I didn't know Grayden even returned." Cyanna grimaces. "He was at a meeting with the king and queen of Kalvorn. I heard he spoke of nothing else at court for weeks beforehand. I was hoping his ship would be lost at sea."

I nod, swallowing. "Apparently, their king said Kalvorn would aid in all Adreania's needs if Grayden surrendered the crown to him." They're fighting over a fae crown neither of them can control, willing to sacrifice their citizens for a relic of old magic, now a status symbol more than anything.

"Men and their quest for power will get us all killed." Cyanna rocks a crib in the kitchen where a toddler sleeps fitfully, wheezing in his sleep. "I may need to call the healer again," she says to herself.

Healer.

Leon.

I gasp, reaching into my pocket and pulling out the locket with my instructions to secure safety. A wave of gratitude for his concern hits me straight in the chest, leaving me breathless. I don't need a safe place; Cyanna does.

Leon can get her out.

I open the locket and hand Cyanna the tightly folded note. "I have a way for you to escape! Take everyone to the fisherman's cove. Find the Black Bell tavern and the captain of the *Hanolis' Sun.* Give him this note. Safety is waiting there! Tell Oliver that Leon sent you. Do not take no for an answer."

Her eyes go wide, filling with tears. "What?"

"Oliver will take you far away from here."

"Oh, Della, I don't know what to say." Cyanna clutches the locket to her chest and lets out a small sob.

I put my hands on her cheeks, wiping away her tears with my thumbs. "I just want you safe. That's all I've ever wanted. Oliver will take you to Leon's childhood home. I will find you again, I promise."

For the first time since I've known her, hope lights her eyes. "I believe you, but you must go!"

I nod slowly, not wishing to leave my cousin, but Nueena waits for me and I've been away too long already. Cyanna opens the back door to her dreary garden, scanning for any spying eyes. When she believes it to be safe, she motions me out and we cross over the dead grass at the back of the house.

We stand in front of the barn door that will lead me out of Adreania.

"Cyanna, we will see each other again, maybe not for a while, but one day. You have done such a wonderful job loving every child the crown has failed. I love you and I'm proud to call you family."

She bobs her head, stepping into my arms, and we hold each other in a tight embrace.

"I love you, Della."

I kiss each tear-stained cheek as we pull apart. Her whisper is raw and broken. "Thank you."

When we break apart, I take a small step back quickly, trying to hide the tears in my eyes as I head back inside. The last noise I hear is Cyanna's soft sniffles as the final lock slides into place, leaving me in darkness.

With the cart empty, it takes half the time to return to my horse. Onyx, sensing my distress, pushes his head against me affectionately.

Leon holds all my thoughts on the ride back to the fae realm. I said goodbye to him. After years of late-night imaginings of what it would be like to feel him against me, it finally happened, only for him to be ripped away.

Not that it would have grown into anything.

I press my forehead to Onyx's warm cheek, centering myself with deep gulps of the forest air before I hitch the empty cart to him.

Traveling back through the dead woods out of Adreania seems endless, and with every passing moment my shoulders sink a little lower, my movements slower. I've been without my magic for too long. By the time Nueena's form appears in the distance, I'm trembling.

Farren whines as he races towards me, weaving in between Onyx's legs as we reach the Divide. Nueena's eyebrows are knitted with concern. Just before crossing, I dismount on shaking legs and step over it.

"Della!"

My magic slams into me with such force I collapse into her and down into the bed of greenery that has burst under her feet, the large ferns and soft clovers cushioning my landing. The jewelsmith powers rush to every fiber of my being, bright as a forge fire; it burns away the emptiness created by entering Adreania, and the feeling of being reborn overwhelms me. My magic reserves are like a small pool, so it does not take long for it to fill up again. The bliss of its return starts at my feet as the magic swirls up through me, going over my hips, through my waist, and down my arms before pushing up again.

Restoring and renewing.

For the first time in hours, I can breathe without an icy grip on my lungs. The air here is sweet and clear.

Nueena and I are a tangle of arms and legs. I roll onto my back, lush clovers grazing my neck, and stare up at the stars and blooming flowers above.

"Nueena," I say in a calm tone that is far from the panic sinking into my bones as I take her hand, "your navlue tree. It's been producing fruit, right?"

Her concern shifts to surprised confusion. "Yes, Camarra says in a few weeks they will be ready to harvest for the coronation. Why?"

"We have a traitor in Ellova."

CHAPTER 8

*I*relive the whole night for Nueena. "When Grayden found me, he tried to make me eat a piece of fruit he said a *friend* gave him. It looked like it was from the navlue tree." It all comes out in a rush. "I know what I saw."

She says carefully, "I believe you but I'm not sure that is possible. No one has access to the throne room besides my family and a few carefully chosen gardeners for historical records. Camarra is only allowed as she is the Court of Green's Guardian. Even then, I was there every moment the Court of Green was, but my parents will investigate when we return. I promise." She is not defensive, even when what I speak of is an accusation that one of her court Guardians has committed treason. "You were gone so long. Did anything else happen?"

I bite my lip but tell her about Grayden.

With frozen rage, Nueena squeezes my hand to the point of pain. I place my own on top of hers and her grip relaxes. She stares at me, mouth open slightly, shaking her head, which sends her curls shifting around her.

Nueena goes very still and declares in a low, menacing tone, "Someone needs to kill him." Anger slowly spreads across her beautiful features.

"And I would truly love to witness that," I say wistfully.

"Del, I'm so sorry. Did you get to see Leon at all?"

I nod. "It was such a strange night. I spoke with Leon at the wine table and asked about his research for a cure. He spoke of the anafaea flower before Grayden came out, screaming like a child about his meeting with King Zilas and going to war with Kalvorn." Leon's scent fills my memory, and I close my eyes to savor it. "He told me he had a safe place that he was going to send me to, me and all those children I lied about having. He promised he'd help my husband find work. He wanted to protect and provide for me. I had no idea he cared that deeply for me. He said we would see each other again. He sounded so sure."

She pulls me up from where I lie in my pain and she tenderly wraps her arms around me. I mold into her arms, and the comfort of her care calms the storm that the waves of heartache brought.

Since the night Leon and I met, whenever sleep evades me, I think of him. When there were only empty sheets to tangle in and Farren's warmth for company, the sweetest fantasy has been a place for us to be together. The ache of that loss inside me is a reminder I spent years seeking ephemeral time with a man I knew full well could never be a part of my future. That no matter what happens, I end up alone.

The agony of longing pulls me close, that bitter dream for a place we could be together, somewhere with the magic I desperately need but where mortals could live free of the devastating consequences being near magic would bring.

Of course I had known our stolen midnight moments were finite. He understood, like I did, that the long glances and soft touches were all that we were given in this life, and still he fretted over me. Cared enough to plan for my safety. I must have meant something to him. He felt I was someone he needed to protect and provide for even if we were destined to never spend more than a few minutes at a time together. Guilt and elation war within me.

I was never alone in my longings. We were both lonely together, separated by realms, wishing for a future that couldn't exist.

Nueena and I break apart and stare at each other. This would be the perfect moment for her to say *I told you this would end poorly*, but she would never. She is too loyal, too kind, although I'm convinced she must be thinking it.

"Well." Nueena weighs her words carefully before she continues. "Now you no longer have to pretend to be Arra, maybe you can find another way to see him again? Where was he going to send you?"

I can only shrug. "He's mentioned living in Versairen before and I was to meet with a sea captain for safe passage. He must have a safe place there." I look down at the small white blooms growing around us. "What would be the point, Nu? We spend a few decades together before he dies? Leaving me mourning him for the next few centuries 'til death takes me from a broken heart over a mortal man as it did with my mother? No, best for me to move on and forget about Leon. Leave tonight in the past."

"If that is what you feel is best, we will never speak of him again."

I look up to find her watching me, eyebrows drawn up with sympathy. I don't want her to worry about me when she has far more important tasks ahead. We should leave. Any more words of passionate healers, insidious princes, and stolen fruit will only bring delay.

She opens her mouth but closes it quickly, turning her head in the direction of Ellova with an exasperated yet endearing smile. Thundering hooves fill the forest; like an arrow from a bow, the rider shoots towards us.

He could find her anywhere.

I stand before Nueena and she slips her hand into my outstretched palm, pulling her out of the flowers.

"Would that happen to be your Zemra?" I ask with a smile.

She lets out a light laugh. "That it is. I was worried about you, and you know how he gets. Once he felt that, there's no keeping him away."

"I'm surprised he doesn't have the Ellovian forces with him."

"Who knows? I'm only an hour or two late. That was probably the next course of action."

Tavien dismounts, relief lighting his handsome features. "Is everything all right?" His riding boots barely touch the forest floor before he draws Nueena to him.

He has his dark brown hair twisted into locs with a lighter brown fading at the tips, all pulled together with a leather band. Two front pieces hang down and touch his golden-brown cheeks near his deep frown.

Around his neck is thick woven leather, a small, jagged amethyst hanging from it. A twin to the one Nueena wears. At their nearness, both Zemra stones glow a soft purple. The physical symbol of their soulbonded matehood holds a small part of each other's magic. Through the connection they share with the crystals, they can sense each other's emotions and needs.

The Zemra magic connects them by mind, magic, and soul.

I love that Nueena and Tavien have found such a rare and precious gift in each other.

"My love, you shouldn't have worried so much. Everything is fine. See? We are both well," she says, smushed into his chest.

"What happened?" he asks in his deep, smooth voice. "Sunshine, I felt your fear." Tavien's nightshirt peeks out under his traveling cloak as he pulls back to assess us. His concerned gaze softens and turns to me.

A stab of guilt joins my current state of assorted raw emotions for making them both worry. "Sorry, Tav, that was my fault. I got caught up in the mortal realm and wasn't able to return as swiftly as I would have liked."

He takes my hand and pulls me into their embrace. "Are you all right?" he asks curiously. "It did not feel like you were."

I nod. "I am now. It was a rough night. Nu can fill you in later."

We all break apart. He looks past us to the Divide and the darkness encroaching into the fae realm. "Is it still spreading into the forest? Something must be done about that damn crown."

They exchange a worried look.

"We have much to tell your parents," Tavien says. "Let's get you both back home, shall we?"

Nueena sighs. "They will not be happy with us."

The three of us mount our horses and head northeast.

"Besides the ball, what coronation planning is left?" I ask.

"I need to meet with Camarra and her representatives from the Court of Green before the coronation."

Confused, I ask, "Before all the other court Guardians?" The last coronation happened hundreds of years before I was born, but when Nyvenah, Nueena's mother, described her own coronation, all the court Guardians arrived together in a procession to start the week-long celebration leading up to the crowning day.

Nueena nods. "It's an urgent matter. There were whispers that something is wrong with the Green Court's growing lands, of soil not yielding as much as in previous years, but neither the court leaders nor Camarra had mentioned anything. As Seed Keeper and court Guardian, she would be the one to report back to my parents. My mother sent her a letter inquiring, and she claimed they wished to wait a turn of the season before declaring anything to us."

"Do you believe them?"

Nueena is quiet again before speaking, choosing her words carefully. "They may be speaking the truth, but they also could have been afraid my mother would step in and try to take control. It would not be the first time a court Guardian has kept something from the High Court for fear we may try to intervene. They know their fields best. They have been growing crops and feeding every fae for millennia. They will have my complete trust when I become Realm Keeper until they prove otherwise. I will hear Camarra out before placing any judgment on her. She is just protecting her court."

I'm almost afraid to ask; a bitter truth lies between us, like death waiting patiently for confirmation of our fears. "The crops have been failing for years in the Iron Realm. The mortals are able to feed themselves less and less each year. Beggars' Row is on the brink of starvation and now ours may be on the cusp as well. It must be because of the crown."

Her shoulders tighten. "I have reason to believe they are connected. The forest should be protecting us from the crown's unending thirst for magic. If the crown is draining life or energy directly from the land in Adreania, it may have pulled all that it could and will now siphon from Ellova."

"How long will the wards last?"

She studies the trees that we pass. "I can sense something is wrong. The forest's magic is slowly fading, which means the protection it offers will go with it. Realm Keeper Zarella used so much of her own magic in the wards, it may not be possible to replicate it if the magic fails."

"You are Zarella's descendant. You may possess the magic needed to restore the forest's protection." I try to sound hopeful. If anyone can, I know it's her.

She looks up at the dark sky and whispers, "I hope so. If only I had the stolen fae crown. It contains so much of the magic we need."

We ride for a while, following the dried riverbed towards Ellova, each step taking me further from Leon. My chest tightens when his face flashes in my mind. Nueena is silent and repeatedly glances over at me with the concern normally found on new mothers with their dewlings. When we finally reach a parting in the forest, I slide off Onyx and hand Nueena his reins to take him to the royal stables for some sugar cubes and their endless supply of hay.

Nueena attempts to hand the leather straps back to me. "Where are you going? It's a long walk back to your cottage. We'll ride there with you."

I need some time to think, to mourn alone. I smile up at her even though it doesn't reach my eyes. "No. I will be fine. I need to walk off this wretched evening anyway."

Nueena nods but appears unconvinced. "See you back at the palace in a few days."

She drops to the ground, and we embrace one last time for the night. I am overwhelmed by how much I love her, that her precious friendship is offered to me, a stronger love than anything else I have ever known. "You're going to make a great Realm Keeper," I whisper from my place below her chin as she towers over me in our embrace.

She laughs as we pull apart and says, "Yes, I will."

A rustle of soft paws crinkling dry leaves in the bushes nearby distracts me. Farren's blue eyes peer up at us.

"Hello, little one," I say to him. "Let's go home."

~

*M*oonlight pours over the Merawood Forest, and memories of tonight's conversation consume my thoughts.

I walk along the dry riverbed that once flowed down from Ellova. Farren's bushy black tail bobs in and out of bushes as he chases fireflies.

Long ago the Airvell River and its healing water flowed to the Elbasan Sea. The swift-moving waters emerged from a rift in the Venneem Mountains of Ellova.

I remove each wide cuff from my wrists and my magic swirls inside me, rushing into my hands, ready to create. The two bracelets mold into a large, smooth, golden ball. The shining mass vibrates as I imagine Leon's face, the metal shifting into a small bust of his likeness in my outstretched palm. It just needs two small emeralds for the eyes. I wanted to see his face one more time, but now that it lies before me, my chest constricts painfully, and I swallow my emotion.

Farren pauses, looking around, ears up in alarm.

I stand behind him, listening. A stillness spreads around the forest as all the creatures that thrive under moonlight go silent. After a moment, I can make out the rough sounds of fast-moving travelers headed straight towards me.

Leon's perfect golden face melts in my hand and shifts into a dagger.

Taking off behind the dense trees, Farren runs up the rocks leading to the higher ground, and I follow, crouching behind one of the boulders. The urgency at which the small caravan is traveling in the middle of the night, through a forest forbidden to most, fills me with dread. The only possible way they can be coming in is from Adreania, but how?

Ellovian magic is fused within the forest soil, used as a protector and defender of its kingdom. The forest's magic will not allow anyone who wishes to harm Ellova in, but panic still shoots its way up my spine.

Hidden from view, I go unnoticed by three figures. Dark brown cloaks are pulled over armor, the men crushing the flowers in their path. A lone workhorse pulls a worn metal cart with a covered flatbed while two of the men walk swiftly beside it.

The full moon's glow is so bright I can see the lone rider repeatedly turn his head behind his horse to peer into the forest at their backs.

Whoever these men are, they are not welcome here, and coming from Adreania, they may be dangerous. Fear burns in me as they pass by my hiding spot, rushing in the direction of Kalvorn.

Jostled by the rough terrain of the forest floor, the mound of fabric atop the cart shifts, and a hand falls limply to the side over the wheel. My heart stops, and my hand flies over my mouth to stop the gasp rising in my throat, my fae eyesight revealing what darkness tries to hide.

Illuminated by the moonbeams between branches, an arm hangs motionless, showing its many years. On the middle finger is a massive gold ring: a large round ruby with two emerald stones cut in the shape of triangles on the decrepit, hooked finger.

A ring I would recognize anywhere.

A ring I forged with my own magic.

A ring that is only ever worn by one person.

Moaning from under the blanket is King Jedrick of Adreania.

CHAPTER 9

The men who have taken Jedrick are heading in the direction of Kalvorn, but if they are traveling there for medical aid, it would be faster by ship. It is at least a day's journey to King Zilas's kingdom, and Jedrick might not make it through the mountains alive.

Could these men be from Kalvorn? When Grayden met with the king and queen of Kalvorn, all they wanted in exchange for endless aid was the crown. Is someone delivering Jedrick to Kalvorn so Adreania can get what they wanted? Or is something far more sinister about to take place?

Whatever the reason is, Jedrick here in the middle of the night is no matter to me. The crown is out of Adreania. The shock that it is so close to the Ellovian palace, so close to the fae realm, overwhelms me for a moment.

I could bring back the crown my great-great-grandmother created.

If I can take Jedrick back to Ellova, the impending war for the crown between Adreania and Kalvorn would be over before it even began. So many lives would be saved. If I could disable the men who captured him and guide the horse and cart to the entrance only I use, this could change everything. With the crown in Ellova, Grayden would have no hold on the throne. No mortal man from Jedrick's family line is worthy of wearing the crown anyway.

If I can get it to Nueena, she will start her reign with unparalleled power. If the crown is as powerful as the myths claim, she might be the only one who can control it.

The men continue on their journey, laughing quietly.

I rise from the hiding spot once they are out of sight. "Farren."

My beloved fox looks up at my whisper.

"Hide."

He does, racing off into the bushes.

I advance in their direction, darting through the trees and around large boulders. I take a secret path and, with no horse to lead through unfamiliar territory, arrive further ahead of them on their course. Patient to strike, I lean behind a thicket of trees. Just ahead, the saplings are slightly wider apart with more of the forest free of the thick foliage, and I wait, hidden, 'til they arrive.

Decades ago, when deciding which court to vow my magic to, the Court of Swords with its many armies was the first to be rejected. I have no desire for bloodshed or war strategy, but with every defense lesson Nueena had to take as future Realm Keeper, I was encouraged to join her. Commander Lillian never allowed us to skip those classes by hiding in the library.

I'll definitely owe Lillian if I survive this encounter. She'll scowl if I make her any jewelry as a token of my appreciation, but perhaps I can make something for her mate.

The men are slow-moving now, the wheels bouncing over large rocks that make the cart difficult to navigate through the trees.

I only have three weapons.

My magic.

A dagger of gold.

My body.

Mortal men have a weakness for soft flesh and do not see women as a threat when they should.

Removing the band that holds my hair, I flip my head upside down, my golden light auburn locks puffing out with soft curls. I reach into the front of my corset and shove my breasts up to a painful point.

The dagger in my hand is too threatening. A more delicate approach is needed. The metal vibrates again, pulling in on itself, separating into small strawberry-sized nuggets like the ones I find in the river that runs through the forest.

Wooden wheels hit the stone-filled path just before I make my presence known.

I start to sing loudly. It's off-key and a poor excuse for a melody, but it's only meant to disarm them. A wide-eyed maiden lost in the moonlit woods.

It's not my greatest plan.

I stumble into their view and fake a show of surprised delight. They slow the horse; the two at the cart have their hoods up but still reveal a sliver of startled eyes. One puts his hand on his sword after stepping in front of Jedrick's hand to hide it from my view.

The false surprise fades and I give them a grateful smile. "Oh! Finally!" I just need to touch the metal of the fitted gauntlets they wear. "I am *so* glad you found me! I've been so lost! Is Kalvorn over this mountain?"

They stare at my hopeful expression.

The leader wears silver armor and stays on his horse with no concern in his words, just mild irritation. "What are you doing out here so late? Who else lives in these woods?"

I shrink my shoulders. "Oh, I'm from Kalvorn. I followed the river up from the port, but I seem to have lost my way. I'm collecting moonflowers and gold overflows from the river. I use them to make doorknobs."

With one eyebrow raised, he asks, "Doorknobs…moonflowers?" He must know no such thing exists.

In unison, the three men look down at the pile of gold in my hand.

"You can have it all if you would be so kind as to provide directions back home. My family must be so worried." I frantically add, *"My children!"*

In Ellova I have seen gold used as doorstops, but two of the men standing before me, with their worn hoods and gaunt cheeks, have a harsher life in Adreania.

So much precious metal must seem like a king's fortune to them.

The two men look up hopefully at their leader for his silent approval. He looks me up and down. My cloak covers my gown, the skirt muddy from the river, and with no weapons in his sight, it only takes mere moments of silent deliberation. He must not view me as the threat he should since he nods at the other two.

A grave error on his part.

Like greedy children lunging for candy, they each attempt to take the gold from me with their iron-covered hands.

That's all I need.

My power rushes from my palms, rising up through the gold pieces, as their metal fingers connect with the now-glowing gold. The magic surges into their armor.

The metal on their wrists tightens painfully as they reach for their swords, but my magic is quicker than they are, flowing up to their helmets. Their visors slam down over their faces, fusing the two metal pieces, blinding them. The metal around their neck tightens.

Not to kill them, just to disarm and distract them.

Both men, having forgotten about me, reach to remove the helmets but the fingers of their metal gloves fuse together, forming a fist.

The magic rushes down, melting the armor over their feet and throwing them off-balance, sending them colliding into the dusty road, the clatter echoing around us.

The rider throws his leg over his horse's back and slams into the ground, his armor rattling, ready to fight. A slicing noise echoes off the trees as he unsheathes his sword, but he makes no move to attack. Standing in front of Jedrick, he positions his legs apart defensively with his sword raised. He shifts back and forth, seemingly undecided about what to do next, before he rips off his helmet and metal gloves, throwing them to the forest floor.

Finally, a man with some intelligence. It won't be enough.

His outraged expression only adds fuel to my delight. He is handsome, or at least he would be if he weren't quite so livid. With dark brown eyes and curly dark hair that falls down to his clean-shaven square jaw, his light tan skin is dusted with sweat. He appears to be in his late thirties, but mortal ages are not any fae's expertise.

"Why are you doing this?" the man demands. "You have no idea the importance of what he's doing, who he's saving."

Jedrick isn't saving anyone. "You have something I want, so I'll be taking over little Jedrick's journey. You can take your friends back to wherever you came from and—" I laugh a little. "—find a blacksmith."

The men entombed in their armor roll around at his feet.

I am giddy with the knowledge that two of the three men have been disarmed, and the only thing standing between me and that crown is a lone man covered in metal. I unhook the bag over my shoulder and toss it in the dirt off to my side. The smile he receives is of near-feral delight.

My great-great-grandmother was exiled for making that crown. Forced every generation before me to live a lonely, cursed life in this forest. I will have redemption for the fae women who have come before me.

I want it back.

His eyes grow wide as he watches the gold in my hands shift back into a glimmering dagger before he glances over to his companions, his massive shoulders sink dramatically in what I'm sure he thinks is the appearance of defeat. As the air inside the helmets has been restricted, the men roll slowly, about to lose consciousness. He moves over to the first incapacitated man, appearing to take my offer and leave, but at the last minute, he lunges at me and swipes the sword towards my chest.

Unfortunately for him, I'm just as fast. I grab the sharpened point of the sword as it flies at my neck.

The sword melts instantly into my palm.

The impact of the hit stings a bit but his sword molds into my hand, obeying me, bending immediately to my magic as I take hold of the melting blade. He tries to drop the handle, taking a few steps back, but it is far too late for that now. Like a snake, the hilt of his sword betrays him and slithers around his hand and up his arm, connecting with his armor. The magic works its way up through it, tightening around his arms and his neck. He backs away from me, trips over a large rock, and falls back with a crash as the metal molds together at his feet, preventing him from trying to attack again.

I cringe at the thump his head makes striking the ground, knocking him out.

The other two men are still unconscious from the tightness around their necks. I go to each one and touch their toes, willing the metal to loosen to allow them airflow. They will have pounding headaches and sore necks when they wake up but will otherwise be fine. The metal that bound them shifts back into the armor's original form. The iron pulls apart at their feet so that when they wake, they can walk out of this forest. The gauntlets' fingers are released from the molded fists so they will be able to remove their helmets.

Farren reappears from wherever he was hiding, coming to my feet, gazing up at me.

My heart pounds while I walk towards the cart, where Jedrick moans. I take a deep breath before I toss the canvas blanket away.

CHAPTER 10

The king of Adreania lies on the cart, his breathing irregular, chest slowly rising and falling. He is securely tied to the cart with ropes over his fine clothing. His eyes are bloodshot, his aged face a worrisome shade of white. When he tries to speak, no sound comes out, his mouth opening before gasping for air.

"Jedrick, it's Lady Arra, your jeweler. Please stay calm. You have been kidnapped, but I'm going to get you to safety." I retrieve the sword that lies in the grass next to the unconscious rider and slice off some of the ropes, careful of his body beneath them.

He stares, but his clouded gray eyes don't truly see me.

Once most of the cut ropes have fallen to the ground, he tries to sit up. Careful of how fragile he looks, I help him ease his body into a sitting position, his legs still secured to the cart. It's against the law to touch Adreanian royalty without express permission, but I'm not sure if he is even considered king here. The forest recognizes no rulers besides Nueena's mother.

He reaches back the way he came before trying to undo the last of the ropes. He is trying to say something, but nothing comes out.

"Please lie back down. The ropes are here to help, to secure you for our journey."

Refusing my plea and brushing away my hand, he stares deep into the forest, down the path he just came from, with desperate eyes. Jedrick tries to shove me away in a pitiful display of strength, so I take a small step back. It's useless but he pulls on the ropes anyway before he reaches out again.

The forest is too quiet. No calls of the owls or tentative steps of deer. It is waiting, watching. A shiver runs down my back, the air colder than it was.

Farren comes up next to me to sniff around, boldly investigating the new arrival.

Jedrick lies back down with a soft thump, his breathing labored, and looks up at me, fear in his eyes. This time he reaches out a hand towards me, but I ignore it. He may be an old man arriving at the bitter end of his life, but he let so many innocent people suffer and die, his hateful son raining down terror. I refuse to ease his anguish with a touch of comfort.

The crown can't be removed until death; he just needs to hold on a little longer. The tree portal to Ellova is not far from here.

His arm falls from my rejection, and I look at the crown. He has to make it; the crown needs to get to Nueena. I move towards the horse's head, pulling its reins in the direction of the fae palace.

Jedrick again points back to the way he had come.

"It needs to go—must be on—a living soul. My, my, my—"

The words look painful to get out as his breaths go shallow, the light beginning to fade in his eyes.

"Grayden is not here, nor is he worthy of it. Your hateful reign is over, and you will die knowing you failed your people."

Jedrick finally looks up at me, terrified. He lays his head down, taking one last choking breath before he goes still, his limp body staring with vacant milky eyes.

Dead.

I hold my breath as the stolen crown falls off his head. For a moment nothing happens.

The dull circlet has fallen onto the cart, which is eroding, the wood turning black. The lush green of the forest floor is gone as the darkness descends at my feet. Black swirls grow from the circlet, racing in all directions as if the grass has been burned. I scramble back as the ground heats, scorched by the violent magic of the crown's wrath. A burning smell reaches my nose, and hot pain erupts in my lungs from the smoke.

Then the whirling darkness spreading from the crown erupts in flames.

The horse leading the cart rears back. I raise the sword I still hold high in the air and slice through the straps holding the terrified creature to the cart. As soon as it is free, it races off into the forest.

"Farren, RUN!"

He takes off like an arrow from a bow, running in the direction of the cottage.

The magic released from the crown destroys the ground around Jedrick's blackened corpse. His body now lies on the scorched forest floor; the cart is nothing more than a pile of cinders. Blackness spreads in hateful spirals.

Must be on a living soul. Jedrick's last words.

Is this what he meant? Was this cursed crown designed to need a living host to channel the magic? I realize with stomach-gutting horror this must be why it cannot be removed until death. The darkness continues to stretch out. It is going to keep spreading; it will burn Merawood Forest to the ground before I can get it to Nueena, who might be able to control it.

My ancestor created that crown. I pray that the magic that formed it recognizes that same magic within me. As Alvina's descendent, I can only hope I can control it, even if half of me is mortal.

Ellova must be protected.

I run into the fire, the ash whirling around my burning boots as I drop to my knees in the burned sphere and reach into the cart's ashes for the crown.

"ARRA, NO!" Someone is screaming my name. No, not my name but the name I abandoned tonight.

Tearing my eyes from the crown for a moment, I gasp as Leon appears, racing up the path before me. A trickle of blood runs down the side of his handsome face, one eye black and blue. Shock and horror roll over me, and I'm torn between Leon and the burning ground.

The longest burn mark yet shoots out around me. I know what I must do.

Grabbing the cold metal, so at odds with the burning ground beneath me, I call all of the magic within me, flowing it into the crown before I slam the wretched circlet on my head.

Oh, Ellova's grave, I don't want this.

Leon is shouting, but I can't focus on his agonized words. The world seems to explode as a splitting headache brings my whole body crashing to the burnt forest floor. The urge to scream overwhelms me, but the pain in my head has stolen any air in my lungs. My own magic is being ripped from me. Not in the way it drains when I cross the Divide, but like claws in my soul. Tearing it out of me and leaving what's left ruined.

My body is going back and forth between numbness and a stabbing sensation I know is magic warring within me for control. My own magic is extinguished; the crown's magic is taking over.

My eyesight blurs from the pain in my head and the billowing smoke around me, but I can make out that Leon is running straight at me. When he is a few feet away, he launches himself towards the ground, sliding on his knees to my side, soot flying around us, his arms going around me. Darkness spreads over my eyes and I feel myself losing consciousness. The world is spinning but the scorched earth has finally stopped spreading, the flames gone.

"ARRA!" Leon's scream is a broken plea in the darkness.

His bruised face is the last thing I see before everything fades away.

CHAPTER 11

My body shivers with a phantom frost, a coldness I haven't felt since I fell into that frozen lake at the Ink Court's snow-topped mountain sanctuary as a dewling. Leon's warm embrace soothes me; his gentle hands trail heat as he checks me for injuries. Lying in the remnants of the burned earth, I gaze up at him. The pain is overwhelming as I lean into that comforting, reverent touch.

His voice is laced with emotions when he whispers, "Oh, my Arra, what have you done?" Leon's rough hands cup my face, his thumbs brushing over my cheek with tender care.

His Arra. I could only wish to be his, and despite the pain I am in, my heart soars at his words.

"Something necessary," I whisper back, rubbing my temple. "What happened to the fire?"

"The flames went out as soon as you put on the crown." He moves some of the copper strands off my face after he finishes inspecting me for possible wounds. We stare at each other for a long moment, his hand resting carefully on my cheek, before he seems to realize how close we are, and he leans back on his calves.

"How do you feel?" His tone is rougher now, like the healer he is, gathering information. His fingers move to my neck and attempt to press down, but I shove his hand away; my heartbeat will reveal I am not like him.

It takes me a moment to respond. "Truly terrible." *For many reasons,* but I keep that to myself. "Can you hunt for my bag? There's some water in it. I need it."

I reach up to attempt to remove the crown, and excruciating pain hits me when I do. Nausea floods me like a sickening punch to the gut.

He finds my bag lying on the ground nearby and picks up everything that has fallen from it, wiping each item on his pant leg to rid it of the dirt before placing it back inside the bag and walking over to me. "The crown will not come off, believe me. Jedrick tried every possible way."

Leon sits halfway behind me. With slow and careful hands, he leans me against him, and I use his bent knee for back support, relaxing into him. He uncorks the small bottle and brings it to my lips, careful not to spill a drop. It's cold, but the magic in the water warms me from the inside. With every sip, the pain recedes, leaving only a sore body and a blinding headache.

"Leon, there must be a way." It comes out small and pathetic.

He is quiet for a long moment. "I have done all the research I could, and to my knowledge, it can only be removed upon one's death."

I nod; the truth strikes my stomach.

Someone in Ellova will know another way, a way mortals are not familiar with. My great-great-grandmother made this crown; she must have created a way to remove it without death.

The stars sparkle above us in the cobalt sky, and the Merawood Forest's midnight creatures begin their moonlit symphony again.

"Arra, what are you doing out here?" he whispers.

"Me? What are *you* doing out here, Leon?" I push the bottle back to him and study his face. "You need to drink some of this. It will help your face. I'm afraid you are more…purple than when I saw you last. What happened?"

He gives me a small smile before taking a long sip. Still beautiful, even with his bloody face.

He sighs deeply, his black-and-gray hair falling in his face. "Those three men attacked Jedrick and me back at the Iron Castle. We were in his locked private chambers. If any of the guards outside heard anything, they would be hanged for treason for not aiding their king. The men came through a secret pathway that had been sealed, created only for an escape route in case of a fire or war. Caught us completely by surprise. One of them grabbed Jedrick and another knocked me out, but I woke up soon after they left." He gestures to his bruised face. "I followed them and managed to almost catch up. Jedrick needed constant medical attention and could not be without a healer." Leon rubs his face slowly, wincing at the pain. "Please tell me, why are you out here in the middle of the night?"

I ignore him and reach up, gently rubbing the cheek not covered in bruises. He leans into the touch, placing his hand lightly over mine. "Do you know who took him?"

"I suspect Kalvorn. That's why we need to leave. We can follow this path." He points northwest, towards the mountains between Kalvorn and Adreania. "You can rest as much as you need, and we will send for your family later. I'll bring you to safety, I have a place for us."

Travel? "No, I don't think so. I need to get home." I want to stand but his warmth engulfs me and extinguishes what little fight I have left.

"Arra, please listen to me. Adreania is not safe!" Anger rises on his face, his breaths coming faster and faster as he speaks. "Grayden will stop at nothing to get the crown back. He knows it can't be removed, but that won't stop him from locking you up! He will keep you as some sort of...pet. The pain he will inflict on you for taking what he thought was his will be unimaginable!"

I finally give in. "I don't live in Adreania, Leon."

The anger clears away. He looks surprised at my admission; his eyebrows draw together. "You don't? But you have a shop there."

"I live here, well, not far, anyway."

"So that is why you were never at your shop."

Now it's my turn to be surprised by him. "How many times have you been by my shop?"

"Quite a few, actually, but there was never an answer," he says sheepishly, rubbing the back of his neck.

"You never said anything? All those nights we saw each other?" Besides his last letters, I don't know why it never occurred to me that he might try to find me outside of the bazaar nights.

"I know, I just...I hoped we could be...friends outside of the castle, but we never got enough alone time for me to ask." He lifts one shoulder. "I figured you weren't interested in that."

"No! I was. I am!" The pain in my head makes it harder to know how to respond to him. Maybe this is the best time to admit about the shop. "I only go there for the royal bazaar once a month. The shop is a...front. It's empty, always has been. If I had known, I would have written or found you. I am truly sorry, but I live here. I always have. My home is within the forest."

Leon gapes at me. "How on earth did you get in? The iron gates? The patrols? Adreania was built to keep its people in and all others out."

If it wouldn't hurt so much, I would laugh at his shocked expression, but the crown's magic pulses painfully. "Yes, that's all true, but I know a secret way. To my knowledge, only a few others knew about it, and most are long dead."

"Where?" he demands, but not in anger or with accusation.

I take a deep breath and rub my head under the crown. "Can we talk on the way? It's hard to think. We can head to my cottage. I have a salve for your face and something I think might help this headache, or at the very least let me sleep."

He looks around the forest. "How far do you live?"

"Not far, maybe a twenty-minute walk."

He looks like he is going to argue but instead says, "We can rest there for tonight if we must, but at first light, we need to disappear. This forest isn't safe. Grayden will come looking for the crown and he will not stop until he has it. He will kill anyone who gets in his way. The king sleeps late, so his disappearance won't be noticed 'til midmorning, but we need to get ahead of any guards Grayden sends out." His eyes leave my face to stare at the crown. For a moment something darker flashes in his eyes as he studies it. "Is it hurting you?" His tone quickly fades to sympathy. "Are you still in pain?"

My nod is curt, and I agree to rest for the night. No point in arguing with him. I will break away as soon as I'm free to get back to Nueena, even if it means slipping him sleeping dust in his tea. That seems easier than fighting.

If Grayden will be looking for me, he will also be looking for Leon. Neither one of us will be safe by sunrise.

Leon's eyes are so green that for a moment I get lost in them.

"I am incredibly grateful you are all right, Arra." He laces his fingers with mine. "So, I take it you were never going to follow my instructions to get you out of Adreania?"

I shake my head. "No, but I am beyond touched that you would care so deeply about my safety, Leon." The water sloshes when I take another long drink and offer him the last few sips.

Leon pushes the bottle towards me. "One more sip. I'll be all right." He watches me take another small drink before I push it back at him. He smiles softly down at me, drinking the last of it. His sleeves are rolled up and his thick forearm flexes slightly as he holds up the bottle. His smile widens when he follows my eyes. With the bottle empty, he places it in my satchel and loops the strap over his shoulder. It joins his smooth leather medical bag. "Can you walk? If you cannot, I will carry you."

I assess my body before I answer. Almost everything aches, and the pull and pulse of the crown's magic makes me want to crawl out of my skin, but walking may be a manageable task. "Yes, at least I hope so." I go to rise but he stands first, taking both of my hands to lift me. I stumble for a moment, and his arms are around my waist in an instant to steady me. My cheeks heat despite the agony within me at the contact as we start walking. He glances down at the three unconscious men as we pass. His eyes linger on the leader.

"They will be fine," I say. "Massive headaches when they wake, but they will recover."

He clears his throat. "I'm glad you didn't kill them. They wanted the crown for the same reason everyone else does. It has the power to change things, on the right person. I am sure they just wanted a better life." Leon, being a man of medicine, is generous with his mercies.

"Did they say where they were going?"

"No, but considering Kalvorn was about to go to war for the crown, we can guess it was them. If it were Versairen, they would have taken Jedrick to the shipyard and set sail there."

We walk in silence for a while, connected at the hip. His arm is tight around my waist. My limbs are heavy, and it makes walking difficult. His eyebrows are drawn together, but I'm not sure if it's due to pain or anger at the situation. He sees me watching him and meets my eyes. A small smile appears, but it fades when he glances up at the crown.

"How's your head?"

The pressure there is almost unbearable; the pain radiates in every part of me. I can feel the magic pounding under my skin, desperate to get out, but I can't release it in front of him. My jewel-smith magic has always felt magnetic and luminous inside me, like hot liquid gold running through my veins. The crown's magic swirls like water and twisting vines in my chest. I swear I can feel the forest thrum inside me as if my very being is encased in its soil.

"It feels like a horse has decided to make war inside my skull. We can't do anything to remove it?" Pressure builds in my head, so painful I feel I might pop like a bubble.

He shakes his head. "I'm afraid magical crowns on unsuspecting women were never covered in my medical training, but I'll write a strongly worded letter to the university about the lapse in my education."

It takes me a moment to see that he's making a joke. I laugh even though it hurts to do so. His eyes go a little wider as he looks at my lips and then back to my eyes after he must have realized where he was looking.

"What does it feel like?" Leon asks. "Besides the pain, I mean, can you feel anything? I once asked Jedrick what it felt like and he said he felt a slight pressure on his head, only feeling pain if it was pulled. I'm curious if the reason it's now gold upon your head but was black on his is the reason it's so much more painful for you. Something has happened. It could be because the transfer ceremony from father to son never happened."

I stop walking abruptly, so he holds me tighter to prevent me from falling. I gape at him. "Is it gold? Truly?"

He nods at the question. "Yes, it has changed from black to a rosy-gold color, very much like your hair. It almost matches. It will be easy to hide, and you *must hide it.*" He stresses the words. "No one can know you have it. That's why we must get as far away from Adreania as we can."

I'm tempted to say that the king's transfer ceremony is only needed because the crown was stolen, but it would not be wise to give away any knowledge of it just yet. He may be the man I've spent my nights lusting after, but that does not mean I know where his loyalty lies now that his king is gone. No matter how much I wish to trust him, years in service to the stolen crown may mean he's loyal to Jedrick even in death, although I can't see him being loyal to Grayden in any way...

"It's just a pressure, like part of my body is underwater, trapped and begging to be released." A wave of exhaustion hits me, forcing me to lean on him even more.

He smells like blood and dirt, but underneath is the scent of his sweet herbs. I inhale deeply, leaning a little more into him. We keep walking. He looks deep in concentration, so I don't try to keep a conversation going. Just beyond the trees, the cottage is tucked away in a sea of sessile oaks. My feet stumble a moment, suddenly unsure if bringing him here was a good idea. He's going to realize I've been lying about so much of what he knows about me. Honestly, it is not something I'm sure I'm ready to share with him yet. It felt so safe in the castle, just him and me with my jewelry table between us. Trusting him is a necessity, though; he is wounded and I can barely stand.

"Here it is," I say, trying to keep the apprehension out of my voice.

Slightly off to the side of my family's cottage is the workshop. It's made of stone, and even with the doors shut, the ever-burning blue flames of the forge glows brightly. The small workshop is shaped similarly to my home, but with more stone and white walls. My small crystal-clear pond sparkles in the distance.

The cottage itself looks as if it were designed by multiple builders who never spoke to each other during construction. The first floor is built with red and light brown bricks. One side has square windows while the other side's window is a large circle. A tower comes up from the middle, and a spiral staircase leads up to a tiny library in the loft space. My favorite part is the twisted brick chimney off to the side of the pointed roof, the steep angle covered in Ellovian sugar pine wood panels painted in soft pinks, greens, and blues.

He looks around at my family's home. This small cottage is nestled among the woodland, in the middle of dense, lush green trees, with flat, brightly colored stepping stones that somewhat match the roof leading up the path to my front door.

A small flag waves in the wind. It bears the Kingdom of Ellova's crest—a tree with six roots, and a large sun behind it. He glances at the flag but doesn't speak on it.

I adore my little cottage, my own personal woodland sanctuary. The Ellovian palace is extraordinary, and home to everyone I love, but here I find peace. I can't stay, though. It won't be safe after tonight, too close to Grayden, who will come looking for the crown. An ache unrelated to the crown hits my chest, knowing tomorrow I will need to remain at the Ellovian palace until this place is safe once more.

"Come on." I pull on his hand and we walk inside my small home. Faint moonbeams stream in through the huge glass skylight in the ceiling.

"Is anyone else here?"

"No, it's just us." Farren waits on a windowsill, watching our arrival with a bored expression, as his food bowl sits empty on the floor below him. He stares for a long time at Leon before looking at me.

The cottage holds no evidence of children or even a husband for that matter. Leon must notice, but he says nothing.

I can always lie when he does inquire of them, but I'm weary of speaking even one more lie when the truth is what he has always deserved.

The space inside has no dividing walls, just golden spiral stairs leading up to the library. Piles of books overflow from the shelves in the small tower library above. A small kitchen is to the right, its windows looking out over the workshop. Chairs stand around a wooden table set for three. Off to the side, there are steps down to a small washroom with a below-ground pool for bathing. A hand-carved side table I won in a palace card game is tucked next to a wide bed, and the stone wall overflows with hanging jewelry I was working on before bed.

An elegant golden mirror hangs next to the door, and I swiftly walk past it without a glance, not ready to see the crown on my head and what it symbolizes for my future.

Best to ignore it for now.

I did not leave that long ago, but it feels like days have passed. I break away from him and make my way to the kitchen, where I pull down a few gold teacups I made long ago. Once I fill the kettle, I open the cellar door and take a few steps into its magically chilled depths to grab blackberry wine off the shelves built into the packed soil. Leon peers down at me and takes the dark bottle I pass up to him.

"Please say this is wine." He holds the bare bottle up to the light.

"Blackberry wine. After the night we have had, we are going to need something stronger than tea."

He lets out a short laugh. "I wholeheartedly agree."

I grab the spiced chicken marinating in a bowl and hand it to Leon, along with a tin of small cookies I brought back from the palace kitchens a few days ago. Leon's hand appears above in my peripheral vision, and I slip mine into his, glad of his assistance to make it the rest of the way up. My well-used copper pan hangs above the sink and I set it on the stove before getting the fire beneath it burning and adding a dollop of butter. Leon adding water to the kettle.

While it heats, I pick up the tin of cookies and open it with a soft *pop*, offering the treat to Leon. Our fingers brush as he takes one, and he lingers for a moment.

"What is this?" he asks.

I take a deep inhale of the buttery tartness before breaking one in half and shoving the piece in my mouth in a graceless fashion, too starving to care. "A lemon and sage cookie."

"Sage, huh? I can't remember the last time I had that." His expression is thoughtful.

Leaning against the counter, he inspects the flaky, pale-yellow confection before taking a bite. He closes his eyes as he lets out a small groan, and I can freely stare at the injuries on that handsome face. The swelling has gone down, but the discoloration on his strong jaw remains.

Leon removes two golden cups from the hanging shelves and pours us two generous servings of wine before holding out one for me to take. We raise our glasses to each other.

"To meeting outside that dreadful ballroom, Leon."

"To finding my way back to you."

CHAPTER 12

Our glasses touch, the sound echoing around the room as we take large gulps of the sweet wine.

My eyes have drifted to Leon's mouth, and he takes another bite of the cookie. Licking his lips, he looks at me and I turn quickly to place the chicken thighs in the now-sizzling pan. A small potted plant of rosemary sits next to the sink, and I pull a few pieces off, ready to throw them in the pan with the butter when the meat is almost done cooking. The kettle announces its readiness with a hissing steam, and I set it off to the side of the stove, silk tea pouches waiting in the cups as the water pours in.

My head aches. I need to get back to the palace as soon as possible. There must be something in one of the Ink Court's libraries on removing unwanted magical items. The crown does not belong on my head; it belongs in Ellova, with the fae. It stole so much magic from Ellova before the war.

If I had the strength, I would leave now, but the journey back to Nueena would be impossible. The crown's magic brings an unending pressure from within that exhausts me, the heaviness making a home inside my body.

All I can do tonight is get enough rest to make it back to the palace tomorrow, so I focus on Leon.

Leaving my side, Leon starts to wander around the room, gazing at the art on the walls. Twisted yarn with frayed ends holds bronze planters above our heads; the plant's bright leaves descend over the edges, draping past a soft emerald-colored couch near the window.

He holds up the charcoal sketch of the necklace I will be making for the coronation ball. The outline is of a teardrop emerald with small diamonds all around it. Putting it down, he moves on to the novel I read before bed. It's a thick cherry-red book about two lovers with not much plot. He flips through a few pages, his thumb saving my place. He raises one neat eyebrow as he reads a passage.

I point to one of the chairs. "Sit down."

He follows my instructions as I grab a medical aid box from under the bed and a clean cloth from the kitchen. I give his boot a light kick to get him to open his legs to make room for me. He leans forward and spreads his knees wide, grinning up at me. I try not to think about his strong thighs as I move between them and apply a thick green healing paste to his bruise and swelling. The paste works swiftly when it touches his skin, and his injuries fade under my fingertips. He is looking at me with an intensity that I want to look away from, but I find myself staring back. I've thought about him every day for two years, but never imagined him here, in my cottage, so close to me.

Once his injuries have healed completely, I wipe the magical salve off and he looks like he always has, infuriatingly handsome. He looks at my lips, and I step away from the intensity swirling in his gaze. The chair creaks, and I see the tight grip he has on the edges of his seat.

"Can you grab me two plates, please?" The question comes out a little strained, and I clear my throat.

He gets up and opens the cupboard with a laugh. "Is everything you own gold? You have more gold in this kitchen than half the court."

"Family heirlooms." Hopefully, he doesn't ask me to elaborate.

Turning back to the stove, I add the rosemary and extra butter to the chicken. I take a swig directly from the wine bottle, drinking deeply before lightly shoving the bottle at his chest. He drinks, watching as I dice up a zucchini and add it to the pan with the chicken. I busy myself with cutting some soft purple cheese and spreading it on the flaky brown bread I baked this morning. Once everything is cooked, I make up both our plates, which he takes to the small table while I bring the teacups. A blue crystal vase sits in the middle of the table with a cheery floral bouquet.

"Do you have any diamond-encrusted silverware around here?" Leon asks.

"No, I prefer to eat with my hands. It keeps me humble." I sit down, pretending not to make a move to get anything.

He laughs at my joke.

I stare at him. "A few years in the castle and you are too good for your hands?"

"Says the woman with a kitchen full of gold."

I make a poor attempt to hide my smirk but go to the kitchen and bring back the cookie tin, cutlery, and a pair of tiny gold teaspoons for the small pot of sugar.

Guests so rarely visit me here. It is nice to have company.

His company.

He eats a forkful of zucchini, even though it's searing hot from the pan, and makes little noises of pleasure. As he makes his tea, he adds heaping teaspoons of the sugar crystals to the dark liquid.

"I haven't had a vegetable in years. This is amazing, Arra. Thank you."

"Which one do you miss the most?"

"Peppers, especially the green ones."

I want to ask more about his life, but he is having a private moment with his dinner, and who am I to stand between a man and his summer squash?

He chews slowly and thoughtfully for a while before looking up.

"I know they have vegetables in the castle. Were you not allowed to partake?"

His face hardens. "I tend not to partake in luxury while others starve."

I shouldn't be surprised but I am. "That's honorable of you. How did you end up as the Royal Physician to King Jedrick, anyway? It's a rare honor, so you must be very good at keeping kings alive."

He takes another bite, chewing slowly before answering. "Clearly not."

A moment of guilt passes through me. "What happened wasn't your fault."

"I know. I had a passion for medicine and saw it was needed, so I went to school. After I attended a small university, I left with excellent recommendations from my professors, and I was able to become an apprentice under a prominent healer at the Versairen Medical Palliation. I stayed there for a number of years before I opened my own practice. When Princess Erenia was unable to conceive, Grayden tasked my mentor with figuring out why. He implied it may be Grayden's fault and was killed for it, unfortunately. That meant a spot opened up and I came highly recommended. I've been with Jedrick for two years, as you know."

A sharp hurt twists in my chest for the lost healer, Princess Erenia, and Grayden's casual cruelty. "He has been vocal about wanting an heir. She hasn't conceived yet?"

"No, and she will not. Not with the number of conception-delaying elixirs she has me prepare for her instead of her morning tea."

My mouth opens in surprise. "You have been aiding her to avoid pregnancy?"

"Of course. The first question I asked Erenia was if she wanted a child. She said no, so that was the end of that. Under Grayden's orders, she comes to see me weekly for her...medication. Mostly we just play cards." He gives me a sly smile as he sips his wine.

"What did you tell Grayden?"

"The truth as to why birth rates are low all over the kingdom. Fruits and vegetables have vitamins and minerals women desperately need to have healthy babies. The sickness we call faerie's revenge ravages his people without aid, we're plagued with drought, and the wealthy overwork the most vulnerable citizens of his kingdom. All of that will have lasting effects, a sickness not seen anywhere else. I believe it has something to do with the crown, that somehow it is draining the life out of Adreania. Grayden seems to think he can change that once he has the crown, bragging constantly that the land will stop being such a barren and desolate place when he is king. He is a fool to think he has any magic to effect change with the crown."

"So he's turning farmers into soldiers to steal what Kalvorn has?"

"That could be, but he implied he had a different plan, claiming he has a way to bring back the lost fae magic. He boasted that there would be so much bounty, it would rot in the streets while everyone went to bed with full bellies."

Grayden's ignorance brings out a hollow laugh from me. "Any idea how he would accomplish such a monumental achievement?"

"Unfortunately, no. I tried to get Jedrick to find out, but he was so tired and old, he couldn't bring himself to care."

Grayden's claim that he can bring back magic while also being in the possession of navlue fruit proves he has access to someone from Ellova? What is he planning and why would he not tell his own father?

"Is Jedrick…? Was he different behind closed doors? He seemed all too happy to turn his back on his people so he could live a lavish life immune to their suffering."

Leon shakes his head gravely. "He was a coward, which is why I will not mourn him. I've known him for years, even when I was an apprentice. He wasn't as indifferent as he seemed in the end. Grayden—" He says his name like a curse. "—was a bully to everyone, even his own father. For the past few years, many laws and rules were placed on the people by Grayden forging the royal seal. Jedrick knew."

I shrug. "Well, the whole reason I sold at the bazaar was to make money for those in Beggars' Row. I only risked venturing into Adreania once a month to bring my cousin food, but I could help more by selling jewelry, so that's how I funded my…assistance. The coins my jewelry earns are enough to provide for the families there 'til I can return."

"So, it was you." His face softens. "For a while, there was an investigation as to why money flowed out from that corner. It was never solved. They were quite loyal to you."

Warmth fills my chest.

"How did you become the Royal Jeweler? That has to be an interesting story. Every jewelry maker I've ever met was a burly, sweaty male. I know I say this every month, but you make such beautiful designs."

"Thank you," I say, looking down at my plate and cutting up the last few bites of the tender chicken, trying for the closest version of the truth I can offer. "I had a family member who served the court as a swordsmith, and my family still held on to the little shop. My last name was known for beautiful work many years ago, so I opened the shop since the reputation had survived. Only open one day per month. Sold out of everything each day with lines down the road. I claimed it was because it took a month to make all the items and everyone believed me. Sold that way for a few years until it caught Jedrick's attention. I was invited to the bazaar years ago and made extra coins there." I shrug.

"Well, now you are unable to return there, and your focus should be keeping yourself safe. I can protect you. I *need* to protect you! Tomorrow, we leave for—"

I do not bother to hide the annoyance on my face at his remarks regarding my safety. "First of all, I don't need protection. I thought we established that. Or did you miss the part where I knocked the three men who were holding Jedrick captive on their asses?"

"Well, I did miss that, actually. I was running a little late, but I'm absolutely sure you were spectacular. I'm simply stating that you have upon your head the crown two kingdoms are about to go to war over. So perhaps you should not be gallivanting in a forest!"

I scoff, which makes him narrow his eyes. "Leon. I. Live. Here. As I have for decades. If two kingdoms are about to go to war over this—" I point to the cursed crown. "—then I need to disappear. You say that Grayden would keep me as a pet, lock me in a dungeon 'til he can find a way to remove the crown, most likely with my head still attached? Who's to say that if the Kalvornian king finds me, he won't do the same? This crown isn't coming off, and I can't risk being found." The anger worsens the pounding in my head.

Leon opens the cookie tin again, handing me one before he bites into his own. "We will find a way to remove it, I promise. For now, we only know two things about the stolen crown: that it once held magic lost to us, magic no mortal can use, and that it was only meant to be worn by an heir of the Fasaile line."

I roll my eyes, chewing on the cookie he gave me. "No, that's false. It has nothing to do with the Fasaile line. They were never involved 'til it was stolen from Queen Inara, who was fae. The crown was created for her and keyed to work with her particular type of magic. Magically forged items can have a mind of their own once the original wielder passes. Magic is fickle. Being Inara's heir has nothing to do with it; it has more to do with the fact that the wearer has the power to control the magic."

Leon stills. I may have given too much away.

Fuck.

He is quiet for a moment, assessing me, before saying, "There is something you are not telling me, isn't there? Like how you would know all this and why the crown is no longer black. Why even now I can feel its magic radiating off you."

I have no answer to that besides the truth, but I can't say that. "I have no idea why the crown would change colors. Perhaps it is because we are out of Adreania? It is said that magic still lingers here. Maybe that is true." I go back to eating my bread, trying to appear bored with this conversation.

His eyes move rapidly. I can almost see him place the pieces together. "Arra, are you fae?"

I force out a hollow laugh, my stomach twisting itself into painful knots. "Of course not. How could I have been in Adreania all these years? Besides, the fae no longer exist, nothing but myths now. Leon, my dear, are you feeling all right? You may have hit your head harder than you thought."

Leon eyes the crown with suspicion. "Something strange is going on. There has to be a logical reason for the shift in color."

"Magic has a mind of its own." I pick up my plate, hoping to end this conversation, and head into the kitchen, where I place my dishes in a copper sink and fill it with fresh water. He joins me, bringing over the silverware and our glasses while I push open a window to let in the crisp night air.

I can tell he has more to say. He opens his mouth but closes it again with a shake of his head. After washing the dishes, he hands them to me to dry, and he watches and puts them back where he found them. Whatever tension remains between us slowly fades away, leaving us in a comfortable silence.

He looks at me every so often with a smile on his face, but he doesn't speak. I fight the overwhelming urge to be honest with him. The panic that he knows too much has subsided; only the desire to have him know my true self remains.

Tomorrow I will have to send him away, but for tonight I can enjoy that he is here with me.

I pull out the only piece of clothing that will fit him: soft sleeping pants that tie in the front that once belonged to my father, one of the few items my mother kept. At the bottom of the drawer, under the piles of sheets and towels, are a few swords he made. My hand hovers over all of them before I pull out one of my favorites. The emeralds on the hilt sparkle in the candlelight, so close to the shade of Leon's eyes. He will need an exceptional weapon to protect himself in the morning. Something inside me twists painfully at the vision of him walking away from me with it.

I point to the space where the narrow stairs hide a door, and he makes his way over to it.

"In the bathing room, pull the left lever for hot water, the right for cold. After you wash up, you can use the same tub for washing your clothes. You will find a bar of oatmeal soap, lathering hair syrups, and a jar with cleansing oil for washing your clothes." I pass him the pants. "Here. You can change into this for now. Announce yourself before you come back up. I need to change."

He nods and heads that way, eyeing me when I put the sword on the table. There's a chest at the end of my bed and I quickly open it, pulling out silky loose sleeping trousers, a sleeveless top, and extra bedding.

A hot bath would be a blessing now, but is Leon the type of man who would snoop through my possessions if left alone here? Maybe he wouldn't, but truthfully, if this situation were reversed, I would, so the bath is forgotten. A few more swigs of the wine bring a new wave of relaxation, and I take a deep breath before I turn to stare at my reflection in the ornate mirror above the tiny writing desk.

The gleaming circlet sits on my head. It is decorated with delicate leaves and small etchings in the fae language, its magic pulsing around me. The crown is obvious even if it is only a few shades lighter than my hair. Thankfully my ears are still hidden. I separate the top part of my hair and hastily braid some of it to wrap around the crown as best as possible. I stick a few golden pins around the circlet.

How in Ellova's name did Jedrick sleep with it on?

With the last of the candles blown out in the dining area, I crawl into my soft bed. Moving all the way to the wall, I lean against the headboard. The echo of the running water makes it impossible to think of anything else besides what he may look like, lying in my bath, rivulets of water flowing down over his muscles. The illusion in my mind of us together in that tub is too tempting to ignore.

The tub is only big enough for one. I would need to straddle him, our faces close enough to kiss as he gently caresses the bar of soap all over my trembling body. He cups his hand in the water to pour it over me, watching the trail of bubbles slide down over my skin, placing soft, lingering kisses on each part of me he cleans. His strong hands line up my hips with his center as I carefully sink down on his waiting cock. The soap forgotten as his hands dip between my thighs, we groan together as the water splashes over the edge of the bath at the frantic motion of our joined bodies. His fingers have the dexterity of a healer on my clit—

The door of the bathing room pops open a crack, causing me to jump. "May I enter?"

"Y-yes!" My voice is a strangled mess.

He stops in the doorframe, his broad, bare chest on display, and studies me in bed. "Are you all right?" That tender tone with his features pulled together in concern sends a blush to my cheeks.

Yes, Leon, I'm fine. You just startled me as I was daydreaming about us, hopelessly imagining you naked as I rode you 'til the floor flooded from our fucking.

Instead, I say, "The line is outside to hang your clothing, right when you walk out to the left. Do not attempt to go into the ominous glowing workshop, all right?"

We do not break eye contact as the words sink in. One eyebrow arches up, but he nods and heads outside with a slight frown on his face. Appearing to have listened, he immediately returns, locking the door as he does, and slowly walks over to the bed. I find him watching my hands as they twist my hair into a long braid for sleep.

He holds his hand out to me expectantly. "I'll take the floor if you hand me a pillow?"

I look between him, his hand, and the exceedingly obvious place I've made for him next to me with the blanket moved down, folding it over to give it a welcoming appearance. Glancing up at him, I ask, "Do you wish to sleep on the floor?"

He pretends to look thoughtful for a moment. "It's a hard choice, really. May I have a moment to think about it?" He holds up two hands like a scale. "Uncomfortable floor?" He lifts an arm up, tipping it upwards. "Beautiful woman." He lifts the other arm up. "Decisions, decisions."

It earns a smile from me. I hadn't imagined it would be this hard to get him into bed. "What a compliment. I'm as appealing as the stone floor."

He smiles back at me for a moment but then gets serious, his green eyes softening, words gentle. "I just want to be respectful of your space."

"That is very kind of you, Leon. When I have a free moment, I shall commission a statue to your gallant chivalry, but between Grayden's vile harassment, the kidnapping, the death of your king, and acquiring an indelible crown, I think we both have had a rather long day and could use a good night's sleep. Which certainly won't happen if you sleep on the floor."

His laugh undoes a little of the woven ball of worry knitted in my chest.

"You also beat up those kidnappers." He slides into the bed but leaves as much space as possible between our bodies.

I leave one candle burning, letting the wax drip on the table, and lie down, dreading sleeping with this crown on. The moment my head touches my pillow, I can no longer feel the crown or its magic, and I immediately bolt up again, gasping. Leon shoots out of the covers, ready with the sword that never leaves my side of the bed. The blade gleams in the candlelight while he looks around for a threat.

"What? Is everything all right?" He moves in a circle, seeking out the source of my panic.

"Yes…my apologies for startling you." The feeling of the crown settles on my head once more, the pressing weight of the magic returning in a rush. He watches from above as I sink into the bed once more. The magic vibrations vanish, leaving only the slight weight of it, as if my hair is pulled too tight, but it's not uncomfortable enough to keep me awake. There is hope for real sleep tonight. "When I return to my pillow, the sensation of magic is almost gone. Well, I know it is there. It makes its presence known…an odd feeling to be sure, but manageable."

He looks at the crown with an expression of frustration, but his gaze quickly returns to one of interest at me. "May I touch it?" he asks tentatively, his raised hand paused and waiting for my permission.

I want him to touch me anywhere else, but I agree. "Of course."

He stares down at me for a long moment before his eyes return to the crown. As his hand gets close, the crown vibrates, like a cat hissing at approaching unwanted affection. He pulls back sharply. "It is blistering hot. Are you sure you are all right?" He presses the back of his hand to my forehead to check my temperature.

I reach up and rub the smooth, warm metal. "It feels fine. The temperature of tea left out."

"Interesting." He lies back down beside me, but this time closer than before, both of us staring at the stone ceiling above. His voice is low as he asks, "Well, that's good, right? Easier to sleep?"

I nod, his closeness bringing a wave of nervousness. How many nights did I imagine he was there beside me while I drifted off to sleep? Countless. He is warm and solid, close enough to touch, to taste, but I keep my hands to myself.

"Um, I didn't want to ask when we arrived, but where is your family? I'm not going to be awakened in the middle of the night by a justifiably angry husband and crying children, am I? Not that I would blame the man. Of course, one must defend one's marriage bed from strange men in it."

I burst out laughing. "Leon, about that…"

"Ah. The family does not exist, do they? I'm going to guess they are as real as your Adreanian citizenship?"

My laugh slowly stops. "Sorry. All part of a carefully crafted façade to gain entrance to the Iron Castle and help its citizens in the only way I could."

He chuckles. "I had my suspicions. You always had the look of a doe faced with an arrow when I inquired about them, and you changed the subject with alarming speed. I wouldn't be surprised if Arra isn't even your real name."

Guilt guides me to honesty. "Um, well, Arra's…Arra is not my name…" The mattress shifts as I face him. He follows my lead and turns; our noses are a few inches apart now. That sweet strawberry and earthy herb scent envelops me. I hope the sheets smell like him long after he's slipped away from my exceedingly long life.

There are so few truths I can offer him, and when he walks away tomorrow, my real name must be one of them.

"Of course it's not." He gives me a small smile, but it doesn't reach his eyes. "Why would it be?"

"Can we start over?" I slip my hand from under our blanket and hold it out to him. He pauses for a moment but takes it. His hand is warm, the simple touch electrifying. A spike of desire brings the urge to take that hand to other places as he moves his thumb over my skin before reluctantly pulling away.

"I would like that very much." He looks relieved, a little tension lifting off him.

"Hello, I'm Izadella Aranelle. Jeweler, that much is true. I like roasted duck, blackberry wine, and adventure books. I dislike peas and being cold. I have a fox named Farren. If I'm not at my cottage, I spend most of my time with two of my closest friends who live not far from here."

Farren hops on the bed at the sound of his name and licks my face.

"Izadella is a beautiful name." Just like with *Arra*, he enunciates it with an emphasis on the *A* at the end that sounds as sweet and rich as melted chocolate on his lips. A joyous flutter starts in my chest again. "So, you just created a whole identity, didn't you?"

"I did what I needed to do for my family, to help where it was needed, no matter what risk it took to do so."

He laughs, but I hear little amusement in it. "I don't know how you were able to create a false identity, sneak into Adreania, and work in the Iron Castle under the nose of King Jedrick. That is not something one does lightly."

Pride swells within me. "Well, with the right motivation, anything can be done, I suppose."

"And what was your motivation?"

"Same as yours. I wanted to help those in Adreania. I needed to ensure my cousin's survival at all costs."

We lie in bed together under the cover of night, staring but not speaking, soaking up each other. Tiredness spreads within me, sleep reaching out its moonlit hand, but he needs to know what his concern means to me. How deeply his desire to protect me has touched me, that his care will always stay with me. "Thank you for being so concerned about my safety no matter who I am. I was truly touched that you would care so much about me and my darling imaginary children. Were they real, I would not be able to properly express my gratitude that they would have been safe. I am sure they would have had a great life where you were going to send us."

He nods. "The destination was a cottage off by the Elbasan Sea in a thriving little village. I grew up there. It has a small farm attached to it with animals and a garden that needs some love and care, but it grows the most delicious vegetables. Or at least it did. The property is not much, but it's home."

My stomach drops. I need to confess to him I sent Cyanna in my place. "Ah, yes, um, about that. I may have sent my cousin and twenty-two orphans to the ship in my place." I quickly add, "I know that's not what you or the sea captain expected, but I *needed* to get them to safety since I wouldn't be able to bring supplies anymore and a war is about to start." I wait for his reaction, hoping it's not anger, and yet somehow knowing it won't be.

He is quiet for a moment but lets out a robust laugh. "When I told Oliver a woman and her children would be expecting his escort, I do not think that is what he had in mind. Izadella, I'm *honored* you would trust me with your family. I know Cyanna. She and the children will have a beautiful life there."

I am so delighted and relieved by his words, the sincerity there. I could kiss him, but I hold back my affections. "You do? How?"

"You are not the only one who spends time trying to help those who call Beggars' Row home. A few nights a week I provide medical attention there, including those at the orphanage."

"Did she know you are the royal healer?" She never mentioned knowing Leon.

He shakes his head. "No, I did not let anyone know. Grayden would have had my head. I will sleep better, knowing the children are somewhere safe and at a place precious to me."

"Is your family there now?"

"No, long gone. I was sent off around seventeen or so, and then I was shipped off to study in Versairen's capital. They left a few years later."

"Seventeen?" I can't keep the horror from my voice. "But that's so young."

Fae children in Ellova are considered dewlings until we are fifty, although we would only appear to be around twenty-five to mortals. A dewling of that age would barely be starting lessons with the Ink Court.

He nods. "Yes, well, my mother needed me to learn medicine. It was a great school and provided the education that led me to become the royal healer. The most coveted position in the medical society. It also meant I got to meet you."

I blush at the comparison and pull the covers closer to my chest to prevent myself from reaching out to touch him. "What's it been like, living in the castle?"

"It had its bright moments but was mostly terrible. Jedrick has been paranoid for years; none of Grayden's four older brothers have survived. Each death was more suspicious than the last. Jedrick believed that Grayden would come for him once there were no other heirs. He feared Grayden, had guards around constantly whenever his son was near. Even if the crown can only be transferred in death, he still knew Grayden would try anything to become king."

"There has to be a way to remove it without..." My throat is suddenly dry. I can't seem to say the word out loud. Oh, Ellova's grave, please don't let me die with this crown still atop my head.

Leon continues, "The crown protects from death, or at least it should. It was meant to. The history books dictate Queen Inara wasn't wearing it when she died. She had removed it, so we know it's possible. It wasn't worth her life or their daughter's. She handed it to Drystan willingly, hoping it would spare her or at least give the daughter time to escape. He killed Inara once he had it. It's said that the little princess was saved, though she was never seen again."

My chest aches at the story even though I have heard it many times.

Leon is silent.

Deep in the White Library, tucked away within the Ink Court, sits Alvina's journal. The Forger's Journal. Since Alvina made the crown, it might have the answers I seek. It has been locked since her death. I've tried so many times to open it, but with the crown's power I might be able to unlock it. The library holds many scrolls recording the lives of the first Realm Keeper, Zarella; Alvina, and Inara.

"We should sleep. We have a long journey ahead of us," he adds after a few more moments of silence.

He has a rough shadow of stubble gracing his face. I want to reach out and rub my fingers over the short, coarse hair. His eyes are half shut. Black hair with a streak of gray falls in front of his face. Would he welcome my touch if I reached out to push it back? I know where I would lead that touch, but we don't know what tomorrow brings, so I hold my hands to my chest.

"Good night, Leon," I whisper while staring into those emerald eyes.

This feels right; he was meant to be here with me tonight, in my bed. It was always meant to be him. The cottage is warmer with his presence. Unlike every other night for the past century, sleep finds me easily. The events of today have drained me; my bones ache, and my heart is heavy, but when his fingers slowly lace with mine, I squeeze his hand and fall asleep with a smile on my face.

CHAPTER 14

irds call to one another, adding to the sounds of the forest waking up beneath the vanishing purple sky. Slivers of early sunlight peek in behind my sheer white curtains.

Delightfully aware of warmth on both sides of me, I do not believe I have ever rested so well. Much of yesterday's pain has faded. Farren is curled up and snuggling in my arms, his snout resting on my bicep. He smells faintly like the dirt he loves to play in, and the sweet blackberry patch he naps under on warm days. My soul swells with adoration at that little face and his purr of contentment.

The love for this small creature spreads through me. He's just as much family to me as Nueena and Tavien are.

The other warmth is Leon. His bare chest presses against my back; one arm wrapped around my waist. My nightshirt has ridden up, so he clings to my stomach, his fingers grasping my soft flesh. The short consideration of moving is whisked away when he pulls me closer to him, his arm tightening. His face finds my neck, but his steady breathing leads me to believe he is still fast asleep.

Farren peers up at me, sleep still in his eyes. I kiss his nose, my lips striking quickly before he can get away from my affections. He side-eyes me and slips gracefully from my arms, stretching before jumping off the bed.

"Don't pretend we weren't cuddling," I whisper to my little beast. He looks at me with a bored expression before slinking off towards the kitchen.

"I wouldn't dare to pretend such things," Leon says, and I can fight the smile no longer. His breathing is slow and rhythmic, still clinging to sleep; his nose is just under my ear. It moves slowly down, and he inhales my scent before brushing his lips lightly against me. I let out a little gasp at his unexpected but not unwelcome tenderness.

"Not you. Go back to sleep." With my arms free of my pet, I place my hand over Leon's on my waist, interlacing our fingers, which is met with a tight squeeze from him. I give in to the cloud of tiredness still in my head and close my eyes again.

"You first." I can feel his smile on my skin as he says it.

I yawn. "One more hour and then we get up."

"Deal." He somehow manages to pull me even closer, and sleep finds me again.

~

The smell of roasted potatoes and bacon rouses me from sleep. The bed is cool and empty this time, now that both of my heat sources are in the kitchen. I pull the blankets tighter around myself and watch a shirtless Leon whisk something in a small bowl. Farren is on the counter, a place he knows he's not allowed to be, accepting small bites of meat from Leon, who chops up bacon and throws it into the mixture.

He has opened the windows for a soft breeze, but the cottage is warm from his cooking. My heart tightens at the way he takes care of me; the view of him in my little kitchen is unexpected. He is whispering to Farren, who looks at him with a surprising amount of concentration. My little pet found someone to feed him and let him get up on the counter; Leon has made a friend for life.

He chops up vegetables before adding them into a roasting pan.

When I finally do sit up, the world spins as the magic rushes up and down, flooding my body. My stomach lurches, bringing with it a sickening swell that makes me gag. The magic is awake and seemingly livid that it found me still in possession of it. I pull my knees towards me and cover my face with my hands as the nausea rises. The oven door shuts in the kitchen, and the sound of his bare feet walking across my floor only gives me a brief warning Leon has made his way over to me. The bed dips as he sits back down, placing a strong hand on the curve of my back, rubbing in deep circles to soothe me.

"I'm all right." Mumbling into my knees, I lean into his touch.

"Are you sure? Can I get you anything?" His voice is soft and full of gentle worry as his hands move across my spine. We stay like that for a few minutes, and I enjoy his touch as the nausea subsides until only the angry pressure remains. Slowly I turn my head to face him.

"Hello." It comes out weakly.

"Good morning." He smiles down at me with concern.

I try to stay focused on his face and not the bare chest inches from me. My eyes betray me, and I glance down to the taut muscles and thick torso. "You know, for a healer, you have quite the physical form. Did you have an excess of available time in your medical education to work on building those muscles?"

"Oh, yes, positions within medicine are notorious for leisurely activities." He nudges my shoulder gently but sobers. "Jedrick required I be trained with his guard as well, just in case I came down as his last defense."

"In case three armed men sneak in and kidnap him, or, I guess, 'kingnap' him." I regret the jest for a moment; maybe that's too far, but thankfully he laughs. It's rich and invites my smile to widen.

"Yes, but based on my previous performance, I shall focus on healing from now on. Perhaps guard duty is not a strength of mine."

"Three against one is hardly a fair fight," I add helpfully.

"Ah, but you handled them just fine. One day you will have to tell me how you accomplished that."

Well, he has a point there. I almost point out that I had magic on my side but perhaps it's just best to leave it. "What are you making that smells so divine? I am surprised you know how to cook."

"What is cooking if not alchemy with different ingredients? My mother made sure I knew how to cook. I should be offended by your remark," he teases. "I wasn't up there with a silver spoon in my hand, you know. It was demanding labor, unlike most of the fools of Jedrick's court, who lay around all day, complaining."

It is my turn to bump his shoulder. "Well, thank you for making breakfast. I haven't had a meal made for me here in a long time." The memory of my mother making rosemary pancakes for me and Nueena over a century ago appears vividly in my mind. The smell of warm butter and rich herbs, her laughter as she watched us play together. Before my father's death broke her heart so completely.

"In the pantry I noticed there was quite a bit of dried meat. A favorite of yours?" he teases.

Most certainly not a favorite of mine but everything is overly sweet in Ellova, like having cake for every meal. The dried meats help with the craving for something savory. "You could say that, but it's probably not as good as whatever you made now. Is it ready?"

Leon moves slowly off the bed and extends his hand to me. I take the assistance, and after I stand, he places a firm hand low on my back to ensure I'm strong enough on my feet. Stepping behind the partition in a corner, I change into tight black pants and a loose, deep green tunic that reaches the tops of my thighs, where my dagger is harnessed. When he sees me, he almost drops the bowl.

"Are you all right over there, healer? Haven't seen a woman in pants in a while, huh?"

He clears his throat, putting the bowl on the counter. "You can say that. Women wore them in Versairen, but the Adreanians are a bit more...traditional."

My eyes narrow. "The word you seek is oppressed."

He nods solemnly. "Yes, forgive me. I would agree that is a better term."

I sit at the table he has already set for us: plum juice, slices of grilled bread with blackberry jam on it, and salted butter on the side.

"You seemed to have been busy in the kitchen this morning. Were you enjoying yourself?"

"I was. I hope you don't mind. These are luxuries I haven't had in years. Jam? Fruit juice? Leafy greens? I feel like a king."

I laugh. "Cook away. Whatever you wish to use is fine. Everything here is easy to replace, and I'm happy for anything you make me."

He turns back to the kitchen. Even though he has spent the morning cooking, everything is clean, freshly washed pots and pans drying on the rack.

"We need to leave as soon as we finish. Grayden may not notice Jedrick's disappearance for a few hours, but I wish for us to be as far away as possible."

Guilt, fear, and dread beat as one in my chest.

"What do you normally do in the mornings?" he asks.

I'm unsure of what to tell him. *Well, Leon, Ellova, the realm thought to be a myth, is real. Most of my time is spent with my closest friend, Nueena, heir to the Ellovian throne. I'm treated like royalty in its palace, there's never a shortage of balls and parties, and I have enough gems to make jewelry for a millennium.*

I go for the barest truth of my life. "I go for rides or a long walk before I start my work in the workshop."

"Has that always been your business?"

"Yes and no. My mother also worked with metals, mostly swords. My father, Nolan, was the business end, from what I understood, though he was also a talented and sought-after sword-smith in Adreania. That was a long time ago, though. Now I spend the month between bazaars making pieces to sell."

"What happened to your parents?" he asks in a low voice.

"My father died when I was young, and the heartbreak from his death took my mother soon after. She died when I was fifteen but thankfully my friend's family welcomed me into theirs." It was over a hundred years ago, but a fresh wave of grief washes over me.

Leon freezes in the kitchen before slowly turning back to me.

He walks over and kneels on one knee before me. "I'm so sorry to hear that. Fifteen is far too young to know such heartache."

I swallow hard, not knowing what to say. "Yes, it was, but please don't burn your lovely meal on my account. It was a long time ago, truly."

"I lost my parents as well, I was too far away to have been able to say goodbye. I know that unending ache. I'm here, though, if you ever wish to speak of them."

Leon squeezes my knees, his hands lingering for a moment before he stands and returns to the kitchen. He pulls the baking dish from the oven and begins slicing into the eggs mixed with meat and vegetables, sprinkled with cheese. He scoops up the potatoes and chopped vegetables in the pan and adds it to the plate, sprinkling everything with flaky sea salt and coarse pepper. He sets down the golden plate in front of me with a flourish.

My mouth waters at his hard work. "This looks amazing, Leon."

"Thank you. It's nice to feel useful."

What an odd thing to say. "You didn't feel useful as the royal healer?"

Leon sets down his plate and joins me. "Jedrick was terrified of illness. He kept mostly to his room; anyone who came into his chambers needed to have washed in hot water and herbs and, at times, even had to wear leather gloves. He had tasters for everything; even his bathwater was drunk before he would soak. Paranoia because of Grayden. Quite a few attempts were made on his life with poison, but the crown protected him even from that. A minuscule amount of my medical knowledge was used. The only time I ever felt useful was assisting the castle servants, or Beggars' Row, but even then, I could only help in the times I could slip away from him."

"He was a terrible king, so concerned with his own illness. What of the sickness that spreads in the streets? How many suffered?"

"You will find no argument from me on that, but I think he was desperate to keep the crown from Grayden. The longer he lived, the more time he could buy the kingdom. Grayden got away with a lot of abuse of power, but with his father alive and hiding in his rooms, he was never truly in charge."

My eyes roll before I can stop them. "Do not try to make him into a martyr, Leon. He watched silently as his people suffered up until the end."

He doesn't respond immediately, so I start eating. The breakfast is delicious, and as I am about to compliment his meal, he speaks in a low, almost saddened voice. "Jedrick was most certainly complicit in all the pain and suffering his family has caused. I'm personally glad he's dead, but I also know how much worse Adreania will be because of it. I am far too familiar with Grayden's cruelty."

With nothing to add to that, we finish the meal in silence. The pounding in my head makes it difficult to hold a conversation even if I wished to say more.

In just a few hours Grayden will rage, finding his father, the crown, and Leon gone. I refuse to think about what he will do to me if he finds the crown on my head and Leon with me.

When we are done, Leon takes the plates to the sink, washes them, and places them gently on the windowsill rack.

"I could use your help," I say. Having him here was something out of a dream, but with this crown on me, everything could soon turn into a nightmare.

He turns with unease written on his face. After drying his hands on a towel, he heads towards me. "Is everything all right?" He looks at my face and then up to the crown.

"Yes, I just need assistance packing up my things for the journey."

Relief floods his face. "Of course. How can I help?" The frown he had worn turns upward into genuine delight. It makes me feel worse for what I am about to do, but I force myself to mirror his expression.

Guilt turns my stomach to ice. "Will you pack up all the dried meat and any vegetables we have here? There are two travel bags in the pantry. Split the food between the bags for our journey. There should be room for your clothing. Hopefully everything is dry. We will leave as soon as you are done."

He gives me a determined nod and pulls the latch up, descending into the pantry.

Knowing I must say goodbye to him forever in a few short minutes sends a stabbing pain into my chest.

Maybe after this short time together, really getting to know each other, he will miss me in the same way I am to miss him for the next few centuries. The sensation of his arms around me when I awoke this morning, safe and warm, is burned into my being. I will never be able to fall asleep again without imagining he is there, holding me.

I may never fully recover from his brief existence in my life, but I hope he has a long mortal life, filled with every possible happiness, even if I won't be there to experience it with him.

How can I say goodbye when walking out of his life feels so wrong?

CHAPTER 15

Not seeing a future without this crown on my head, everything of personal value must be packed up. Until Nueena and I can find a way to remove this blasted circlet, I will only truly be safe in the palace.

I hate having to leave so much of my life behind, so many treasures collected for the past century.

Misery makes its way into my chest as I search for my most precious possessions. The first items packed are faded love letters with my parents' names in swirling cursive on the front, tucked into a jewelry box my father made. All the jewelry my mother forged and saved for me. A bottle of sweet oils, a tea set wrapped in one of the dresses Nueena left here last month. My sketches rolled up for travel, the few books and journals I kept here. I open the crystal top of my pale-yellow perfume and dab a little under each ear and down my neck. Sweet rose and geranium with a hint of lemon. The last item is a small oil painting in a golden frame of Nueena and me. The rest will be safe here for now. I spend much of my time in the Ellovian palace with Nueena and Tavien, but knowing I might not be able to return to my home in the near future strikes me with grief.

Alvina, my great-great-grandmother, built this cottage, and

survived her exile for creating the crown with her daughter here. That daughter raised her daughter and then her granddaughter, my mother, within these walls. I only had fifteen short years with her, all of them spent here. Five generations of fae women have made this humble cottage a home.

Nueena took Onyx back to the palace stables when she left, so the only way to get to the tree portals is on foot.

I risk leaving Leon for a few minutes and slip out the front door, hoping he does not follow. The crisp morning is alive with songs from the stone dove nests above. The family of rabbits feast from the garden, neatly kept thanks to Nueena's tender care and magic. My boots are slick with dawn's dew as I make my way across my yard. Just past the garden wall is a large pond of clear water, the last bit of morning fog still gliding atop it.

Besides the colored glass doors and windows, the entire small round forge's walls are lined with smooth gray stones. An identical twisted brick chimney stands above it all.

Long ago, this was a great forge; its divine flame birthed mighty fae weapons and dazzling jewelry fit only for royalty. The story of its power is that of myth, but now the fire that dances in the legendary furnace is slowly fading. To forge an item with the blue flames is to instill within it deep magic. Swords that could only be touched by the wielder keyed to it. A family heirloom that would turn to ash if stolen. Fae would travel from the farthest corners of Ellova and beg Alvina to infuse the flame's magic with what they needed. Her powerful metal-wielding, her jewelsmith powers, and the magic from the forge made her weapons unbeatable.

How would Alvina react to the knowledge that the crown is, once again, coveted by another heartless Fasaile man willing to kill for it. Only this time, instead of her best friend, the wearer is me. I'm terrified, so one can guess she would be as well.

The crown was the last item ever forged with its magic. After it brought such ruination, she was never sought after ever again.

I slip into my workshop, welcomed by a wave of familiar, ever-burning heat of the forge, magic, and a mosaic of colors. I sit on the end of the forge, the flames rising higher in greeting.

With one hand I swirl my fingers into the flames and with the other I grasp the crown, desperately trying to remove it. Again, I try to remove the crown with one hand, but it sits firmly on top of my head.

Since Jedrick's death, I held on to hope that being in here, the crown might acknowledge the presence of its birthplace, but it continues to release the same vibration of magic that flows up and down my body, pressure trapped within me. I rub my temples, desperate for some kind of relief. Angrily, I give it one last hard tug, which only results in almost passing out from the sharp pain.

When that does not work, I close my eyes and call the magic of the crown to me, willing it to obey my jewelsmith powers, to release itself. The only result is another headache.

Alvina's blood flows in my veins. If the crown were to respond to anyone, it should be me, here in this room, so why won't it come off?

Fuck.

~

Acceptance takes root in me, and when I return to the cottage, Nueena's crown in hand. Leon is ready to leave, both packs over his shoulder. He waits patiently as I take one look around the cottage for anything I may have missed. A sense of dread coils deep in my gut as we walk out the front door. The cottage locks itself with long-lost protective magic; once I leave, it will allow only Farren in and out at his will.

The sun is bright in the blue morning sky. If I were a cloud-keeper and could control the weather like Camarra, leader of the Green Court, I would have the skies rage with me, sending thunder and lightning to embody my misery of parting with Leon.

We walk in the direction of the Airvell River, Farren running ahead of us. Leon breaks the silence with small comments on the thriving trees and abundant wildlife but mostly we do not speak. I attempt to seem casual, as if I am not about to abandon him.

We pause to fill our travel bottles in the cool waters. Leon starts to walk again but I stop him, my hand on his arm. "Wait."

"Do you need to rest? What can I do?"

The concern and care he has shown me makes this even harder. I miss him even while he stands here before me with those warm eyes.

I pull on the straps that attach the sword to my pack. The sword my father forged over a century ago in his small metal workshop in Adreania. I always loved the emeralds that surround the hilt, but leaving Leon with something to remember me by and to give him protection means more to me at this moment.

I hold it out to him. "This is for you."

He takes it from me, admiring the gemstones and checking its balance. "Do you need me to carry it?"

"No, Leon. It's a parting thank-you gift, for everything, but this is where we separate. If you head around the mountain between Adreania and Kalvorn, in about a day you will reach the Elbasan Sea. There you will find a small dock. My mother would take me there when she needed some supplies. It's run by Kalvorn but you will be able to find a ship to take you home. You can fund the journey with the bag of gems I placed in your bag. You can charter a whole ship back to Versairen, if you like." I try not to let the dread of this goodbye seep into my voice. "It's been a pleasure, truly. I hope you can return home to a life free of Adreania, and build a new, happy life. You have been gone for a long time."

Forcing myself to hold eye contact, I shove down the desire to pull him towards me for a goodbye kiss. I extend my hand out to him for a farewell handshake and one last bittersweet touch. He makes no move to leave, and my heart skips a beat. His eyes travel slowly from my face to my outstretched hand that still hovers in the air, waiting for him, before trailing back up to me with an amused expression.

He slips his hand into mine. "And where do you think you are going?"

"My travels will take me elsewhere, but I hope one day we can meet again." My attempt at a friendly, reassuring smile falters.

I try to end our farewell handshake, but he twists his hand in mine, entwining our fingers together. His thumb brushes over my fingers, our palms pressed together.

"Izadella," he says patiently, determination lacing every word, "I will not leave your side for the foreseeable future. Whether we head towards the docks or the highest mountain of Widowmaker's Peak, my place is beside you."

Damn it, Leon, why must you make this so difficult?

I muster all my courage for a firm answer. "No. I'm sorry, Leon, I am, but you can't come with me to where I'm going."

"Oh?" His voice is gruff. "And why is that?"

I take a deep breath, already exhausted from this conversation, my head drumming with a dull ache. "You will not be welcomed there. I am truly sorry. It's best if we part here. Trust me, please."

The smile he has worn all morning is gone, that strong jaw set in a firm line with all of his focus solely on me. Taking his free hand, he points to the embroidered symbol on the clean shirt he put on this morning. It's a dark reddish-brown sword facing straight down and inside a black ring tilting to the side. The ring surrounds the weapon at a high angle. One side of the ring is between the hilt and the handle, the other by the blade's end.

"Do you know what this means?"

"Yes, the symbol of Adreania." It comes out of me in a whisper. The intensity with which he is staring at me steals my breath, rooting me to the spot.

His eyes bore into mine as he takes a step towards me, the forest around us fading with his nearness. Neither of us remove our entwined hands. "That is partly true, but see the sword here?"

Leaving the intimacy of his gaze, I track his hand as he ever so slowly drags a finger down the deep red thread that creates the blade.

"Those of us who have sworn loyalty to the crown that rests atop your head bear the red sword. We do not marry or sire children; our life is fully dedicated to the throne. My life no longer exists outside of this loyalty to you. It is an existence of devotion, fidelity only to the wearer, 'til death."

Anticipation and dread send my heart thundering as he takes another step towards me, his hand still in mine. We are chest to chest now when I start trembling, and I know he can feel it.

"The red thread that embroiders the sword did not use a dye to give it that color; I bled over the needle that sewed it. Do you know what that means?"

I shake my head.

He tightens his hold on my hand. "It means, Izadella, that *you* have my blood and my blade. *Forever.*"

"Oh." *Oh.*

"So you will have to forgive me if I do not abandon the vow I made and watch you walk away from me. I swear it, not only as a man of medicine, to heal you when you need me, to protect and defend, but to care for and serve you in all ways. You are my queen, and I am yours to command, in whatever way you need."

His scent is overwhelming, and a warmth I've never known fills my chest at his sweet words. He leans down and my eyes flutter shut, but the moment our lips are about to touch, I jerk back, releasing his hand as if it burned me, the full realization of his words hitting me.

Queen?

CHAPTER 16

I stumble away from Leon, and my confusion matches his. He takes a step towards me, leaves crunching underneath his boots, arms outstretched to catch me if I fall.

"What's wrong?" He looks around the clearing for an attack but quickly returns to my gaze.

"Queen?" It is a broken sound, even to my ears.

His confusion grows at my shaking question. "Yes, queen." What he offers as an explanation is of no help to me, and when my open-mouthed shock does not morph into understanding, he pulls an iron coin from his healer's bag. Holding it up before me, he reads it aloud. "'Loyal to whoever wears the crown.'" He turns the coin over to show the same sword and crown symbol. "It means whoever wears the crown is the ruler of Adreania. You are now the rightful que—"

Lunging at him, I cut his deranged words short as I slap my hand over his mouth. "Leon, do not finish that sentence! Adreania may have a rightful ruler, but it is not me! Do you understand me?"

My heart hitches at the whisper of pressure as his lips press into my palm, sending an electric current through me, before his hands rise up to cover mine, slowly removing it but not letting go.

"The truth may be unexpected, but that doesn't make it false.

120

However unintended this all was, the law is clear. You are the queen, and my life is sworn to you."

"No, Leon. Maybe that was true long ago, but it's not now. No matter how awful Grayden is, with his father dead, that makes him king. That is how the line of succession works. Please, I've given you everything you need for your journey home to Versairen. Food and gems to trade, to buy the silence of everyone you meet. Please, you need to go." He is making this so much harder than it needs to be.

"Never." He takes the pack off and tosses it to the forest floor. "That crown makes you queen of Adreania. It may just be a historical object to you, but it symbolizes something much greater: power. Kalvorn is about to go to war for the crown! You need to be somewhere safe. I can take you there." Desperation bleeds into his voice.

"So, I am your queen?" Frustration is building in me.

"Yes."

"Truly, you will do whatever I say?" Air is suddenly harder to pull into my lungs.

"Truly," he answers earnestly, gifting me with a small reassuring smile.

"Then I order you to leave! Any foolish oath you made to that poor excuse for a king is complete. Pick up that bag and go home, Leon."

The aches in my body are nothing to the pain in my chest when I see his expression. When I can no longer stand to see the hurt I've caused, I pull my hand back, stepping out of his space.

Leon's fists clench at his sides. "It's been long enough, so surely the king's absence has been noticed. Instead of his father, Grayden will find an empty bedchamber, his father gone, and a suspiciously missing healer. Once the guards have searched the castle only to return to him empty-handed, what do you think he will do?"

My voice is trapped within my chest.

He continues, bitterness blooming in his words. "Do you know what they will do to me when they find me? Kill me. Oathbreaker and defender of the king disgraced. Death will be the only justice in

Grayden's eyes. Once he is done raging, he will send forces out into the city, and when the crown is not found there, he will never stop looking for it. I have no doubt he will seek revenge on Kalvorn immediately, who already has an army waiting to attack, turning his sick and dying people into soldiers for a crown that is useless to him and revenge for a father he never cared about."

"Leon, you tried to stop whoever took Jedrick. You went after him when they left you for dead."

His face hardens but I do not feel his anger is directed at me, just the situation he now finds himself in. "You think the man who threatened you two nights ago would care that I *tried*? He will only see failure, and the punishment for that is death. It is no longer safe for you or me! He will be sending out forces to comb this forest shortly, no matter the risks. They may already have sent guards to the port to stop all ships from leaving for Versairen. He could have spies anywhere. I've already failed one royal. I refuse to fail another one, especially one I actually *care* about."

I want to scream that a fate worse than death awaits him if he follows me to the fae realm, that the magic will drive him to madness. "I'm sorry, but—"

The rumbling of horse hooves slamming into the soil nearby grows louder, heading straight towards us.

Leon holds my father's sword out at the same time I remove my dagger, hiding it from view in my back pocket. He moves to stand in front of me. "You need to run. I'll find you again," he demands, scanning the forest. "Go, *now*!" When I make no move to flee, he pleads, "Please! *Please* hide."

I should run, leave him. It was my plan all along, wasn't it? But as two riders race towards us, I do not have it in me to abandon him. That constant pull to Leon tethers me to him, keeping me at his side. Above all, he is my friend, and I will not sacrifice him to save myself, no matter how much he begs me to. "I'm not leaving you here to fight them off yourself, Leon, so either you fight with me, or *you* run."

"Damn it, Izadella!" He says it through gritted teeth. "I'm trying to protect you."

"And I've told you I do not *need* protection," I hiss back.

We glare at each other before turning back to our unwelcome guests.

The horses come to a slamming halt before us, and the two men dismount, weapons out.

Grayden's fucking guards, his initial carved deep into the black leather of their clothing. Violence seeps off them with their cruel laughter.

The taller of two speaks first. "Healer, I was wondering how long it was going to take to find you. King Grayden suspected it was you. How pleased he will be that he was right when we drag you before him for your betrayal."

"The next time I see Grayden will be on his death day," Leon spits.

"Aye, she looks familiar. Is she from court?" the shorter, blond one asks, eyeing me. "Don't you make the jewelry for those pompous courtiers?"

The first one sneers at us. "The king is going to be delighted when we bring you both back to the castle. He has a particular plan in store for each of you." His cruel smile towards me turns my chest to ice.

Leon moves again in front of me and snarls, "You will not *touch* her!"

The tall guard only laughs before he charges at Leon with his sword. Leon is faster and blocks the first attack. He slashes at the guard, causing a laceration on his shoulder, but with the next attack the guard's sword slices through the flesh of Leon's arm, a line of blood seeping into the cut fabric.

"We need them both alive!" the blond guard shouts. "The king will have our heads if we kill his playthings."

Before I can scream, the guard launches himself at me, his hand stretched wide to grab my arm. I reach back for my dagger with speed only the fae possess. The dagger and his hand collide in the air, the onyx-eyed fox handle flush against his palm, the blade protruding through the other side. He shrieks as I yank the blade out, the blood spattering the forest floor.

He presses his pierced palm to his chest, drawing his sword as he charges at me. My fox dagger stands no chance against his broadsword, and he wears no metal. I call to my magic, desperate for the dagger to morph into a short spear, but nothing happens.

No, no, no!

The jewelsmith magic refuses my call, the crown's magic pushing down on it, overwhelming it. I try to manipulate the foreign magic that pulses beneath my skin, but I can't. No call or demand for it produces anything. Desperation builds and builds. I can feel the magic wishes to be free, like a blocked river of power within me.

Farren appears with a flash of fury and black fur. With a fierce little growl, he bites the guard's ankle. The man attempts to kick Farren away, who jumps back only to latch onto his flesh again. Fear and rage redden my vision, and I do not give him a chance to go after my fox again. I slice and stab at his chest over and over again, my golden dagger flashing like lightning. Every drop of blood is justice for his attempt to hurt Farren.

The guard wails, his good hand trying to press into the wounds. "Stupid bitch!" he screams, tears running down his bloody cheeks while he looks down at his brutalized body and collapses to his knees.

With Farren safe at my side, I take my attention off my attacker and run towards Leon. He still fights the other guard, my father's sword dripping blood that runs down his elbow. His shoulders shake with exertion. Leon kicks the guard in the groin, momentarily halting his incoming attack. It is no time for amusement, but I let out a laugh at the way the pathetic man's eyes bulge from his skull when he is unable to block Leon's heel.

"Where is the crown?" the tall guard yells at Leon. The sounds of clashing swords echo off the trees as they continue their fight.

A body from behind collides with mine. I feel the sharp pressure of the blade on my neck, the other guard's bloodied hand clenched in a fist around my waist, my blouse soaking up the blood.

I meet Leon's eyes that are wide with fear for me. The guard he was fighting seizes his opportunity to take a cheap shot, punching

Leon in the jaw. He grunts in pain but swings his blade, catching the man in the chest, and crimson washes down the leather, causing it to shine. The guard keeps attacking, both of them leaking gore. Leon knocks him to the ground, raising the emerald sword for the final blow.

"Finish that strike and she's dead!" The man holding me tightens the blade against my throat. "The king has plenty of other mistresses. We can tell him we only found you trying to escape."

Leon halts, sword frozen midair.

"Drop the sword and get on your knees, healer."

Leon does what he is told, his eyes never leaving mine. The panic is bright and overwhelming, and I start to tremble. I scream when the guard's fist slams into Leon's perfect face. They are going to haul him back to Grayden bloody and bruised, tortured and imprisoned for someone else's crimes. With Jedrick dead, no one will believe he tried to help the king. It will not take Grayden long to discover the crown is on my head. What will he do when he finds me to be fae?

"Tie him to the horses and have him drag behind us for a while to show him what awaits him when we arrive at Grayden's castle."

The other guard moves towards Leon, and I scream.

My scream is filled with all the anger, fear, and frustration that has built over the past day, and the blistering rage overwhelms me. The rage that these poor excuses for men have come into my forest and threatened Farren's life, Leon's life, my life. Threatening us with the torture at Grayden's vile hands.

I'll never see Nueena again, not be there when she is crowned Realm Keeper. Every plan we made for our future will be ripped from us.

The magic within me breaks open. It's unfamiliar, and wholly different from my own, a living thing shooting down my legs and into the soil beneath me. A rumbling begins under me, thick roots bursting out under the two guards. Green and purple vines with thick thorns wrap around the men. They try to escape, struggling with the stalks that surround them while they yell in pain at the sharp spikes from the plants digging into their skin. I can feel the vines like I can feel my own limbs as they twine around the men, raising them up off the ground. Painful blisters rise on their skin where the poisonous plant touches.

Now free from the guard's clutches, I stumble, the world spinning around me. Leon races towards me, and his arms cradle me, holding tightly against him.

"Are you all right? Tell me you are all right!" he asks desperately, but when I open my mouth, nothing happens. I stare up at him, his beautiful face tainted with the assault from the guards. Blackness closes in on my vision. There are two loud thumps. The ground shakes for a moment before everything fades away.

CHAPTER 17

ool water pours down my throat, a strong hand holding
my chin up. When my eyelids flutter open, I am greeted by
Leon's worried frown. I'm pressed to his chest but now I find us on
the forest floor.

"Where are you hurt?" he asks. "Did they touch you? Your neck
is red, but it will heal. I have some herbs in my bag." His concern is
palpable, and it makes me smile. Damn it, this sweet man cares
deeply for me.

I reach up, moving the hair that has fallen in his face. "You
worry too much," I say softly.

His shoulders drop in relief, and he chuckles. "Perhaps if you
stopped fainting on me. I've aged a hundred years in the past day."
He tilts his head down with a lopsided grin. "Can you see more
gray? I can feel it growing when I'm with you."

I laugh even though my body feels like I've been trampled by
Onyx. Leon helps me sit up, but we do not let go of each other.
"Gray looks good on you. Exceedingly dignified."

"I'm glad you like it." He turns serious and my stomach drops.

I know what the next words out of his mouth will be.

"Izadella, again I ask, are you fae?"

How can I hide what I truly am now? The crown has changed

colors, and he already told me he can feel magic radiating off me. I glance at the two unconscious men who lie in a heap on the forest floor, wrapped in vines and roots, the thorns still pressing into skin.

I stammer, "Leon, what—"

"Izadella, you screamed, and they were attacked by murderous plants that rose from out of nowhere, and when you fainted, the guards slammed right back to the ground. The logical conclusion is that you or at least the crown controlled whatever happened here. You have great and powerful magic within your reach. Which is why I suspect you to be fae. Are you?" He waits for my answer with wide eyes.

I want so badly to tell him the truth.

So, I do.

"Not fully, no, but my mother was. My father was mortal. The crown is reacting to me but it's not my magic." I pull up my hair to reveal my hidden pointed ears still pinned back.

Leon's grip tightens and he stares at me in wondrous shock, a slow smile spreading on his handsome face. He clears his throat. "Thank you for being honest." He drops his head, his forehead resting on mine. Breathing heavily, he quietly says, "I'm just glad you're alive."

Something brushes my arm, and we both look down at Farren, who reaches his nose towards me, his paws on my thigh. Leon releases me enough that I can pull the fox onto my lap. Farren licks my face, and my heart squeezes with affection and lingering fear.

"You could have been hurt, little one. Next time you run back to the cottage and hide," I say softly as he continues his trek across my face with his rough tongue. It's impossible to be upset with my brave boy. I pet him 'til a grasshopper enters his line of sight and he hops after it. Leon helps me stand but doesn't let me go.

"I have more questions for you but for now—" Leon reaches up and brushes a stray lock of hair behind my ear, trailing his thumb over its point and down my flushed cheek. My little gasp has him grazing the top of my lip. "The image of that bastard's sword on your neck, his bloody hands on your body, it will haunt me 'til I die." His words are as intense as the way he is staring at me. "We need to leave now. Together. It's not safe for us to be apart. Please don't fight me on this, Izadella. Let me protect you. I *need* to protect you."

The grass at my feet holds my attention while I let his words sink in, unable to look at him. Silence falls between us as minutes pass by. Could I bring him with me to Ellova? How long could he even stay before the magic of Ellova rips his sanity from his mortal mind? I'm going to lose him in the end no matter what. At least in Ellova he will be safe, even for a short time. Mortals are forbidden in Ellova but...

Nyvenah will understand.

Nueena will understand.

The crown deserves to be back in the fae realm, and I cannot get there without taking him.

I nod. "If you wish to stay by my side, then we go east to the Venneem Mountains. *No* place is safer than where I'm going, where I am from. You cannot stay there long, though. There is a reason King Drystan could not be with Inara in the fae realm. The whole reason she needed the crown to store magic so she could be with her treacherous husband in Adreania. Mortals like yourself will be driven mad by the magic in Ellova. Do you understand? It's a place mortals are not meant to be because it's too dangerous to stay there. If you come with me, you must understand it's only temporary, that I will stay there and you will need to leave, for your own good. If you do not agree, we must part ways here."

I look back up to find his gaze assessing me, eyebrows drawn together to match his deep frown. After a moment he nods. "I agree."

He steps away from me and walks towards my father's sword; the emeralds look more like rubies now. Leon kneels, picks up the blade, and heads to the guard nearest to him. He raises the sword to end the man's life.

"Leon! Wait!"

He turns back to me, frustrated. "They forfeited their lives the moment they tried to take you from me. We can't let them live. If anyone else finds them, they will tell Grayden who we are. They know us."

"I know, but I don't want their blood on your hands! You're a healer, not a murderer."

This only frustrates him more. "You heard them. They would have been all too happy to hand you over to Grayden to live a life worse than death. You don't know him like I do. When they wake, they will hunt you again."

It's too horrible to even imagine, but taking a life stains a soul and I want Leon whole. "There has to be another way."

His shoulders sink in defeat, but he walks over to his medical bag that lies covered in dirt.

"What is it? What will it do?" I ask as he pulls out dark vials and jars and mixes them with a plum-colored liquid, adding a few spoonfuls into an empty vial.

He goes to Grayden's guards and pours the concoction down each of their throats. "It's a substance made from Vedesdron plant. In small doses, it can be used as a sleeping aid. With this amount, mixed with other herbs, it will result in a coma-like sleep for a while, but when they awaken, it causes powerful hallucinations and memory loss. If they survive their injuries, they will have nothing to report back, useless to Grayden, but alive, thanks to you." Leon rises from the men. Their bloody and blistered bodies convulse before lying still once more.

He holds out his hand to me. "Lead the way."

For a moment I do not take it. This is a terrible idea, but that pull inside me demands I keep him near, so I slip my hand into his and gently tug towards Ellova. It's unfair how many secrets I must keep from him, but if he fails what is to come next, we will be forced to part before the sun has fully risen.

"Are we going somewhere other fae will be?" He asks carefully.

"Yes. Like I said, it's safe. For now, that is all you need to know."

"That's fine. I just wish to know about you. The fae have magic. What do you possess?"

The trees around us get wider, growing closer together. Every few feet a tree has delicate green gems embedded in the thick bark.

"I have metal-wielding abilities, or at least I did before the crown. We are called jewelsmiths. My powers are weak as I am part mortal, so I tend to focus on jewelry, but I do enjoy creating daggers and swords."

"What do you mean, before the crown?" he asked carefully.

"I can't use my own magic anymore. The crown is blocking it and I cannot seem to control its well of magic. I can feel it trapped in me, waiting to be released. It's like a door I do not have the key to. Whatever it is, it's painful."

"It appeared to me that strong emotions played a part."

I nod.

"There must be a way to control it." Leon looks thoughtful. "We can experiment."

He seems to examine every section of the forest's many plants and trees when he is not searching for expected danger. He is quiet in his observation of our surroundings, stopping a few times to collect samples of foliage with medicinal properties in tiny glass vials.

I had thought most of these plants were only found in this forest. "I'm impressed with your forest knowledge. Most of these do not grow in Adreania."

"My education was thorough. Some of these grow in many different places, but I have come across the ones that do not, in medical or geography books."

Most of the walk is done in companionable silence; the pounding in my head makes it hard to hold a long conversation. Leon swings from being enthralled with the nature around us to checking on me, offering every medicine he has.

The forest is darker here, the thick leaves blocking out most of the light, but sunbeams break through the gaps. The trees have large jewels twisted in the trunks.

I turn to Leon, who is assessing the wood, and release his hand. "We have reached the Verge. It's the outer ring of protection to where we are heading. You are able to stand here because you have proven to the Merawood Forest you mean no harm. The forest is alive in many ways, protecting against anyone with evil in their heart towards Ellova and those who call her home. These trees that forever stand guard still have the bones of Ellova's enemies wrapped around their roots."

I'm not sure how much to tell him. He will see the palace when we arrive. I wish to tell him everything, but how much would Nyvenah want him to know?

I settle on, "Mortals are forbidden. You will likely not be welcomed and I cannot promise what will happen from here. Our ruler will listen to why I've made the choice to bring you here, but I cannot guarantee her decision. Whatever she decides, I will stand by. I am loyal to the royal family above all else. Whether she says you are to be a guest or prisoner in her dungeon, that is her right as Realm Keeper. For many fae, the only mortals they know are from a history steeped in conflict and misery."

His mouth opens slightly, and he takes a step forward. "Of course, I understand. Does Ellova still exist? Truly? Is it part of the Merawood Forest?"

"Yes, it exists, but no, Ellova is part of the fae realm. The Merawood Forest is not part of it. The forest protects Ellova. The Verge is Ellova's greatest protection. You have to make a vow; swear you mean no harm to Ellova and all who call it home. It is the only way it will allow you to pass through. If you are unwilling or the Verge rejects your oath, we part here forever. It will be out of my hands." That he is here unharmed by the forest around us, proves he has no ill intent towards Ellova or me, but that may not be enough.

Leon does not hesitate. "I will make any vow, any oath, to stay by your side, Izadella."

"Will you swear it in blood?"

CHAPTER 18

*H*e is taken aback momentarily, clearly not expecting the cost, but his voice is steady when he straightens his spine. "That I will, Izadella."

Ellova's grave, I love the way he says my name. After years of *Arra*, my real name is magic on his lips. That familiar flutter blooms low in my gut at the reverent tone. The *A* at the end is drawn out when he says it, making it sound like music, like worship. I yearn to hear him moan it, scream it, say it a thousand times more. Over and over again until his voice is nothing but a broken whisper of devotion.

My voice, however, breaks, and I stutter, "G-Good. I shouldn't bring you to where we are going. The loyalty you are swearing is to me too. This isn't an ordinary blood oath. Once you pour your blood on Ellovian soil, it will bind you to it." I take a deep breath. "I shouldn't trust you, but somehow, I do. There's a pull towards you that I can't explain." I slowly pull out the dagger that is strapped to my thigh. Farren weaves in and out of my legs, looking up at us.

With a determined expression, Leon watches the morning sunbeams glint off the blade. "I feel it too, whatever is between us," he whispers. "I've felt it since the night we met."

Something shifts at the acknowledgment of something deeper

than a frivolous crush or temporary lust. The feeling of something dangerous and beautiful. "Hold out your hand to me."

He thrusts his hand forward, palm open, before I even finish speaking. "I trust you, too, you know," he says in a lover's tone.

For a moment I get lost in his green eyes before focusing on his hand, tracing the lines on his palm. My fingertips graze his rough ones, the touch electrifying.

"Each tree in this forest stands sentry. Guarding and protecting, ever since the war. Only those who seek to harm Ellova are dragged beneath its soil, their flesh a feast for the things that crawl under moonlight. With your blood spilled here, it proves you walk with me into Ellova without evil intent."

Leon doesn't even flinch when the knife brings forth his crimson lifeblood. We wait together as it pools in his palm before I continue. "Now press your palm into the ground at my feet and tell me what you vow."

He lowers himself, his eyes never leaving mine, hand plunging into the soft soil. "I vow no harm to Ellova, but furthermore, I vow to heal you, protect you, and defend you, Izadella of the Merawood Forest. You said my previous oath was fulfilled, so I vow a new one. Ellova has my blood, but you have all of me."

He says those last few words in a tender tone, and I suck in a harsh breath. The heart he just vowed to protect beats so rapidly it could burst free of my body with my next movement.

A faint glow rises from the ground where his fingers grip the soil, his blood mixing with dirt and clovers. The glow brightens and light flashes under the soil before darting out like bolts of lightning beneath us. The light fades as quickly as it arrived, and when Leon stands, holding up his hand, the scar is a thin faded line. Hope bursts within me.

I take my finger and softly trace the evidence of his oath. He gently pulls my hand to his lips and places a lingering kiss on my knuckles.

He can follow me into Ellova, meet my family and friends. Just a little more time with him.

The pain in my head lessens. It must be the excitement that he will get to meet Nueena by night's end.

"Are we ready to depart?" he asks.

My silent nod is all I can offer. Perhaps I should remind him he will only be able to stay for a short time, but he's looking at me like I'm holding the sun in my palm, and somehow, I doubt that would have changed his mind.

The forest is a fierce protector, but it is also an enormous gossip.

When we turn to head east, we find ourselves surrounded by every possible creature that calls this place home. Rabbits, foxes, and deer sit among the bushes, and a blue hawk flits about above them. Birds of all types fill the trees, along with soft white opossums and squirrels, the branches leaning towards us. The grackles, my personal favorite, have iridescent feathers that gleam in the sunlight, and they are the first to take their leave, realizing the early-morning entertainment is over, and the rest follow, scurrying off or taking flight.

Some sections of the woods are thick, and we must wind our way around the broad trunks. While I walk unbothered by the forest, Leon trips over everything the forest puts in front of him, much to his growing annoyance. I cannot help the snicker that escapes me as another root rises up to meet Leon's boot.

In one particularly dense part of the woods, two trees cross over each other that certainly weren't there a second ago.

As if he were speaking to someone of great importance, Leon politely inquires, "Excuse me, may we be permitted to pass, please?"

The two trees uncross themselves, letting me walk through them, but the moment before Leon tries to follow, they launch themselves forward, crossing again. "They don't seem to like me much or have developed a taste for my blood and require more of it," Leon says through gritted teeth at the trees that separate us. He tries to go around, but two trees near him cross over their branches to delay him.

I can only shrug at this, placing my forearms on the branches to lean on something for a short rest. "The trees within the Verge don't like outsiders. It goes against their protective instinct." I give the branch an affectionate pat. "It's not them; it's the protective enchantment using the trees to express itself."

"Did my blood sacrifice not suffice?" he grumbles, and a short branch whips out, smacking him upside his head. Something not unlike a growl escapes his lips.

I'm still giggling when I put my forehead to the branch.

"You are doing a wonderful job of protecting Ellova, but we need to travel quickly to Nueena. I promise he means no harm." Something brushes my cheek, and I look up to find a vibrantly deep-yellow flower hanging from a branch at my eye level. "Oh, it's lovely, thank you!" I pull it free of the branch and place it behind my ear, watching the trees uncross themselves to allow Leon to pass unbothered.

"Why, exactly, were these trees not inclined to defend against Grayden's guards?"

"Try not to take offense. This is just how the forest in the Verge is. Had we been attacked here, they would be dead. In the echoes of Ellova's history, mortals have meant death and destruction. The protection is wary, and the magic is only doing what the enchantment requires of them. Your vow means the forest didn't feel it needed to end your life, but it seems all mortals are still unwelcome here."

He concedes but side-eyes the tree closest to him. "I can hardly be offended at magic seeking to do its job."

The sounds of the early-morning forest surround us. A flash of blue wings takes flight, and when I look back, other birds and a few of the furrier residents here shadow us.

Leon follows my gaze to the unusually wide tree covered in thick ivy before us. "What is this?"

"A tree portal. It's a way to travel," I say to Leon before I kneel next to Farren. "Do you wish to stay here or come with us?"

Farren twirls, his fluffy tail sliding across my face before he leans against me.

I scratch behind his ears and kiss his little forehead. Another fox who has trailed behind us makes a noise at Farren. My fox scampers to follow but runs back for one last long pet and a soft head bump before racing off.

"He won't be joining us?"

"Farren rarely accompanies me to Ellova. He enjoys the freedom the forest offers. He knows the way if needed, and the cottage wards allow him to travel in and out at will. If danger is near, the protection wards will seal him inside. Long ago there was a winter crueler than any before it and we stayed safe with friends in Ellova. He was so upset he destroyed my favorite pair of shoes, two dresses, and eleven books. Little terror. Now he is free to go where he likes."

It would not be safe for me to come check on Farren, but Tavien or Viella, Ellova's Spy Guardian, would if I asked.

The thick trunk hides a large hollow in it, only revealed when I pull back the ivy that drapes over the massive tree. It's pitch-black inside and I pull Leon in with me, dropping the tangle of leaves to hide the opening again. I step up to the back of the tree, my left hand still in Leon's.

Before he can ask, I explain, "It's a portal tree. We need to travel as fast as possible and this is it. I've never used them by myself as they take quite a bit of magic to command but it's worth a try. Don't let go of my hand, all right?"

"I trust you," he says in the darkness, giving my hand a gentle squeeze.

I feel around on the bark until I find a hand-shaped carving and line up my fingers with the grooves. I close my eyes and remember the terror I felt as those guards closed in on Farren and Leon, the fear of being Grayden's prisoner, of never seeing Leon or Nueena again. I beg the portal to propel us forward, for the crown's power to release some of its reservoir of magic. A pulling sensation swirls down my hand, the tree's portal enchantments siphoning the magic. My stomach lurches forward as the magic is accepted and the inside of the tree lights up from within and then goes dark, the ground behind us rolling. Seconds pass by before the ground shifts behind us from grass to light brown dirt and the movement of the tree stills.

"It worked," I whisper with surprised elation. The throbbing in my head from the magic's pressure has lessened, too. We both turn and Leon pushes back the curtain of ivy as we step outside. The forest is behind us, and we stand at the base of Ellova's mountains. "Let's go."

We both look up at the rough side of the large rocky mountain and the impossibly steep incline of the path ahead of us. The protective glamour hides the true entrance.

"Are you sure you're feeling well enough for this?" he asks, apprehension on his features.

"I've climbed the Venneem Mountains many times." We are so close to the royal natatorium. The thought of the cool, healing waters in the private pool pushes me forward.

"Venneem Mountains? I've only heard it called Widowmaker's Peak. You know, I've put a great deal of effort into staying alive up until this point. I'm not sure I'm ready to die here." His eyebrows are drawn towards each other, but when he turns to me, his next words are teasing. "Even if I do adore the company."

I bump my shoulder with his and start walking. "It's glamoured." This is the first secret of Ellova I've spilled. I wonder how many more of Ellova's truths I will reveal to this mortal before his time here is up.

We ascend the side of the mountain, careful to use the crude steps carved into the dirt. Looking up, it is all jagged rocks until it reaches the top of a steep cliff. Behind it are more mountains as far as I can see.

Leon keeps looking up with a puzzled expression. "Izadella, what's at the top?"

I ignore him. One minute and it will all be revealed to him. A few more steps up and the mountain flattens off to a small landing with barely enough room for the two of us to walk on.

Leon reaches a protective hand out when a few rocks slide down the now nearly vertical mountainside path. I entwine my fingers with his and pull him sharply to the left.

"Stay close to me. Climb any more that way and you will find yourself falling off an invisible cliff into a pit and never know why."

The glamour's barrier shimmers, though I'm unsure if he can see it or if it takes fae eyes, so I don't say anything about the magic when we pass through it. I hear a quiet intake of breath as he looks up at what has been revealed.

We still have further to climb, but the dirt and rocks are gone. The mountain is a lush green path with trees around the large stone stairs now available to us. His mouth is open slightly and he's looking between me and the new mountain.

"That's why they call it Widowmaker's Peak. If you don't know where the mountain door is, the magic will shove you off it and deposit your broken body at the base. Part of the magic that protects us, an ancient fae guarding spell."

He only nods. "Is this the entrance to Ellova?"

"No, at least not an entrance anyone else can use. The real entrance is elsewhere but there's no time to get to it," I explain, and we start up the smooth steps.

He looks at me, ready to say something else, but the crown buzzes inside my body again the closer we get, making it feel like bees are making a hive in my head. We continue in silence until we again reach a part of the mountain's wide, flat ledge covered with soft grass, finally at the door to Ellova, to Nueena, to home.

When Leon turns around to look at the view behind us, a "whoa" slips out of him.

CHAPTER 19

The view is incredible. No matter how many times I've stood here, it never fails to amaze me. The mountaintop overlooks the lush Merawood Forest that starts the fae realm, a sea of deep green under a crystal-clear blue sky. The tallest tree towers in my backyard as a marker to my home.

Like an ink stain on parchment looms the unrelenting black iron wall that hides most of Adreania. The Iron Castle stands to the left, before the Elbasan Sea. The deep green-blue waters peek out between breaks in the wall.

To the right is the border of Kalvorn. Mountains with snow-dusted peaks separate the realms.

Three kingdoms built to keep all others out.

Leon is looking at Kalvorn with an unsettled expression. "Grayden wants to go to war with them. He's already preparing his armies. He will say it's to seek justice for his missing father but all he truly wants is more power, to invade, and to steal. More lives he can reduce to ash."

I huff a laugh. "Grayden is an atrocious excuse for a man, but he doesn't have the manpower, the support of his people, or the crown. I'd like to see him try."

"Do you think Ellova would intervene or fight with Kalvorn if he did try?"

I wish I could say yes. "The fae do not concern themselves with the bloody affairs of mortals. They have kept out of sight for a reason."

On the landing is a little hiding spot Nueena, Tavien, and I sometimes visit to sneak away or stargaze; the large tan pillows we sit on are propped up against the stone walls. A small drink cart is tucked behind a large rock with crystal goblets, unopened wine bottles, and a forgotten wheel of cheese. I head to the door hidden by hanging purple flowers. He follows me but I turn back, rounding quickly on him.

"Remember your blood oath, healer. You are a guest and that is a privilege. One I can take away at any moment."

He nods again and takes a step closer to me, sending my heart racing at his nearness. "I will be on my best behavior."

I need to speak with Nueena before anything more happens between us. He stares at me with an intensity that makes me wish to hide from him and yet, at the same time, shove him against the violet buds and finally see what a kiss from him would taste like, feel like. He gazes as if he can see straight into me. Can he sense how fast my heart is beating?

"Um, turn around, please," I ask, needing to break the connection.

He does so quickly and without question. I push aside the hanging flora to reveal a round wooden door. Old and cracked, no handle, just a small, hollowed circle in the center. I slip off one of my bracelets and place it into the circle. It glows for a moment, recognizing the key, and cracks open. I return the gold band to my wrist and push the door open all the way.

Gratitude that I've finally returned and the sharp sense of coming home overwhelm me, bringing back the ache in my head, causing me to sway before strong hands wrap around my waist. Leon draws me against his broad chest before I can collapse over the threshold.

"I didn't say you could turn around. For a healer you have poor listening skills." There is no venom in my words. The back of my head makes a home between his neck and shoulders. I should step forward but the pressure of his hands on my waist is alluring, his chest warm against my back.

The bright sensation of being safe and treasured entices me to relax against him.

I risk the betrayal of emotions clear on my face as I turn my head and look up at him. Most of his hair is still tied up, but a few strands have come undone on the trek up the mountain, one gray lock falling in front of his distressed face.

"Apologies, my dear." A flutter starts low in my belly at the words *my dear.* "When you didn't say anything, concern got the best of me. It feels pointless to ask as I know you are not, but are you all right?" He takes his hand and presses it to my forehead. "No fever. Clear eyes. Can we stop and rest?"

"No, we need to go. Come on." My first step is steady and I'm careful not to stumble as I walk.

Before us is a long, dark hallway straight into the mountain. I summon some light crystals. A speck of brightness appears in front of us, slowly growing in size. The white marble walls reflect the faint glow of the small ball of luminescence that bobs merrily before us.

He stares at it, so I offer some explanation. "Inside is a crystal that produces light. They can get bigger or smaller on command, or by using magic, depending on how powerful the person using them is. Not a specific magic, more of a right the fae have. You may need to ask me for assistance with running water or doors, as they run on the same magic."

He smirks. "Far more convenient than oil lamps and candles."

We walk in silence again before I stop abruptly, turning to him. "You can keep your name, but if anyone asks, make no mention of Adreania. You are part of the Ink Court. That is the court of healers and scholars. You are here visiting from the Eastern Library."

He nods.

"Good." We continue down the long tunnel. Above, a few small fae spheres of golden light join in the illumination of our path, bouncing along with us.

I will one of the lights to grow larger and brighter for Leon. It flares merrily, a chance to show off. It burns luminously before I pull the magic away from it, taking the light with me. It returns to floating above me, with the faint glow of before.

"What is Ellova like?" he asks nonchalantly, but I can hear the edge of unease to his tone. It must be terrifying for a mortal not only to learn the fae are real, but to travel to an entirely new realm, future unknown. He has had to leave his entire life behind him and now is someplace new with only me to guide him.

No explanation of my home will do it justice. The beauty of it, the kindness of those who live there, and the magic that flows freely, so all I can say is, "That is something you will need to experience yourself."

Leon chuckles. "Helpful."

I can tell him one thing. "Ellova is everything Adreania is not. Wealth is not hoarded like a spiteful dragon. No one in Ellova is without their most basic needs. Everyone is taken care of; no one knows of empty bellies or cruel leaders. Ellova has structures in place to help take care of others, and if they cannot take care of themselves, others will. No one is just looking out for themselves. The needs of the whole come before the wants of the individual."

"Sounds like a dream." He looks thoughtful at the vision I have painted for him.

We finally come to another round door, and my eyes fill with tears. Home, finally home.

An identical door stands before us, and I throw it open. It slams into the side of the wall, but I'm already walking towards the enormous pool of water in the center of the marble and gold room. Giant plants of all shapes, sizes, and colors grow in golden planters along the wall. Gold pillars hold up a glass dome roof, sunbeams streaming through it. One wall is made entirely of stained glass images depicting the six courts, bathing the room in a rainbow of color. The soft chimes of the alarm I have knowingly triggered can be heard from the hall.

Slipping off my dusty and sweat-filled tunic reveals a small undershirt made of a deep-yellow lace. "We need to wash away our travels."

He pulls off his filthy shirt and boots. The fluttery sensation from earlier returns and heat rises within me as I take in his shirtless form. His muscles draw my eyes, and the low vee at his hips makes my heart pound.

I turn away so he cannot see my blush, but I can sense his eyes on my body. I kick my boots off but leave on the leggings, and dive into the pool.

The clear water is cool and welcoming. The magic penetrates me; the tingling of soft healing around me soothes my bruises, the tight muscles relaxing after the agonizing ordeal that has been the past day.

I break the water as the first honeyguards arrive. Leon dives in behind me and swims to my side.

The High Court protectors, honeyguards, surround us and have arrows ready to fire, swords drawn. When they see it's me, they all lower their weapons. A few give a wave or a shout hello as they stroll back to their post nearby. As they leave, their leader, the commander of the Ellovian armies, enters.

Commander Lillian strides over to me, her determined footsteps echoing off the ornate walls. The long sword that never leaves her side swings gently on her hips over leather pants, shining onyx epaulets reaching to sharp points. Her all-black attire stands out among the lush green of the plants surrounding us and adds to her vaguely threatening appearance. She has no color to her pale cheeks, as she would not have needed to rush here like her guards.

She's tall and slim with long, wavy dark brown hair. Her beautiful sharp features make her striking to look at; her nose has a slight roundness to the tip below high cheekbones, her dark lips in a frown.

"I would ask you to use the main entrance or announce your arrival beforehand. I do not need the wards going off in the middle of my lunch." There's not much bite to her voice, though, more of a vague annoyance.

"Hello to you too," I tease.

"This him?" she asks with a sharp nod to Leon, but she doesn't actually look at him. He looks quickly at me with a smug smile spreading on his face before dunking under the water.

"Maybe," I say and float on my back, bobbing on the surface. I hear Nueena before I see her, the vibrations of her heels as she enters the room echoing through the stone and into the water. She kicks off her shoes and sits at the edge of the pool, her legs dipping into the water as I swim over to her. Her hair is in hundreds of little braids with rubies and scarlet beads woven through. The gown she wears is not the soft purple of her own court but instead the deep red of the Court of Swords. She must have been meeting with them at the Larissian Fortress today about her coronation.

"Della, is that *your* blood?" She gapes at the soft pink rivulets of water that trail down my skin. Nueena waves her hand, and the remnants of the gore are gone. "What happened?" She searches my face before skimming over my body for any visible injuries. "Is everything all right?"

"Nu, something has happened." My words are soft. I raced here to tell her, but now that I'm standing in front of her, the words won't form. Where do I even start?

"She brought a pet," Lillian adds unhelpfully, looking down at Leon swimming low in the pool towards me.

Nueena peers around the floor of the room. "You brought Farren? He hates the—" The words die on her lips when Leon returns to the surface. He pushes his wet hair back with both hands and looks between us and then to the shining crown on her head, and he bows deeply, his nose nearly touching the water.

The ancient crown upon her braids is made of mangled metal scraps left over from the swords forged to protect the realm of Ellova during the war with the mortals, a crown that once belonged to Zarella. From afar the pieces seem randomly placed, but up close there are intricate designs. It comes to a point above her forehead, polished so brightly my reflection is mirrored back at me.

She grabs my arm and squeezes it with excitement. "Is that—?" Her head swings between the two of us in quick succession. The delight on her face bleeds into concern. "Del...I...I trust you have a reason for bringing him here, but I don't think that was a good idea. You know mortals are forbidden." She looks between us.

I turn to her, grasping her hand, which she squeezes back. "I need to talk to you," I whisper. "Lillian can stay but send your honeyguards away."

Nueena nods and turns to Lillian. "We will no longer be needing guards."

Two fae women and one male leave us without a second glance.

"Please close the doors and wait outside," Nueena adds as they exit.

The male nods and gently closes the wide doors.

Once the door is closed, Leon and I swim over to the carved staircase that leads out of the natatorium pool to meet Lillian and Nueena by the main doors.

I pull out two thick bathing robes from a large chest. Leon takes one. It has six tree roots connecting with a sun and a tree, the Kingdom of Ellova's crest, embroidered on the back, and we each slip one on. The magic heats from the inside, drying out our clothes and hair.

I guess it's time for introductions.

"Ummm, this is Leon. This is Nueena, Future Realm Keeper of Ellova."

She gives him a sincere smile. "It's nice to finally meet you."

"I feel like I've been spoken about for a while." He looks at me with a confident smirk. "I had no idea I made such an impression." Leon will likely never let me forget this and I can only imagine this is just the start of my friends bringing up my small obsession with him in his presence.

I look away to conceal the budding flush that paints my cheeks. "This is Lillian, Nueena's commander."

She does not extend her hand.

"Nice to meet you both," Leon says.

Nueena is the first to speak. "We have heard wonderful things about you, Leon, and I am glad to finally meet you, but what happened that brought you so far from your home?" Her concern warms my chest.

I take a deep breath in a pathetic attempt to steady myself, but it only adds to Nueena's troubled expression. I start to undo the braids that keep the crown hidden. Nueena and Lillian's faces shift from curious interest to shock when the crown is slowly revealed. Nueena's hands migrate to her mouth, and she holds her breath until all of my hair is down. Fully on display on my head is the stolen fae crown, no longer black, the similar shade of my copper locks.

Nueena is the first to speak. "Is that—? What? How? When? Del, what—"

I save her any more questions. "I was heading home after we parted last night and two men showed up in the woods, pulling along a cart carrying Jedrick. I knocked them unconscious and tried to bring Jedrick here, but he died. When the crown fell off onto the forest floor, the ground started to decay instantly and caught fire. It spread so fast I was terrified it was going to burn the forest down, destroy the wards, and corrupt the protection of the Verge. The burnt ground spread out like claws, scorching everything, just like the markings we saw yesterday at the Divide. I didn't have time to think it through; I just grabbed it and put it on." The tale comes out fast and broken, distress in every word. "It seemed like the only option, but now it's stuck, and it fucking hurts. Then Grayden's guards found us. Theirs is the blood you saw. The crown's magic fought back and saved us."

Nueena is silent as she stares at the crown in wonder.

When I am met with silence, I continue to blabber on. "Maybe your mother knows something we don't. We can search the whole library in the Ink Court. There must be something. Some way to remove it. It's gold again, not black, so already it's an improvement." It all spills out and panic takes over my voice, pitching it higher and higher.

"Um, Izadella?" The three of us turned our heads in Leon's direction. "Are the plants normally like this?"

We follow his line of sight. All the plants have turned slightly brown and are wilting on the edges. Another surge of panic rises up in me as the brown spreads on the leaves. A pathetic whimper escapes me: the plants' decay is my doing.

Nueena ignores the plants and pulls me into a tight embrace, and I sink into it. We hold each other for a moment before she steps back.

"Ellova's grave, calm yourself, Del. The crown is out of Grayden's hands; it's in Ellova. That's the most important part of this. We can figure all the rest out later! I'm just glad you are safe." She presses her cheek into my head as I melt into her again, holding tightly as relief floods me. I knew she would understand, but I still feel overwhelming relief. She raises her hand, sending a wave of magic towards the plants. I look back at Leon, who is examining the plants, where black ends have returned to their green and plump state.

"Interesting" is all he says, holding a leaf between two fingers, turning it slowly over.

Plants changing colors is not something I can worry about at present.

"We need to speak with my parents," Nueena says, "now." We break apart and I pull my hair into a pile on my head, hopefully concealing the crown from anyone else we may pass in the hallway. She turns towards Leon. "I do not wish for you to feel unwelcome here, but some concerns will arise with your arrival."

"I understand. Izadella has informed me that mortals are forbidden, and I fully understand the health risks of staying too long. There was also mention of a possible dungeon," Leon says, trying to lighten the somber mood around us.

Nueena purses her lips to hide a grin and moves in front of me and Leon. "I need to glamour you both. The crown is emitting too much magic. Any fae will be able to sense you have more magic than you should for being half-mortal. It could raise suspicion." She turns to Leon. "And you are not emitting any magic, so that also needs to be concealed."

Leon agrees, "That would probably be best."

She raises both hands and, in a fluid motion, swipes the air, sending a burst of light above me. I turn back towards the large mirror. Lilac sparks fall like stars over the golden crown, dissolving into my skin and clothes. The faint tingling sensation fades when the last of the light flickers out.

"Have your parents returned from the Larissian Fortress yet?" I ask Nueena.

Lillian rings a bell for assistance and looks back at Leon before answering, "No, but they are on their way back. Should be arriving any moment. We can discuss this in Nyvenah's chambers." Mistrust is crystal clear on her sharp features. "In private."

I almost laughed at the exchange. "Welcome to Ellova, Leon."

CHAPTER 20

The main hallway on this level is mostly empty, with its shining marble floors and open windows. Most of the residents of the Ellovian palace are away at the midday meal. Lillian leads us at a quick and steady pace back to our rooms.

I link arms with Nueena and she squeezes my hand, leaning in to whisper in my ear. "Is he as wonderful as you thought?"

I cannot resist the urge to look back and whisper, "Yes."

Her smile is as giddy as I feel.

Leon takes everything in as we walk through the High Court's palace. Every few steps, pillars wrapped in flora hold up a half-moon ceiling of opalescent glass where sunlight streams through in pastel beams. Much like the natatorium, potted plants line the halls. I follow his eyes as he gazes up to the chandeliers made of glowing crystals encased in light. Wisteria flowers, frozen in time, hang gracefully outside the windows, blocking the view of Ellova's capital city, Lavencia.

The last staircase in the west tower leads to a similar hallway lined with family portraits. Our small group passes a few portraits of myself with Nueena and the royal family. Leon turns his confused eyes on me.

The last and largest painting hangs in a golden frame just outside of our rooms: a portrait of Nueena and Tavien dancing in ceremonial gold attire at their Zemras celebration to honor their new matebond.

Lillian turns down another hallway and waits at the wide double doors, its carved archway made of gold, flanked by two twisting trees. Sensing our arrival, the doors open on their own, welcoming us to the royal west wing, the tower I share with Nueena and Tavien.

Nueena leads Leon into our large, circular sitting room. She gives a little sigh of contentment at the sight of our main living space and summons four large fae lights to illuminate the spacious room as hot tea is set for us.

A golden arch identical to the front entrance leads to each of our private rooms. There is a fine dining area with crafted chairs around a driftwood table with a towering floral arrangement in various shades of purple and green in the center. Behind the table, but before the balcony, sit the soft couches, and piles of books and unrolled scrolls lie over edges and on the floor.

Lillian, who keeps a watchful eye on Leon, says, "Have a seat."

He does, but not before he looks out over the balcony and the Merawood Forest below.

Lillian's eyes darken.

I walk to the other side of the room, where twin doors lead to my quarters. "Leon, I'll be right back. I just need to change, and when Tavien returns, he can assist in finding you new clothing."

To reach my sleeping space, I must first walk through our private library. I look over my shoulder to find Leon watching me as I leave his sight.

Most shelves are packed with our personal libraries, but they overflow with a lifetime of collections and keepsakes of our adventures over the past century. It was once a detailed and organized space, but over the hundred years we have lived in the shared apartments in the west tower, it now holds countless trinkets—broken swords I keep meaning to repair, vases, wobbly floral teacups from our childhood tea parties we just can't bear to throw away, shoes that fell out of fashion, a jewelry box made of the shells we collected over summers at the Shell Court's seaside palace. It was lovingly named the *room of many things*, as any attempts at organization failed us and we would spend the time revisiting the past, forgetting to finish cleaning it. It has a small bathing room in one corner for guests.

I drop my soiled travel clothes onto the rug of enchanted marigolds, the petals soft beneath my toes. We don't have much time, but I tie up half of my hair with gem pins to hide the crown until I am before Nyvenah. I brush my lips and cheeks with crushed pigment the tint of ripe peaches.

In the smaller connecting room that doubles as both workspace and closet, I pull a fresh gown from the pinewood armoire.

I change into an off-the-shoulder, low-cut dress with two high slits in the front. Its gossamer sleeves almost touch the ground, a popular Ellovian fashion. The deep yellow material is made marginally more modest by sheer fabric panels hanging beneath the gaps, covering my legs. It's a style far more revealing than what Leon is used to, and I smile, imagining his reaction.

A swirling gold belt I created a few decades ago completes the ensemble. I shuffle through the tangle of delicate metals in my ornate jewelry box and take out a gold bracelet.

I try the pull of my magic, sensing it separate from the ancient magic of the crown that is held within me. The crown's magic feels like an ocean, while mine is a shell clinging to the sand, crushed by its waves. The pressure in my head builds again at my attempt to drag out even a speck of my magic. It weakly comes to me when I call, and as I gather it, I close my eyes, giving it all my focus.

My breath comes in uneven gasps at the sight of the unaffected metal. I beg the crown for my summons to yield any results on the cold chain. I've held on to a desperate hope that when I returned to Ellova, when I returned to all the magic held here, my powers would resurface.

This metal-wielding magic within me was the only thing I had left connecting me to my mother. Despair floods my aching chest when my attempt to manipulate the gold leaves me empty.

Just like in the forest, whatever power was in me that caused metal to mold and shape at my will, the force that gold and silver obeyed, is gone. The crown's magic has truly suffocated my own.

It's impossible to hide the growing panic in my voice as I call out, "*Nueena!*"

From outside the door, wooden legs slide hastily against a marble floor and Lillian's harsh demand echoes: "Get back here!" A moment later, the door slams open and Leon darts in. He looks around and then at me, up and down. He opens his mouth, but Nueena is just behind him.

"What is it?" She gives him a questioning look before they both look at me.

"Leon—" I try to sound calm. "—thank you for your care, but I need to speak with Nueena." After a moment I add, "Alone."

He appears as if he wants to object, but reluctantly leaves with one long glance back, Nueena shutting the door behind him.

"My jewelsmith powers, metal magic, I can't use it. It flickered out like a candle. It didn't work when I was fighting Grayden's guards either." I hold up the chain of gold and focus on it. Nothing I do has any effect on the limp jewelry. "I keep trying, but it won't…"

Nueena looks at the crown with confusion. "When was the last time you could use your magic?"

"Moments before Jedrick died. I used my magic to melt the armor his kidnappers were wearing so I could escape with him, but he…Nueena, what if my magic is gone forever?" My heart aches at my woeful words.

She pats my arm. "Let us go talk with my parents. They will have more answers. And besides, we need to brief my mother on some significant events, like the arrival of the first mortal in a millennium and Inara's crown. First, we need to find out how long your pretty mortal can survive here, and how to remove this." A curious kind of hunger gleams in her golden eyes when she asks in a small voice, "Can you feel it? All the magic stored there."

"Yes, and it throbs. It feels like it is trapped in me, willing to tear me apart to get free. We need to find out how to get this crown off. If anyone can control it, it's you! The well of magic trapped inside is extraordinary but it's suffocating to me." Another painful realization pierces my chest. "Will my court still consider me a jewelsmith if I can no longer use metal-wielding magic?"

"Of course they will! In no world would Lazalai cast you out of her court. Magic or not, the Gem Court will always be open to you."

Together, we walk out of the room. Lillian stands between us and Leon. From behind him, we can see the tops of the Black Castle and the forest that keeps Ellova safe. A hint of the Elbasan Sea is visible.

A loud chime fills the room, but Leon is the only one who glances up for the source of the noise. Lillian turns to Nueena. "I am going to meet your parents at the entrance and send guards up to watch him." Leon pretends not to notice her side eye when she leaves.

Nueena returns to her quarters, giving me and Leon a moment alone.

As soon as her door shuts, Leon asks, "You live here? In the royal family's personal suites?"

"Yes, most of the time. I do enjoy the solitude of my little cottage, though. It's been in my family for years, and the bustle of the palace can be overwhelming at times."

"I gather Nueena is a princess?"

"We do not have titles like *king* or *queen* in Ellova, so the term *princess* is not used here, but yes, she is the royal heir."

"It appears I am missing some key moments. Are you considered royalty here as well?" His eyes are bright as he waits for my response.

"No, no. However, Nyvenah, Ellova's Realm Keeper, the closest to your version of a queen, welcomed me into their home when I was young, still a dewling. Nueena and I have shared this part of the royal west wing for many years. I wield no power here; I'm not even a part of her court. I belong to the Gem Court, but I am treated like family."

Lost for words, he stares at me.

I laugh at his astonished expression. "Please do not bother being impressed. A fair amount of fae here consider me more of a pet than any type of royal."

Leon asks in a honeyed tone, "Will they see me as *your* pet?" He still holds my father's sword, the end resting on his shoulder.

Before I can answer Leon, the door to the chambers opens and two figures arrive at the same time. Leon swings the sword down, ready for whoever has arrived.

"A MORTAL?" Viella, Guardian of Ellova's spies, all but yells it as she places her short body in front of Tavien in a protective stance, her fists bursting into blue flames.

Tavien's massive body towers over her, and he glances down in fond amusement before patting her short blonde head. He chuckles at her. "I think that may be Della's little mortal friend she is so fond of."

Viella's green eyes widen with delight, and she practically skips over to us, shaking out the flames with a dramatic flick of her wrist. Her pale skin is untouched, and when the fire is gone, I take a large step to the side and watch Viella hug Leon, much to his polite confusion.

"Welcome to Ellova, Leon! We need to get you into some new clothes. I'm afraid you look rather terrible. Izzy always says how handsome you are; let's not make a liar out of her." She takes a step back, freeing him from her surprise embrace, while she assesses the breeches he wears.

"Er, thank you?" He gives her a half smile before looking up at Tavien.

"I'm Tavien, Nueena's Zemra. I have clothing that might work," Tavien says, adding, "at least for now. I think a trip to the market is in order." Tavien shakes hands with Leon before turning to me and pulling me into a quick side hug.

I see Leon stiffen out of the corner of my eye at the contact. Nueena, now dressed in a long purple silk gown, comes to stand next to her love. Tavien holds her for a kiss. Half of her braids are up in an elaborate twist atop her head behind a crown of amethyst. Nueena's Zemra stone is now nestled in the center of her crown, and it glows the same way Tavien's does.

Tavien's loose shirt is the same soft material as her gown and is worn over black breeches. Tavien is taller than most fae men, so even with her heeled boots, Nueena is shorter than he is. She hands Leon a bundle of clean clothes.

"Leon." He finishes his introduction with "Izadella's friend."

"Friend?" Tavien's smile is catlike. "Is that what we're calling this now?"

Nueena elbows him in the side but laughs anyway.

I inwardly grimace at my friends' endearingly annoying insistence on bringing up my persistent feelings for him, but Leon is clearly amused by this and gives me a cocky grin.

Tavien turns to Nueena. "I spoke with Lillian. Your parents are waiting for us in the throne room. Viella will keep our friend here company while we discuss the..." He cocks his head to one side while looking at the crown hidden under my hair. "...situation?"

"I need to stay with Izadella. Anywhere she goes, I go," Leon says as Nueena and Tavien start towards the door.

"I'm sorry, Leon," I say, "but there are some things I must speak with the Realm Keeper about. But if they would like to hear your side of the story, and I'm sure they will, I will come back here and bring you."

He opens his mouth to argue at the idea of us separating.

"The library has some wonderful books. Get cleaned up. Vi will call for some lunch for you, and I promise I'll be back as soon as I can. Viella is wonderful, you will like her, and she can answer any questions you have. Take a hot bath. My bathing room has everything you need."

Two of Lillian's personal honeyguards come in to stand at the door. They are both highly trained and vicious fighters when needed, and I know she sends these two in particular as a statement. One of them gives Leon a little wave, but her acknowledgment seems more mocking than friendly.

Leon narrows his eyes at the guard. "Right." He moves closer to my ear. "Are you sure *you* will be all right?"

Unable to resist the genuine concern in his question, I reach out and place a hand on his forearm, his hand quickly covering mine. "Quite all right. I promise you are completely safe here."

Leon moves even closer to me, his lips brushing my ear. "It's not my safety I'm worried about."

CHAPTER 21

At the heart of the Ellovian palace is a spacious courtyard garden. At the center, surrounded by its countless blooms, is a stone and crystal sanctuary. It was once a holy temple for the fae goddess Ellova but now holds the Realm Keeper's throne room.

Guards with baldrics the color of plums greet us as they open the large doors. The long room has open crystal windows filled with the early morning sunshine. The surrounding flowers peek in and the lively morning sounds of the palace float by. Vines wrap around the columns that hold up the ceiling and the soft purple material that drapes between each one.

Our steps echo throughout as we walk across the light green floor with dark green marbling towards the driftwood table just before the throne.

Nyvenah, Realm Keeper of Ellova and Nueena's mother, sits upon the Ellovian throne, which is made of twisted trees and intricately entwined ivy. Above her head, gemstones in the color of each court are set in an arch. Her consort and Nueena's father, Alachite, waits off to the side next to a floating tapestry of the fae and mortal realms. The elaborate tapestry map is sewn with delicate shimmering threads, the realm of Ellova on one side with the mortal kingdoms of Adreania, Kalvorn, and Versairen across the Divide.

On Nyvenah's right grows the navlue tree with its deep purple branches, its beautiful fruit dangling from it, ripening, a deeper shade than the one Grayden tried to feed me. The green rind darkens with every day that passes as Nueena's power reaches its peak, its closed flower buds waiting to bloom.

My stomach twists with dread at the memory. Another situation I will need to tell them about.

Just beyond the Ellovian throne stands a grand gray statue of the goddess Ellova, ten feet tall, a flowing dress frozen behind her, with patches of moss clinging to the bottom in spirals. Her marble eyes are open, her expression kind. Long hair reaches her feet, curling at the edges. Atop her head is a floral crown with flowers enchanted to never die. Her beauty is carved into the stone, ethereal to all who see it.

Last to arrive is Lillian, who strides in and with a wave of her gloved hand sends all guards away, shutting the door behind them.

"Welcome home, Dewdrop," Alachite says to me as I approach.

Alachite and Nyvenah smile warmly at us, but their concern is clear beneath it. Lillian must have told them something alarming has happened.

"Hello, my dewlings." Nyvenah rises gracefully from her throne, stepping down to greet me.

We kiss each other on the cheek in greeting and her arm wraps around my shoulders as we walk to Nueena.

Nyvenah is still dressed in her regal red garb from her visit to the Court of Swords this morning. Her dark brown skin is a stark contrast to her moonlight hair. Her thick braids are pinned in a swirl around her head, with a large gold crown covered with emeralds and amethysts on top. She is hundreds of years old but could pass for a mortal of fifty or sixty years. Small wrinkles are permanently etched around her eyes, which are now focused solely on me.

"Welcome home. How was the Court of Swords?" I ask. "It's always lovely this time of year."

We all sit at the ornate table together. Nyvenah folds her hands atop it, facing me. "Fine, fine, more preparation for the coronation.

Lillian said we might need to return sooner than we thought to bring Ellova's armies here. I am somewhat nervous as to that cryptic message, but she said you had something to share. Are you all right, Della?"

Saying yes feels like a lie, so I pull out the pins holding up my hair, one by one. All eyes are on me. Nyvenah's and Alachite's expressions grow increasingly worried with each one I drop on the worn wood, my hair falling to reveal the reason the Merawood Forest was enchanted with protection.

The golden crown that destroyed the lives and friendship of Nyvenah's great-grandmother, Realm Keeper Zarella, and her closest friends, Inara and Alvina.

I can see my reflection in one of the wall mirrors.

I tell them everything that has happened since I found Jedrick defenseless in the forest: the attackers who abducted the king, Jedrick's death, the crown about to burn down the entire forest, the pain of putting it on, Leon showing up, and Grayden's guards attempting to take us. I take great care to explain that bringing Leon was a last resort and a matter of life or death.

Nyvenah and Alachite take it all in with stunned expressions, but it's Alachite who speaks first.

"You did the right thing. It seems without a living conduit, the crown cannot handle the great magic trapped within it. Powerful objects are often unpredictable. Everything outside of the Venneem Mountains would have been destroyed, and that threatens our safety."

"Yes, you did what you needed to do to protect Ellova," Nyvenah agrees with her mate. "It's vital that the protection of the Mera-wood Forest holds, especially if Adreania comes seeking what is no longer theirs."

My eyesight blurs, grateful tears about to make their way down my face. Nyvenah stands and I follow. She opens her arms auto-matically, as she has done for a hundred years. Like most fae in Ellova, she is much taller than me, and she wraps me in a strong embrace filled with comfort from the only mother I have left. We stay like that for a long moment, her scent of jasmine and rose-water sweet in my nose until she pulls back and holds my face in both hands, looking into my eyes instead of at the crown.

"It will be all right." Her expression is one of loving maternal concern, her white eyebrows twisted in sympathy. She holds me for a few moments longer before I step out of the familiar embrace and we take our seats once again.

Tavien reaches his hand across the table, squeezing mine when I take it. "Ellova went to war with Adreania to try to get that crown back, only to lose. It's finally here; no matter what, that's enough. It's been returned where it needs to be."

I squeeze his hand back before we let go and I face Nyvenah again. "But it can be removed, right?" My words are laced with both panic and hope as they spill out of me. It has to be able to; it just has to. But when Nyvenah and Alachite look at each other with matching expressions of concern, that hope burns away.

Alachite gives me a small but reassuring smile. "We know so little about the crown. It was stolen too long ago and its existence in Ellova was short. The most important thing is that it's out of Adreania's grasp."

An endless stream of questions run through my mind, but I settle on one: "It turned from black to gold as soon as I put it on, so that must be encouraging?"

Everyone nods slowly and Nyvenah looks thoughtful. "The change in its color may be one of two things. First, it may have recognized your heritage as part fae. Magic flows from mother to child, recognizing bloodlines, but the crown was not forged to be worn by just any fae."

"It was created and crafted for Inara," Tavien added, "keyed to her and her magic, but perhaps it has chosen you. Keyed items have a mind of their own at times."

The pounding worsens when I shake my head. "So far it has brought nothing but pain. I need to find a way to relieve the pressure. The magic is heavy on me and feels like I am being suffocated by its power. The crown feels...wrong, so wrong."

"Then it hasn't chosen you," Tavien says. "You would know peace wearing it. When I hold my family's keyed sword made by

Alvina, it has a sense of wholeness there. As if it were forged just for me."

A pensive Nyvenah nods. "There is always a possibility that since you are a direct descendant of the Forger, it recognizes you as an heir of its maker. Metal-wielding of a jewelsmith is one of the rarest gifts and magic has a long memory. The top scholars at the Ink Court may have more answers, but we must limit who knows this. Nueena's coronation is fast approaching."

Nyvenah and Alachite glance at each other, worry passing between them. Nyvenah sits straighter in her chair. She looks at me, her tone more serious than she has ever spoken to me, the voice of a ruler. "The crown holds a vast amount of power. We may not know how much, but in the thousands of years it was siphoning magic, we can only guess that you may have in your possession magic far greater than Nueena's."

Confused, slightly taken back at her tone, I can only agree. "It's certainly possible."

"The throne chooses the Realm Keeper based on power. That is the way it has always chosen Ellova's leader," she says reluctantly, but her eyes are hopeful, understanding there. "We all want what is best for the fae realm. That is why its leader must have the most power, to protect and provide. Do you have any desire to test if that magic *could* crown you Realm Keeper in the upcoming days? It would be somewhat of a loophole to succession, but we would not stop you. The throne chooses."

My mouth falls open at the very suggestion I would attempt to take the throne for myself, and I jump to my feet. "Absolutely not, never. *Never.* Nueena is this realm's future! Not me." I'm horrified that she even had to say it. That I seize the throne from my closest friend is implausible, bordering on madness. "Nueena was born to rule; it's in her blood. She is everything Ellova needs."

Nueena gives me a soft, assured smile.

Nyvenah looks relieved. "That is what I assumed you would say. I am pleased to know I was right. I know this goes against your loyalty to the Gem Court, but I would ask that you keep this from them, at least for now. We are too close to the coronation for this kind of disruption. They may challenge for power if they know a member of their court is in possession of Inara's crown. I have nothing but fondness for your court's Guardian. Lazalai is wonderful, but if the other courts found out about this, it may interfere."

Bile rises up at the idea of my court trying to claim something that isn't theirs to demand. "Of course! I would never do anything to interfere with Nueena's crowning or her place on the throne! I have no intention of telling anyone from the Gem Court. They get my craftsmanship, not my secrets. I just want it off my body to have it destroyed or in the hands of someone who can control it."

"We will find a way to free you of it, Dewdrop. It may take a while, though," Alachite says honestly. "Alvina was a great forger, but she did not make many keyed objects. There may be limited information on it. The Ink Court takes care to document the vast majority of our history, but many keyed items may have been lost throughout the centuries and only been recorded in personal libraries. Those with keyed items often kept them hidden."

I try to keep the disappointment from my face.

"Our sword is in my family's trove. I will bring it. Perhaps it will shine some light on the situation at hand," Tavien reassures me.

High pillars of marble with gold accents hold up the ceiling, and between each one are enormous potted plants, their vines spilling over. In one corner sits a small bar with a variety of liquids and fruit purée with golden goblets. I walk directly to it, grabbing a cold goblet and stirring in strawberry wine with muddled basil.

It smells like Leon. Tastes like what I imagine kissing him under the stars would be like, wrapped safely in the promises he's made to me. I turn away from the cart, still drinking deeply, hating my next words.

"Another issue is that I can't use my metal-wielding." It's the most painful part of this mess. Losing the ability to use my own power leaves me hollow, as if I'm missing a vital part of myself. I hover my hands around my gold belt, close my eyes, and will with everything in me for it to melt so I can change its shape, but nothing happens. It stays solid and cold beneath my pleading touch, but I can feel magic trying to get out like something is leaving me slowly, clogged and thick but flowing, so why won't the gold obey my touch?

Nueena clears her throat. "Um, Del?"

I open my eyes to find everyone staring at the plants that surround the room, which all have grown a few feet, with flowers blooming on branches and new vines twisting. A smaller pot cracks in half, its tangled root system splitting it open onto the floor.

Fuck.

The edges of my eyesight have gone dark, and I'm suddenly overwhelmed with the desire to sink to the floor and sleep. Tavien is closest; he reaches me just in time to hold me up.

"Thank you," I whisper as he directs me to a mossy green couch and helps me get seated.

"The crown's magic has overshadowed yours," Nyvenah explains. "It's much stronger and you are only half fae. The crown has been pulling magic for thousands of years." She makes her way to her throne, and the moment she sits, she grimaces before her features smooth out.

"Mother?" Nueena's eyes widen with concern as she moves closer to Nyvenah. "Are you all right?" As Nueena approaches, the gemstones embedded in the throne flare to life, growing bright. "I wish we could move up my coronation." When she is within arm's reach of her mother, small white flowers bloom from the tangled ivy, releasing an enticing floral perfume.

Nyvenah shakes her head. "Sunflower, I can handle it for a few more weeks. I must wait for the full rejection of the throne before you can ascend. I know it's difficult to watch. I hated seeing my mother's slow rejection, and she hated seeing her mother go through it, and her mother hated to see the throne reject Zarella, but this is the way it's done. We must wait for the navlue flowers to fully bloom before we can start the coronation." She shifts uncomfortably again before returning her attention to me.

I glance at the navlue tree, dreading telling them about Grayden and the fruit he had. The navlue fruit is ripening but the pale purple flower buds are still tightly closed.

"I do have a question, Della. How did you know what King

Jedrick looked like and who Leon was?" Nyvenah tries to appear indifferent, but the question is laced with suspicion, her eyes narrowing at Nueena and me.

I keep my expression blank, and Nueena moves to stand behind me. We've talked before about how they would react if they ever found out. She straightens her back, ready to face their reaction with me.

"Well," I say, leaving Nueena out of it, "I have been sneaking into Adreania with a stockpile of provisions for a place called Beggars' Row."

Alachite and Nyvenah are tense as they listen to my confession. Nyvenah's face is frozen in fear.

"My only living mortal relative, my cousin Cyanna, ran an orphanage there with twenty-two children. They were desperately in need of help. The children she's raising were starving and sick, so I've done what I could. I have gone once a month for a while. For the first few years I stayed at the orphanage, but while the food was helpful, what they truly needed were coins. I didn't have their currency, so at first, I just sold my jewelry to the noble houses out of an old family shop. Once I made a name for myself, I got an invitation to the monthly royal bazaar, where I had been selling my pieces. At the end of the night, I distributed the coins to the families there. I know there were risks but they were suffering so much."

"Oh, Della…I cannot *begin* to explain how dangerous that was! How *foolish*! The arrogance inside you to believe you would be safe in that monster's kingdom!" Fear no longer graces Nyvenah's beautiful face, only rage.

"I took every precaution. But even before I was forced to put on the crown, I was never going to risk returning after my last night there."

Nueena is ready to defend me and my choices. "We have so much here, and those who live in Adreania have nothing. She couldn't just turn her back when she found out children in her family's care were dying there!"

"Why?" Alachite says, ignoring Nueena, fury simmering in his eyes. I look between them. Alachite so rarely gets angry; this might not end well.

"Because I do not possess the ability to ignore my family's suffering."

"No." His tone is ice. "Why aren't you going anymore after that last night? You said you were not going to risk returning. Besides the crown. What. Happened?"

I may be over a hundred years old and proud of what I have accomplished in the past ten years of the lives I have saved and the children I have kept fed, but I exchange a guilty look with Nueena like we are dewlings again, caught stealing treats from the kitchens.

"Because Jedrick looked like he was on his last breath and Grayden was about to take over as king."

Alachite crosses his arms, waiting.

"Jedrick was a lazy and apathetic king, only wanting to give in to drink and bleed the coffers dry, ignoring the pleas of its people, but Grayden...he seemed to believe the cure to the sickness that spreads in Adreania could be found in Kalvorn. He plans to lead both Adreania and Versairen to war against Kalvorn."

Alachite sees right through me, one eyebrow arched, unconvinced that was the reason we left. "So, because he was planning a war that would not affect you, you decided your safety suddenly mattered? Our spies keep an eye on the activities of our enemies. He has little weapons, starving cities, and a malnourished army. Not much of a threat to anyone."

"Leon was concerned for my safety. He had a plan in place to get me out of Adreania when he thought I was a mortal woman with children. He had hired a ship captain to bring me to his childhood home. I sent Cyanna and her children in my place. With Cyanna safe, my work there was done, and I could not risk seeing Grayden again."

Nueena continues for me, "Jedrick wasn't going to last the month, and Grayden is insidious. An heir to make King Drystan proud. Cruel, merciless. Whatever he is planning, he deserves to die. He also showed far too much interest in Della."

Nyvenah's blue eyes are glassy and Alachite looks even more

enraged. I shrink even more under their gaze, hating that I will need to tell them exactly what Grayden's plan were for me.

Ellova's grave, I just want to crawl back into my warm bed and sleep 'til Nueena's coronation. See if Leon will hold me like he did last night, hold me so tightly and tenderly this will all fade away. I look up at the mural painted above us to avoid the eyes of anyone around me.

I'm so tired.

Alachite opens his mouth to speak, but Nyvenah claims the next words.

"I know that this came from a good place." Nyvenah closes her eyes and takes a long, deep breath to calm herself before speaking to us again. "Della, it was a precious gift to help raise you. I love your heart, that you care so much for those poor mortals. The Forger and your mother would be immensely proud of the woman you have become." She speaks through gritted teeth now. "But you have been reckless with your life to go into the forest alone and cross the realms."

Alachite slides his eyes suspiciously to his daughter. "Why do I just know you went with her?"

Nyvenah lets out a little gasp when Nueena does not deny it. The room shakes with it, the evidence clear on the windows, which all have jagged cracks running down them, threatening to shatter. Above Nyvenah, the crystal lights shudder, burning so brightly they nearly explode.

Nueena quickly confesses her part in all of this. "I never went to Adreania, never once crossed the Divide, but yes, I did travel with her there to ensure she returned. She begged me not to. It was my choice to accompany her through the forest. Nothing ever happened. It's as empty as it has always been since the war ended. I also provided all the food she brought to Cyanna from our kitchens."

Nyvenah takes another deep breath. "My dewlings, who apparently place so little value on your own lives." Her eyes widen and she whirls around on Tavien, who is leaning back in a chair, balancing on two back legs, and twirling his dagger. He appears unfazed by this whole conversation.

"You *knew* about this? Soulbonded mates are meant to protect their Zemras!" She glares at him, demanding an answer.

He only shrugs. "You know as well as I do that Nueena is not one to be controlled. She does what she wants, what she feels is best. I trusted her to keep herself safe; she would not jeopardize her place as heir. Nueena will make an exquisite Realm Keeper because she has a heart for justice and kindness, unable to turn away from suffering, something most of the mortals have been experiencing daily for years. Nueena understood why Del would return month after month. Nu would have done the same for any of your family. If it were her sisters on the other side, if Vaylin and Kaylena were mortal and starving. I would never stand in her way; I would advise you not to either."

Nueena and Tavien stare at each other, smiling with twin adoring expressions. He has a proud gleam in his eyes when he gazes at her, and she sends the look right back. They share a quiet moment even with all of us around, connected on a deeper level, the way only Zemras can be.

Nyvenah stares at Tavien in surprise.

"Besides," Nueena argues, "if I did not accompany Del, I would have never seen the darkness spreading into Merawood Forest with my own eyes. The protections around the Divide were failing, the crown siphoning the magic there again, but now that we have it back, we can work on restoring the protection enchantments."

Alachite comes behind Nyvenah, wrapping his arms around her waist. He kisses her exposed neck, and she leans back into him, shoulders relaxing. She sighs deeply while rubbing her eyes before she steps out of his embrace and stands in front of us. "If you both were still dewlings, there would have been strict punishments for this, but as you are both fully grown, all I can do is express my deepest disappointment for your carelessness and disregard for your own safety. I hope neither of you do *anything* like this in the future without speaking to me first, but I do understand your reasoning."

Nueena and I nod. It would be best if we move on from my journeys into Adreania and I address the room.

"Someone else is after the crown, and while it's safe here, we need to know who kidnapped Jedrick and how they planned to use it. Kalvorn is going to go to war with Adreania to try to take it. It's possible Kalvorn has also discovered a way to release its power. It could explain why they suddenly are willing to start a war for a crown that has been powerless for thousands of years. Maybe they know what Grayden does, a way to unlock it."

Nueena turns to her parents. "It must be King Zilas then. This was a power play. Del said that Grayden met with him shortly before and Kalvorn demanded the crown in exchange for aid. They met on the Elbasan Sea this week; Grayden refused and plans retribution."

What if Kalvornian guards come searching for me now that I have what they were willing to go to war for?

I open my mouth to speak but close it, not knowing how to phrase what I need to tell them. Then I try again. "There's one more thing you need to know. When I last saw Grayden, he offered me fruit. Fruit, I believe—no, I know—was from the navlue tree. It looked just like the same fruit in every coronation painting."

Nueena's parents stare at me.

"Della, that's not possible," Alachite says.

"He said it was the sweetest thing he had ever tasted." I wet my lips, trying to rid myself of my dry mouth at my own words. "Right before he shoved it in my mouth. He wasn't lying. I know what it was. Grayden claimed he found a way to use the crown, to bring back its magic once he is king. I didn't believe him, but he had the fruit. They are connected; I just know it. Whoever broke into the throne room and gave Grayden that fruit is working with him."

"We have been betrayed," Nyvenah finishes for me. Her words are icy, anger burning in her eyes.

"I believe so." I hate to be the one to tell her this.

"We will add extra guards to the throne room," Alachite says, watching his mate carefully. "When all the court Guardians are here, we will decide what action to take once the one who seeks to share our magic with that murderous prince has been caught." Turning to Lillian, he adds, "Please bring the mortal man here. I think it's time we meet him."

She nods once, but her expression clearly indicates she thinks this is a bad idea.

Leon is going to meet those who raised me. He is still a stranger to me in many ways, but I can't stop the hope that rises in me that they like him as much as I do.

Nyvenah looks at me, her expression thoughtful. "Alvina forged the crown that was stolen and it brought on ruination, but you brought it back to us, my sweet dewling. How proud she would be."

"Thank you," I say softly.

"May I touch it?" Nyvenah asks suddenly. When I agree, she raises her hand to it. Like with Leon, it vibrates angrily at her incoming touch. "It's burning hot. Can you not feel that, or is it part of the pain you spoke of earlier?"

I reach up and run my fingers over it. "It feels warm, but mostly it gives me a terrible headache. Like all the magic is trapped in my body and it is trying to tear itself out of me."

Alachite is next to learn of the crown's molten rage at being touched.

Everyone in the room watches Nueena's approach, her gown flowing behind her like water. My stomach tightens with anticipation.

"At least the crown is no longer draining the magic around it. I feel nothing being siphoned by the crown. Having the crown on your head seems to have solved the issue of it stealing magic." She stands before me with her hand slowly rising. I wait for the vibrating to start, but it's not the angry quivering as it reacted with Nyvenah, Alachite, and Leon.

I'm surprised when she ignores the crown. Instead of reaching for it, she takes my hand in hers, our fingers intertwined. She closes her eyes and a jolt ricochets throughout my body, followed by a violent pulling sensation deep within me. We gasp at the same time. The magic flows into her, slowly at first, then rushing to get out of me. She tightens her grip. The pressure that had been building, pushing against my skull to a painful point, leaves my body until I finally relax with welcomed relief.

Her lashes flutter open and my heart stops. No longer golden-brown, the eyes that stare back at me are glowing gold as she absorbs the magic that has been suffocating me.

Everyone in the room is quiet as they watch the exchange of magic between us. The stream of magic slows within me, sputtering to a stop. Her long lashes flutter again, and her eyes slowly fade back to the color they have always been. That same golden-brown I woke up to one hundred twenty years ago on the day we met.

"Are you all right?" I ask. "How do you feel?" It comes out as a whisper.

"Energized, full, unlike anything I've felt before." She speaks as if she is in a daze before panic dawns on her face. "We *must* find a way to release it. Your mortal body will be destroyed with that much magic. I was only able to absorb a fraction of it. You won't be able to survive this, Del. It's going to kill you."

CHAPTER 22

our mortal body will be destroyed with that much magic.
Nueena stares at me with panicked eyes and squeezes
my hand. It takes a moment for her words to fully
sink in.

The crown is going to kill me.

Dread seeps into every bone in my body, tears making their way
down my cheeks because I know Nueena speaks the truth. Even
though she's taken the crushing pressure out of my body, I know
it's still too much for me to handle, too much to control. I'm just a
half-mortal jewelsmith.

"We will not allow that to happen," Nyvenah insists. "There
must be a way to remove it." She keeps speaking but a rushing noise
in my ears blocks out sound.

If we can't find a way to remove it, how long do I have? Weeks?
Months? The crown holds thousands of years of siphoned magic
within it. How am I even alive now?

A matching tear slides down Nueena's face and I pull her tightly
to me, hating the tears on her face more than mine. My fingers dig
into the soft fabric of her gown, clinging to her as desperately as
she clings to me. That is how Leon finds us when Lillian brings him
into the throne room. The somber mood hangs like a shadow.

Lillian taps the tapestry map, rolling it up so it hides everything from view, but Leon doesn't even glance at it or at anything else in the room, his eyes frozen on me and Nueena.

"What's happened?" he demands, watching me wipe away Nueena's tears, his posture accusatory.

Nyvenah stands at her full height and steps in front of us. "Hello, Healer Leon. I would ask you to calm yourself."

Leon nods and bows deeply to her. His expression is neutral, but his body betrays him. The tension radiates from him.

"I'm all right. Nothing has happened. Just tired." I move beside Nyvenah and force a smile to reassure him.

He is not convinced but stays quiet.

Nyvenah gracefully takes her seat at the head of the table. She gives me a sympathetic look that promises my impending demise by the crown will be discussed later. "Have a seat, mortal. I've heard you have had quite the journey to us, so this will not take long. I do, however, have a few questions."

When he doesn't immediately move, I walk over to him and together we all sit. Goblets appear for the vessels of water and juice in front of us.

Leon sits nearer than necessary.

Tavien and I make brief eye contact, and he brings his crystal goblet to his lips to hide his smile.

"What would you like to know, Your Majesty?" Leon asks, making no move to drink anything in front of him.

She shakes her head and waves her hand. "None of that. Nyvenah is fine. Della has explained your circumstances, but I would like to hear your side of the story, the events from your perspective, and perhaps a part of your own personal history, so I have a clear understanding of your role in all of this."

"I was the personal healer to King Jedrick up until last night, when he died."

Nyvenah nods. "And how did you become his healer?"

"I was an apprentice first and was with him for the past two years, keeping him healthy."

"What made you decide to stay with Izadella? She tells me that you did not wish to part with her and were quite insistent on accompanying her here. Why was that? The king was dead. You were free."

He pulls out the same coin he showed me in the forest.

Everyone in the room seems uncomfortable with even that small amount of iron, and he puts it away.

"I am loyal to whoever wears the crown. That loyalty ends upon my death, not the death of the wearer. Izadella is now queen of Adreania. Wherever she is, there you will find me."

She stands and walks gracefully over to the portrait of Realm Keeper Zarella, her great-grandmother, whom she looks astonishingly similar to.

"Are you aware of the true story of this crown? Not the lies I'm sure have been passed down for generations." When he shakes his head, she goes on. "The fae wanted nothing to do with the mortals. They lived their existence outside the mortal realm, and that was the way it was always meant to be. Thousands of years ago, a young king named Drystan appeared in the Merawood Forest. Apparently, he had seen Inara in the woods while he sought a cure for a sickness that had spread through Adreania, and he claimed he loved her. Inara was naïve and had never met a mortal. Deception was not something she had ever known. She believed him when he told her he wanted her for his queen. She wanted to be with him, but the fae are incompatible with mortals. We need magic to survive, which is the very same thing that will drive you to madness if you remain here."

Leon's jaw tightens but he calmly states, "I've been made aware of the consequences, Nyvenah."

"Inara created an elixir that brought healing to his kingdom. This only caused him to want her magic even more. Inara and Drystan met in secret, and he convinced her to marry him. Inara was not royalty here, but he wished to make her his queen. When she told Zarella and Alvina, they warned her to stay away from him and that the mortals were not to be trusted. She desperately wished to be with him but there was no place for them. Devastated she might lose Drystan, Inara pleaded with Alvina to make her a crown that possessed the magic she would need to stay alive in the mortal realm." Nyvenah turns her head to me, pausing in her tale to see if I wish to tell him this part.

I share what I can about my family's history in all of this. "Alvina was my great-great-grandmother. Against her better judgment, she created a crown that Inara could wear so that magic could flow to and from her. The crown was only ever intended for Inara. Alvina keyed it to her, and after her death, the crown, like all keyed items, will choose who can control it."

Nyvenah continues, "When Zarella found out about the crown, she forbade Inara from seeing Drystan, but Inara refused to be parted from him. Alvina was torn between her two best friends, but chose to help Inara, believing in the love Inara thought she'd found. The crown called magic from Ellova to her so she would never perish without it. It allowed her to live in the mortal realm, only for her to be murdered by Drystan a few years later. Their daughter was never seen again. That foolish king looked long and hard for the princess once he realized the crown was useless to mortals and his half-fae daughter was his only hope to wield its magic. He remarried and started another line, Grayden's line. The crown was not and will never be a marker of royalty for the traitorous Adreanian heirs and holds no bearing on any sinister succession. No matter what your iron coin declares, it was a gift of fae friendship, keyed only to Inara. So, while Izadella has the crown, she is in no way the queen to the mortals unless, of course, she chooses to be, so you may be free of your loyalty to her." Nyvenah's voice is sympathetic, but her meaning cuts into me.

While Nyvenah speaks, Leon's face hardens. The kindness in those green eyes is replaced with a cold determination. "While I understand the origins and intended purpose of the crown, you must understand, to the mortals there, it *is* the symbol of succession and has been for thousands of years. Ellova may not recognize Izadella as queen but to every citizen of Adreania, she is, whether or not she wants the title, and I will not be parted from her."

His hands are balled into fists, thankfully, outside of the view of everyone around him. I long to reach out and grab his hand.

"I understand your concern for Della. If you are as loyal to her as you say, you will not breathe a word to anyone about this realm, but I'm afraid that I cannot allow you to stay. Mortals are forbidden," Nyvenah says, and her tone is soft with genuine regret.

No.

No, no, no.

Nueena turns her head quickly at my sharp intake of breath. I had told Leon that I wouldn't intervene, that I would stand by my Realm Keeper's decision, but it can't end like this.

I want him here. *Need* him here.

It felt so right, and the thought of him leaving sends panic burning into me. I know he can't stay, that we can't be together, that death will claim him in the blink of an eye, but still, it hurts. I can feel my heartbeat racing faster and faster. I must say something.

"Nyvenah, please let me—" I am willing to beg for whatever time we have left.

Leon turns his attention to me before he opens his medical satchel, cutting my plea off.

"I did suspect," he says with a slight arrogance to his tone, "that it would come to this. You have no reason to trust me. I do wonder something, though, if you could grace me with a reply. Say you do get the crown off Izadella's head." He turns to Nueena. "Which, at the moment, is unclear if that is even in the realm of possibilities. What is your next step? Are you washing your hands of mortal woes?"

Nueena is quiet for a moment but answers him. "Once I am crowned Realm Keeper, I will find a way to return to the mortal realm as Del has done every full moon and let them know that I will assist with their survival. There are food and medical shortages. I will not let the forgotten children of Adreania starve. They have suffered enough under millennia of kings who cannot be bothered to care."

Leon nods. I think I see a spark of respect in his eyes at her answer. "That is what I assumed. You can bring all the food you wish, but without a cure to the sickness, nourishment will only go so far. There are ways to truly help those who need it most in Adreania. It was once a good place to live. Realm Keeper Zarella also cared for the mortals, at least enough to let the river flow from Ellova to Adreania. Their crops grew and the healing waters of that river allowed the mortals there to thrive before it was all taken away."

Tavien places a hand over Nueena's, just patting gently, before she interjects, "Is there a point to all this? I'm hardly in the mood for a history lesson from someone who hasn't even been here long enough to see a sunset. Drystan had murdered Zarella's best friend. One of the consequences of that action was loss of that particular fae gift. She was well within her right to retract the Airvell River for revenge." She may sit next to the current ruler, but she commands the room, power all around her.

Leon continues, "It is an observation of a kingdom that I have helped heal for many years, long before I came to be Jedrick's royal healer, and there's only one thing most of them want—a cure. A grieving mother cares little for who sits on a throne."

Nueena and her parents exchange looks, and I'm desperate to ask him what this all means.

He makes eye contact with each person in the room. His eyes linger on me the longest before he speaks again. "I do, however, have something that may assist you, if it is your wish to see healing brought back to Adreania. I wish to give it to you as a sign of good faith, that I am loyal to whoever wears the crown, and the loyalty that I vowed will not be in vain. So, I have a gift. It is in a fae language, but Zarella's name is written over and over again."

He rises from his seat and reaches into his satchel. Lillian is on her feet the moment he stands, her hand on her sword, ready to cut him down in a single blow if he produces anything out of that bag that would threaten the family she vowed to protect.

Leon pulls out a leather-bound book weathered and faded with age. Its yellowed pages stick out at odd angles, and the cover is torn on one side. It's faint, but some sort of old engravings are stamped on the front.

He holds the fragile pages with respect and with both hands, gingerly passes it to Nyvenah, who holds it with reverence as she flips through, placing her hand over her heart when she stops on a page in the middle. "Inara's diary? Where did you find this?"

"When I was not assisting the king, I was working towards finding a cure. The castle holds many libraries where I spent my nights researching and reading everything in the history section, or at least what had yet to be destroyed. A few months ago, on the last shelf hidden by other ancient tomes, I found a large book with its pages hollowed out, and this was inside it. Your guess is as good as mine as to how it got there and who hid it."

Nyvenah's mate and daughter come to stand behind her to read over her shoulder. My heart pounds with satisfaction as I witness the family that raised me learn a new priceless piece of their history.

Leon returns to me, sliding his chair even closer to me, our knees almost touching. Without a word, I take his hand in mine and squeeze it in gratitude. He does not let me pull away; instead, he interlocks our fingers and with such gentleness rubs his thumb up and down my hand. We sit there together, fingers interlocked, in silence while we give them a few moments.

Nueena looks up suddenly. "Thank you." Her eyes are glassy, her gratitude genuine. "There is so much of our family's history here."

Leon looks incredibly pleased at Nueena's reaction. "You will find a bookmark towards the end. While I could not read it in its entirety, as a man of medicine I could, in part, read the ingredient list and instructions for the Anafaea Elixir. I believe the flowers shown here are that of the anafaea flower, as well as some plants that only grow here. Inara was the creator of the elixir. I do not believe it was the same illness, or at least they had different symptoms, but the legend around the anafaea flower is that it could cure many ailments. I believe it's worth seeing if the elixir can be recreated."

Nueena answers without looking up from the faded flora illustrations. "You are correct, but what does that have to do with you?"

"My proposal is that you allow me to attempt to create the elixir. I will need assistance, of course, but if we're successful, we have a chance to cure the plague. I've been the king's healer for years, and many who have grown up in the shadow of the Iron Castle have known me for much longer as the only healer they can call upon in the middle of the night. I don't *know* if it's possible to make the elixir, or even if it would indeed cure the plague, but those people need it. Especially the children. I *have* to try. Please allow me the opportunity to help them, and then I will leave, never to speak of this place or whom the forest keeps hidden." He finishes and waits.

There is no movement or sound in the room, and the weighted stares of the entire royal family are on him.

Tavien is the first to speak, turning to me with a laugh. "I see why you are so taken with him."

Heat paints my cheeks, and when I again make a feeble attempt to free my hand from Leon's, his hold tightens, his thumb moving in a gentle dance on my skin.

Once Nyvenah has collected her thoughts, she straightens and draws her hands together. "While I am Ellova's Realm Keeper for another of the moon's full turns, this decision is not mine to make. The culmination of this would be the start of Nueena's legacy. I will leave this decision to her. I trust her to make choices that protect Ellova."

Nueena, still a little dazed, smiles at us. My heart leaps with excitement.

I know that smile.

t Nueena's delighted expression, Leon and I squeeze our hands under the table at the same time.

"My first act as Realm Keeper will be to allow you to stay and have an active hand in the elixir creation. The flower has been lost for so long, but this may give us a clearer vision of its creation. Now we know what it looks like, so there is hope that we may grow it. I wish to see healing and restoration in the mortal kingdom. Once Adreania's people are healed, they can make a stand against Grayden. Especially if the crown is indeed a requirement to reign, he will have little ground to stand on."

"Once Inara's diary is verified by the Scroll Keeper of the Ink Court, of course," Alachite adds. "I will bring it to her now. Some translation will need to be done as well."

"Thank you." Leon's gratitude and mine are expressed at the same time and I want to laugh, but Nueena's smile fades slightly to concern as she takes in our close proximity. The soft clicks of Nueena's heels on marble are the only sound as she walks over to us. From her new perspective, she gazes at our entwined hands. This time when I pull my hand away, he reluctantly releases me.

Leon stands and faces Nueena.

"This is all on one condition, Leon. The blood vow ensured you did not enter with malicious intent, but that doesn't mean you are safe here. You do understand that the magic here will start to affect you? It will tear at you. Your mind will betray you and madness will come for you. Mortals were never meant to be here. That's why they are forbidden. When that moment arises, you will withdraw from all work completed and accept that any vow of loyalty to the crown will be completed. If Adreania is not safe, you will need to find a new life far from here. Since mortals have been forbidden since Drystan, I do not have a timeline." She turns to me. "Del would be the only one with any idea of when that would be, but I will leave that up to her if she wishes to share it with you."

Leon tries to meet my eyes, but I avoid his gaze at the vague mention of my parents. I only hear him say, "I understand. When that happens, I will return to my family's home. I will keep a log of how I am feeling, and I'm sure Izadella will keep a close eye on me for the foreseeable future as I become her shadow. I will not leave her side until I have no other choice."

The way he says it, I can sense a small smile there. I can hear it in the way he says *her side*.

When I look up, Nueena holds out her hand to him and they shake.

"Izadella trusted you enough to bring you here against the laws we have in place. Lillian will be all too pleased to bring justice if you prove that trust was treasonous."

"I would expect nothing less."

Confident in her ability to make good on Nueena's words, Lilian adds with a sardonic smirk on her darkly painted lips, "Any suspicion of betrayal to either Ellova or Della, you will be thrown into the dungeons, where your wilting mind will be your only companion while you rot."

Nueena cheerfully claps her hands together. "Wonderful. For now, if he is staying, he needs clothing and any other necessities."

All the suffocating fear that was coiled begins to loosen its grip around me. Leon can stay for the time being, and the royals are grateful for him returning a text so precious it will be seen as sacred by sunset.

"We can take him to the market now," I say.

Before we leave, Tavien strolls over to the window closest to him. He raises one hand, and a blueish-white fire bursts from his palm. The glowing flame flickers up the shattered glass, which burns brightly. Before the first glass is finished, he sends a flaming sphere to each fractured window. One by one the flames are extinguished at the tops, leaving the glass shiny and new.

"Oh, thank you, my dear." Nyvenah affectionately pats Tavien's cheek as she exits.

Tavien comes to stand at Nueena's back with an automatic hand on her hip and holds two golden ear cuffs with delicate points at the top. Typically worn as adornments for more extravagant celebrations, they will hide Leon's rounded ears from anyone who looks too closely. I made them as a gift for Tavien many years ago, and I am touched that he thought to bring them for Leon.

Leon thanks him and places the cuffs over his ears. I reach up to mold the metal to fit him, but nothing happens.

Right.

I'd forgotten for a moment that gold is no longer mine to command.

Never mind, it will work for now. Leon notices the way my face falls, but thankfully says nothing as he follows me out of the throne room.

~

The sounds of the city center of Lavencia, Ellova's capital city, grow louder as Tavien, Nueena, Leon, and I pass into the crowded market that completely surrounds the Ink Court's circular library. Facing the round library are tall marble structures standing on one side of the market's entrance. Shoppers stroll through the dozens of shops that encircle the trading quarter as sunset nears. Daily vendors have set up shop in the curving cobblestone road. Freshly baked bread and roasting meat cooked over an open flame permeates the air, the scents mouthwatering.

"How was your time with Viella?" I ask Leon.

"It was interesting. She is—" He looks thoughtful.

"My dear friend." I narrow my eyes at him in case he plans on saying anything unkind about her.

"I was going to say energetic. She seems like she gets more done in an hour than I get done all day."

Relaxing, I laugh at that. "Yes, she certainly does."

"Will she continue to be my babysitter? She is incredibly sweet, but she asks a lot of questions at an alarming rate. She almost got my whole life story out of me."

I giggle at that. She is particularly good at her job, and unfortunately for Leon, he had no idea who he was speaking to. "I'll try to keep you near, but I cannot promise anything."

A young male carrying a tray of flaky jam tarts to a nearby booth stops to offer us some and wishes Nueena well for her coronation. I grab a few, passing one each to Nueena and Tavien, and Leon takes his own with a polite thanks. He chews slowly as he walks beside me, taking in the lively crowd.

Most of those selling have some symbol of their court on display, with banners in the shop windows or hanging from their carts.

Nueena and Tavien stop to speak with some vendors, but Leon and I keep walking, taking in the succulent smell of seasoned meat roasted on red sticks wrapped in a large purple leaf for travel with a sweet and spicy sauce dribbled on it. I steer him over to the elderfae with drooping pointed ears and small spectacles.

"Hungry, you two?" he asks kindly, flipping the sizzling fare.

"Very much so, thank you." Leon nods next to me.

A long paper is pinned to his cart, listing the trade options he will accept in exchange for his delicious fare. The items range from *a joke* to *a new roof for a friend's shop*. I search the list and see *Gift for a new Zemra mating - female*. I rifle through the jewelry I've brought and pull out a small pair of pink-and-yellow diamond stud earrings. The seller peers through the cooking smoke and nods hastily.

The elderfae chooses the four sticks with the juiciest portions, adds extra sauce to ours, and hands us the purple leaves to carry our meal. I thank him with a bow. Leon sees this and does so as well.

"So, coins are useless here?" he asks quietly when we have walked further away so as not to be overheard by the vendor.

"We don't have any currency. It's all by trade, barter, or gift."

"So, if we had nothing to trade, it would have been a gift?"

"Yes. We are hungry; we had a need, and he provided it. If it were a larger, more pressing need, he would have sent a trade reminder to my court to settle the cost."

"Surely those earrings were worth a hundred times the cost of four meals."

I wish I were surprised by his questions, but after spending time in Adreania, I know how greedy mortals can be, how different it is here. He may be a selfless man, but he has known many who are not.

"Since the trade was not equal, he will balance it out. Watch."

The vendor raises a small yellow Gem Court flag.

"Now anyone walking by will be offered a meal. The flag is yellow for my court, but if it had been Nueena, the flag would have been purple."

"Fascinating. What a wonderful place to live."

Most trade something small with the vendor: a new ink pot, a glass of wine from a vendor next to him, a bag of apples. But a few fae see the flag and enjoy a meal without the need to barter for it. A father with three dewlings takes just enough home for his household, the little ones at his feet each carrying their own meal. A small group of young scholars from the Ink Court rush the cart, delighted for the free meal after their classes as if they didn't have a delicious evening meal within the library before us.

"Fae magic is infused with the land and water, so everything grown in Ellova is naturally flavored with sweetness. All food will taste overly sweet to you, like a dessert. Even if it looks savory like meat and cheese."

He takes his first bite. "This is delicious! It is remarkably sweet, but the heat at the end balances the flavors."

"Fire peppers."

He watches everything around us. "Why do most of the vendors have banners with shades of green?"

"There are six courts. The Court of Green is mostly agricultural—those who tend farms, guard livestock, keep gardens, and grow or bake anything. Mostly food-related, really."

"What are the other courts?"

"Well, besides Nueena's, which is called the High Court, no court is greater than the others. Every court plays a vital role here. The Court of Shells is shipowners, sea crews, dock workers, fishermen, and sea guards, anything with relation to the waters around us."

Two guards walk by, laughing at something. Their red capes flow behind them.

"What about them?" Leon asks before taking another bite.

"They are from the Court of Swords, protectors. Ellovian Guards, sentinels, blacksmiths, personal guards, and the defenders of Ellova."

Leon looks thoughtful. "Is one born into their court, or is it by profession?"

"A little bit of both. You can be born and do the task your family did, or you can move around. Mostly, it all has to do with the powers fae are born with. All fae have some magic, but some are more inclined towards certain gifts. Gifts show up as dewlings. Most fae are drawn to where their power would be best used and where they can be taught by elders who share those gifts."

Leon peers in the window of a bright apothecary with a touch of yearning but turns back to me to ask, "When did your powers first arise?"

The sudden sadness at the reminder of the magic I've lost hurts, but it is a happy memory, so I share it. "I learned I could manipulate metal at a young age. My mother could not understand how I kept crawling out of my crib until she saw the bars bent while I played with my toys in the kitchen in the middle of the night." I let out a pitiful laugh and he joins in with sincerity.

"Have you always been a member of the Gem Court?"

"The Gem Court has always recognized me as a member of

their court, even though I don't live in Ellova all of the time. The metal-wielding of a jewelsmith is a rare gift and the Gem Court is home to artisans and crafters. Viella has been a member of every court over the centuries. We have plenty of flexibility here if someone chooses to go elsewhere. Each court has a unique need for all gifts and talents, but some are simply better suited for certain ones. The courts ensure everyone is cared for and all fae talents are used. Nyvenah and the High Court are entrusted with the care and stewardship of all of them."

Shops are set up under bright-colored fabric or enchanted flowers. The small stores have vibrant window displays, and their sellers stand in the doorways, holding their goods out to entice the evening visitors. Cheerful cloth makers hold up fabrics dyed bright colors, and near them a spice maker gives out a dash of her blends for those interested in a taste.

I walk slowly so Leon can take everything in. He looks from shop to shop with wide eyes. This is nothing like the markets of Adreania, where most cannot afford anything being sold.

In the Court of Green's rows, farmers have tables piled high with ripe fruits and seasonal vegetables from the east fields, their horses resting nearby from the long journey with heavy carts. The warm scent of spiced meats mingles with the bakery smells of fresh cakes. A cart selling peppers has its small blue flag up. I send up a thought of gratitude for whoever left extra from the Court of Shells.

I point to a fresh green pepper. "One please."

He hands the plump vegetable to me and lowers his flag. I return to Leon, who has his back to me, watching a fae woman hold out small jars of honey from her family's farm to those who pass by, a black Ink Court flag waving behind her.

I tap him on the shoulder, and when he turns around, I present the smooth pepper to him. "A gift for you." I'm delighted when he seems genuinely touched by the small gesture.

"Thank you." He takes a bite and offers it to me. "Would you like some?"

I shake my head with a soft chuckle. "No, you enjoy that."

Leon is so handsome when he smiles my heart skips a beat, and I force myself to keep walking to avoid embarrassing myself.

Bright yellow fabric connects on the roofs above, welcoming us to the Gem Court's section of the Lavencia market. I exchange greetings with the shop owners I've known for decades, but we keep moving until we reach our destination, not wanting anyone to ask me for something that would require my magic.

I enter the large shop made of blue stone, the Calendula, with its flower-lined windows that feature canvas-molded mannequins wearing elegant flowing gowns.

We are greeted by the assistants cheerfully sewing real flowers on corsets and helping to pick out fabrics in the front corner with patrons. There are four trees in each corner with clothing pieces hanging on every branch. Intricate lace tops and gowns with billowy iridescent skirts on display. With the coronation soon arriving, the shop is crowded with those looking for extravagant garments to wear to the festivities.

Tavien walks Leon over to the more masculine cuts, and they discuss colors. Nueena and I smile at Hiliyah as we peek into her private office. She stands behind a dress on the stand, watching an assistant, Cora, use her magic to pin up a skirt. Sharp silver pins hang frozen in the air near her hands, waiting to be used, and around the room, fabric swatches of every color hang by invisible strings.

Hiliyah has her long curly brown hair tied up in a large bun on her head and is holding sketches of the gown being worked on by her seamstresses. Her youthful tan face lights up when she sees us.

"Hello, hello." She moves to join us, but Nueena stops her.

"Please continue. We're looking around. Finish your design."

Hiliyah nods, and with a wave of her hand, a floating roll of fabric glides to her. She returns to supervising the construction of a gown the color of a raven's wings, the bust covered in dangling teardrop gemstones that swing at any movement. A gown for someone in the Ink Court.

Nueena notices me looking back a few times. "How do you think Leon's handling all of this?"

Turning to face her, I shrug. "He's mostly curious and asking a lot of questions. It *is* tremendously different here. I just hope he can stay for a while, and that we have more history on any other mortals here besides my father." I shove down the rising emotion at mentioning him.

"Being born in a place like Adreania, I imagine anything is better," she says, misery for the misfortune of others in her voice.

I don't have it in me to respond, so I pretend to see what new gowns are available, but I watch Leon. He picks out black pants, knee-high boots, and a green tunic the same color as his eyes.

When Hiliyah does come over, she takes in Leon's form topped with the ear caps.

She looks at me with a questioning expression and I sigh before giving her a small nod. Her face lights up as she turns back to Leon.

"The healer, is it? I've heard so much about you. Della, you were right; he is incredibly handsome." She gives him a bright, mischievous smile before winking at me.

All my friends' inability to feign ignorance of this man's existence or at the very least not rush to spill my secrets is expected, if not a little vexing, but the pleased grin Leon wears at yet another one of them knowing about him washes any true annoyance away. He chuckles at my embarrassed sigh.

I may need to stop introducing him to those who already know of him before his ego explodes.

"This is Hiliyah, Royal Gown Designer and my dear friend," I say as they shake hands. "This is Leon, a fact that you already made awfully clear you know."

"You have a beautiful shop," he says with clear sincerity.

She beams at his praise of the colorful surroundings of her store.

"Thank you. You can change here." Hiliyah grabs a dark green vest off a branch and points to a small changing area for him. He gives me one last glance before disappearing behind the thick yellow curtain.

She turns to me, lowering her voice. "Kole was here earlier, snooping."

I sigh and she takes my hand, leading me to the front of the shop near the main windows, not wanting Leon to overhear. I keep my voice low just in case. "What now?"

"He was asking what you are wearing to Nueena's coronation ball. I told him if he wanted to share shades with you, he would have to ask you himself, but he did try to bribe one of my assistants with a variety of valuables."

"Thank you for not telling him, and please apologize to whoever he bothered for me."

"Stop being polite, Della. Tell him to sail his ship far from you, or at the very least to stop coming in here. Next time he comes in, I will use my most horrid fabric and make him a shirt so ugly that his own mother wouldn't even dance with him."

I laugh at that, but it dies on my lips as the damn male we were talking about strolls in.

Captain Kole.

CHAPTER 24

Kole and his co-captain, Everett, join us, both dressed in the deep blue and seafoam green of their Court of Shells sea sentinel uniforms. They have been best friends for almost as long as Nueena and I have. The four of us attended schooling together at the Ink Court. Kole's sandy blond hair is pushed back, while Everett's light brown strands are windswept. They're both smiling, but Everett's is the only one that reaches his blue eyes.

Everett, whom I actually like, is taller than Kole, handsome with boyish good looks, and no matter how much time he spends under the sun on the high seas, his skin stays fair. The sapphire-studded sword I made him years ago still hangs on his hip. "Della!" he exclaims happily.

"You're back!" I say, greeting Everett warmly as I step into his embrace; he smells like ocean salt and bergamot. His lips press quickly to my cheek before he steps away to hug the others.

Everett and I have been friends for a long time, but I will forever question his friendship with Kole.

"I'm on shore duty 'til the coronation is over to spend time with my mother. Since my little accident, she wishes me to stay as close as possible, so I'll be around the palace. If she could attach me to

190

her in some fashion, I fear she would." He lets out a little laugh at his overbearing mother. "I'll join you all for dinner sometime this week." He eyes Leon, and Nueena and I share a quick glance at the mention of his mother, Camarra, the Guardian of the Court of Green.

"I wouldn't say getting thrown overboard on a training expedition and going missing for a few days in the middle of winter is a 'little accident,'" Nueena says sympathetically. "Your poor mother, no wonder she's eager to have you near."

"I'm fine; I'm fine. The water wasn't that cold." Everett winks at me in a friendly manner but I know he is playing it off. We were all desperately worried for him.

"This is Leon. He is also here for the coronation," I say, watching Leon coldly shake the sea sentinel's hands.

"I'll be here too. Couldn't let him have all the fun." Kole laughs at his own joke.

Hiliyah rolls her eyes.

Kole opens his mouth again, but Everett cuts him off. "Della, I finished the book you lent me. It was an entertaining read on a long ship ride. I'll bring back your copy before I set sail again."

"I have the next one if you wish to continue the series. Stop by the west tower when you can," I say, ignoring Leon's fixed gaze on me when I mention my rooms.

Kole ignores our conversation, butting in without remorse. "I was scheduled for another journey, but I requested to continue my work at the palace and will be home for Nueena's celebration. What shade of blue will we be wearing together?" he asks in this cocky tone that implies my answer doesn't matter much.

"Well," I say in clear mock politeness, "you can wear whatever blue you like, but we won't be sharing shades." Sharing shades, a type of claiming through fashion, was one way to show other dancers you are spoken for. Formalwear cut from the same fabrics.

Everett laughs and mumbles to him, "Told you."

Kole ignores him. "Surely you can't attend Nueena's ball alone. Who will you dance with if we don't go together?" He laughs a little at the thought.

I shrug. "Well, Nueena will be busy, but Tavien is always up for a spin around the dance floor. He is an excellent dancer and never minds when I step on his toes."

Kole is unamused at that, but his cocky grin is quick to return. "But of course, you will save me a few dances. Last time you disappeared before I could find you, or if dancing isn't on the table, we can find a few dark alcoves during the revelry to entertain ourselves…"

Kole smiles at me with what I'm sure he believes is a charming grin and moves a bit closer, his black pepper and patchouli scent overwhelming, but stops to look over my shoulder. Leon slides behind me, pressing into my back, and a firm hand is placed just above my full hips. Everett's smile slides off his face as Leon's fingers press into my waist.

Leon ignores Kole completely and gazes down at me with open adoration. "I'm ready to go back to *our* rooms when you are." We stare at each other for a long moment; his protectiveness is an electric sensation passing between us. He pulls me closer, a possessive edge to his touch.

I nod. "Um, yes, we should go." I'm uncomfortable with the way Kole is looking at both of us, so I attempt to be kind. "That color you have on now looks nice. You should wear that to the ball."

"Is it the color you will be wearing?" he asks with a wicked smile that Leon quickly wipes from his face.

"No," Leon says flatly, "she will be wearing green with me."

All of us turn to stare at him. Kole is momentarily silenced before he looks down with narrow eyes at Leon's hand on my hip and says, "We shall see."

Everett takes all this in before he gives Kole a friendly shove, pushing him towards the exit. "I'll see you later," Everett calls behind him and as the door is about to close, I hear an angry "Just let it go!" The door slams behind Kole, rattling the glass.

"I'm going to make him the ugliest tunic possible," Hiliyah declares.

I close my eyes and sit on a cushioned stool. A headache stabs the back of my head, and I sway a little. The crown's magic thrums painfully. The sound of motion and a wisp of air in front of me lets me know someone has bent down to my level. I open my eyes, unsurprised to find a fretting Leon.

"What a delightful gentleman. I do not understand why he is not attached," Leon says with a scowl.

When I don't laugh, Hiliyah clasps her hands together with apprehension. "I knew that would shut him up. I won't make you share shades if you don't wish for it."

"Thank you. That will not be necessary." The act of matching formal clothing is a treasured part of our culture and should not be tossed about lightly. Once Leon completes the elixir, he will leave here with it to help the mortals in their recovery, and I will be left alone again. Sharing shades will only give each of us false hope of what this means and send the message we have a formal attachment to anyone who sees us together. That is, if the magic hasn't driven him into madness by that time.

Leon's gaze is intent on me, but I refuse to meet his eyes as I stand and walk to the counter with Hiliyah and Nueena. I lay a long piece of satin down and place the contents of my bag on it. "He will need at least five of everything; a new travel cloak, brown; and two sets of boots. One outfit fit for any royal activities he may attend with us."

Hiliyah looks Leon up and down before selecting items for her trade: ruby hoop earrings, a large jade ring, a gold watch enchanted to never be wrong, and a diamond-studded nose jewel. "I will have his new clothing delivered in the morning."

"I'm going to command the entire Ellovian army soon," Nueena says. "Say the word and I can have Lillian station Kole on seawall duty on the ice coast."

It's impossible to hide my smile at the visual of the handsome Kole freezing, his perfectly combed blond hair and frostbitten pointed ears sticking out from a massive white fur coat, shaking with rage at his new assignment. "As truly amusing as that would be, it won't be necessary. Besides, let's not have your first act as ruler to be reassigning one of your best captains for my benefit. You might appear to be playing favorites."

The three of us look at each other before bursting into laughter.

"Would you like Tavien to duel him?" Nueena's suggestion only makes us laugh harder, the sounds carrying throughout the shop.

While Tavien is much taller and stronger and a skilled swordsman, the only time I've ever seen him ready to duel anyone was when finding an essential history text that someone had spilled a goblet of wine on and abandoned in one of the royal libraries.

"You know," I remind her, "I don't need your commander or Zemra to fight my battles for me. I can handle it. With a sword I forged myself, I might add." I send her an unamused look in an attempt to appear annoyed, but we all end up laughing again.

"I know, I know. I'm just saying you don't have to deal with him alone." Nueena's sweet offer is genuine. "Obviously not Kole, but perhaps it would be nice for you to take someone special to my coronation ball. You have never shared shades before." There is a hopefulness to her question as her gaze slides to Leon, who stands across the room, his eyes on me.

I avoid his stare and instead watch a cluster of white flowers bloom on the hem of a lilac gown a fae woman is trying on. "Kole is harmless, just persistent and oblivious."

Well, mostly he is.

I *hope* he is.

Kole's attempts at courting me have never been genuine, never seeking a mating bond. Metal-wielding is rare to be sure, but my powers are weak and come with a shortened lifespan, not highly sought-after traits for a partner in a place where the most powerful fae women and life-givers are courted first.

He wants what he can't have after my many refusals. The captain has spent the past fifty years undeterred by my rejections and seems to forget the fact he would live long after the painfully mortal part of me wins out against my fae side, my life flickering out before he would even see mid-life.

Or perhaps that is part of my appeal.

~

e leave the market; busy vendors shout last-minute deals for goods they wish to barter for before heading home. Dewlings squeal delightedly as they play a game in the streets while parents close the doors to some shops, the sky behind them brushed with bright orange and budding purples. Worry and confusion are my constant companions on the short journey.

We are halfway back to the palace when I realize I don't know where Leon is sleeping tonight, and it surprises me how badly I want it to be in my bed, my stomach filling with flutters at the thought.

After the rainy balcony garden confessions and the intimacy of sharing my bed last night, will that continue to be an expectation? Does he want that? A calmness wraps around me at the thought of Leon and me together, no matter the form it takes. I attempt to shove down those feelings. Any attachment we form will only bring pain when we part, but the memories of the midnight moments in his arms send a wave of warmth through my chest.

Leon is deep in conversation with Tavien, but he looks over at me every few minutes of my melancholy. Every glance is a reminder that a war rages inside me. To enjoy every moment no matter how fleeting, contrasting with the crushing urge to push him away and save myself centuries of heartache.

Nueena solves my problem of deciding where Leon is sleeping. She had a bed brought up and placed in the library adjoining my rooms; a tower attendant arrived while we were gone to set it up.

Tavien explains the wards to Leon. "You have full access to the library at night, but for any other rooms here, you will need one of us with you, and that includes the entrance and Del's rooms. Avoid unnecessary conversations with the palace attendants or anyone who might notice you are mortal. One of us should be with you at all times unless you are here."

Leon nods. "I will not give Izadella a moment of peace with my presence." He says it in jest, but I wonder if he has any idea how true that is.

We say our good nights to Nueena and Tavien, and Leon follows me into the library. The bed has been placed as close as possible to my door, and with mine just on the other side, it means there will only be a small wall between us tonight. He follows me as I show him around the space and point out what books he might find interesting that are in a language he can read. The way he watches me pours heat into my veins and I see a vision of us tangled in my sheets, the library bed forgotten as his body encompasses mine under the stars.

A large sapphire necklace set in silver lies haphazardly over a stack of unread books. "Did you make this?" he asks, still looking at my creation.

"I did."

"Do you like being a part of the Gem Court?" He traces the gemstones.

I nod. "I did until this new addition to my head. I loved working alongside so many talented artisans and makers. They never cared that I was only half-fae; it was all about my work. Not every court is as welcoming, but some place more loyalty to their court than Ellova. If it gets out that I kept this from them, it will be seen as a betrayal."

"No one will find out," he says with a confidence that makes me want to believe it.

"I hope so. Good night, Leon." I make it two steps towards my door before he asks another question.

"If I lived here, what court would I be in?"

The image of him in healer robes, the Ink Court crest on his broad chest, is a beautiful picture, so I humor him. "Healers are part of the Ink Court. It's the court of educators, scholars, scribes, and healing." He would fit so perfectly there, his talents needed.

"I know Nyvenah said any loyalty I have, any vow I made, no longer matters here, but I meant what I said. If you are planning on staying here, then so am I. How does one join the Ink Court?"

I stare at him, perplexed. "I'm sorry. Courts are an entirely fae tradition. Leon, staying here isn't an option. We have gone over this. The magic will drive you to madness. I've seen it happen."

He moves close to me. "Did something similar happen to your father?"

I suck in a breath. "Something like that, but this is a completely different situation. Nothing is the same. It's been quite a day; we should get some rest." Not wishing to discuss my family further, I head into my rooms.

Leon trails behind me and leans against the door frame. "May I?"

A tiredness I can feel in my bones makes me hesitate. There is an intimacy to him even standing outside my bedroom, but whatever is deep within me that craves his nearness is the part of me that nods, lowering the protective wards, allowing him access. Leon enters at a leisurely pace, eyes roaming the gilded frames holding portraits and landscapes of Ellova, gowns thrown over the plush purple chair in the corner, and a sword that leans against the window.

His presence fills the space, and I cannot look away.

The bed is seated in the middle of four trees coming up from the floor, sheer drapings so light the pale amber is almost white hanging from the branches. A long work desk is a tangle of controlled chaos: bowls of materials to make jewelry with, quills, abandoned teacups, a dagger with its entire handle covered in gemstones.

He picks up the bottle of perfume I wear every day and brings it to his nose. "Floral, with something citrus underneath. Roses and geranium? With a hint of what I would guess is lemons." He breathes it in again. "Definitely a summer lemon."

"Impressive. A man who knows his scents."

He places the bottle back on the desk with care. "Jedrick was a late sleeper, and I enjoyed tending to my medical garden in the misty mornings, the one we met in. I have roses and geranium planted there too."

My heart skips a beat. When I was in that garden in the Iron Castle, I saw those flowers. "Is that right?"

He picks up the dagger on my desk and finds it perfectly balanced before setting it back down. "Oh, yes, I planted them almost two years ago. Geranium leaves can be used as a pain reliever when placed in teas, and rose oil is good for the skin." He turns and walks over with soft eyes to where I lean against one of the bed trees. "The scent also reminded me of you. One night a month never seemed like enough."

His intense green eyes search my face. I marvel at his perfect nose and strong jaw, the dark shadow of stubble a little longer than yesterday. His black hair, dusted with salt-and-pepper streaks, is loose and calls me to brush my hand through it.

It would be so easy to bring him down for a kiss and drag him down to my bed, to pull him completely into my life.

As if he can hear my racing heart and knows my thoughts, his eyes go to my lips. I know he is waiting for me to bring them to him, but his ears stop me. The roundness to the tip reminds me of the shortness of his life compared to mine, the risk to his sanity, and the crushing weight of the knowledge that loving him only for him to die is something I may never recover from.

If I survive this crown at all.

Fae die from broken hearts; their magic decays within their chest. We call it an enervation death. It's rare and incurable. White scars like lightning strikes appear across their skin as a mark of the magic's corruption. Eventually, their hearts simply stop beating. So instead of kissing him I ask, "How are you feeling?"

He breaks our eye contact by looking upward in an internal evaluation. "Worried about you, full from that delicious dinner, and restless from the past two days. Why do you ask?"

"Just worried for your well-being. Please tell me if you start to feel anything strange, all right?"

"And then what?" he asks carefully.

"What do you mean?"

"Say I feel the magic pushing me out or driving me to insanity. What then?" He looks down at me again with pinched brows. His eyes roam mine, searching for something.

Not wanting him to find what he's looking for, the longing, the fear, I cross my arms and look down at my bracelet, inspecting it for nonexistent flaws. "I would make sure you are returned safely.

You went to school in Versairen and you said it was safe. Maybe there's still a place for you there to teach. Or perhaps your childhood home, where you wanted to send me? You could go there even if Cyanna is there, right?" My heart aches at the reminder that he was trying to protect me before all of this started. When I was just someone he saw once a month for a few brief, stolen moments, someone who spent years lying to him, and yet he is here.

"And you will stay in Ellova, even after the elixir is made?" I want the smile he wore in the market again. Now he stares at me, slightly dejected, when I finally look back up at him.

"Yes. I have the crown, and Nyvenah needs to figure out some details, and Nueena's coronation is in a month. I need to be there for her while she transitions. Even if Grayden is removed, I imagine Nueena would want me to be safely here while in possession of Inara's crown."

His jaw tightens slightly at this. "Some things can't be rushed. Why is she taking over anyway? Why now? Nyvenah seems healthy and able to continue ruling for many years to come."

I shake my head. "Nueena's magic is about to surpass her mother's. The throne belongs to whoever possesses the most magic. She will be the youngest Realm Keeper ever. By hundreds of years."

"What type of magic does she have?"

Sighing, I put up my hands. "Look, we are—" I stumble over the words, realizing I have no idea how to describe him. What do you call someone you have years of feelings for with only brief monthly conversations and now bonded together by a life-changing moment? I do not have such a word, so I go with what I would like us to be. "—friends, and I want you to understand my home, but you are still an outsider here and there are things I can't share with you."

With earnest remorse, he says, "Of course, of course." He shakes his head. "Forgive me? I'm sorry, this is all so...new. So, we are friends, then?" A small, playful smile emerges, and I can't help but mirror his expression.

"Well, yes, of course. We have known each other for years,

shared a traumatic experience, and both love blackberry wine. That's the foundation for all good friendships."

He takes a step closer. "What if I desire to be more than friends?" That herb and strawberry scent invades my space.

I want to step into him and run my nose over his neck, inhaling that tantalizing smell.

"Ummm…" I ball my hands into fists, forcing myself to stand still and not act on my wanton desires. His eyes leave mine for a moment, noting my clenched fists in my gown.

He takes an impressive step back, straightening his spine, and places his arms behind his back, looking very regal. Mistaking my hesitation for disinterest, he says, "My apologies, Izadella. I probably shouldn't have asked. I had hoped I made my feelings obvious at the bazaar, as poorly timed as it was." His smile is strained.

I take a step closer, and he mirrors me, shoulders relaxing. "Yes, yes, you did, abundantly so, but so much has happened since then. This has all been overwhelming and I'm terrified of what it will mean if the crown cannot be removed. Your lifespan is so much shorter than mine and what I feel for you already scares me. This crown declares unwanted monarchy, so I now have a whole kingdom on the brink of starvation to be responsible for and war with Kalvorn on the horizon and I'm sor—"

He presses a finger to my lips, and his gentle touch pauses all my fears from spilling out of me. "I understand, Izadella. It's all right. I regret asking. I just never thought we would end up here, together. I didn't know if I would ever see you again after that night, and I've been distressingly infatuated with you since the first midnight we met, but I'm happy to give you time, if that's what you need."

"Time is something we don't have, I'm afraid," I whisper, but I lose the internal battle to not touch him and move towards him. His arms open with no hesitation, wrapping around me and pulling me close. I lean my head on his chest, sighing deeply and stealing his comforting scent.

"Thank you," he whispers into my hair with a soft press of his lips.

His warmth, his comfort, his scent. I could get drunk on it all.

"For what?" I ask, my hands digging into the muscles of his back.

"For sharing whatever time we do have. For not running off in the middle of the night when we were sharing a bed in your cottage." There is a deeper press of his lips into my coppery waves, and I close my eyes, memorizing the feel of it. "For trusting me with your secrets. We do not have to have it all figured out tonight. One day at a time."

I pull back to look up at him.

An urge rises to weep at him that once I get this crown off me, he will be dead in forty years, and I'll just keep living and living and living. To wail that he needs to stop looking at me with such longing, hopeful eyes and saying words like that with warmth and kindness. His shy smile does something to the inside of my chest and the world fades a little when he laughs, but the words don't come. I lower my arms and reluctantly take a step back from him.

Too much of a coward to push him away.

Too weak to resist the hope that loving him might be worth the pain in the end.

"I'll let you sleep," I whisper, even if it's the last thing I wish for.

He nods slowly and returns to the other room. I hear the rustle of his sheets, and I slide into mine, alone and aching. Thoughts of my own looming death are my only company.

CHAPTER 25

*J*ust before dawn, still wrapped in sleep, I hear movement in my room. Footsteps, slow and deliberate, move past the foot of my bed. With the wards securely in place, it can only be one of the few who can enter freely no matter the unreasonable hour.

Nueena bends down with a finger over her excited grin and motions for me to dress. As she does most mornings, she goes through my jewelry stores to select her jewels for the day. Today she's chosen a moonstone ring and a matching necklace that complement her pale lavender gown and look beautiful with her dark brown skin.

I sit up carefully now that I know the magic will rush back once I do. My head spins briefly, the crushing weight sitting on me again. My body is sluggish, but I get up and dress in a pale-yellow skirt and black corset with matching yellow stitching and ruffles over my shoulders.

I quickly write Leon a note not to worry, and together we tiptoe through the small library, past his sleeping form.

We stay quiet until we reach the outside hallway, where Tavien is waiting and holding two large teacups of morning-dew tea for us.

Nueena takes her teacup from Tavien with a kiss on his cheek. He yawns and heads downstairs. "I translated the parts of the journal we believe have information about the elixir. It will take time to translate the rest, but as time is not our ally in this, creating the elixir will be my priority."

Nueena pats the satchel at her hip. "I have a copy of the sections we need."

The tea is a vibrant burst of flavor. It's sweetened with sugar cubes and slowly awakens me as we walk through the dimly lit palace. The water the tea is brewed with is from the Airvell River, filled with magic and healing properties. I feel a little better with each sip. A few stars still linger through darkened windows. Many of the palace hallways we travel through are quiet and calm in the early hours, with only a few attendants who finish up midnight tasks or prepare for those who will rise soon.

"How are you feeling, after yesterday's conversation before Leon arrived?" Nueena's tone is soft.

I straighten my shoulders. "We will find a way to get the crown off me. Alvina's blood runs in me; we will figure out the way to unlock it. We also have every possible scroll available to us, and the forge it was made in. We are just missing something."

She is quick to agree. "We will!"

I link arms with her, and she pulls me close. "Are we going to the Royal Garden?"

Nueena is practically vibrating with excitement when she nods, braids bouncing. "Tavien found that the elixir needs many different types of herbs and flora. I have already contacted the head botanist at the Court of Green to assist in the search, but a few of the plants are rare and have not been seen in centuries. Possibly even some only Ellova herself grew. We need the anafaea flower, leaves from the salvidah plant, and blutells from the Airvell River."

We take one of the passages heading down to the ground floor, and two attendants stroll by us with platters of jam-filled pastries for the morning meal. We grab a few on our way to the bottom of the west tower. Outside the palace is a hidden garden, tucked away amongst trees and flowers, their petals closed 'til morning.

According to myth, the Royal Garden was where the goddess Ellova created the first faeries out of her blood and bones, soil and sand.

Considered sacred, it is only open to a few and is one of Nueena's favorite places. This holds the memory of where she and Tavien shared their first kiss. It is used to grow rare plants, if needed, for ceremonial or medicinal purposes. We stand before a stone archway marking the entrance; the door is made entirely of entwined ivy and thorns. The enchantments that guard this place recognize us as those who are welcome within its walls, and the thorns slowly twist away from each other, revealing the lush garden, the vines spiraling up the archway and around the towering stone walls that circle this divine sanctuary.

Over by the garden's stone statues, plants and flowers of every color grow below a mosaic table and chairs where we occasionally have tea in the last afternoons near a set of swinging seats that hang from the branches of a thick tree.

One part of the garden has been cleared, now filled with fresh dirt ready for new planting. "I have a theory, and it might not work, but I want to try." Nueena's golden-brown eyes hold an extraordinary amount of hope in them.

Tavien holds the diary open to a faded page, a sketch of a small plant with deep violet buds. "There are four key ingredients I need, but as of now, we have no way to produce two of them. The main problem is the anafaea flower, but we also need the leaves of the missing salvidah herb. The blutells will be no trouble to find, and the base ingredient is the healing waters of the Airvell River."

Nueena explains the rest, speaking quickly. "But I want to see if I can grow the flower. Since we had no idea what the anafaea and salvidah looked like, I had no way of imagining it, but since Inara's diary had drawings and other details for the other ingredients, there may be hope, but it must be grown here."

We slip off our shoes and walk to the center, kneeling on the cleared soil. Tavien holds the book for her to memorize the flower. She digs her hands into the packed earth, and they start to glow, the light shining out through the gaps in the soil. Her eyes are closed, mouth mumbling what sounds like a prayer or plea to the goddess Ellova herself. I watch as the large empty planter sparkles with tiny dots that shine brighter and slowly reach upward. Small green leaves extend outward, transitioning through three different stages of growth in a matter of minutes, which should have taken weeks or even months.

"Nu! You did it," I whisper as the seedlings expand, growing a dark green stalk topped with white buds.

She opens her eyes, and her smile takes over her face at the swirls of white flowers that surround us, a faint glow to their petals. The anafaea flowers that lie before her are beautiful, and she runs one finger over the nearest one's leaves.

"How is this possible?" I ask, awestruck.

A plant that can cure most anything.

A plant that will save so many lives.

Nueena's back straightens with pride. "I can grow anything as long as I can see it in my mind, but without knowing what it looked like, there was no hope of growing it again. Magic always seeks an outlet, eager to grow and create. I just needed to direct my magic into the soil, mold it, imagine the seeds in my hand growing, blooming. I could feel my magic mixing with the magic of the garden. Whatever magic is left from Zarella in the roots and soil."

I nod. "Sounds like how my metal-wielding works. When can we harvest it?"

"It needs to fully mature for seven nights under the moon," Tavien says, beaming as he surveys the new floral life his Zemra created. "Then the real work begins. The elixir will not be easy to make. I'm still collecting texts to bring some clarity on what is needed. We need to wait 'til the bud turns dark blue and fully blooms. In the meantime, we can start to collect or research the other ingredients, like the salvidah plant."

"Are we not a little too old to be playing in the garden?" At once, we all turn to Lillian, who wears an amused half smile at us kneeling in the dirt.

"Never too old for gardening," Nueena says as I stand and hold out two hands, pulling her up. She walks through her new blooms, careful of each delicate one. When we step onto the winding stone pathway, she flicks her wrist at the bottoms of our dresses. The dirt falls to the ground, leaving perfectly clean fabric and skin. "And to what do we owe this early-morning visit, Lils?"

"You are all requested in the command room if you are done here." Lillian turns around, sword swaying at her hip.

~

The ray of sunshine that is Viella greets us with a perky "Good morning." As she opens the command room doors for us, her eyes linger on Lillian. "Hello again." Viella winks at her.

Lillian's cheeks turn slightly pink at that.

Nyvenah and Alachite are sitting at the table, eating their morning meal. Nueena places a kiss on her father's cheek and then her mother's moonlight hair before sitting down next to her. The command room overlooks Ellova in every direction. The circular space is lined with tall arched windows in a crystal dome tower with natural light pouring in from the early-morning sky, tinting the room in shades of pale blue and purple.

With a wave of Nyvenah's hand, breakfast appears on the plates laid out on the table. Roasted rosemary potatoes, round lamb sausage, fruit, and sweet pumpkin pastries.

The four of us who just arrived begin to eat as Viella, Spy Guardian for Ellova, says, "My spies from Adreania have returned. Grayden has been crowned king. He is making few outside appearances, and when he does, it is with a poorly made imitation of the crown. He has been speaking to large groups from one of the balconies, telling them that the cure to the sickness is in Kalvorn and they must be ready for war."

"You may need to intervene," Alachite says to me.

The fork I was using crashes into my ceramic plate. "Me? How?" My body curls in on itself, dread pulling my limbs inward.

"Well, we had a spy bring back a copy of their laws." Viella holds up a faded scroll. "It clearly states, 'Loyal to whoever wears the crown.' It appears the treaty, the laws made when Inara and Drystan married, never changed." Viella says, her bright smile gone. "It is also all over their currency, flags, banners, really everywhere,"

I try to think back to any time I had seen the law, but it was always dark when I went, and I paid little attention to the decor of a castle I hated to be in.

Nyvenah sips her tea. "Revealing yourself to be queen may be enough to stop whatever plan he has until we can make contact with Kalvorn."

But what if it's not? What if I make myself known and the kingdom chooses Grayden?

"My spies also reported that Grayden did meet with the king and queen of Kalvorn again and it did not go well," Viella adds. "We need to gather more information on Versairen and see if they truly will aid Grayden in a war against Kalvorn per the treaty of their princess who is married to him."

I push the plate away, too nauseated to eat anymore. "You have someone from Versairen here—Leon. He had plans to send me there because…" Nyvenah and Alachite raised me, loved me as their own. This will not go over well. "The last night I was in Adreania, Grayden threatened me—"

"Threatened you how?" Alachite's voice is low, his eyes narrowing. It makes me want to sink into my chair like a dewling.

I take a deep breath, pushing away the feeling of Grayden's hands on me. "Grayden had shown interest in me for a while. He made some threats of what was to come. When he became king, I was to return to the castle immediately or my children would be killed."

"Children?" Nyvenah's confused expression bounces between Nueena and me.

My stomach twists painfully again. "A few years ago, he took an interest in me. The night we met, he requested that I stay after the bazaar and join him in his chambers, but I lied and said I was married with children. I don't think he was used to the rejection. He implied that my…um…choice in the matter would end when he became king."

Nyvenah places her hands over her mouth, horrified, and Alachite is so angry on my behalf it radiates off his body.

Best to change the subject and continue my point to all of this.

I hastily add, "After Grayden threatened me, I ran out and Leon followed me. He had made a plan for me to escape. He told me to take my imaginary family to Fisherman's Cove, where I would find transportation to Versairen. He had a new life planned for me there. He knew Grayden would destroy everything when he inherited the throne in a quest for more power, and Leon wanted me to be somewhere safe. He told me a small plot of land would be waiting. I could have lived in his childhood home, and he said some of the local jewelsmiths could help me start over." My head falls. "He promised I would be safe and taken care of; even my imaginary husband would be given work and the children educated in Versairen. I sent my cousin there instead." I don't realize a tear has slipped out until the teardrop strikes the table with a splash.

"Hey," Tavien says softly, "Imagine Grayden's face when he finds out the crown is on his jewelry maker's head." That brings a wobbly smile to my lips, and some of the weight I've been carrying within me washes away.

Alachite puts a hand over mine and gives it a gentle pat, the anger receding. "You were right to bring Leon here, Dewdrop. He clearly cares deeply for you."

I can only nod at that. "You should speak with him. He knows so much about Adreania and grew up in Versairen. He will be a wealth of knowledge on both kingdoms."

Nyvenah looks at her commander. "Lillian, please go get him."

Viella watches Lillian with a fond smile as she leaves the Command Room, the large doors closing behind her.

"You care deeply for him too," Nyvenah adds softly. "We all see it. I do not wish to see you hurt. Your mother—"

I can't let her finish that sentence. "I know."

My mother loved my father to the point of death and that is something I cannot forget, cannot repeat.

"If it is going to be an issue that he's so near, he can have new rooms outside of your wing. Perhaps some distance will help while he's here," Nyvenah offers, maternal worry in every word.

"Thank you, but that is probably not necessary. Since we don't know how long mortals can even stay here, I need to keep an eye on him." I don't say that the thought of him moving rooms, sleeping far from me, sends a bolt of dread through me. He needs to be near me while he's here. This might be all the time we have in the world.

Nueena and Nyvenah look at each other, but Nyvenah speaks first. "You know more than anyone that a broken heart will kill a fae. Just because we have a luxuriantly long lifespan, it does not mean we are guaranteed it. My friend was only four years past her Zemra ceremony before her soulbond mate drowned in the Elbasan Sea. She expected at least eight hundred years and died two months later." Nyvenah's eyes are filled with tears. "I cannot see you die of a broken heart like she did. There are many reasons mortals are forbidden here."

Nueena and I were just dewlings when it happened, and I desperately attempt to block out the memory of her close friend's vacant eyes at dinners, the glowing veins like lightning strikes marking her skin, the outward sign her broken heart had fractured her magic, days before they'd found her dead, curled up on the rounded soil of her Zemra's grave.

"Are you sharing shades for the ball?" Nyvenah asks quietly.

I shake my head, looking down at my lap. "We're not courting, and I'm not in love with him, Nyvenah. It's just a little crush on a kindhearted man." What I speak is the truth, but guilt floods me as if it were not.

The press of Nyvenah's lips displays that she remains unconvinced. "Della, have fun with your little mortal if you wish. Just be safe."

I know she says all of this out of concern for me. I'm concerned for myself. I nod. The door opens and Leon appears with Lillian, who appears less than thrilled.

His clothing had been delivered. The leather of his riding boots shines; his breeches and white tunic are perfectly cut to his form.

He looks directly at me as his greeting smile turns to dismay at yet again finding me upset. I shake my head, but his frown only deepens.

"Leon, please have a seat. We have some questions." Nyvenah waves her hand for him to sit in the empty seat next to Tavien and not me. Leon glances at Lillian, who pointedly sits in the chair to my right, Nyvenah's meaning not going unnoticed.

"How can I be of service?"

"We need to know more about Adreania and Versairen. Specifically, if you believe they will join forces and attack Kalvorn?"

"I do. Grayden is adamant in his belief that Kalvorn holds the key to their survival. Food is about to run out and sickness claims most of the kingdom. His vast inner court is protected for now, but soon they will feel the pain the rest of the kingdom has felt for decades. While he has a kingdom on the brink of ruin, Kalvorn is thriving. He wants what he is not willing to care for. If nothing changes, Grayden will rule over nothing but a kingdom of ash and bones."

"Will those who call Adreania home truly go to war at Grayden's word?" Nueena asks.

Leon's heartbroken expression pains me in ways I can't explain. "They will. They would have no choice. Refusing would mean imprisonment or death, and they would likely have a better chance of surviving the war than Grayden's fury, but the casualties would be great in either case. What little food is grown in Adreania is wilted and bitter even at the peak of harvest, which is why so much is imported from Versairen. Something is corrupt with the land, a certain wrongness one feels when in the Iron Castle. Despair is all around; it seeps into their souls. I have a theory that the sickness that continues to spread is related. If Grayden says all their troubles will be alleviated with a war, they will have no choice, but believe me, they hate Grayden. If provided with any alternative to him, they will take it. Their children are starving."

Leon pauses. His hands on the table curl into fists. He stares out the large windows in the direction of Kalvorn. "When Grayden left for two weeks to speak with the king and queen of Kalvorn, the castle was an entirely different place." His eyes soften. "Princess

Lyrora ensured the staff got days off, we celebrated, and servants' weddings were finally held. We got a taste of what it would be like without him, to work in the castle without fear. Those who live outside the castle only know the pain and struggle of living under Jedrick's rule. All who live inside it know it's going to be devastating under Grayden."

Tavien follows Leon's gaze over the forest. "Will Versairen agree to war with Kalvorn?"

"Grayden's wife, Princess Erenia—well, I suppose she is queen now—is the eldest daughter of the king of Versairen. Part of the marriage agreement is if one goes to war, the other will aid. I cannot speak whether or not the king of Versairen actually desires war. Erenia certainly does not."

"How do you know that?" Nueena asks.

Leon faces her. "Both princesses in the Iron Castle are my friends and close confidantes. Erenia would never wish harm to come to the innocents of Adreania or the soldiers from her motherland. She and Lyrora are the best parts of Adreania."

An ugly twist of jealousy darkens my face. Only Tavien notices and pats my leg in reassurance.

I have no right, but a bitterness blooms within me, and it claws at my chest. Leon and I only spoke once a month. Life in that palace was miserable. Leon and the princesses deserved to find any light in the darkness, to find comfort in friendship. I have no right to be jealous.

But I am.

A palace attendant comes in and leans over to speak into Nyvenah's ear. She nods at the attendant's words. "We will have to complete this conversation at a later time."

Lillian opens the door to Everett's mother, Camarra, the Seed Keeper and Guardian of the Court of Green. She is barefoot and wears a long, flowing sage dress with a golden belt. Small pouches hang from it with wildflower seeds and loose tea leaves. Camarra's dark blonde waves are pulled up into a bird's nest on her head and are home to a yellow canary that sits on her shoulder, chirping every so often.

"Hello, my Keeper and her kin." Camarra's voice is light and airy, unhurried.

"Camarra, welcome. Please join me for breakfast," Nyvenah says.

They kiss each other on the cheek.

"Della, Everett was telling me he was with you yesterday. How delightful that he is back for a while. You two have much to catch up on." Camarra beams at me.

"I hope to see him later this week," I say, noting that Leon sits up straighter at my words.

Nyvenah turns her back to the Seed Keeper, her eyes widening with meaning to me.

Time to leave.

Even though the crown is hidden under my braids, I need to avoid any court Guardians, who are more sensitive to powerful magic, as they hold it themselves. I rise and look at Leon, tilting my head towards the door. Leon immediately rises as well, following me out while Camarra is distracted by Nyvenah.

Leon turns to me in the hall when the door has shut behind me, a wide grin on his face. "Good morning, Izadella."

CHAPTER 26

y heartbeat skitters at my real name on those smiling lips. "Hello, Leon." I get a little lost in those hopeful eyes he has pinned to me. "H-how are you this morning?"

His smile grows even bigger. "Remarkably well. Intrigued where you went off to so early in the morning. I assume if you wanted me as a prisoner, I would have been brought to the dungeon and not trapped in a lavish royal tower with a most impressive library and a full spread of breakfast."

"I would say you're somewhere between a prisoner and an esteemed guest. I need to show you something."

He sticks out his elbow in a gentlemanly fashion. "Lead the way."

I hesitate just for a moment, but his earnest expression makes me want to melt into a puddle in his hand, and I take his arm as we head outside.

We continue our walk, a slight sweet breeze in the air, and arrive at the royal gardens.

Before I can tell him he might not be able to enter, as the gardens are heavily restricted, the vines and thorns twist themselves apart, allowing us to walk through. "Oh, wonderful! Nueena must have given you entrance already."

Leon moves to the statue of three fae women gowned in moss off to one side of the garden. Flowers grow all around the statue, small blooms in the lightest shade of purple. "Who are they?"

The stone fae women sit in a half circle, bright smiles carved into their beautiful faces. Long pointed ears peek out behind the stone hair with everlasting crowns of flowers on their heads.

I point to each stone woman. "Inara, future queen of the mortals. This was long before the crown ruined it all, though. At the center is Zarella, Nueena's ancestor and the first Realm Keeper." Zarella holds her stone crown in her hands. "Last is Alvina Vanabalt, the Forger, my ancestor. The monument was built by my court as a gift to Zarella for her crowning ceremony. The three of them loved this garden."

"It is nice to know Inara had a good life before her dreadful one in Adreania," Leon says as he takes in the statues.

'They were closer than sisters, their friendship torn apart. Queen Inara sacrificed herself to save her daughter. Alvina was exiled from Ellova by Zarella. The crown wreaked havoc. Zarella's quest for revenge and retribution over Inara and her missing daughter led to war with the mortals, a failed attempt to get the crown back that took the life of many Ellovians." I've heard this story so many times, but each retelling feels like a new puncture wound on my already tattered heart.

"A blood-soaked, tragic history," he says.

"I love seeing this statue, though," I add. "It's a reminder that they had a beautiful friendship long ago."

Leon watches me carefully. His fingers lace with mine and he brings the back of my hand up for a light kiss. "I'm sorry Alvina was exiled and that your family suffered so much for it."

He kisses my hand again and this time his lips linger there, his gaze above sympathetic. The breath has left my lungs. His lips are so soft, and I miss them when he guides my hand back down, but when he tries to unlock our fingers, I weave them back together, not willing to let him go so soon.

I lead him away from the painful past and over to my hope for the future.

He marvels at the garden, the rich colors of the blossoms and the plump leaves, and silently watches the gossamer-winged, lavender butterflies flutter around the flowers, drinking their delicacies. We walk to the wooden planter box that holds the anafaea flower.

"These are most of the ingredients we need to make the elixir. Tavien says they need to mature a bit, but hopefully it'll be a reality soon." We both sit down on the low edge of another planter a few feet from where the anafaea grows in swirls, and he places our joined hands on his lap.

"How long have Tavien and Nueena been married?"

My heart lurches, knowing I have to explain Zemras, and I try to keep the longing off my face as I explain. "We don't have husbands or wives here in the way that mortals do. Mates are the term we use for someone who is in a committed relationship. It's a term of respect and claiming. You must be together for a long time before you can state someone is your mate. They don't always last forever because fae lives are long, but it's mourned when it ends and meant to be a permanent union."

"So, they are mates?"

"Yes, in a way, but so much more than that, they are Zemras. A deeper, stronger bond than a mating claim, a soulbonding of eternal union. It's veiled in secrecy, but if you truly believe that someone is your Zemra, your soulbonded mate, there is a place you can go. It has age restrictions and laws, consequences for even attempting to find it without the blessings of your courts' Guardians. Impossible to find without the knowledge of the Zemra guides who take mates to the hidden temple."

No longer able to hold Leon's gaze, I look up to the sky and watch the birds soar leisurely overhead. I close my eyes and relish the warmth of the sun on my face before continuing, "If you and your mate are granted access to the temple and you have a chance to prove that you are truly soulbonded mates, your souls are forged together. Zemra soulbonds exist to connect two fae souls on an eternally deeper level for paramount emotional, spiritual, and physical intimacy. Zemras can feel each other's panic or joy, which is amplified directly through the crystals they wear. Any strong emotion Nueena feels, Tavien does too, even states of mind. If she's hungry or tired, he can sense it. They can even share pain, so one is not a burden. Power can be exchanged over time."

The weight of Leon's gaze on me is heavy, and when I can no longer ignore his eyes on me, I turn my back to him.

"Is that something you desire?" he whispers, tracing his thumb along my hand.

I laugh, but it's a bitter and broken sound. "Courting is taken peculiarly seriously here. Fae men often highly desire to continue a strong family line. Powerful babies are needed to ensure that. Magic is passed down through birth to dewling; the more powerful the mother, the more powerful the offspring. I'm only half-fae, so it wouldn't work for me, not that anyone has wished to try. My power is rare, yes, but I do not possess much of it."

He places my hand in his and brings it to his lips. "Izadella, you are so much more than your magic."

Emotion swims in me. "I know, but more than that, I will only live a few hundred years. I'd be lucky to reach five hundred before the mortal part of me dies. The fae were once nearly immortal when the magic flowed freely, before the crown stole so much magic from us. Now their lifespans are shorter, but not nearly as short as mine. Any mating claim with me would forge promises of torment for the male, condemning him to grieve long after I'm dust even if we never chose to see if we were Zemras. I probably lack the necessary amount of magic to even attempt to enter the temple. Never seemed worth it. To be with someone, knowing I will end up hurting them in the end. Why would I be worth that type of pain?"

He drops my hand as if burned and stands up, the sun behind him blinding me to his emotions. "Is that what you think will happen with me?"

I repeat the question in my head and try to come up with an answer. When I stay silent, he goes on.

"So, you do not wish for someone to mourn you, and that is the reason you deny yourself a chance at love? You think a lack of magic determines your fate?" He's not angry when he says it. His words carry an undercurrent of anguish. "Forget the crown; forget how magic affects mortals. Say it was just you and me, with nothing but time to stand in our way. If the roles were reversed, and you were the mortal and it was I who would live long after you, would you still tell me it's not worth it? That you weren't worth mourning? Should I simply focus on the elixir and leave as soon as I am able to save you any heartache? I can. I will. I do not wish to cause you a moment of pain. Only if that's what *you* desire. Is that what you want?"

I gape at him as he lowers himself gingerly and pushes my thighs apart, kneeling between them.

"No. Yes. I don't know." I sound small and pathetic even to my own ears, being torn in so many ways, saddled with too many burdens to think clearly.

He sighs and moves to stand, but I pull him down again. I'm desperate for him to understand me. My fingernails dig into him, and only the thick material of his tunic stops me from drawing blood.

"Listen to me," I say. "You have been my silly little infatuation for the past two years. I have worn my best dresses, spent endless hours working on your every commission so it would be perfect, and repeated our conversations over and over again before I fell asleep."

His eyes are wide, and he pulls me closer as I spill my secret longings at his feet.

"Once, you left your wine glass on my table and I kept it. Nueena and Tavien teased me mercilessly about it for weeks on end. When any male did show interest in me, even for a meaningless lust-filled night, I turned them down because it never felt right. I thought you were forever unattainable, nothing more than a gift I got every full moon, even if everything I said to you was a lie, because it felt unbelievably real, this tether between us. I was prepared to harbor these feelings, hide them away for years."

Leon pulls me closer to him, and now it's his fingers that dig into me as I continue to pour out too much of myself, leaving my tattered emotions bare to him.

"Yet you are here, and everything has gone wrong, and I feel like I cannot breathe properly when I am torn apart on the inside from wanting you and wanting to protect what little of my heart you don't already possess. I don't know how to save you from the fate my father met. Seeing you driven mad just for us to have a painfully short time together would break me. So, please, do not ask me what I would do in a different situation because I do not feel like I will survive this one." My breaths are shallow and rough, the tightness in my head returning.

Nothing in the garden has changed around us. The butterflies continue their gliding path around us, the gentle breeze caresses the flowers, and yet something has shifted between us, irrevocably altered.

His hands slip from my waist, and he cups my face with such tender care I want to weep.

"I understand. I just couldn't stand the thought that you believed yourself unworthy of anything." He pulls me forward and his soft lips are pressed into my forehead. The gesture is sweet and loving, unburdened with all the complications I carry. "We need not worry about it today. I just want…no, I *need* you to know that any amount of time with you would be worth it—*is* worth it, and you were never alone in your midnight infatuations. The days leading up to the bazaar were agony for me, waiting to see you again. Erenia once tried to suffocate me with a pillow in the middle of tea when I spent an entire afternoon talking about you. She had to listen to me wonder what type of cheese you liked, how you might like your tea, and if you preferred the sea or the mountains."

I burst out laughing, and Leon looks at me with wondrous delight at the sound. He caresses me closer, resting my forehead in the curve of his neck, his long hair tickling my cheek.

I deeply inhale his scent—healing strawberry oil and herbs, the most wonderful scent in the world—taking lungsful of it, not caring if he hears it, although by the chuckle vibrating through him, it does not go unnoticed.

"I love soft cheese over warm bread straight out of a stone oven with tea so hot it burns, no sugar. Just a splash of milk. As for the sea or the mountains, sea. I wish we were there now. Warm beaches, salty air, cool waters. Just you and me."

His lips press into my temple with a delicate kiss. "That is good to know." I can hold back no longer as I drag my nose along his neck, absorbing him, demanding more.

Lost in the warmth of his touch, I almost miss the feeling of something slithering up and around Leon's arms. He notices at the same time I do, both of us pulling away, glancing down at his body. The vines, with their little plump strawberries dangling, make their way around him.

I turn so quickly I almost fall off the edge of the planter, but Leon's hands return to their home low on my hips to steady me.

Oh, please, do not be what I think you are.

A large strawberry plant has grown behind me and has slowly attached itself to Leon's limbs. Not tightly, just moving at a leisurely pace, twisting around his ankles and arms.

"Hello," he says to the plant currently trying to wrap itself around him, and reaches down to pull a plump, ruby-red strawberry off the vine. "Well, this is new."

Biting into it, he closes his eyes and lets out a contented sigh as a bit of juice runs down his chin. Since his eyes are closed, he is surprised when I swipe the trickling juice with my finger. He watches as I bring it to my lips without thinking.

His eyes darken. "That, my dear Izadella, is a dangerous game."

My cheeks must match the strawberry in his hand, given the heat of them, and I drop my gaze, trying to pull the vines off him so I can shove them back into the strawberry bush.

"I told you, Sunshine."

We both turn to find Nueena and Tavien staring at us, our nearness, and the strawberry plant clinging to Leon. Nueena and Tavien wear identical, slightly concerned expressions. Continuing to form further attachment to Leon will only end in heartache; we all know it, but I can't seem to stay away.

Leon stands and offers me his hands for assistance while I try to explain, "Um, well, I think I grew strawberries, or the crown did, at least. Ignore it. What's going on with Camarra?"

Nueena's amusement dips at the Seed Keeper's name. "A discussion for later. Our presence has been requested at Bardhana."

~

We walk together to the northernmost part of the palace and out to a large courtyard laden with enormous trees. Leon watches the fae saunter in and out of the various portal trees, their large branches shading those who emerge from the archways carved within the bark.

Unlike the one we used in the forest with its ivy-hidden hollow, these trees' arches are made of emerald and gold. Onyx steps lead up to the entrances. Nueena selects the largest tree, and we follow her in. With one hand, we each take hold of the handrail that circles the interior and plant our feet for the short journey. The moment her palm touches the rough interior, the bark lights up, the tree accepting Nueena's magic and propelling us forward as the light goes out.

My insides roll at the rumbling beneath us. Leon's warm chest presses up against my back, and his hands find their place low on my waist, pulling me closer. His teasing thumb trails small circles on the side of my hip. I reach my free hand behind to cup his cheek for a brief touch; his stubble tickles before his head moves and follows with the softest press of his lip to my palm. The tree's motions slow as we move away from our stolen moment.

Light pours in through the back archway as we turn around, stepping out. A cold breeze nips at us as we arrive on one side of an enormous mountain, snow lightly falling around us, the early-morning sun casting a torrent of color as it cascades off the opal and moonstone walls. Balconies and windows pepper the mountain's face.

Its massive circular doors shimmer from the pale pink-and-white crystal that it's made with. The etchings carved on the door tell the story of the creation of the fae realm, of Ellova: a celestial being grew tired of the heavens and came down, taking corporeal form to experience a new life, bringing with her wild magic, myths, and legends molded with long-lost truths of Ellova the goddess.

The doors to the Ink Court's capital, Bardhana Library, open on their own, sensing our presence. Ink-gray banners hang on the quartz walls with the crest of the Ink Court embroidered in gold thread: a quill piercing a thick tome, surrounded by the moon phases.

Large balls of captured sunlight appear, swaying lazily above us. The hallway is filled with paintings preserved with magic, so they are as vibrant as the day they were painted, despite having hung here for thousands of years. We pass by small shops, living spaces, and room after room filled with books and scrolls. Dozens of spiral staircases and ramps lead up to housing and dining halls.

Nueena and Tavien stroll hand in hand, discussing trade agreements in front of us. She waves to some dewlings dressed in small pastel scholar robes, who eagerly wave back before a teacher hurries them into one of the carved-out lesson rooms. Some of the residents and courtiers turn to look at our arrival, pausing on the steps or wishing Nueena well for the upcoming coronation.

Our journey is so deep into the mountain there are no windows, the space brightly lit with hundreds of the sunlight-filled crystals that hang all around us.

"How many fae live here?" Leon asks, staring into each one of the many small bright libraries we pass. Room after room of knowledge and history.

"A few hundred, but not all at once," I explain. "There are Ink Court libraries all over the kingdom that most scribes travel to and from, depending on their research. Each court has a few hundred scribes that document what's going on in all the courts. Not much happens here without it being documented. We take record keeping and education seriously, as you will see."

I smile at him, but he's not looking at me, his head twisting back and forth to try to take it all in. He has a slightly greedy look in his eyes, a starved man sitting at a buffet, desperate to devour the knowledge this library offers.

When Leon does turn his attention back to me, it is with a wistful half-smile. "My favorite place growing up was my family's library. In the last row, on the top shelf, there is an old green book. If you pulled it, it led to a secret reading room. I loved to hide there, ignoring my brother's and cousin's insistence that I play outside with their friends." Leon reflects on this sweet childhood memory with a slightly dreamy expression.

I turn, walking backward in front of him, brimming with excitement to show him the main library. With a ridiculous smile on my face, I ask him, "Are you ready?"

"Ready for wh—" His question dies on his lips as we enter another set of enormous jeweled and white wooden double doors.

Leon has stopped walking, staring up with his mouth slack. It opens and closes a few times before he can get the words out. "I've never seen anything like this. How is it organized? How do we get any of the books from the top? Is it open to everyone? Who carved the shelves?"

I laugh at his flurry of questions. "Yes, it's open to everyone. The ancient fae who started the Ink Court carved the library." The rest he will need to see for himself, so I take his hand in mine, pulling him along to follow me.

The main library in Bardhana houses millions of books, the shelves built directly into the mountain and extending so far up one can barely see the top. The most rare and fragile are stored up high, away from the constant traffic of hands and the floating lights. Many of the shelves are painted or ornately carved, touches added by countless fae over the centuries.

Nueena comes to a stop in front of one of three large tree desks to the left of the main doors. Reyna, the Scroll Keeper and Guardian of the Ink Court, a petite fae with chin-length dark brown hair waits for us with two guards. Her shoulders, chest, and thighs are covered in floral and moth tattoos of vivid colors alongside intricate fae markings, including the Ink Court's crest tattooed just below her neck.

Reyna is in a sleeveless and cropped tunic that shows the tan skin of her midriff and leggings that have been cut off at the tops of her thighs. Along her arms, on her shoulders, and in her hair are five large glowing light green moon moths lazily flapping their wings. They seem undisturbed as she moves.

Reyna hugs Nueena first before turning to me in greeting. I wrap my arms around her, careful of her moths and their delicate wings. Each moth is thousands of years old.

"Reyna, this is my friend Leon." My hands move in elegant motions of the Ellovian hand language."

She smiles warmly at him. *"Hello, Leon."*

I show Leon the proper sign and he greets her.

Before we step away, Nueena waves her hands to inquire about Reyna's own family and work, making signs and symbols in the air in front of her. The tattooed librarian passionately updates Nueena on her latest research.

"Thank you for meeting us on such short notice. I need your assistance with research, but it must stay between us. It is of a delicate nature. So, you are the only one I can trust with this request." Nueena ensures her hand movements are concealed if anyone is watching us.

Reyna's face shifts into determination as she responds, *"I will help in any way possible. Does this have to do with your coronation?"*

Nueena shakes her head. *"No, this is more of a historical request. We seek knowledge of the mortal elixir that Inara created, her magic, and anything on the stolen crown and the war that followed to try to get it back."* She hands Reyna a small scroll sealed with wax in the High Court's colors. *"My mother has written down a few texts she believes may help us. We can also use anything about the Merawood's magic."*

"This is Reyna," I explain as Leon watches the expressive hand movements Reyna gives Nueena with great interest. They both laugh at something Nueena signed. "She's Head Librarian and in charge of the Ink Court. You will see her again for the coronation ball, when each court Guardian presents a gift to Nueena as a show of good faith in her future leadership of Ellova. She is Deaf; that is why we are communicating with Ellovian hand signs."

"Is that a language everyone here knows?"

"Of course. All fae are taught as dewlings so everyone can

communicate with one another. Is that not the case where you are from?"

"No, it would only be used in households and small communities."

The Scroll Keeper grabs a leather satchel off the wall and hooks it carefully over her shoulder, so as not to disturb the moths, before dipping her hands in a fine white powder and scaling the white stone walls of the library.

We all watch as she ascends row after row, swiftly and with graceful precision, carefully choosing where she puts her hands on the rocky shelves.

The moths take flight, fluttering around to land on a few books, guiding her to the ones she is intent on collecting. After a few minutes, high above us, she removes another book from where a moth has landed and places it in her bag. She does this a few more times, climbing all over the place, following the moths, before making a quick descent to us.

Once she is safely on the ground, she hands us the books. Nueena, Tavien, and I all do the sign of gratitude for her efforts, and the moths fly down and gently rest once again on her.

Reyna looks curiously at Leon, who gives her a small wave before he follows us out.

Tavien walks us up a flight of stairs to his spacious private office. Bookshelves stuffed with ancient tomes line the rocky walls adorned with multiple portraits of Nueena. The oval-shaped desk in the center is covered in notes, scrolls, and sketches of plants.

He hardly works here anymore. His private library and personal collections of the histories he has written moved to the palace, but it still smells faintly of him. Leather-bound books, smoke from a cheery fireplace, and Nueena's perfume.

Nueena and Tavien look at each other and she gives him a small nod.

Leon peers down at the sketches, but Tavien slaps a hand on his shoulder, steering him out of the room. "Leon, I must show you something."

Leon gives me one last glance. Nueena and I watch the two of them leave, shutting the door behind them. My concern deepens when protective wards flare up around us, locking in any sounds.

She takes a seat at the small table to rub her forehead for a moment and gazes at me, or rather, at what is concealed behind the twisted hair hiding the crown.

"Del, we have a problem."

CHAPTER 27

"What is it?" Panic rises at the thought of another problem. Unable to stomach any additional calamities, I drop in a green velvet chair, suddenly exhausted once again. When Nueena doesn't respond immediately, I guess. "Does this have anything to do with Camarra?" Court Guardians never show up in the middle of breakfast in the command room, but she is known for being quite the free spirit.

Nueena is quiet for a moment as she thinks about my question. Lips pursed together, she looks down, suddenly looking more tired than I have ever seen her.

"So, it *is* the Court of Green? Is something wrong with their growing lands? Nueena, please say something."

She finally looks at me. "Camarra has confirmed the rumors of soil not yielding as much as in previous years. She promised Nyvenah that she wanted to compare this year's harvest with the last and had to wait until the season was over to do so. She was quite apologetic and swears there was no ill intent in keeping the information from us until now."

I let out a huff of frustration. "She should have immediately reported that to your mother. That is critical information for the Realm Keeper to know."

Nueena nods. "That's what Camarra was told. Camarra has no idea what's happening, but I have a theory, and I think the crown is the reason. That's why we're here. We need to read everything written about it. The Ink Court has preserved the Forger's Journal. I've asked Reyna to bring it to us, but we will take it back to the palace."

I sit back in my chair; face twisted in confusion. "Nu, you know I can't unlock it, nor could my mother. We both tried many times. You were present when I tried fifty years ago."

"I know," she says delicately, "but I am hoping with the crown it will open this time. We need to learn if there is a way to remove the crown, or even why the crown cannot be removed. It's unwise to open it here, with how unpredictable the crown's magic can be, so we will have to wait until after dinner."

"You know I will try." I look down at the pale blue carpet of the study, embarrassment warming my cheeks. "I should lie down when I try, in case I faint again like the last time."

"I'm sorry, Del," she says gingerly.

I scoff at her. "Do *not* apologize. I'm the one who made this mess. Well, I do blame Jedrick for not staying alive long enough for me to bring it to you. That was incredibly insensitive of him."

Nueena's eyes soften at my joke. "You stopped Kalvorn or whoever took him; it could have even been Versairen. They could be pretending to agree to go to war as an elaborate ploy to get the crown, who knows? Maybe the king of Versairen didn't want his daughter to suffer anymore under Grayden. What matters is that it's here, but it can't stay with you, *on* you. You are half-mortal. We need to worry about the magic driving you into madness, too. I can funnel the magic out when you need, but Del, I can feel its fury when I touch it. The crown has had thousands of years to collect power, and it's screaming for release. It will likely only accept me being a funnel through you for so long. If I'm being honest, I do not understand how you are all right now."

"That's not the word I would use. I feel lightheaded and drowning. The magic is a crushing weight within me while pushing me away." Ignoring the sensation of the magic can only last for so long;

it's a building pressure. "Nu, we should discuss what will happen if it does take my life." I loathe giving voice to my fear, but no matter how painful the thought is, it is a possibility.

Nueena looks taken aback. "We won't let that happen."

"But if it does, your mother and you are the only ones who may be able to control it, or we must have a plan to destroy it. It has stopped siphoning magic, so if the crown is connected to the failing soil, we should see improvements, but who knows what else it is capable of. It's a keyed item, wholly unpredictable."

She gives a somber nod. "I understand what is at stake, but we will figure it out. Tavien will retrieve his family's sword for us to study, we have the Forger's Journal, and Reyna is seeking information with every library at her fingertips."

"It might not be enough."

"All we can do is hope."

Reyna waits at the door with a box wrapped in silk in her hands. Nueena drops the wards, and I open the door for her. She passes the box to me, and I am only half-aware of the conversation they are having. I do not need to unwrap it; I have it memorized. It's bound in leather so old it is soft to the touch. Part of one edge is burned; wrapped around the whole book is a long leather cord and an enchanted gold lock that has always eluded me.

~

*T*avien and Leon return, Leon having found a book on fae plants and their medicinal purposes. He scribbles a note in a small leather-bound book he carries with him before looking up. "So, this library is the capital?"

"Of the Ink Court," Nueena answers without looking up from her scroll.

"So, with there being no currency, how does one from the Ink Court buy things if nothing is sold here?" A scholar in pastel robes walks by the glass windows of the study, books piled high in her arms, and Leon points in her direction. "Say she saw a dress she liked. How would she get it?"

"When she needs a new gown, she would simply be given it by someone like Hiliyah. Work robes are provided by the court." Nueena writes something down.

Leon looks unconvinced by this. "But how?"

Putting his book down, Tavien patiently explains, "Ellova is a community. The Ink Court taught Hiliyah to read and write when she was in school. Every young dewling is educated by a member of the Ink Court. It all balances out in the end, but the transactions with the Ink Court have long-term value, rather than a short-term trade. Hiliyah herself may not be reimbursed for a single dress, but she benefited from the education she received, and if she has dewlings, they will also be educated at no cost to her. Members of the Ink Court are taken care of by the other courts, as their place in Ellova is to share, preserve, and pass on knowledge, and that has great value here."

"Yes, but how does Hiliyah buy more fabric in that case?"

Tavien answers for me, "We all care for each other. Ellovians are not selfish like mortals, and they have never known scarcity, so they have no fear of running out of necessities. Your society says, 'If one dress is free, take them all,' but here, you only take what you need." Without looking up from his book, Tavien takes a folded cloth from his pocket and wordlessly hands it to Nueena, a moment before she sneezes.

"Thank you, my love," she says.

"No one pays taxes to the crown like in Adreania," I explain to Leon. "We share what we make and give what is needed. Courts create fast networks to ensure everyone has what they need."

There are no windows to the outside, but the constant trickle of fae leaving the library lets us know dinner is soon. "Shall we pack up?" Nueena asks.

We leave the cozy study and head down towards the entrance. Tavien and Nueena stop to speak with many of the librarians.

Leon watches the busy library break for the evening meal as we leave. "It's wonderful here. So peaceful and full of life." He doesn't have to say it; the wistfulness in his voice makes it clear what he is thinking. Ellova is a kingdom unlike Adreania in every way. Here everyone is cared for, none left to starve or suffer alone.

Leon and I are alone outside next to the dimly lit portal tree, waiting for Nueena and Tavien. "Hopefully Adreania will be a better place soon. They will see through Grayden's lies. Once the cure is ready and all those you helped are healed, you can tell them of a different way to live. Adreania could learn much from Ellova, from my culture. You could be the one to show them."

Leon nods. "Grayden will hold on to whatever power he has by whatever means necessary. If you come back with me, we could show Adreania a different way. I—"

I cut him off. "Now is not the time."

With my fae sight I can see his fist flex in frustration. "You deny something that is rightfully yours now. The crown sits on your head."

"You act as if I can just walk in there and demand the throne. Grayden has an army who will still obey him. I was never meant to be a queen. I would probably hate it anyway. Lyrora would be a kind queen, or they could elect new leaders."

"Izadella, you would make a *magnificent* queen. Any kingdom would be extraordinarily lucky to have you lead them. You snuck into a dangerous realm where you would have been killed if you were discovered, to bring food for those who needed it. Went to a castle cursed with hatred to get coins so those who didn't have much could survive. Do you not see how much bravery, how much heart that took? The compassion, the fortitude. All beautiful, admirable qualities to have in a queen." He whispers the last part, eyes shining with pride.

My knees shake at the way he is looking at me, with such reverence and admiration. The hope in his eyes is nearly blinding; it warms and terrifies every part of me.

"Let's just focus on the elixir, all right? Then we can decide the next steps. I wish to help Adreania; I do. I don't wish to see its citizens killed in a war over a crown that I have. My father was Adreanian, and my cousin and all she cares for are Adreanian, but for now—" I take his hand in mine.

He stares down at our intertwined fingers and squeezes.

"—this is all we can do. Hopefully it will be enough to convince them I do wish to help. I want to see a thriving kingdom ruled by someone who cares for them. This is the first step."

"Adreania will be forever changed because of you, Izadella."

I squeeze his hand back. "Because of all of us."

Because of us.

CHAPTER 28

The palace is a flurry of activity as we make our way to the dining chamber, greeted by the mouthwatering scents of meat roasted in open flames, and fresh bread smothered with butter and dusted with cinnamon.

Round tables with silk cloths of every shade of green in honor of the court that provided our food are set with golden forks and knives and huge goblets. Nueena and Tavien fill their plates and walk off to sit with Viella and Hiliyah.

Lillian comes and takes the Forger's Journal again to secure it for the time being. The rest of the tables are filled with students eating after lessons, families dining together, and friends greeting each other before sitting down. Some scattered fae sit alone to read a book or knit.

"Everyone eats together?" Leon asks, watching honeyguards sit with scholars.

We all nod and make our way to the vast rows of food on display.

"We do occasionally eat in our private dining rooms, but most evenings we share meals here, together," I answer him.

A few fae males stand in line before us, gathering their choices. I hand Leon a golden plate before turning to him in a whisper.

Though I am near enough hearing would be no issue, he moves closer so that my lips brush his cheek when I speak.

"I have dried meat and cheese from Adreania back in our rooms too if everything is too sweet, but give whatever you want to try a taste," I say it slowly, allowing myself to savor my cheek on his.

Giant shells from the Elbasan Sea are heated with enchantments to hold a vast spread of this evening's steaming fare. Sizzling lamb stew with roasted purple carrots, flower petals over peas, and cheese-covered rolls with cooked dough made of corn.

Taking a slice of a spiral, flaky pastry filled with cheese and spinach, I add it to my plate of duck crisped with spiced butter, carrots drizzled with spicy honey, fried rice molded into a sphere, and a hearty scoop of seared zucchini. I add more spices I've brought back from Adreania to try to fight the sweetness.

The long table shifts from meats like maple pork and rainbow trout with the head still on, to brown bread and wild rice dishes, to the end filled with desserts. Most desserts are not my preference, considering how sweet the other foods are, but I'm partial to the shortbread cookies with jam and add a couple of those to my plate.

A tray of Nueena's favorites, little jiggling lemon cakes, are placed out and I grab a few for her.

Leon's plate is piled high, and he looks at everything with a greedy expression. Most of his plate has vegetables on it. Grilled asparagus with fatty pork meat wrapped around it, its juices dripping on his smashed rosemary potatoes and dark greens in a dill sauce. Carved pieces of duck are laid out next to long fire-roasted squash and chicken stuffed with sweet spinach.

Once his plate is full, we make our way back to the table where Nueena and Tavien sit with Viella and Hiliyah. They are all discussing fabric trade routes from the seaside capital city of Meridia Cove over the sounds of laughter and the scrape of plates.

"Hello!" Hiliyah and Viella greet us in unison and quickly return to their discussion.

I place the lemon jelly cakes on the side of Nueena's plate and she makes a little noise of delight, swiping some of the sweetened whipped lemon zest cream off the top with her spoon, savoring the taste.

Leon eats his meal with enthusiasm and compliments every-thing he tastes, savoring each bite. "This is truly delicious. Such richness to the flavors, complex with the layered spices and the untouched sweetness."

His enjoyment is endearing, but I am quick to ask, hoping he is not simply being polite, "You do not find it too sweet?"

"Sweetness is present, especially when I expect a savory taste, but the flavors work so well together." He takes another large bite, and I fork a potato from his plate and pop it in my mouth. It tastes sweet to me.

Hiliyah jumps into our discussion. "No one else agrees it tastes sweet, but Della is sensitive about her food here." She says this as I pour a pot of sweet, milky almond tea into a few cups for us and hand her one.

I bite into a table roll. It's less sweet but still has a light honey aftertaste, even with the extra spices.

Lillian joins us again with a head nod. She has changed out of her armor and wears casual black clothing, taking her place next to cheerful Viella. The commander pulls Viella close, kisses the top of her short blonde hair, and starts to eat off Viella's plate in silence. Viella leans into Lillian's chest and gives her a detailed and enthusi-astic account of her day while Lillian listens intently.

After we finish, Leon ascends again to the dining table, coming back with bloody sausages, hard-boiled dove eggs, fried crab cakes, creamy purple cheese spread on thick brown oat bread, and green apple slices drizzled with a thick caramel glaze.

He sits next to me, smiling. Breaking apart the apple, he passes me the bigger piece and watches, grin sliding off, when I lick the caramel off my fingers. He makes a choking noise, and all my friends try to hide their smiles.

Toward the end of the evening, Leon asks how we all met.

"We met as dewlings," Nueena explains. "The night my mother gave birth to my middle sister, she was screaming in agony. It was the loudest noise I had ever heard, and I thought she was dead. Her healer had fallen ill, and they'd had to call for another, but a storm delayed their arrival, so she had hours with no magic to dull the pain. The sound of birth is exceedingly violent for a dewling to hear. Later, I snuck into the room. There was so much blood that I couldn't imagine a world where she would survive. The healers said if she only had the crown, it might heal her. I had seen the maps, so I knew where Adreania was, and if getting the crown would save her, I had to try. It was devastatingly foolish of me to even try to get near the mortals."

She pauses her story to look over at the table not far from us where Nyvenah and Alachite sit with Vaylin, the sister from Nueena's story, and their other daughter, Nueena's youngest sister, Kaylena. Vaylin, having returned home for the coronation, lives at the Court of Swords capital, where she is a healer. Kaylena, still a dewling, only born a decade ago, jumps up and down with excitement over a large slice of chocolate cake that an attendant has placed on the table in front of her.

Nueena smiles, turning back to us. "I'd discovered the mountain door you arrived in weeks prior, having no idea where it went. I had been afraid to look before, but that night, I went through it. Practically rolled down the hill in the rain without knowing about the glamour to hide the palace or how to return home again. I just ran and ran. I was lost for hours. Thankfully, the trees blocked my way when I tried to stray from the Merawood Forest, and they led me to the forge by Della's cottage." She turns to me.

It's my turn to bring the memory to life. "My mother found her asleep in the forge curled up next to the flames and tucked her into my bed 'til she could figure out what to do. Our family was still in exile and my mother had never been to Ellova, so Nu lived with us for three days. I thought she was going to stay forever, and so did my mother. My father came to visit as he did a few days each month and did not even question it. Declared he had two daughters now and took us hunting. She became a member of the family that day."

Nueena laughs. "I knew someone would find me eventually, but I was too scared to tell them where I was from. I asked them once about Ellova and they said it was hidden and they couldn't find it, even if they wanted to."

Tavien puts his arm around her shoulder and kisses her head before Viella cuts in.

"The whole damn kingdom searched everywhere for her, but eventually, Lillian and I found the door. We were honeyguards at the time, no longer dewlings, eager to prove ourselves. Lillian thought Nueena might have slipped through it. She was right, of course." Viella beams at her mate.

Tavien continues, "I could feel where Nueena was, even though we had never met. My father was one of the few who believed me that I could sense her, and I was determined to find her. My father knew the commander in charge of searching the Merawood Forest, and I begged them to let me join the search with Lil and Vi. Led them straight to that little cottage. There was my future Zemra, playing with a little mortal girl with hair the color of pumpkin soup. She looked up as if she were expecting me, just waiting for me to bring her home."

Tavien brings Nueena's hand up to his mouth and places a tender kiss on the inside of her wrist. She smiles up at him, their gazes the same, like each of them hung the stars for the other. Sensing they may be preoccupied with the memory, Leon and I lean towards each other, giving the royal pair space for their moment of reminiscence.

"So, what happened after that?" Leon asks.

"I was devastated she had to leave. I had found a friend and a sister all at once and didn't wish to part. I had never met anyone my age before, but they took her back to a rejoicing and relieved city as well as a new baby sister. Later, Alachite would come find us. He learned we were related to Alvina Vanabalt, who got exiled for making the crown and made a home for herself in the Merawood Forest outside Ellova's borders."

My eyes drop to my plate as I move the last of my food around, recounting the past of my family, the fae line of the Vanabalt women. The dinner plate in front of me blurs. So many years have passed, but the weight of Alvina's exile and her bloodline's fate still holds grief, not enough time to rid me of the sorrow. "My great-grandmother did make her way back to Ellova for a time, long enough to conceive, but the past was still new, and she found no reprieve from being Alvina's daughter, so she returned to the cottage and had my grandmother, alone. They bore the banishment well and survived on their own. Anyway, Alachite said his daughter demanded we be reunited."

Nueena leans over me, returning to the dinner conversation, her chin on my shoulder, and chuckles at her dewling antics. "I was not ready to be parted. I refused to eat until my new friend was allowed to visit. I was just a dewling with no interest in history or politics."

I lean my head to rest on hers. "When Alachite and Nyvenah came down to thank my mother for her help and ended the exile of my family, my mother was given instructions on how to find the door." Nueena knows what I am about to say next, so she links her arm with mine in comfort. "She died a year after we got the news that my father had died. I was fifteen, too young by both fae and mortal standards to live alone in the woods, and Nyvenah moved me here. She and Alachite made sure I was taken care of. No one dared say my family line didn't belong anymore, so I lived in the palace 'til I was ready to be on my own at the cottage."

Leon takes in my history and simply says, "Drystan destroyed much the day Inara died, but I'm glad you have each other."

～

Tavien lights the fireplace in the west tower with a wave of his hand after the four of us return from the evening meal. The Forger's Journal sits unwrapped on the table inside the shared lounge area. Leon sits close to me on the couch.

"Are you ready?" Nueena asks. She had been the one most eager to try to open the journal tonight, but now she glances back at me with reluctance clouding her beautiful face.

"I'll be all right," I reassure her. "Even if I faint again, it will be worth it. It could have the key to removing the crown."

Leon shifts nearer to me, and when I glance over at him, his lips are in a tight line. He reaches deep into his medical satchel and pulls out some sort of mortal listening device.

Faster than I have ever seen him move, Tavien launches himself to his feet, blocking Nueena from Leon. Tavien's hands erupt in blue flame-like swirls, and he sends out a glowing burst of magic. I am surrounded by sapphire and white flames that move like smoke around me, forming a barrier between me and Leon. More magic shoots out from Tavien and encircles Leon's hand that is holding the contraption in a sphere of cerulean light.

Tavien's face is sharper than I have ever seen. "Don't touch her with that! Why do you have iron here, Leon?"

Leon freezes, absorbing the sight of Tavien's magic before cautiously moving his glowing hand away from me. "Tavien, all my medical equipment is made of iron. It's the only metal we have in Adreania. My deepest apologies. It is only to listen to Izadella's heartbeat so I can monitor her to ensure she doesn't lose consciousness again."

I wave my hand through the protective shield and Tavien dissolves it; the whirling, sheer flames rise before they disappear. Leon's hand is still encased, so I slip my hand in and hold up the device to show Tavien. "I'm all right, Tavien, truly. See, I'm unharmed by iron. Leon can do what he needs to."

Tavien relaxes slightly and sits back down next to Nueena, nodding. "It will be destroyed after tonight. I will not allow it near Nueena."

Understanding his mistake, Leon apologizes again. "Of course."

It's quiet for a moment and I ask, "Why don't we get started?" to loosen the tension in the room. Everyone agrees. Nueena rubs her Zemra's back with an affectionate smile at his protectiveness. His hand is tight on her thigh as Tavien takes a steading breath.

The journal lies before me, and I cover the lock with my hand.

Leon gently places one end of the device in his ears and the cool iron chest piece below my collarbone. His other hand slides low on my back to steady me. "Ready?" he asks, so close I feel his breath on my cheek.

Ignoring his nearness for the moment, no matter how much I wish he were nearer, I focus on the lock. The crown's power surges up, eager to be loose outside of me.

The lock remains sealed, ignoring the torrent of ancient force willing it to open.

The more the magic is unable to break free, the more agitated it becomes, the pressure of it building. My heart starts to race, and Leon's firm hand moves to my hip, shifting me closer to him.

"Are you all right?" he asks me in a soft, concerned tone.

"Yes. The best way I can explain it is that the magic is a corked bottle of sparkling wine someone has shaken."

This book might hold the knowledge we need to remove this cursed crown from me. It's a piece of my family's history; it might be able to tell me why Alvina created the crown in the first place, knowing Zarella forbade Inara from being with her mortal lover. I cannot, *will not,* allow for this lock to go unopened. I would rather destroy the whole book than let its secrets remain locked for centuries, sitting in that library when I desperately need an answer.

The agonizing thought that I may need to die to rid myself of the crown pushes me onward, and I shove the magic deeper into the lock with all the frustration and heartache the crown has brought me.

If we do not find a way to remove this cursed crown, it will kill me, and I refuse that tragic ending. I will fight to any breaking point to rid myself of it.

For a long moment, nothing happens, but slowly beneath my clenched fingers, the gold begins to shake and vibrate. It shifts under my hand, determined to stay locked, but I will not yield. My heartbeat is a wild animal in my chest.

"IZADELLA, STOP!" Leon screams, trying to pull me back, but I ignore him. Tavien throws another shield up around Nueena and himself.

With one last burst, a blast of magic ripples out of me and the lock explodes in my hands. Leon throws himself over my body, shoving both of us into the couch cushions as darkness floods my vision.

CHAPTER 29

My hands sting and the acrid smell of burning metal pierces the inside of my nose, forcing me to cough in a poor attempt to clear my airways of the invasive scent. When the air smells more like home again, I try to return to my fitful rest. The bed is soft, and something warm is wrapped around me.

Strawberries. It smells of strawberries.

Just like Leon.

I inhale deeply, pulling the scent into my lungs to chase away the bitterness, and slip back into sleep. I dream of the sweet berries and stolen kisses on rain-soaked balconies in secret dark gardens and of hot, sweat-slicked skin on cool sheets under moonlight. It takes me a moment to place the sensation that my arm is being stroked by a soft hand. It feels nice.

"Del?" The feminine hand stops brushing against my skin and squeezes carefully. Nueena. "Del, honey, can you hear me?" My head is resting in her lap.

"Nu, I want to fuck Leon."

Someone laughs quietly near me, followed by a soft cough. "Perhaps this is a private conversation?" says a man's voice, joined by the masculine laughter of another.

"Yes," Nueena says, trying to stifle her giggles, and she pushes some hair behind my ear. "I'm sure you do, but we can talk about it another time."

"Do you think he wants to fuck me too?" I ask somewhere among dreams.

"If he wants to, I'm sure he will let you know." Her words are kind and soft and sound so far away.

"Mm-hmm." That would be nice.

I cough again, my body aching at the movement, and the room comes into focus, everything rushing back. Oh gods, the realization of what I confessed brings heat to my face, and I let out a small laugh intended to hide my embarrassment over my words.

Leon helps me sit up carefully, and my head rolls to one side. A cup is brought to my lips.

"Drink up," Nueena encourages me, and I drink it greedily as she assists with the goblet of water. When I've finished it all, she offers a wobbly attempt at a reassuring smile.

Leon transforms into the healer he is.

"What hurts?" The sweetest concern is carved into his features. Leon's firm hand threads behind my neck to keep me still as he places two fingers on my neck, checking my pulse. He looks so serious, as if I'm moments from fainting again, making it impossible to hide my amusement at his sober gaze.

"Leon, I'm fine. The crown's power overwhelmed me for a moment." I place my hand on his and run a gentle caress over it to soothe him.

Now it's his turn to look sheepish. "Apologies. I'm ever eager to touch you, it seems." He helps me stand before taking his warmth and strength with him as my neck mourns the loss of his grip.

I avoid Leon's piercing gaze. "The journal?" I ask hopefully to avoid any more discussion on my health or sleep-filled confession.

The journal lies open on the table.

"We haven't gone through it yet," Tavien says, standing next to Leon. "Didn't seem right while you were unconscious. How are you feeling?"

I rake my fingers through my hair. "I feel like that book had better hold all the answers. I would love to be free of this blasted crown and its burning desire to render me unconscious."

Leon's helpful hand stays near, hovering close as I move to sit on the end of the couch. I pull the journal closer, and together we turn page by page. To everyone's disappointment, it's mostly filled with sketches of swords and jewelry. Garnet rings, a sword with a handle made only of onyx, sapphire studs, and jeweled bracelets. In fact, most pages have no writing besides a quickly scribbled name of what I can only assume is the fae she made them for, and a list of what was traded in exchange for their creation.

With only a few pages left, the hope starts to bleed out of me like an open wound before Tavien turns the page and there it is: the crown drawn out in great detail.

The sketch is artful, beautifully done with an artist's flare. It sits on a sketch of Inara. No markings on the page, no ancient Ellovian to translate, nothing but art that means nothing to me.

I frantically flip the page. The anticipation strangles my chest, crushing the hope that the next spread would hold something, anything to help me, but it's just filled with sketches of the same small golden ring with three strands twisted together at the top drawn over and over again. More fucking jewelry.

I want to tear the book apart, rip each page out, shred it into scraps, and have Tavien set it all on fire.

Alvina was a fool, but so was I.

That's it, then. We have run out of options. Nothing to guide me out of this, to give me the hope I'm desperate to find. Leon must sense my distress as he starts to rub my back. I had truly thought Alvina would have left something here about the greatest magical item ever made, but she didn't bother to leave a single sentence of instruction, not even a question in her mind that it could all go wrong. Inara was killed for the crown that will kill me.

Filled with defeat, I turn the page, but there on the back of the ring sketches are paragraphs of writing in soft feminine handwriting, written in an older fae language. Tavien translates it aloud.

"Zarella has forbidden me from helping Inara in any way, but she came tonight with pleading eyes. To be with her lover, to find a way to keep magic within her, so that they can be joined as one. How can I resist those tear-filled green eyes? She deserves happiness, and if she thinks she has found it, how can I stand before her with denial on my lips?"

Tavien moves to the next section.

"I do not trust the mortal Drystan, who claims to love her as deeply as she loves him.

"I've made her a crown that will hold all the magic she needs to survive in Adreania, but she will need more than just a crown if she is to rule. This is a gift I will forge for her, a symbol of our friendship and the trust I place in her.

"The crown will be keyed to her alone. It will answer the command of no heir and obey no bloodline, loyal only to Inara.

"Once her soul has faded from this world, the crown will yield only to whoever is truly worthy. No mortal or fae may take it from Inara once it's on her head; only she can remove it willingly. It will protect her from all who seek to end her life early, but if she is killed through blood or blade, the crown will unleash a curse, slowly stealing the life from the land, piece by piece, until it is ash.

"The only cure will be Inara's elixir, and she will not be there to create it. Once the crown has chosen one worthy to wear it, it will cease its havoc on Adreania.

"It's just as we suspected. The crown is responsible for the decay in Adreania," Tavien says.

Down below in harsher script, dated a month later.

"Drystan claims he wants a queen, but what that bastard truly wants is our magic. He wishes to glamour her, to hide her fae nature and make her appear like them, mortal, as if anything she is needs to be hidden. How can you claim to love someone and wish them changed so much?

"I did what Inara asked and made a glamour ring for her. It will give her the appearance of a mortal form."

As the writing goes on, it gets more and more frantic. Deep scratches into the paper tell of someone desperate to get down their thoughts, weeks after the last entry.

"*Zarella has found out about the crown and what I have done for Inara, who I helped Inara become.*

"*Inara has left Ellova. I hope she is happy. Zarella will not speak to me.*"

Tavien scans the few dozen pages until he stops reading and looks up at me with sorrow in his flame-blue eyes. "This may be hard to hear, Della. This is almost three years later."

"Please, don't stop reading. I need to know."

He nods, continuing.

"*The bastard killed her. Her precious daughter, Arelia, is missing. Zarella has sent troops throughout the forest to try to find her, but there is nothing we can do. They cannot find her. THIS IS ALL MY FAULT.*

"*Inara is dead.*

"*He killed her.*

"*He killed her.*

"*He killed her.*

"*The crown is locked on Drystan, but he cannot control it. With no wearer who can control the flow of magic, the crown will take and take and take, pulling magic forever. We can feel it siphoning, stealing.*

"*I do not know how to stop it.*"

Dried teardrops and ink spills blacken the page with a glimpse into her grief.

"*We would need to kill him, but the crown defends against harm. Many fae have left Ellova, no longer wishing to live under Zarella's rule. She is readying for war to get back the crown before it drains all the magic in Ellova.*"

Weeks later.

"*I am with child. I have a feeling it will be a girl.*

"*My bones ache from the loss. The healer said my grief and guilt could cause me to lose my child. It would be a fitting punishment for all that I have done.*"

Months later.

"*I gave birth. Zarella allowed me to stay in Ellova until Naewyn was born but I have been exiled, never allowed to set foot in my home again. It is what I deserve. I deserve worse but Naewyn does not. I am so sorry, Naewyn. May Ellova one day welcome you with open arms.*"

"Zarella's troops could not get into the castle. Drystan has many men ready to defend him. Many Horn Court soldiers died."

There are more sketches of jewelry and a young babe.

Two weeks later.

"Zarella came tonight. She has sealed off the Merawood Forest, using her own magic. I could not bear to look her in the eyes. She held Naewyn for a long time. We did not speak of Inara's missing daughter, Arelia. She said when she leaves tonight, she will use the last of her magic to seal off Ellova forever, hide it with ancient glamour, and the forest magic will stop anyone looking to harm the fae.

"Zarella had come to say goodbye.

"She left Naewyn a gift she can only open when she is no longer a dewling. I wonder what it is..."

"What was the gift?" Leon asked.

"The key to get into the mountainside door you entered through," Nueena answers quietly.

This betrayal of deliberately creating the curse attached to the crown was another way Alvina failed this family and her realm. For a brief moment, I thought her journal was going to redeem her, that history would be kinder to her once we had seen she tried to do something good, but that wasn't what we found at all.

Returning the crown would wash away a sliver of her transgressions, but there will be no redemption here and only my death at the end of all this. Her shortcomings will be paid for with my own body. To restore the crown to its rightful place in the fae realm means I will never see the crown wielded by someone who can control its wild magic and finally use it to bring prosperity instead of destruction again.

Rage fills me; bitterness draws me near with its claws. Leon places his hand on my shoulder, his concerned eyes on me. His touch calms some of the storm within me fighting to break free.

My heart stops when Tavien turns to the next page. Something is pressed between Alvina's agonizing words that makes all of us take in a sharp collective breath.

An herb.

"Could it be?" Nueena whispers, hands over her mouth.

Light from the fire highlights the herb's dark green scalloped leaves, preserved in magic with something written underneath it, teardrops warping the page at the bottom. Nueena picks it up and twirls the stem gently between her fingers while Tavien reads aloud the words beneath it.

"The last thing Inara ever gave me, salvidah leaves for my healing. It is all I have left of her."

This cursed crown is going to kill me, but we can stop it from taking any more lives. I may not be able to control it, but the crown is stagnant atop me, not pouring out magic but at least no longer taking anything either. I stand, pulling on Nueena's hand. "Come on, Nu." I all but run to the greenhouse attached to our wing.

The west tower greenhouse's large planters are filled with flowers and towering plants.

I kneel next to the first planter, Nueena following behind me. "You can create all the salvidah plants we need tonight, and we will be one step closer to a cure for the mortals. Adreania needs this. They deserve better. They always did." My breathing becomes labored. I try to ignore the pressure from the crown, the heaviness of what I just heard, and the burning in my eyes from unshed tears. Making the elixir is all I can do to correct the mistakes Alvina made. It needs to be the last thing I do before the crown claims my life.

As I hang my head, I see Nueena about to comfort me, but Tavien places his arm across her chest, stopping her.

Leon kneels next to me. His eyes are full of understanding and empathy. "It's not your fault," he whispers. "You took back your ancestor's creation, and it will no longer harm the mortals."

"Yes but think of those it has killed. The crown stole the life right from the land and starved them. It stole their essence as punishment for Drystan's crime. Enough is enough. I need to help them before the crown kills me too."

He connects our foreheads, and I breathe in his luscious scent.

"We're going to figure it out together." We reach for each other at the same time, locked in an embrace on the cool green stone of the floor. Leon's distracting touch is soft on my hip and shoulder, but I shove down any rising feelings.

I want to believe him. I truly do. But the crushing weight of the crown, the unimaginable power trapped within me, is an immutable reminder that my mortal body will perish beneath it.

The last life the crown will take.

CHAPTER 30

*T*avien pulls Nueena to his chest, his head resting on her head for an intimate embrace, before she moves to the planter.

"Ready?" I ask Nueena.

The salvidah herb is held to her chest when she speaks. "Yes."

With a wave of her hand, Nueena clears the planters, leaving behind a blank bed. Her eyes flutter closed as she digs her fingers into the fresh soil. I close my eyes too and send up a prayer to Ellova that this will work.

We *need* this to work. So many lives depend on it.

"Open your eyes." Leon's lips are near my ears, and I shiver from the sensation, but I do as he says and gasp. Light shines before small green buds that stretch and rise slowly from the dirt. Hundreds of the lifesaving herbs are growing under moonlight.

Nueena shrieks with joy when she sees them, happy tears erasing the grief from before. Leon and Tavien release us at the same time as Nueena and I launch ourselves at each other, our laughter filling the small greenhouse.

"We did it!" Nueena cheers.

We all stay there for a minute, wrapped in silence, feeling the weight of being so close to the cure and the relief at the sight of the thriving sprouts.

I turn to Tavien. "When will they be ready?"

"They are not fully matured yet. Thankfully we don't need them for another few weeks. They will need to be watered once a day 'til we harvest them."

"What is the fourth ingredient?" Leon asks, his reassuring hand lightly stroking my back.

"It's an underwater plant," Tavien answers. "It only grows in a few places, any body of water that comes from the Airvell River. I looked at a few maps. Quartzridge has a spring that should have enough, at least while we test the first batch. I figured since we have to go there for one of the crowning ceremonies, we can wait 'til then."

When the excitement wears off and the stars in the sky fade, we realize the late hour and make our way off the floor. I take the hand Leon offers me, but stumble when I try to stand. He wastes no time and lifts me off the ground, ignoring my gasp of surprise, arms behind my knees and back, heading to our rooms.

Tavien and Nueena chuckle and follow behind us.

I would protest the unnecessary assistance, but with no fight left in me, the weariness that has wrapped itself around my bones leaves only the desire to pull him closer as he ushers me into our rooms. Nueena pulls the blankets down on my bed and Leon lays me down so gently he must think I'm made of glass.

Nueena turns off the lights above and they both wish me good night as they leave. I hear them murmuring in the next room. The library light next to me blinks out a few moments later after a rustle of clothing and the creak of Leon's bed.

The emotions of the night are still warring within me, an ache in my body from forcing the lock open, the weight of knowing death awaits. Hope fades like a sunset on my worst day; bitterness has replaced what little there was.

"Once the crown has chosen one worthy to wear it, it will cease its havoc on Adreania."

One worthy to wear it.

It *allowed* me to wear it, but that does not make me worthy to control it. After every king's death, it was passed on to another unworthy man. The only difference is its hue on my head and that magic can flow out of it now. Not that I can control that. I imagine a worthy person would be able to control it once again, wield its magic the way Inara once did. I curl in on myself under the blankets. Wouldn't being the kin of its maker mean anything to the crown? It might not find me worthy, but at the very least, is it too much to ask it not to kill me too?

Will the crown even let me live long enough to see the elixir heal the mortals? To see Nueena's coronation? Or will the magic have demand more than I can give, taking my life in its place?

The bed is as empty and cold as I feel despite the pleasant night air that the open window brings in.

I lower the wards, granting access into my bedroom. "Leon?" I say it so quietly I do not think he hears, but he appears. The small light that follows above reveals him to be shirtless with low soft pants.

"I'm here." He kneels beside my bed.

Sorry, I know we agreed we would just be friends, but I want to sleep in your arms again and do not wish to be alone but worry not if you do not want to be bothered.

"Will…will you stay with me tonight? Only if you wish, of course. It's just that everything hurts and—" I don't know what else to say. I'm one hundred and thirty-three years old for fuck's sake; I should be able to sleep by myself. I'm quite well-practiced at it.

Before I can finish, he sits on the bed, swinging his leg over. I use the last of my energy to move, giving him space. He lies down, the bed sinking before me, but he keeps his distance.

I am too weary to play this chivalrous game with him and move to practically lie across his bare chest. His deep rumble shakes me when he laughs at my boldness.

Leon's skin is soft and warm, and his muscles flex under me. He pulls me closer and entwines his legs in mine, holding me. He slips his hand under my top to rub sweet circles on my back. I'm overwhelmed with the sweetness of the intimacy; just his presence soothes my troubled heart. It floods my body with warmth even as I'm reminded why I need his comfort tonight.

"I had placed so much hope on Alvina having left behind some way to remove the crown, but the book only confirmed my fear that we might not be able to find a way to end this curse without—" I can't even say it. I thought I had hundreds of years left. Not a life as long as Nueena's or Tavien's, but another few centuries with them. Time to travel and create beautiful jewelry, to dance under the golden glow of the Gem Court's temple, and to dine on fresh seafood in the Court of Shells summer festivals. To see Nueena become the great leader she was always meant to become, a Realm Keeper who ruled with grace and justice, mercy and compassion. To watch her and Tavien celebrate their Zemra union every year under the stars for decades to come.

To maybe find love one day.

I sit up quickly with tears in my eyes. "What are we waiting for?" I ask him. My words have a hysterical edge to them. I reach for the band around his waist, but his hands cover mine, stopping me.

"Izadella, what are you doing?" His grip tightens when I try to undo the laces.

"What's the point of only being friends if this crown is just going to kill me? It'll probably happen before the magic drives you mad. I want you. I always have, and you desire me, too. I've seen the way you have looked at me for years."

He hardens beneath my frantic touch and makes no move to deny it.

I lean down and press my lips over and over again to his chest, looking up at him. "Let's be together, even if it's just for tonight. Maybe it's all the time we will have." I have given him so many reasons why we shouldn't be together but now I can't seem to remember them.

They seem so unimportant here in the dark with death and madness hovering nearby.

I grind against him when he will not let go of my hands. His groan fills the space and suddenly I am flipped onto my back beneath him. One of his arms is under mine keeping his weight off me, one leg between my thighs. With his free hand he wipes the tear that is tumbling down my face. When my face is free of my obvious pain, he kisses each cheek. Not a quick, friendly peck, but the one only a lover can give. Slow and tender, like his touch.

"As tempting as it is, I will not take you with tears in your eyes." He moves some of my curls away from my face.

I savor each and every one of his touches, my heart leaping into my throat at his thoughtfulness towards me and my erratic desires.

"But we might not have time," I whisper into his chest. All I want is time with this mortal man, endless amounts of it.

"You will not die before we have a chance to explore the depths of our passions for each other. Tonight, unfortunately, is not for that." His smile is so kind I want to weep all over again. "Although I do dream of that moment."

His lips brush my temple. His chest rises and falls in a contented sigh. "Good night, Izadella." He rolls over so once again I am draped over his chest.

"I believe you." I fade into sleep and dream of him 'til dawn.

~

I wake to Leon's soft breaths on my nose and one loose arm around me. The aches in my limbs have faded overnight and I am surprised at how well-rested I feel considering last night's events. The sun is just rising behind him; his outline dipped in gold. When I slide away from him, he moves closer in his sleep, seeking out the warmth I have left behind, his arm sliding up, finding only my pillow. A frown pulls at his lips in his sleep.

I grab a white blouse cut at my waist and a dark green skirt. After changing in the library, I slip out of my room, surprised to find the main living area already occupied. Tavien lounges on one of the couches; papers, and books are strewn about, as he lazily flips through a faded leather book with one hand and sips a steaming cup of tea.

"Morning, Tav," I say, yawning, flopping down on the space across from him.

He grins over the rim of his cup, setting aside the book in his hand. "You feeling all right?"

I lean forward to the table where a teapot is waiting and pour myself a large cup of tea, mixing in fresh milk. The tea is sweet enough on its own, so I ignore the bowl of sugar cubes. The teapots never keep the tea quite as hot as I would like. "I've certainly been better. I slept surprisingly well last night, though."

He nods and flicks his wrist at me. A single blue flame erupts from his finger and floats over to me. It wraps itself around my teacup, and the tea boils for a few seconds before he calls back his fire.

I let out a contented sigh, holding the cup up to him. "Thank you."

He holds his cup up as well and we pretend to clink our glasses from a few feet away.

"What are you reading about?"

Tavien holds up one of the worn books. "Reading some of my family's personal historical journals about the war over the crown and looking for history on our keyed sword."

"I've never been more thankful for the Ink Court's obsessive documentation than I am right now."

He chuckles. "It *is* our true passion."

We both drink our tea in comfortable silence 'til I can no longer hold in my question. "What do you think of Leon?" I try to sound indifferent but am not sure I succeed, hope overtaking my words.

Tavien leans forward on his knees; eyes focused intently on mine. "I like Leon. I do. He seems like an honorable man, and you clearly harbor intense feelings for him, but please be wary. Nu and I are worried about you. The hovering shadow of death does not make for a pleasant third partner."

"I thought you might say that." My hope bleeds out of me, disappointment taking its place, and I try to hide it by taking a long sip of my tea, ignoring the burning sensation down my throat.

"We want you to be happy. Nueena and I have wished for years you would find what we have and the four of us would have centuries of time together, traveling and living our lives as two pairs. I just hate that you found someone with an hourglass attached to him. I like him, but I love *you*. I'm sorry, but he's not worth dying over, Del." His blue eyes are full of sympathy.

His words pierce me like flaming arrows even if I know they are meant to protect me.

Tavien puts down his own tea and grabs one of the empty cups, filling it and adding sugar and milk.

He turns around to face the door behind him that just opened, his Zemra strolling in. Nueena's shimmering blue gown moves like a flowing river down her body from its high collar; the sleeves are open and made from a fine fisherman's net covered in shells at the top that glides down over her arms to reach the floor. Pearls wrap around the cuffs. She joins us on the couch, sitting next to Tavien, who hands her the teacup. While she drinks, she leans her cheek up to Tavien, and he presses his lips to her high cheekbone.

"Good morning! Do you have coronation meetings today?" I ask.

"I have a few meetings with some representatives from the Court of Shells and their Guardian today on the coast. They are building a new ship for my personal use so I will be shown some of its construction, but I will be back in time for dinner."

A knock at the door has Nueena waving her hand to unlock it. Lillian and Viella appear just as breakfast materializes on the table.

"Good morning, my loves," Viella's velvety voice greets us. Lillian follows her in. I move to one end of the plump couch, and they join me.

Lillian grabs one of the newly arrived pastries. "One of the rooms on this floor has been cleared and turned into a temporary apothecary for the elixir." She turns to Tavien. "It has everything you've requested."

"I hope Leon's ready to work," Nueena jokes. "There's much to be done with creating the elixir, and it needs to be done in an extremely short amount of time." She bites into an apple slice.

Before I'm able to speak on his behalf, a voice from behind me says, "I am."

We all look at Leon, who is dressed. His green sleeves are rolled up, revealing his strong forearms. His eyes stay on me while he walks over, ready for the day. He takes a seat on the couch arm nearest me, looking down at me with affection. "When do we get started?"

CHAPTER 31

An empty room has been transformed into a fully stocked apothecary. The wide-open windows face north, the mountains the only view with the scent of wildflowers drifting in. Three large tables hold hundreds of glass vials. The other ingredients needed are spread out on the workstation in large containers and long jars. Measuring cups and spoons of all different sizes join the organized chaos of the room.

Leon and Tavien go over Tavien's extensive notes for every part of the elixir, including what he thought the measurements might be, but some experimenting would be required.

"I'm still waiting for a few more books from the Ink Court, but we have enough to get started," Tavien says, looking pleased. "Everything else we may need is here in this room or can be bartered at the market."

I sit on one of the stools, mixing some ingredients under Tavien's careful instructions, and watch them work. Nueena has left for the day. She invited me to go with her but I'm eager to stay at Leon's side, no matter how lovely the coast is with its crystal cobalt waters and crisp salty air.

The royal family has a lovely sandstone palace in the Court of Shells. Nueena's family and I used to spend a few weeks together there every summer. Maybe when the elixir is complete, I can take Leon there for a few days. Perhaps it's wishful thinking, but after the dreary life he led in Adreania for so long, he deserves some time lounging on sandy beaches with fruit wine chilled in ice crushed from the snow-capped mountains in the far east.

Tavien and Leon work in a synchronized flow, Tavien with his wealth of knowledge and Leon with his mastery of medicine. Breaking only when the midday sun reminds us to eat, they create with unrelenting focus.

A large pot sits over the fire, boiling the sweet water from the Airvell River. Leon slowly adds in ingredients and I'm entranced with how swiftly and precisely he works, grinding down dried leaves and pouring in different healing tonics to the base of the elixir. Leon narrates everything he does for me, why certain ingredients need to go in first when creating a medicine such as this, why some of the ingredients are needed at all. He's never worked with a few of the fae plants before but only needs a quick explanation from Tavien to understand their purpose and how to extract what is needed.

Leon tells me and Tavien of his time as a healer for the mortals, his own recipes for medical miracles. He is especially proud of a tonic he created to help mortal women stop bleeding after birth.

Tavien shares about growing up in the Ink Court surrounded by books with his historian parents. His thirst for knowledge as a dewling was fueled by the libraries surrounding him, and he started school a few years earlier than his peers.

"Then I met Nueena in that forest and I only ever wanted two things: to know everything there was to know, and to be near her. I demanded to attend the palace school. Thankfully my parents and the royal family agreed. We have been inseparable ever since."

Leon looks up from the large paste he is making. "How long have you been Zemras?"

Tavien laughs. "Much longer than we should be. Technically we broke into the temple. Our parents were furious when we came back soulbonded. The laws surrounding Zemras decree one must be at least seventy to even be seen by your court's Guardians and the temple guides. Nueena was forty-four and I was forty-seven."

"Fae are considered dewlings until they're fifty," I add to Tavien's story, "so it is incredibly young by the standards of our society. Similar to mortals twenty-four and twenty-seven."

Leon looks thoughtful. "Why were your parents so upset if they supported your relationship so early on?"

"Because we broke a sacred law and even the Realm Keeper's child must be punished."

Leon's eyes widen at that, and he opens his mouth to speak, but the door opens and Nueena leans against the doorframe. She wears the massive crown that the Court of Shells gave her last month at their crowning ceremony. It's made entirely of creamy white pearls, delicate light green gems, and pale purple sea glass of all sizes. She embraces Tavien and they share a long kiss before she heads towards me. I stand, giving her my seat. Tavien follows her and pulls out the pins that hold up the delicate crown. It's beautiful work; their crown maker did a fine job reflecting their court on the headpiece. But I'm confident Nueena will favor my court's crown above all the others.

"What did I interrupt?" Nueena asks, her shoulders relaxing as he pulls off the crown. Her braids are gone, and her hair is in long tight curls down her back.

Tavien remarks, "Ellova's grave! That's heavy for a crown!"

She rolls her neck to relieve the pressure. "They don't call it the Crown of a Thousand Pearls for nothing."

Tavien rubs her shoulders, and she leans back into him, eyes closing, releasing a long breath as he works on the knots in her neck from wearing the crown all day. "We were just telling Leon about our unsanctioned visit to the Zemra temple and the repercussions."

Just as Tavien did, she laughs at the memory of young love. "Oh, yes, that."

"What was the punishment for breaking the Zemras law?" Leon asks her with a concerned frown.

"Complete separation for one month. Which doesn't sound so

dramatic, but soulbonded mates need each other like air in the early days, and being apart is *agony*. Like your heart is being ripped from you. My mother had to stay at the seaside palace; she couldn't bear my anguish. Said she could hear me no matter how far away I seemed to be. The only reprieve was the letters we wrote to each other that Del snuck us."

"I will always need you like air," Tavien says, pulling out her last hairpin and massaging her scalp.

She gazes up at him with adoring golden-brown eyes and blows him a kiss before facing Leon again.

"Why such a harsh punishment? You were in love." Leon looks between the two of them, but I don't miss the way his eyes flash to me for the briefest moment at the end.

"It's meant to be a warning for any other fae who might want to follow in our footsteps. Praise Ellova, we were correct; we were Zemras. But not everyone who enters that temple is as blessed. Guessing wrong has a lifetime of consequences. But that is a story for another time. Dinner is ready." She takes Tavien's hand and pulls him out of the room. Leon holds the door for me, and when the door shuts, Tavien sends white flames that glide up the wood frame with a guarding spell before fizzling out.

Dinner is waiting for us in the west wing. Tavien and Nueena sit close as we share with her our day, and she describes the beautiful ship with her name carved in the seafaring wood.

She brought home fresh fish that the palace chefs cooked with caramelized onions and red peppers alongside a thick fish stew. We dine on bread baked with corn, crumbled white cheese, and leeks, our plates full of crunchy green beans and a mound of yellow rice. At the end of the meal, I reach for the shortbread cookies to smother in jam, but Tavien and Nueena look at each other with mischievous smiles.

"Actually," Nueena says, "we have a special dessert." A silver tray appears, and she dramatically removes the lid, revealing four small strawberry tarts. A buttery, flaky pie crust at the bottom, with juicy strawberries lying in a bed of thick cream piped in a swirl. A small decorative leaf sits delicately on top of the sweet dessert.

Oh, please don't be made from what I think you are.

"We call it Della's tart. We didn't want all those strawberries from the garden to go to waste." Tavien presses his lips together to stop from laughing at his own joke.

Leon and I lock eyes as he tries to hide his own smile. "It does look delicious."

His intense focus on me sends heat rising to my cheeks. Embarrassment wars with longing. Those little strawberries remind me of his hands on my hips and his lips brushing my hair as he kissed my forehead in the garden, of our confessions among the clovers, of his reassurance and patience.

A loud bang rings out and the potted rosebush behind him bursts open with a flash of emerald and crimson, as yet another unwanted strawberry plant grows before tumbling to the floor, a few of the fruits rolling away.

Laughter erupts around me, and through my mortification I find myself laughing too.

~

The following morning, Tavien's family's keyed sword arrives by one of his cousins, who thankfully assumed it was for him to wear at one of the coronation events and asked no questions.

I clear off one of the smaller tables and Tavien sets the package down to unwrap it. Nueena, Leon, and I gather around as the sword is revealed. It's a stunning weapon with an onyx hilt.

I reach out my hand to touch it and a blast of invisible heat has me pulling my fingers back. Leon and Nueena are also met with a blistering warning.

"Typically, keyed items are to a sole person, but this was forged by my great-grandfather, who ensured only his line and legacy can use it," he tells Leon. "One day when there are no longer any Delwinns, the sword will choose a new wielder." He picks it up and holds the blade to the sunlight streaming into the apothecary, admiring the workmanship.

Nueena slips off her Zemra stone that dangles on her neck. "My stone holds some of your magic. I wonder if it will let it near." Tavien's brows knit with worry as she slowly presses the stone to the blade. Nothing happens. She pulls the stone back, touching the sharp point. "No trace of heat. So, the sword recognizes your magic within the stone but not when it's on me. Fascinating."

"The crown may be doing something similar, recognizing the Forger's magic enough to let you wear it, but since you are neither the one it is keyed to nor the past wearer's chosen successor, you are stuck in the in-between," Tavien concludes.

"Lovely," I say, the words dripping with despair.

Two sharp knocks strike the door and Lillan joins us, Viella at her heels. Lillian has no interest in the Delwinn's family sword, but Viella gets close. "Keyed sword?" she asks.

"It is," Tavien says.

Viella takes a step back. "It's a beautiful weapon. I would love to beat Lillian with it in a sparring match." Lillian opens her mouth to argue but Vi continues, "We have word from Adreania. Grayden has officially declared that war is coming. He is publicly accusing King Zilas of Kalvorn of his father's death. The king and queen of Kalvorn adamantly deny any involvement, of course."

"How much time do we think it will take for war to start?" I ask, fear reaching into my chest. How much longer are those who live in Adreania safe from Grayden's death sentence on the battlefield? I cannot let countless Adreanians die.

"He has every available man training, resources being compiled. Possibly months, but anything can happen. Adreania has not gone to war for many years. He has much to prepare for. Grayden is not a patient man. He will rush into this, and it will not end well for his people. He wants that crown back and revenge for his father. It will make him rash," Viella says with a frown.

I think back to Leon's words. *You would make a magnificent queen. Any kingdom would be extraordinarily lucky to have you lead them.*

"Grayden would rather rule over rubble than give it up." I take a deep breath. "If I were to try and stop this, if the mortals were to support my claim as queen, as crown wearer, what would I need to do? How can we stop him?"

They all stare at me.

Nueena is the first to speak. "Della, your safety needs to come first."

"I know, and I do not want to be queen of Adreania, but to sit back and watch so many suffer at Grayden's hands, that's not something I can do anymore." It may be the last thing I ever do.

Leon stares at me triumphantly and it sends a thrill within me. "We will come up with a foolproof plan, one that keeps you safe while taking back the throne."

I turn to Nueena. "What about the Airvell River? The one ran through the Merawood Forest into Adreania. Zarella's wedding gift to Inara, for the mortals. When they had the water, their crops flourished, and their animals never got sick. Could we let it flow again? If I have the crown and give them back the river, it may be enough for the mortals to turn on Grayden. He promised them magic. I could actually bring it."

Nueena purses her lips with sympathy. "It's still there, just behind a dam. No matter how betrayed Zarella felt, she still wanted Inara to be in a prosperous and safe kingdom, so she reluctantly opened the river out of love for her best friend. During the war with Adreania, Zarella took the river back, vowing it would never flow freely there again. My mother would have restored the river if she could. Zarella put a powerful enchantment surrounding it. It would require more powerful magic than my mother or I possess."

"Perhaps," Tavien surmises, "if you could control the crown, it has enough magic to break the enchantments, but—" He lets his words fade away.

"But I can't even open a lock on a book without fainting?" I finish for him.

"Right, for now," Tavien says apologetically.

I rub my face, suddenly tired, the pounding in my head starting up again. "If I get the crown off, I have no claim to that throne, so I can do nothing to save the mortals, but if I keep the crown, I cannot escape the hourglass that is held over my life, and I can't help anyone if I'm dead. It's maddening."

"You're not going to die," Leon and Nueena say at the exact same time.

Leon continues, "I know you don't believe me, but I believe in you. We will find a way out of this."

"Yes," Nueena agrees, "we will."

~

The next few days follow a familiar pattern. Tavien and Leon work on the elixir, tirelessly mixing and collaborating. One ingredient is listed incorrectly, and the liquid turns gray, some reaction gone wrong, forcing them to start from scratch. Reyna is brought in, and they are able to find where they went wrong.

The crown continues to be a painful reminder of what is at stake. Each day I feel a little worse, needing naps in the afternoons. The compression of magic builds and builds, and Nueena often takes my hand and relieves the pressure.

Nueena and I wake early on the seventh day. Together we watch the rising sun illuminate the sea of anafaea flowers. The moon fades with morning's light, dewdrops sparkling like stars on the petals.

"Now we can finally remove the key ingredient." Nueena kneels in the soil, inspecting the flowers' centers.

I reach into one flower and pluck the dark blue bulb from its center. It is incredibly light, made up of ten petals enclosed around each other in a soft sphere. At its base, longer petals hang over the sides of the stem. "What do we do with them?"

She stands in front of the healing flowers. "They need to be removed and dried out. We leave for the Gem Court today, but they should be ready to pulverize when we return." She motions with her hands, and the midnight bulb petals rise one by one, swirling in the air as if it were raining in reverse. Each glistening petal follows the motion of her hand skyward, twirling together near the palace walls and turning towards the north tower, where Tavien and Leon await them.

We link arms and head back up to our wing.

"Last crowning ceremony before your actual coronation. I know the Gem Court plans to put your last four to shame."

She throws me a small conspiratorial grin. "I have no doubt about that. Your court throws the best parties. After the past few days, I believe we've all earned a little time for revelry to drown out anxieties of the future." She tightens her arm around me, and I squeeze back.

"What weighs on your soul, Nu?" I look at her, but she stares straight ahead as we climb the tower stairs. Her faraway look worries me. She has so much pressure on her; a fair amount of which she places on herself. The weight of her royal future always had her striving for perfection, a lifelong pursuit of excellence to be ready to rule Ellova.

She sighs deeply. "My mother leaves behind a great legacy. She ruled with honor and earned the respect of every court for centuries. I know it will take some time for me to command the same. Some think the throne has chosen me too early. The courts may not give the grace they so freely gave my mother."

I take a moment to collect my thoughts. Nueena is not one for empty words. "The choice of the throne is not for them to agree or disagree with. You have sat beside her for every Guardian gathering, council session, and court meeting for decades. You even sat outside with your ear pressed to the door when you were too young to attend." I reach over and playfully flick her pointed ear. "Nyvenah has taught you everything she knows, and you have memorized how your grandmother and even her mother handled each situation and complication. Once Nyvenah returns from her well-deserved vacation after your coronation, she will sit on your council, guiding you. The fae of Ellova do not require perfection from you, Nu. They only desire for you to rule with integrity and compassion. Both are traits you overflow with."

She leans over and kisses me on the cheek as we reach the top step. "Thank you, Del."

When we join Leon and Tavien, they have already set out the petals on the table. Tavien's palms light and he sends a blue ring of flames circling above the anafaea. Not burning, but as the room heats, the flowers begin to wilt before he calls back his flames. "They will be ready by the time we return. For now, we have a royal event to pack for."

"What should I expect for my first crowning ceremony?" Leon asks.

Nueena, Tavien, and I all look at each other and grin. In unison we all say, "The best party of your life."

CHAPTER 32

I should have packed days ago for our journey to the Gem Court.

Two large trunks lie open on the floor, half-filled, as I throw in a pair of golden silk shoes that match the folded gown already packed. I open and close three drawers before I find my aquatic attire and toss it in to join the rest. My best necklaces are wrapped up and safely tucked away, but the jewelry boxes I fished them out of are haphazardly pushed back into their places.

"How long will we be in the Gem Court?" Leon's eyes follow me around the room. He sits on my bed, and even when my back is to him, I know he looks nowhere else.

I frown at my open armoire as I rifle through my extensive collection of golden-yellow dresses. "Two nights. The last four crowning celebrations lasted almost a week. Thankfully, since we have delicate matters to attend to here at the palace, it has cut the trip short." Restlessness stirs within me, and I try to shove down the building panic. *It will be fine*, I repeat for what seems like the hundredth time that day, taking a deep breath.

When I walk past Leon, he reaches out his hand, grabbing mine and pulling me to a stop in front of him.

"This is your court. Are you not excited to return?" He stares up at me from the bed, studying my face. He phrases the question delicately, not exactly probing.

I can tell he wants a real answer from me, but I stay silent, pressing my lips together with a shake of my head.

"Please, tell me what troubles you."

I don't wish to bother him with my own fears, but he seems eager to share this burden. "I'm always happy to return to my court, but if it ever comes out that I'm in possession of the greatest magical item ever created…"

"Are you safe there?" Leon asks with a possessive edge to his voice that thrills me.

"Yes, of course, nothing like that. It's Lazalai. I've always considered her a friend, and I think you'd like her as well." I pause, trying to think of the best way to phrase it delicately. "Ruling Ellova is not dictated by birth, but by power. Nueena's family has the strongest bloodline and have been in power for millennia. There's no specific rule that the power needs to be contained within a person without the aid of a magical item. One of my fellow courtiers could make the argument that I, or my court, would be within our rights to challenge for the throne. I would never, of course; I can't even control the magic, but I'd rather avoid it coming up at all."

"Do you have to go? We can stay here and work on the elixir together." His thumb brushes my hand in a comforting touch.

I snort at that. "No, no, Nueena and I have been inseparable since we were dewlings, rarely one without the other. For me to miss her crowning celebration in my own court, with a crown *I* made, would raise far more questions than anything else. I wouldn't be surprised if Lazalai showed up here as soon as she realized I wasn't there, pounding on the door, demanding to know why I missed it. It's the celebration of the century, and if there's one thing my court knows how to do, it's celebrate."

Community is a pillar of Ellovian culture, not an easy place to hide. No one can disappear here; no one goes unnoticed. It's the way we ensure no one is forgotten, that everyone's needs are met.

That care was part of the reason the courts were set up in the first place, to form deeper bonds. I could travel to every corner of Ellova with nothing and find shelter, food, and friendship with anyone whose flag waves yellow. When I found myself heartbroken and alone after the death of my parents, the love shown to me by the Gem Court and by Lazalai, Nueena, and her family held me together. I love that about the fae. I always have, but now I wish I could fade away from memory 'til this crown is removed.

Leon gently squeezes my hand, bringing me back to him. "How can I help? Please, give me a task, Strawberries."

I smile at the nickname.

Before I can think better of it, I push back a loose gray strand that has escaped his tie. My hand rests on his cheek, the stubble prickly beneath my palm. He leans into the touch, closing his eyes. His desire to help and his ever-eager kindness are like fire lapping at my soul, searing away my ability to stay away from him.

"If I say 'strawberry,' it means we need to leave, maybe not the court as a whole, but wherever we are. It means I wish to avoid someone or something."

He kisses the inside of my palm. "They will never even know we were there."

I laugh at that, and we both turn at the sound of voices in the main living space.

Spinning back to my closet, I pull out two yellow gowns and hold them up to each other to compare.

"I like the one with the yellow gems." He gives me a sly smile. "Really brings out your…hair."

I let out an embarrassing giggle more fitting of a dewling. "Is that so?" I hang the other dress back up and bring the citrine gown with me into the bathing chamber and slip it on. The gown is made from a dark yellow shimmering material that is sheer in some places with a dangerously low scooped neckline under a wide piece of fabric that goes around my neck. Strings of citrines hang down and cover the daring thigh slit, the gemstones touching the floor. The strands of gemstones are cool on my thighs and swing as I walk. Half my hair is up in braids and golden pins that hide the crown, and the rest hangs loosely. I don large citrine earrings to complement the dress and add heeled shoes with long strings that wrap up my calves.

When I step out, Leon's eyes go wide at the exposed skin, his hands clenched into fists with the sheets at his side. He is quiet for a long moment before he gives his head a little shake.

"You look beautiful," he says, his voice strained. He clears his throat.

I give a little spin in the large mirror in one corner of my room, and the gemstones twirl around me. The structured bodice underneath holds up my breasts and the pleated fabric over it reaches nearly to my waist. Leon's eyes meet mine in the mirror and I smile at him.

"Izadella, I—" he starts but a knock on my door interrupts him.

Hiliyah stands there, holding my gown for the ceremony in a travel garment bag. There are indents in the bag, sharp points that outline the front. She looks at me, delighted. "One of my favorite designs for you!"

"Hi, Hil." We kiss each other on the cheek, and she hangs my dress off the door of the open armoire. She takes out a few men's dress shirts for Leon from another garment bag, all in various shades of gold, and hands them to him.

"Thank you," he says. "Now we find out if yellow is my color." He winks at me, the gesture so playful I'm momentarily stunned.

Hiliyah laughs. "Everyone must wear the crowning court colors during the ceremony." She turns back to me. "Everything you need is in there. One of the Gem Court gown makers can assist you with the corset, although—" She looks at Leon. "When I designed it, I didn't consider a dancing partner, as you never mentioned having one. You so rarely dance at these events, and I went for the dramatic over function. I'm sure Leon will be willing to try."

"The gown will be perfect! Everything you make is," I tell her, and she helps me carefully place the garment bag in my trunk. The three of us leave the room as four palace attendants come to collect everything we need to take with us to Quartzridge, the capital of the Gem Court.

We meet with Nueena and Tavien, and together we travel down the palace steps to the main entrance, where Nueena's family stands, waiting for her. Her younger sisters greet us first with excited waves. The youngest, Kaylena, runs up to me, her long braids flying behind her with sparkling gems and colorful beads. She leaps up and I catch her, spinning us both around.

"Delly! Where have you been? Can you make me a new necklace? I want a necklace to match my dress for today," Kaylena asks, playing with my jewelry as she eagerly tells me what her necklace should look like in great detail.

The familiar sensation of dread descends upon me, knowing I'll disappoint her with my answer. "I'm sorry, honey. Maybe next time." I feel a stab of guilt at her pout and for lying to her, but she's much too young for me to explain.

I set her carefully on the ground and she finally notices Leon, who stands behind me. "Who are you?" she asks him.

He kneels to her level. "Hello, I'm Leon. Izadella's friend."

Vaylin, the middle sister of Nueena and Kaylena, joins us. While Kaylena would be about five in mortal years, Vaylin is thirteen years younger than Nueena and just celebrated her one hundred twenty-first birthday. She leans against me and whispers, "Is that the male you and my sister always talk about?"

I bend down to her ear and whisper, "Yes, he is, but you can't tell anyone."

Vaylin makes an excited noise and looks at Leon. "Is he coming with us to the Gem Court?" Both sisters look at him appraisingly and he nods.

Before they can ask any more questions, Nyvenah calls them back. "It's time to leave, my dewlings."

Kaylena runs back to her mother and takes her hand.

Lillian and Viella talk in hushed tones, and when Lillan whispers something in her ear, Viella blushes, lightly slapping Lillian, who wears a rare half grin as we approach. We make our way to the portal trees, taking a different tree than before to Quartzridge. Our group is large, honeyguards and High Court attendants joining, so we walk through the portals in small groups.

We step into the tree, and as the lights go out, Leon takes my hand, and I give it a quick squeeze. The portal spins and spins and finally stops shaking. The hollow door fills with golden light.

"Welcome to my court, Leon."

CHAPTER 33

The Quartzridge crystal palace sparkles in the late-afternoon sun, the entire structure made of gold and crystal, with yellow flags atop golden spires. Vibrant music and thunderous cheers greet us as we step into the atrium. Nueena waves at everyone there to welcome her to my court.

Lazalai stands in front of the crowd between two Gem Court honeyguards, who hold large yellow flags embroidered with our crest. She claps her hands in delight and reaches for Nueena, pulling her in for a tight embrace.

"Welcome! Welcome!" Lazalai's voice is like honey. When she's done speaking with the royal family, she turns to me and Leon. She is older than I am, with laugh lines at the corners of her eyes, but she has a youthful beauty to her. Covering her pale, ample chest is nothing but draped necklaces over a slip of bronze fabric; her dark hair is pinned up with an elaborate headpiece with stars hovering above her. Her sheer skirt has a six-foot-long train trailing behind her, and a thick belt hangs low on her spacious hips, draping more gilded chains over her center.

"My dear, how I've missed you!" She embraces me tightly. Some of the heaviness I've carried releases as she holds me, the sensation of coming home replacing it. I hold her tighter as she whispers in my ear, "You've been gone too long, my golden girl."

Although Lazalai has been Guardian of the Gem Court for centuries, she has felt like a trusted aunt during my time here since I was young, and she still does. I was always welcomed at Quartzridge, even before I chose it as my court. My talent is continuously celebrated, my company enjoyed, and here I have a creative community centered in unity to offer support.

"Lazalai, this is my friend Leon," I say and try for a bright smile.

"Welcome, Leon." She does not ask more questions, for which I am thankful.

Leon is polite as always. "Thank you. Izadella has told me many wonderful things about your court."

"Your room has been cleaned and ready for you," Lazalai says to me before turning back to Nueena and her family. "Our finest accommodations overlooking the lake have been prepared for you. Leon, I'll have one of my attendants find a room for you. All the rooms in the palace are full, but we have some lovely guest quarters in the lake houses."

Leon frowns, his eyes sliding to mine.

"Oh, that won't be necessary. He can stay with me."

She raises one of her eyebrows and looks between the two of us, a devious grin on her full red lips. "Oh, well, this is exciting. Two historical events in one week, I see." She links arms with me as we walk further and leans in conspiratorially. "You'll have to tell me all the details. He's quite delicious. If you feel like sharing, I'm sure he would be a hit in the underground lounges."

I'm about to respond to her jest, but Leon beats me to it.

"There will be no sharing." He tries to sound lighthearted, but he cannot hide the hardness in his eyes at the very idea of it.

This only causes Lazalai to laugh harder. "I'll let you all get settled before dinner. Goodbye, Leon." She winks at him before wrapping her arms around two handsome guards' waists. One kisses her exposed shoulder before they head off, her hands squeezing each of their ass cheeks.

I turn back to face Nueena and Tavien. Nueena is laughing so hard Tavien has to hold her up. Even Lillian is smiling at us.

Leon's frown deepens.

"Come on." I grab Leon's hand, pulling him past the musicians composing songs about Nueena's greatness.

The main part of the palace is alive with art and creativity as we walk through the atrium. I wave at the fae I know, but I am thankful they don't try to stop me. While this is my court, I've spent far more of my life at the High Court palace, and I have few close relationships with those who live here. We walk past artisans of all kinds working on blown glass, needlework, painting, and poetry. One firefae holds glass in their hand until it glows bright orange and shifts into a vase. Another uses frost magic to turn a tray of water into an ice sculpture of Nueena. There's a mix of music from musicians all over, tuning their instruments or writing songs.

"Each of the hallways leads to a different subsection of the palace." I point out the window to the large lake. Temples and luxurious homes surround it, each decorated or designed to show what they create there. One home with tall pillars is covered in murals of every color. Another is made entirely of gleaming metal. At the far end of the lake are rows of vivid tents. "Most artisans trade their work at the lake pavilion if they don't travel to other courts. Ellovians come from all over for their creative works."

The air is tinged with the sweet smell of herbs and flowers from one of the perfumeries we pass.

My room in this palace has a large, gilded four-poster bed with matching furniture, exactly the same as when I was originally assigned it as a dewling. I show Leon inside. Yellow dresses hang in the closet with a collection of jewelry I made when I was young and Lazalai taught me how to control my powers. The large windows overlook the crystal-clear lake, the sound of laughter and singing drifting in. Besides a few portraits I had commissioned, there's not much of my personal belongings here. Our items have already been put away, and Leon looks out the window before quickly looking away. I think I know what he is trying to avoid. I peer down out the window and my laughter is soft.

Many of the swimmers and sunbathers are splashing freely in nothing but the skin they were born in.

"Afraid of a little skin, healer?" I taunt.

"Never. I just don't wish for you to think I'm staring."

"If you do have an issue with nudity, you may not enjoy this court. Plenty of places here are clothing optional, especially when swimming. It won't be the last naked fae you will see, especially after the sun goes down."

There's a knock on the door and a palace hand walks in with a platter of fresh fruit juices and wine. The fae woman is lovely, her lips painted gold and matching the long blonde locks that cover her chest. She wears the same type of sheer dress that is favored here.

Leon suddenly becomes interested in the paintings on the wall.

"Hello, crown maker. If you need anything, I'll be taking care of this floor. Just shout for Iris." She places the tray down with a conspiratorial smile at me. "May I see the crown? Just a peek?"

Leon freezes as I walk over to the chest and remove a few items, pulling out the rich redwood box and lifting the lid.

She leans down and makes a noise of delight. "It's beautiful!"

"Thank you. There are a few enchantments on it, so try to get a good view during the ceremony."

She nods enthusiastically. We have never met each other before, but nothing bonds those in the same court faster than wanting to upstage the other courts during Ellovian events. "It's stunning! I cannot wait to see her in it."

"Me too."

"Thank you for showing me. Enjoy your evening."

Before she can close the door behind her, I add, "Please tell Lazalai that I'm not feeling well and may not make it to dinner tonight."

She is instantly concerned. "Would you like me to send for a healer? I saw a few of them swimming in the lake."

"No, no, that will not be necessary. My companion is a healer. If you could just bring up some dinner when you have time, that would be lovely. Thank you, Iris."

Her eyes shift between me and Leon. She nods in understanding and gives me the same smug grin Lazalai did. "Of course, not feeling well. I understand. I'll send up dinner." She leaves with a flick of her hip.

"Why are we avoiding dinner?" Leon asks. "Or are you truly ill?"

"Two reasons. First, I want to avoid Lazalai as much as possible for now, so she doesn't ask questions, notice you're mortal, or figure out that my magic is glamoured."

"How would she be able to tell if you have a glamour?"

"Each fae releases a unique pattern of magic. If you're close with someone, they learn to recognize it, and I have known Lazalai most of my life. Plus, she's a powerful fae."

"And what's the second reason?"

"This is a communal space where we prioritize collaboration. I can't access my magic while I wear the crown, and the people here would expect me to use my jewelsmith magic. Everyone lends their powers to everyone else's creative endeavors. It's encouraged, expected even. I don't wish to disappoint anyone."

"I can understand that."

I fidget nervously. "Sorry, there's not an extra room for you so you can have your own space. It tends to be crowded here; it's not unusual to share rooms. We keep talking about extending the palace, but it would mean putting a pause to the nightly parties and we simply haven't gotten around to it."

"We've shared beds multiple times since leaving Adreania." Leon steps closer to me. "I do not require my own space, nor do I wish for it. I would much rather be as close to you as possible, especially since we're in an unfamiliar place. While we may be in your court, surrounded by your people, your safety is still a concern of mine."

I open my mouth to tell him it's unnecessary, that I'm safe within these gleaming walls, but I know he'll argue with me, so I simply say, "Thank you."

He looks surprised at that and nods once.

We are not alone long before Nueena and Tavien arrive, closing the door behind them.

Nueena waves her hand and magic flows out of her. "Sound enchantments to keep our voices to ourselves." She sits on my bed, kicking off her shoes. "I think it's best if you both head to the spring early in the morning. The start of the celebration is tonight and hopefully most of this court will sleep late tomorrow. Della will be expected to be at dinner, and as royal crown maker, she has to be there for the ceremony tomorrow. There may not be much time to slip away after that."

"Do we need to hide what we're doing here?" Leon asks.

Tavien shakes his head. "No. As a member of this court, Della has free rein to go wherever she pleases, with anyone she chooses. Now, if anyone asks why you were collecting water blutells from the Airvell Spring, you can simply say it's for an art installation or for medicinal uses on my behalf."

"How much do we need to collect?" I ask him.

Tavien hands me a leather sack the size of a large watermelon. "Fill this up with the leaves and get as much of the root as possible. Everything you will need is here. I suggest going to bed early if possible. It's a long ride to the spring."

~

*L*eon and I spend the evening dining on my balcony and eating tender cuts of meat on skewers, still sizzling in their juices, alongside steamed vegetables and brown bread with designs baked with white flour on top. We end the meal with tea and share a small poppyseed cake with lemon frosting.

Once the meal is done, we sit side by side in plush chairs in the small adjoining sitting room and read. The only sound is a crackling fire and the soft whoosh as pages turn. Leon reads from the large tome in his lap, taking notes and filling pages of his journal for reference.

I feel his eyes flit to me every so often before they return to the book, and I find myself staring at him when he is too engrossed in his work to notice.

When the fire has gone out, I take that as a sign for us to attempt to go to sleep, and nervousness spreads.

I toss back the rest of my wine to steady the nervousness trapped within me.

Leon has a point. We slept in the same bed back at the cottage the first night, and he slept in my bed back at the palace.

I'm filled once again with the gnawing sensation of excitement and dread that is now so familiar when it comes to him. How many nights had I fantasized that he was beside me before sleep took me? It delights me to know that falling asleep next to him allows me to hear his breaths and feel the warmth of his body. His tousled hair and sleep-filled eyes only make me like him more.

After we've gotten ready for the evening, we slide into bed at the same time. He doesn't offer to sleep on the floor, and I don't suggest it.

"What exactly did Lazalai mean when she said sharing in the lounge?"

It was funny this morning, but it only makes me blush now. "Well, those who live here tend to be more generous with their bodies than the other courts. Many choose to keep company for the night and indulge rather than focusing on longer-term commitments. The underground lounges offer more unique pleasures for the evening, usually with multiple bed partners. Sex is considered an expression of creativity, and we are known for our art as much as our pleasure seekers." I laugh. "I told you this court is known for our parties, and there are many, *many* different types of parties."

He chuckles. "That's the conclusion I came to, but I just wanted to be sure and to let everyone know I'm uninterested in being shared. You have all my attention." In the caressing low light of the moon, his eyebrows pull together. "Of course, I wouldn't attempt to stop you if that is something you're interested in participating in. I can only speak for myself. I—"

I find his hand under the covers and trace each finger with my own. "That's not something I'm interested in either."

His exhale sounds relieved.

"Good night, Leon."

He locks his finger in mine. "Good night, Izadella."

I dream of crimson couches in dark lounges, the space empty except for us. Of thrusting hips and tangled limbs, rough hands and soft lips.

CHAPTER 34

"*B*arley is the only horse we have available," the tired stable attendant informs us with a yawn. "More stables on the other side of the lake are available for trade, but they might not be open for a few hours. Most of the palace horses were taken to a nearby pasture to graze during the festivities."

Leon and I share a glance. We don't have time to secure a second horse.

"One horse will be fine. We can ride double," Leon says.

We wait on the platform for the stable attendant, who returns a few minutes later with a large horse. Her pale golden coat gleams in the sun.

I take the reins with a smile. "Thank you."

Leon wastes no time, launching himself on the back of the horse. His smile is radiant as he holds his hand out, helping me nestle myself in front of him. The tall slits of my dress reveal my bare thighs. There's no saddle, just a thick blanket.

"Riding is one of my great passions, but I so rarely have an opportunity to indulge," he says, excitement in every word.

I hand him the reins and try not to lean against him. I don't want to invade his space, but his legs give a swift squeeze around

Barley, and she takes off, sending me flying back against him. His arms tighten around me.

"Lead the way," he shouts over the wind into my ear, and it sends shivers down to my core. He is leaning forward, tucking his head above my shoulder.

I point in the direction of the forest that houses the spring, a well-worn riding path in front of us. After a couple of miles of swift riding, Leon slows our horse to carefully navigate the forest, and we emerge into a meadow of bright wildflowers at a leisurely pace.

"How are you feeling this morning?" he says, leaning into my ear.

"Better than I have felt in days." I almost feel like myself. There was no pounding in my head when I awoke this morning, the crushing pressure of the magic weight lessened. I should have returned to my court sooner.

"I'm glad to hear that. This place is something special."

"It truly is."

"It's breathtaking here," Leon says wistfully, "so unlike Adreania. Everything here has a warmth to it. The fae here, the food, the architecture. It's all around. I never realized just how cold the castle was, how lifeless it was, 'til I came here. The Iron Castle has a heaviness that claws at you, cutting deep and crawling into your bones from its never ending winters." His arms get a little tighter around my waist. "You were the only thing that would brighten my day. A sliver of sunshine at midnight breaking through a life full of black clouds, even if it was just for a moment."

Sorrow slices into my heart, severing it in two at his words. I squeeze my eyes shut and place my hand over his. I need to keep this perfect man at a distance, but he makes it so difficult. "Leon, I—"

Before I can respond, he asks, "Did you spend much time here when you were growing up?"

I sigh. "Yes." My words are breathy. "Our powers develop slowly over the course of the fifty years we are considered dewlings. There are plenty of jewelry makers in Ellova, but the gifts of a jewelsmith are rare. It wasn't exactly something I could teach myself how to control. I would touch a necklace, and it would turn into a puddle, dripping silver on the floor. Hold a knife at dinner and it would turn into a snake sliding around the table. The palace lost quite a few dishes and statues to my touch, as I was unable to shift them back to their original forms. Once, Nueena and I were playing dress-up in Nyvenah's closet and I accidentally turned her favorite crown into a golden dove. Flew right out the window, never to be seen again."

Leon's sudden burst of laughter echoes around the small valley we are riding through. "Was she angry?"

"No, of course not. She's too kind for that. I went on to make her countless jewelry pieces, including many crowns, to try and make up for it. Eventually it was agreed that Nueena and I would spend a summer here when we were old enough. I trained under Lazalai, who has a similar power. Even though she was a busy Guardian, she always made time for lessons." That familiar touch of guilt lingers at the memory and what I'm keeping from her now. "By the end of the summer, I could control my magic. I also learned to do embroidery, paint with oils, create glass mosaics, and make wine."

He smiles. "Sounds like you had an enchanting childhood."

"What was your childhood like?"

"Expectations were high, but my childhood was a happy one. I was especially close with my younger brother and our parents, who gave us a great life. I spent most of my time reading. When I was thirteen, my mother moved my brother, my cousin, and me from our estate to the house I had wished to send you to. We lived there for a number of years."

"Where was your father?"

"He stayed to run the family business in the city. My mother thought country life would be best for us, plenty of room for us to run around. It was chaos in the way only three boys can make it. My brother and cousin were the wild ones. I preferred reading or spending time with the town healer, just observing. The other two got into trouble as if their lives depended on it. At seventeen, I left for the capital of Versairen for my medical training. My family were clear that a successful healer position for me would bring them great pride. I haven't seen them since."

"That's a long time to be away."

"It is, but they knew how important it was for me to be a healer."

"So, you have always wanted to help others?"

He lets out a little laugh. "I was born for it."

"You must miss them."

"It's been a long time. My parents have passed, but I hope to see my brother and cousin soon. Maybe you can meet them too."

"I'd like that." I feel so safe with his hand tight on my hip, securing me, with him sitting so close as we ride. His warmth and the scent of wildflowers in the air make me feel like I could tell him anything and he would understand no matter what it was.

Up ahead, through the trees, I can see the Airvell River that rushes by and the small stream leading into the rocky area where the waterfall cascades down into the natural pool, thick ivy climbing up behind it.

"I loved swimming here with Nueena. Those who live in the crystal palace prefer to swim in the lake, so the spring is often empty. We would swim for hours."

"My brother and I loved swimming when we were growing up, too."

Finally, we arrive at the small pool of turquoise water. A few white water lilies with round leaves decorate the surface. We can see the bluish-green plants we need at the bottom. Leon slides off the back of the horse. He comes to help me down, and Barley nibbles on the surrounding shrubs. Bright greenery shades the spring; this hidden place is filled with the healing waters of the Airvell River. Lizards with bright blue heads and orange bodies lounge on rocks, soaking up the sun, while bright teal dragonflies dance over the water.

Leon lifts his shirt and slides it over his head, and I am momentarily lost in his body. His bare chest with its taut muscles, the deep vee on his hips demanding my eyes lower. When I finally look up at him, his half grin sends butterflies erupting in my chest.

"Hello." His voice is as smooth as chocolate.

In an embarrassingly strangled voice I say, "We should get started." At my feet, a vine is coming up through the ground to reveal my lustful thoughts. I stomp my boot on it before Leon can see it.

He starts to chuckle, but it dies on his lips when I take off my dress, his eyes going to the tight, yellow band around my chest, tied with a bow in the front. The same fabric is sewn into bottoms that wrap low around on my hips.

Now it's his turn to stare, his eyes darkening as he drinks in my body, my soft middle, and the dark places the fabric covers.

His fingers twitch at his sides.

"Ready?" I ask loudly and cackle when he is startled by the question, looking a little dazed.

I open the small box Tavien had given me and pull out one lochkiss bubble, offering the other to Leon, who takes it curiously.

"Lochkiss. It lasts for weeks, so there will be plenty of time to collect what we need and return for more if needed. It's going to give us the ability to breathe underwater. The spring is deceptively deep; you just can't tell with how clear the water is. We'd run out of air long before we reached the blutells, so we will need these. With these, we will also be able to speak and hear each other under the water." I pop it in my mouth and chew. It has a gummy texture, but no taste.

"Anything else to know?" he asks, chewing cautiously.

"When you go under the water, just breathe normally. The lochkiss will turn water into air for you. You can also control buoyancy. Imagine yourself heavier or lighter to stay at the bottom or rise to the surface."

We tread into the water, and with the heat of the bright midmorning sun above us, the cool water is a pleasant touch.

"Anything behind the waterfall?" he asks, focusing on the flowing water.

I pause for a moment. "An underwater cave." When his eyes light up with excitement, I reluctantly add, "I can show you before we collect the blutells if you would like to see it."

"Only if we have time."

"Come on and stay close." I dive in, indulging in the freeing sensation of being weightless, the rest of the world fading away. It's just Leon, the healing water, and me.

Leon cuts through the water at an impressive speed, swimming in a large circle around me before chasing a small school of fish. My laughter sends bubbles rising to the surface. He looks back at the sound and returns to me, offering me his hand so we can swim together.

He follows me, diving deeper. The cave opening is just to the right of us.

The entrance is wide enough for two, the tunnel only taking a few seconds to swim through, leading into a small, hidden grotto. Slats of light break through the arched rocky ceiling with moss crawling up the walls, vines hanging down. A small but beautiful waterfall comes down from the Airvell River. The grotto is damp with a hint of minerals clinging to the air, so much hidden from the sun.

This place does not hold happy memories like the spring does. I'm transported back to when I was an angry dewling seeking solace here. Unable to control my powers, mourning the loss of my parents, lost and afraid. I came here to hide, to be angry alone so no one would think I was ungrateful, my pathetic attempts not to be a burden to Nueena or her family. Guilt grabs at me. How is it possible that over a hundred years have gone by and I'm in the same place I was before?

The only difference is, instead of mourning my parents, I'm mourning my own life, threatened to be cut so much shorter than I was promised with fae heritage. Mourning the inevitable loss of Leon. Mourning the loss of what could have been if things had been different.

I should have sent him in here alone.

I use my strength to sit on the rocky ledge, my legs still dangling in the water, and stare into the depths below us.

Leon swims up to me and pulls himself out of the water with far more grace than I did. He sits close, our thighs fully touching. "Are you all right?"

Ellova's grave, this man is always so attuned to my moods. Tears spring to my eyes.

He picks up my balled fist. He doesn't speak, just brings it to his lips. He kisses my first knuckle and uncurls that finger, repeating the process 'til every finger has been kissed. Turning my palm up, he closes his eyes and presses his lips into the center, then my wrist and the top of my hand. Each tender kiss absorbs a piece of my anger until I sag against him.

"I'm sorry. I shouldn't have brought you into the grotto. This place holds memories I would rather forget. We should start collecting what we need."

Before I can slide back into the water, he stops me. "What memories?"

I sigh, not wishing to expose even more of my heart to him, but wanting him to understand my fear too. "I lost my parents suddenly. One after the other. I felt utterly betrayed by my mother's death in particular. It wasn't until later I learned that the fae can die of broken hearts; the fae call it an enervation death. I never knew love could end so tragically. Then, on top of it, I didn't truly understand how my magic worked. I was a grieving dewling dealing with emotions that were affecting my magic."

"That is too much for someone so young to handle. You were a child. I'm sure your mother didn't want to leave you alone to figure this all out by yourself," he says, tucking me into his side, arm tight around me.

It's easier to say the next part with my head on his shoulders, not looking into those deep green eyes. "I know now it wasn't her fault, but I blamed her for loving someone she knew she was going to outlive. Having a child with him. Knowing I would lose my father when she would lose her husband. Knowing there was a possibility she would die from a broken heart, leaving me alone. Maybe she didn't know that at the time; maybe she didn't care. Maybe she didn't think about it, but it felt like a betrayal at the time. Still does, actually, but knowing you now, I think I'm beginning to understand."

I try to fight off the memory of her last few days. The bright white scars that spread all over her skin, like she had been struck by lightning. An enervation death is excruciating. Her grief-stricken sobs still haunt me late at night. Knowing her magic was decaying from the inside, slowly killing her, and yet her cries were not for herself. They were for my father and me. At his loss and what I was about to lose. Her.

I was left with nothing in this world but a tainted family name and an empty cottage.

The rushing waterfall echoes off the slick walls and fills our silence. Then Leon lifts my chin up, forcing me to look at him. His eyes are so soft, such understanding there.

"I can't tell you how or when, but we will figure out this mess. Together. We will get that crown off and we will find a place to be happy. You are a treasure. Nothing will keep me from you, Izadella. Do you understand me? Our story does not end with us dead or apart. It was never going to."

The warmth of his words pulses through my veins. I believe him. I don't know why, but I do. "I trust you."

He pulls me closer, and my heart stops, expecting him to kiss me, but he turns his head up and presses his lips to my forehead. It's such a tender show of affection my heart melts to a puddle of emotion as I lay my head on his chest.

We stay there for a long while, wrapped up in each other, his arms so tight around me as if he were holding the pieces of my broken heart together to keep it from shattering.

I'm already missing his warmth when I reluctantly pull away. "We have an elixir to create and a crowning ceremony to prepare for. We should probably leave."

"We also have a ball to attend, which I've been assured features quite a bit of dancing, and we both know I will never turn down a chance to hold you close all night." He slides back into the water and waits for me.

There will never be enough. I want all my days to be surrounded by our friends and nights to be alone with him. How could I live without this man? That's exactly what I'm afraid of... that I can't.

I follow him into the water. I might follow him anywhere.

We both kick off, swimming to the center of the spring. The blutells sway gently and I dig my hands into the soft sand, picking up the whole plant and placing it in the bag Leon holds open. We work together, carefully pulling up the aquatic plants in the corners of the pool. After the bag is full, we swim towards the beckoning sunlight. The bag is enchanted to preserve them until we return home.

We break the surface together with a splash, Leon shaking his head and spraying me with the droplets.

"Hey!" I laugh and splash some water back at him. His eyes light up and he chases me towards the shore as we send water splattering at each other. He chases me through the water; when he gets too close, I dash away from him.

He finally catches me and grabs my arm. I let out a playful scream, trying to get out of his grip so our game will continue, when suddenly my vision spins, the water moving around me in response to the power of the crown. The crown's magic overwhelms me, and I stumble. I watch in horror as a wave forms and launches itself at Leon, who is swept under the water. It pulls him to the center of the spring. I try to command the magic back, clawing at the power pouring out of me, but it rushes out, ignoring my pleas.

Leon thrashes in the water's vicious hold. Devastation rips through me at the realization that this might kill him, that he came to Ellova to protect me and I would have utterly failed to protect him from myself. Water swirls around his throat, tightening its grip.

"LEON!" I scream, racing after him.

CHAPTER 35

$\mathcal{I}$ beg the crown over and over again, but the magic ignores my anguished cries. The magic is so far out of my pathetic control, attacking the man who has my whole heart in his gentle hands. The relentless water keeps Leon in tortured suspension in the air, entombed in the spinning waves.

Please, stop! Please, please, please, let him go!

STOP, STOP, STOP!

PLEASE!

I take gasping breaths to calm myself, and the magic listens; the water finally drops him.

"I'm all right," he rasps as I reach him.

There are black spots in my vision from the dizzying pain the crown is causing, but I throw my arms around him, the lochkiss keeping us afloat. "I'm so, so sorry. It was the crown. I don't know what happened. All of a sudden, the magic just started to attack. I couldn't stop it."

My head is on his rapidly heaving chest. His pounding heartbeat stabs at me with each ragged breath he takes, knowing this was my fault.

Weak arms wrap around me, and wet lips brush my forehead. "It wasn't your fault—"

I cut him off. "Of course it was! I—"

"Shhhhh, stop, stop. You don't have control right now. The magic was just protecting you. I can't say I enjoyed being on the receiving end of the crown's wrath, but I am glad it's keeping you safe." His grip tightens, not painfully, just enough to emphasize his point.

I pull back my arms on each side of his waist, fingers digging into him. "Leon, stop being so understanding! I almost *killed* you."

"It's a good thing we took the lochkiss *before*." He pushes some of my sodden hair behind my ears. I hope he doesn't notice the evidence of my tears with the dripping spring water, but he does. Of course he does.

He cups my face, his thumbs wiping my cheeks. "Oh, Strawberries." He looks at me with such kindness and warmth, understanding staring back at me. "It's all going to be all right. I promise." His words are gentle, kind.

He's always so fucking kind.

Anger blinds my tear-filled eyes. "Do not patronize me. I do not want your pretty lies, Leon," I cry. "You keep saying that! Just accept it's not true. Accept, like I have, that everything will not be all right. Every possible situation has us dead or alone!"

His expression does not shift. He's weathering my misplaced fury flawlessly.

The terror and joy, lust and longing, that has been building in me takes over and I move without thought, without doubt, blinded by need, towards him. He eagerly meets me halfway.

Our lips brush and I almost collapse from the explosion of relief and lust within me.

The feeling of his body tight against me, his lips on mine, exploring, tasting. Gentle and sweet. Slow. Like we have all the time in the world, and my magic didn't just try to assassinate him.

Like the overflowing passion and pining between us isn't trapped by an hourglass, the cascading sand of our time together quickly escaping.

Thanks to the lochkiss, Leon lies flat on the surface of the spring, pulling me closer, draping my body over his as I deepen the kiss. I open my mouth in a greedy invitation and his tongue rushes in to meet mine. His kiss is no longer careful and unhurried, but demanding, feverish, claiming my mouth with his over and over again.

I straddle him and we slowly sink to the bottom of the spring.

Fish swim out of our way as we descend, and his back meets the soft sand of the pool's bottom. My hair floats up, fluttering in the current. His kiss becomes slow and reverent until he breaks free from me, pulling back. We stare at each other before he moves in again and kisses me, hard.

Delicate touches transform into urgent pleas, gentleness vanishing from his kiss.

He kisses like the only thing he wants is to consume me, forging our bodies and souls together. My hands cup his rough jaw while he pulls me closer.

I love kissing him. It's everything I'd hoped it would be, sweeter because it's real and not just fantasies from a cold, lonely bed. His touch is demanding, as if he never wants space between us again. Fiery joy pours into me, burning away the hurt that has lain here for a hundred years.

I want more, *need* more. Kissing is not enough.

I want him thrusting roughly inside me.

I want those soft lips on my skin.

I want to tear off his clothes and taste him.

Leon tangles his hand in my hair at the base of my neck, his arousal evident between my thighs as I grind against him. His fingers tighten and he gently but firmly pulls me back, making me moan. He breaks our kiss with a loud gasp, his eyes widening at my pleased expression.

"Such a little tease," he says, little bubbles escaping with his words, and pulls me down to continue, his hands leaving my hair to trail down my body, his mouth moving to my neck. I let out a blissful groan, melting against him.

He releases my throat with a pop. The spot he has abandoned

pulsates; he has left a claiming mark on me. I hide my smile in the curve of his neck, delighted at how possessive he is.

The spring's sunbeams dance over his skin. I want him so badly my center throbs, but continuing will only make everything worse. I was supposed to be keeping my distance. I needed to care *less* about him, not more, but he's too intoxicating.

"Don't stop," I whisper into the water. "Please, don't stop."

His mouth captures mine again and he rolls us, my back pressed to the soft, glittering sand as he settles over me. The aquatic plants around us tickle my skin. One of his hands slides up under the cloth at my chest, cupping my breast, and he moans into my mouth at the contact. His fingers grasp at my nipple.

"I need this off." He groans his request as he pulls at the bow holding it together. The yellow fabric falls away, releasing my breasts, and floats lazily towards the surface. The spring's gentle current glides over my newly exposed skin. Leon wastes no time leaning down and taking one tip into his mouth, kneading the other breast with his hands, teasing me. I'm gasping; he is achingly eager. Every touch and taste is exquisite.

I claw at the fabric around his hips, reach into it, and caress his thick cock, pumping. He groans, releasing my nipple and resting his forehead between my breasts.

"Izadella, I—" His words are cut off in a strangle as I increase the speed of my stroke. I tease the head of his cock with a brush over his tip, and then slide my hand around him, noting how his body reacts to my touch. I need to make him feel good.

Leon's lips recapture mine and he hooks my bottoms to the side, sliding two fingers into my burning core. "Fuck, Izadella, so tight for me." I spread my thighs wider as his thumb grazes my clit, ecstasy taking over. We moan into each other's mouths.

His touch is greedy, the perfection of it driving me closer and closer to release, plunging into me in a knee-shaking rhythm.

Leon's slick fingers leave my core and swirl on my clit, his other hand still tugging in my hair as our tongues tangle together.

I grind myself on his touch, desperate for my own release and for his too. The sensation of his cock in my hands, his hips thrusting against my palm, drives me wild until I'm feverish with desire for him. I squeeze gently as he moves against me, his hand inside me matching the rhythm of my pumps. He breaks the kiss for a moment, his mouth returning to my breasts, sucking and teasing each one. He groans his own pleasure into my skin when it becomes too much for him.

His fingers plunge back into me and thrust over and over again as his thumb glides on my clit. His touch is intoxicating and I'm melting in my simmering pleasure, almost ready to burst with his searing fingers.

Leon's frantic touch overpowers me, the pleasure peaking, and I scream. My thighs splay open further as he keeps up a breathtaking tempo with his trembling fingers. He groans before his lips find mine again, and we kiss through our joined pulsing euphoria. He pulls away briefly to bury his face into my throat, lavishing the sensitive spot there with attention as his fingers glide back into me, and he lazily pumps into me again, prolonging my waves of bliss, that teasing thumb of his circling my overstimulated center.

I am weightless, truly weightless, and the lochkiss floats us up to the sparkling surface. We are still holding each other as we gasp in the fresh air, lying at the top of the spring as if we weigh nothing, sunshine warming our skin.

His fingers slide out again and he brings his glistening fingers to his lips, licking and sucking my release off. When he is done, he turns to me for a deep kiss.

We float there, spent and sated.

"We should head back," I whisper into his chest.

He swallows hard. "Gonna need a minute." His breaths are rapid, his voice cracking just a little.

"Sorry," I whisper, and I mean it. I should have had more self-control, kept my hands and mouth to myself. The water drips off him and I follow the rivulets down his body, wishing I could follow its path with my tongue.

He whispers back, "Don't be. You are a treasure, Izadella. My treasure."

We lie there together, bobbing atop the pool's surface, his hands tracing lazy circles on my back and thighs, for a long time before he kisses my cheek and we swim back to shore. He grabs the fabric I used to cover my breast and gently ties it around me before pulling me in for one last long kiss. Together, we mount our steed and head back.

We barely make it back in time to prepare for the ceremony. I'm putting the finishing touches on my hair in the bathing chamber alone when I hear Nueena and Tavien come in, and then Leon's soft laugh from behind the door at something Tav said. When I step out of the bathroom in my ceremony gown, the room goes silent except for Nueena's delighted gasp.

Hiliyah has outdone herself.

My strapless gown is made with a golden fabric that flutters around me. It is tight on my waist and hips before flaring out, but that's not what the three of them are staring at. The top of the gold corset is shaped like a giant crown that cages in my chest, the arch from each point sticking out. It is heavy, covered in yellow diamonds, lemon quartz, and golden garnet. The highest peak of the center presses into the space between my breasts. It would make any close dancing nearly impossible, but the visual is stunning.

Nueena comes forward, touching one of the yellow gemstones that top each arch.

"The perfect gown for the royal crown maker," she says, smiling at me.

I laugh. "*My* dress? Look at *yours!*"

Her gown's base is the same fabric as mine, but that's where the similarities end. The bodice is covered with a sheer fabric that rises up off her shoulders; strands of yellow pearls form small dangling sleeves. Across the top, gems have been sewn on, so it gives the illusion her skin is sparkling. A diamond-shaped cutout under her chest leads to her waist, where gossamer layers flow down. The skirt is sewn together with yellow gemstones and gold thread, so it glimmers when she walks. It is a gown strung from sunlight and highlights her dark skin beautifully.

Nueena does a happy spin, her gown shimmering in the light. "Now all I need is my crown," she teases.

"Ladies, you both are breathtaking, but we must be leaving now," Tavien says, coming behind Nueena with a hand on her back, leading her out the doors. He doesn't take his eyes off her.

I turn to face Leon, who is still staring at me, slack-jawed. His gaze flickers over the gold lining my eyes and gold dust on my cheeks and shoulders.

"You look stunning, like a queen." His eyes have a faint shine to them.

"Thank you." I stretch out my hand to him. He takes it, and together we head downstairs into the waiting crowd.

The ballroom where the crowning ceremony will be held has been decorated to reflect all the artistic talents that call the Gem Court home. Chandeliers hang dripping with diamonds beneath the intricate oil paintings on the ceiling with scenes from our court's history. Yellow roses wrap around the golden columns. Those who attend tonight wear their finest clothing in every shade of yellow.

Dancers twirl with ribbons while musicians play music they wrote just for tonight to celebrate Nueena. The walls are covered in portraits of her. Watercolors and oil paintings, lifelike and abstract. Glowing glasses of sparkling wine glint in everyone's hands as they toast to her.

Excitement is so strong I feel feverish. Many months ago, I was asked to create the crown for tonight. I had hoped, of course, to be asked, to share this moment with Nu. Historically, it is done by a master artisan, one whose years using their skills exceed my own, but Lazalai showed up at the palace one night and blessed me with the task.

To create a crown worthy to be given to our future Realm Keeper on behalf of the Gem Court was one of the highest honors my Guardian could have bestowed upon me.

Lazalai said that it would mean the most to Nueena if it came from me, and judging from the scream Nueena made when I told her I would be her royal crown maker, Lazalai had been right.

"I have to go to the dais. Stay nearby," I say to Leon over the music and head where I need to be for the ceremony, next to my crown, which sits beneath a satin cloth, waiting to be presented to Nueena.

The royal family stands at the top of the grand staircase, ready for their grand entrance. Each family member's name announced is met with thunderous applause from the crowd as they descend one by one.

Last is Nueena.

"Future Realm Keeper and ruler of the High Ellovian Court, daughter to Nyvenah and Alachite Verrelia, Nueena Verrelia, with her Zemra, Tavien Delwinn of the Ink Court."

Nueena and Tavien walk down the golden staircase hand in hand, Tavien's face bursting with pride for his Zemra.

The excited crowd parts to let Nueena pass, their joyous cheering endless as they toss marigold petals at her feet on the path to her throne. Nueena embraces Lazalai when she reaches her on the dais, and they both look at me as I pull off the cloth, revealing the crown I created on a plump pillow.

I'm overwhelmed with gratitude that the crown was completed before my magic was overshadowed. If I had delayed or abandoned the honored responsibility, I would have disappointed Nueena, and the entire court would be asking questions.

Nu and I face each other, wearing twin smiles so wide and

joyous our cheeks will ache tomorrow. We mouth, *I love you,* at the same time, and our laughter is drowned out by the celebration around us. Everything that makes her an amazing friend will follow her as she steps into her role as ruler of the fae realm.

Her compassion, unending loyalty, and caring heart.

Her deep wish for everyone to know happiness and a life full of joy.

Nueena loves with all of who she is, endlessly and without restraint, and her friendship is a bright light woven into my life and the future of Ellova. My devotion to her is so deep in my soul, wrapped up in who I am. Adoration and pride burst out of me, my love for her luminous in my chest. I'm *so* honored to stand up here with her, to stand beside her 'til the end.

The crowd goes quiet, ready for their Guardian's words as I pick up the crown and gently hand it to Lazalai, who is giddy with excitement.

She holds my creation out to the crowd, the room erupting with cheers. "We pause our midnight amusements and salacious entanglements for a momentous occasion. Our dear Nueena Verrelia will soon be crowned our Realm Keeper. As long as she rules Ellova, we, her court of artisans and crafters, will stand beside her in support. She has always seen the value and dedication, the passion and intensity in our creativity and craft. Nueena deeply appreciates the strength and vulnerability it takes to create. She knows the significance art has on our culture and the value it plays in shaping our society. She has a vision for Ellova worth trusting. The fervor with which she will rule, the attentiveness to her court's needs, and her glowing compassion for all will be the foundation from which she will lead us all."

Nueena sits on the opalescent throne.

"And now, our gift to you." Lazalai stands beside her, gently placing the crown upon Nueena's curls.

As soon as it touches her head, it glows. I hold my breath as the enchantment begins, the golden crown coming to life, each closed flower blooming, as dozens of gold butterflies rise and flutter around her, leaving a bright trail behind them before they fly out around the crowd. Gold dust falls from their gilded wings to sprinkle atop everyone. The dust glides over each courtier's hands to form a single golden band on their fingers. Their gasps of delight warm me through as surely as the relief I feel that losing touch with my magic did not affect the enchantment. Many hold up their hands to the lights above, sending a wave of twinkling lights before Nueena.

Nueena looks back at me with tears streaming down her face. I give her a small nod of understanding at the look of thankfulness in her eyes. I motion for her to hold her hands together. When she does, all the golden butterflies dance back to her, kissing her fingertips before flying up and forging their open wings to the crown.

The gleam of my gift fades and so do the enchantments. The music shifts to a fast-paced melody, and the dancing starts, the lights lowering. Fae move and flow to the beat, bodies grinding on one another, as more wine is poured and passed around.

"Della, the crown is perfect." Delight glows on Nueena's beautiful features.

I point to the large amethyst nestled in the center of the crown. "The gem was part of Tavien's family trove. He selected the stone himself."

"Only the best for my Zemra," Tavien says, coming up behind her, wrapping his arms around her and pulling her close, pressing his face into her neck.

Leon stands with his hand outstretched as I walk down the stairs to him. "Let's dance, Izadella." He spins me around and pulls my back flush against him to avoid the spikes on the front of my gown. We join the mass of dancers on the darkened ballroom floor. Our hips move as one, shifting and flowing together. When I am not tucked against him, he is spinning me and pulling me back to him.

Every so often he kisses my shoulder or breathes deeply into my neck. His contented sighs during the slow songs and exploratory hands during the fast ones have my body alight.

I'm glistening with sweat and gasping for air when Leon finally glides us off the dance floor. "Let me get you something to drink."

I nod gratefully, and Leon makes his way through the crowd and out of my sight.

A hand slides around my waist, pulling me close, but instead of Leon's sweet herb scent I am met with patchouli and black pepper.

Kole.

CHAPTER 37

*K*ole spins me around to face him. "I knew you'd save a dance just for me." He looks far too pleased with himself and much too close as he uses his larger body to push me towards the dance floor.

Annoyance rolls through me, and I make no attempt to hide the expression from my face. Kole just smirks at me.

"You really must *ask* before one can accept the dance, and you," I say, shoving him away, "did not ask."

This only makes him laugh. It's not a malicious laugh, just one where he seems to think we are both in on the same joke, as if my expressed desire not to dance with him is some sort of playful game. I instinctively glance around for Leon. Not that I can't handle the fae male in front of me, but I'm worried about Kole's face meeting Leon's fist if he doesn't move away from me by the time he returns.

Unfortunately, Kole is a powerful fae and any retaliation on Kole's part could turn deadly for Leon.

Kole is wearing golden cuffs, which would've been perfect if I still had my powers. I could've molded the metal together and he'd be forced to spend the night begging any fae with metal magic or a blacksmith to help him. They wouldn't have, knowing no jewelsmith would have done that without cause and it was likely a result of wandering hands.

The dance floor is hot and the other dancing couples press close to us, which doesn't give me much space as I make a second attempt to remove myself from his grip.

The only reason I don't punch him in the face myself is the fact that Everett is his best friend and we've all known each other for so long. Kole simply wants what he can't have and enjoys the game of chase. The less interested I am in his advances, the more he takes this all as a challenge.

When he does let go, I ask, "Where is Everett? He should be keeping a tighter leash on you."

He just laughs again. "Everett stayed behind at the palace. You know he's no fun at parties."

"Believe me," I say, "I'd much rather be at a party with him than with you."

That wipes the smug expression off his face. He opens his mouth to say something crass, no doubt, the way his eyebrows are pulled together, but Kole's bitter scent is washed away by healing oil and herbs. Leon hands me both crystal goblets and moves to stand in front of me. Kole sneers at him, looking him up and down. Leon just glares back.

"Do you know," Leon says, "when I choose a dance partner, I like to pick someone who looks like they *actually* want to dance with me. You should experience it one day."

Kole takes a step towards Leon but Leon remains unwavering, still as a statue. "Stay out of this. I don't know who you are or which court you crawled out of, but she doesn't need a bodyguard," Kole says with a snarl, his face turning red.

I stand on my tiptoes and whisper, "Strawberry," in Leon's ear before I kiss his cheek, marking him as my dance partner.

Kole looks between the two of us, confusion taking over the anger. Leon turns to me with adoring eyes and pointedly says, "Let's go find a *dark* alcove to entertain ourselves in."

Kole's jaw drops at hearing his own words thrown back at him.

Leon and I walk away, our arms around each other's waist. I can still feel Kole's eyes on us as we leave the ballroom, which is probably why a moment later, I feel Leon's hand sliding down my back and grabbing a handful of my rounded backside.

We walk through a well-lit hallway; every inch of available space covered in art frames of every shape and size. Two fae men passionately kiss up against a giant portrait of some long-past court Guardian. Leon and I pass many dark alcoves, but most are occupied, the sounds of moans and fae enjoying themselves coming from inside.

"Is he always like that?" Leon asks, irritated.

"Yes. He's always been annoying, but it's only been within the past decade that he's gotten more bothersome. He doesn't want anything serious with me, just some careless fun. I promise, he's harmless."

"A man that does not accept a woman's no for any reason is not *harmless*. He has just *been* harmless up until this point."

"Are you hungry?" I ask, knowing the feast that awaits us will erase Kole from both of our minds.

He leans down with a sly grin, his lips brushing my ear as he says, "For some things more than others, but I've already licked my fingers clean so I suppose dinner will have to do."

The heat of my blush joins the dusting of gold over my cheeks.

~

*D*inner is an extravagant event. Five extremely long tables run down the length of the atrium with an assortment of Ellovian cuisines sitting on hot rocks to keep warm. None of the dishes or chairs match, each carefully crafted by individual artisans to reflect their unique style. As we walk between the tables to find our place, we pass firefaes crafting images with flame in the air and dancers spinning around them, their hips moving to the beat of the music in glittering skirts.

I've missed this place, every night alive and welcoming. Something in the air here makes me want to dance and paint and create. If I ever get my powers back, it'll be the first place I'll come to. I hadn't appreciated what all my court offered when my magic was still intact.

Lazalai sits with Nueena, Tavien, and the Verrelia family at the head of a table running the length of the dining hall. Since I'm looking to avoid any lingering conversation with Lazalai, Leon and I sit tucked towards the middle, my back to her.

We eat off each other's plates, sitting shoulder to shoulder and thigh to thigh. I bring him small bites of foods he hasn't tried yet. He barely takes his eyes off me, settling his hand on my inner thigh, brushing his thumbs up the fabric, which brings the memories of his fingers pumping into me, building an ache there. He must have the same memories; his smile widens as I blush.

The wine we have been drinking brings a flush to our cheeks and a wobble to our words. The alcohol has helped the pounding ache at my temple, but now I'm lightheaded, feeling better than I have in weeks.

"Let's take a walk," I declare with a hiccup.

Now that most of the dewlings are tucked in bed, bottles of a vibrant fuschia liquid are passed around.

"What is it?" Leon asks, intrigued, as we pass through the doors of the dining hall. A pretty fae woman passes Leon a glass with a wink, and I immediately hand it off to another passing fae before Leon can taste it. She has a male on each side of her, both gazing at her with lustful longing, as we head into the gardens. "Thanks!" she says delightedly, taking a drink before dripping some into each of their waiting mouths and walking off, leaving us alone.

I pause; my back pressed to a marble pillar for support. Leon stands before me, moonlight making him glow as his hands wander on my waist.

"It increases sexual pleasure and is meant to mimic Zemras' experience when they have sex," I whisper. I may have had my hand around his cock earlier, but a sudden shyness overtakes me, and I become very interested in our shoes.

"Sex with a Zemra is different, then?'"

"Well, of course! It's a soulbond." The world around me is getting fuzzy, my body swaying on its own, drunk off wine and Leon's nearness. "Zemras can feel each other's emotions, especially their pleasure. Their arousal is heightened with shared orgasms, shared magic."

Leon takes my chin in his hand and brings my gaze up to him. His eyes darken, his grip on my waist tightening.

"What if that is something I want to share with you? Being Zemras? What if that is why we have been drawn to each other from the start?" He is staring at me with such intensity I laugh bitterly; it's too much.

"Leon." I say his name to give me a moment to figure out how to respond. "Zemra bonds are a form of magic, *fae* magic. You are mortal. It's not possible for us to be Zemras." Having a Zemra *is* what I want, what I've longed for, but it's not worth the pain of dwelling on it.

"We don't know that. We could try." His words are as tight as his jaw.

The look in his eyes, full of hunger, sadness, and desperation, sobers me. Suddenly I'm too hot, pain returning to my head.

"Leon, there are laws. It requires Lazalai's approval. You don't have a court to approve us speaking with the temple guides. Besides, we would need to be mates for decades before a temple guide would even consider speaking to us, and you know we do not have that time."

"Nueena and Tavien did it. They snuck in, and they figured it out. Why can't we? Why are you not willing to even attempt it?" His shoulders sink. "Are you waiting for someone else?" he asks, bitter betrayal crossing his handsome face.

I gasp, "No, no." I'm frantic to make him understand. "Zemras share magic, Leon. Magic is deadly to mortals. A soulbond to me while I'm still wearing this crown would kill you. It would not be the slow descent into madness you are putting yourself through now. With this much magic? You'd be dead. Instantly. I don't even understand why we're having this discussion! We are not *together*, Leon. We don't get a happy ending! You are here to assist with the elixir as long as you can and then you are leaving. Leaving Ellova, leaving this realm, leaving *me*." My voice cracks on the last two words but I can see something crack in him too.

The world around me blurs again. This time it's not from the wine or the headache threatening to consume me, but the tears running down my face. He offers everything I've wanted and it's agony to turn him away.

"I understand," Leon says stiffly, his hands retreating from my hips.

My stomach drops. "Leon, I—" *Please don't leave me.* It's on the tip of my tongue to beg, to scream, but that wouldn't be fair to him. He stares at me, waiting for me to finish what I was saying, but I can't ask him to stay. It's not fair to him; it never was. He's free to walk away from me, from this place. I suck my quivering lip between my teeth to hide what a mess I am until his back is turned.

I can't have him, but I can save my dignity.

Each fading footstep pierces my heart as I slide down to the floor, heart breaking all over again. Agony rips into me at the sight of him walking away, but Leon returns just as quickly as he left, crushing me with relief. He holds a goblet of water and kneels in front of me.

"Drink this," Leon says quietly, "and let's get some sleep, Strawberries."

I gape at him. "What?"

He presses the goblet into my shaking hands. "Drink. It's been a long day, and I would like to go to bed, preferably with you."

I have no words, so when he pushes the water upward, I drink deeply, his stern features softening with each sip.

Leon helps me rise on unsteady feet and offers me his elbow, which I gladly take. As we walk back, fellow artisans stop to congratulate me on the crown or appreciate their new rings. A reminder to them that their loyalty belongs with Nueena.

When we arrive at our rooms, we undress silently, his back to me. I almost tell him to stop being so prudish since he had his fingers inside me this morning, but maybe a reminder of what we did is not what he needs right now, so I crawl silently into bed. My back to him. He follows a minute after. I ache for him to pull me close, but I have no wish to be rejected, as I deserve to be.

He slides behind me, our hips pressed together, his lips moving slowly on the curve of my neck. "I recognize what you are to me, Izadella. Fate has destined our souls to be forged together. No Guardian's opinion matters, and no temple is necessary to prove what I feel for you, what I can sense deep within me. I don't need to hear it back tonight. If we part ways tomorrow, know that my soul is forever bonded to you, even if we never receive a soulbond."

A part of me demands to say it back, to spend the last few decades of his life trying to put into words these indescribable feelings I have for him, the knee-buckling need within me to never part from him, to howl the ways in which I desire him. That urge to forge my soul to his, it is its own kind of madness, one magic plays no part in.

I open my mouth to speak, but fear grips my throat. To admit it, even to myself, to declare my unyielding desires would be a dance with death.

CHAPTER 38

*L*eon is quiet the next morning. His smiles are soft, and his touches are frequent, but a wrongness lingers between us. It hangs in the air, tormenting me, but nothing can be said that I haven't already voiced. How we feel about each other does not change our situation. I'm ready to accept it, prepared to grieve and scream and cry and try to find a way to live a half-life without him.

Leon seems determined to fight fate 'til the end.

I can't decide if I want to kiss him for it or fall to my knees to beg him to abandon me. I don't know if I'm strong enough to continue resisting when he makes his desires so clear.

We spend our last day at Quartzridge by the sparkling lake, the four of us lounging in long, woven chairs, sipping on cold juice, and enjoying the sun. Nueena's sisters splash in the water nearby; Kaylena's happy screams join the chorus of singing birds and several musicians' soft melodies. I sit next to Nueena in an attempt to keep some physical distance from Leon. Nueena and Tavien both eye us with concern, having noticed the tension.

"How was the Airvell Spring?" Tavien asks cautiously.

"Collecting blutells went well. The bag is in our room. The part where I almost killed Leon did put a damper on the day, though."

Tavien reaches out and takes Nueena's drink to prevent her from spilling it everywhere right before Nueena sits up so quickly her chair shakes.

"What?" she demands.

Leon sits up as well. "She did no such thing. The crown thought I was attacking her and reacted; it was not her fault. Something I keep trying to tell her."

Nueena and Tavien glance at each other before Tavien narrows his eyes at Leon. "Why, exactly, did the crown feel you were attempting to do her harm?"

Leon looks briefly offended at Tavien's tone but is quick to explain we were just having fun, and I was never in any real danger. Nueena relaxes, lying back down and taking her drink back from her Zemra.

"Well," Nueena says, "this does prove the crown will protect against even perceived threats."

The crown needs to make up its fucking mind. Does it want to protect me or kill me? The way everyone's sympathetic eyes slide to me tells me it's clear they all had the same thought.

We have one last meal before we will travel back to the High Palace.

Lazalai sees us off and I can no longer escape her presence. "Will you stay a few moments after our royal family leaves?" Her signature happy disposition is not there, and her question implies it was not a suggestion.

I have no choice but to agree.

"I'll see you back at the palace later tonight," I whisper to Nueena, who nods, and I hand the enchanted bag of blutells to Tavien so he can get them to the apothecary.

"I'll stay with you," Leon interjects, visibly displeased with his instruction to leave with them.

I shake my head. "You have work to do with Tavien." Leon opens his mouth to argue but must think better of it and nods instead.

Lazalai and I wait for the last of the party to disappear before we turn to each other. "Let's walk, my dear." She loops her arm with mine. "I'm not sure what is going on, but you've been avoiding me, and after a century of adamantly avoiding romantic entanglements, you have Leon following you around like a lost pup. I'm worried about you." She stops and faces me when we reach a low balcony overlooking a lush garden. "Are you all right?"

"I'm fine, just overwhelmed with all the coronation preparation." I smile at her. "I would come to you if it was something you could assist with."

She rubs her temple. "Della, I *know* something is wrong. I can sense it. I won't demand honesty if you will not freely give it. I know much of your loyalty and life lies with the High Court, but you have a home here too. You've made vows to this court, and to me." She takes my hand. "I'm here if you need me."

"I know. I've always known that." Guilt mixes with affection for my Guardian. "Thank you for everything." I pull her in for a hug, unwilling to add to the lies, but I have no truth to offer her.

She pulls away and with a mischievous grin asks, "So which court is Leon from?"

"He's a healer, and we are not together. Or not in the way you think. He's working with Tavien and only here for a short while. Once he is finished, we will part ways. I really must be getting back to them."

"You might want to let him know that," she says, her eyes kind and her words sympathetic.

"What do you mean?"

"He looks at you the way Tavien looks at Nueena, just with more open longing. It's sweet." She reaches up and cups my cheeks. "You deserve to be happy for whatever time is offered. Don't let the ending ruin the beginning."

To assuage my own guilt, I stay with Lazalai most of the evening, reminiscing on our past and all the current court drama, knowing that I have at least completed my task of acquiring the blutells and that Tavien and Leon can make progress while I'm here. When I finally return to the High Court, the royal wing is empty. As I lie in bed, the moon is high in the sky before I hear the library door open. I hold my breath, waiting to see if Leon will join me, but then his bed creaks when he sinks into it, and my heart follows.

Maybe this is for the best, but my bed has never felt so cold.

~

The early-morning sun is bright and spilling through the windows as I take deep breaths through the sharp pain in my abdomen. After slowly making my way to the bathing room, I strip off my stained nightgown, drop it to the marble floor, and pull down one of the large shells, letting the hot water flow out of the wall into the small bathing pool in one corner, next to the large green translucent windows.

I pour in fragrant oils and dried sea foam from the Meridia Cove tide pools.

Large bubbles cover the top of the water as I sink into it, twirling my hair around the crown in a twist. Some falls back in my face but I do not have the energy to fix it. The warmth helps to ease the pain crawling up my spine.

I'm resting my eyes when a knock sounds and Nueena pokes her head in. She's wearing a purple gown that wraps tightly around her with a deep neckline that crosses below her neck. The long train of it follows her. She's barefoot and takes a seat at the edge of the pool, her legs tucked under her.

"Bleeding started during the night?" she asks.

I can only nod and rub my hands over the soft flesh of my stomach, letting the warm water soothe the muscles. "Unfortunately. It will be over in three days, plenty of time before the ball." I try to control my breathing through the pain. In and out, in and out.

"Want me to get the healer for some herbs?"

"No thank you, they never work anyway. What's on your schedule today?"

Nueena picks up one of the oils, inhaling its sweet scent. "We are meeting with some court representatives about the ballroom decor, wine tasting at the Court of Green's vineyard, and attending a birthday celebration for the Court of Shells' Guardian at their pool pavilion this evening if you are feeling well enough."

I groan, not from the pain within me but from missing a trip to the vineyard. "I think I will take a rest day. Will you tell Leon I'm not feeling well and keep him entertained for the day?"

She laughs. "If you want a man to leave you alone when you are ill, you shouldn't have chosen a healer. He can come with me and Tavien, of course, but I'm sure he would much prefer to be by your side."

I lie in bed in fresh linen pants lined with folds of fabric and a soft wrapping around my breasts to help with the temporary ache in them. The bath helped some of the pain, but it still feels like a hot dagger has been sheathed through my insides as the cramps continue. Maybe I should try to read in bed, but the ache in my chest completely unrelated to my bleeding threatens to hurt even more.

I recognize what you are to me, Izadella. Fate has destined our souls to be forged together. No Guardian's opinion matters, and no temple is necessary to prove what I feel for you, what I can sense deep within me. I don't need to hear it back tonight. If we part ways tomorrow, know that my soul is forever bonded to you, even if we never receive a soulbond.

This man! This beautiful, protective, and kind mortal man. Leon is everything I never hoped to find. How could the sweetest words burn so painfully? He gives his heart so freely to me, asking for nothing in return except that we try. Try to find a way to make this impossible relationship work. To give him my heart as freely as he's given his.

As if my thoughts summon him, the bedroom door that is rarely kept closed immediately swings open after a frantic knock without waiting for a response. Leon swiftly walks in and looks me up and down, assessing me.

"Why didn't you call for me?" That strong jaw clenched tight.

Guilt trickles in. "Leon, everything is all right. It's not something I wanted to worry you about."

"Are you ill? Nueena said you weren't feeling well and tried to recruit me to approve ballroom decorations and go swimming." He hovers over me with impatient concern on his handsome face.

"You have excellent taste. I'm sure you'll be helpful." It's meant to be a tease, but a cramp hits and I suck in a breath involuntarily.

He looks even more alarmed at this.

"Calm yourself, Leon. It's just my bloodline bleeding, nothing I haven't been dealing with for a century. I promise, it's fine. Please go enjoy a day about the palace. Nueena and Tavien will keep you fully entertained today, and the pool at the Court of Shells pavilion is divine. Let the Ellovian royals show you a good time."

He sits on my bed. "It won't be a good time if you're not there. Now, what hurts?"

I sigh. Fae are open when it comes to our bodies, but I've heard mortals have different ideas. Though, as a man of medicine, Leon is likely far more understanding. "Just temporary pain. Please go with them. There are parties happening all over the kingdom, and as Nueena's guest, you have an invitation to all of them."

He is about to argue with me again, but we both look towards the strong knock on the open doorframe. Nyvenah stands there with a smile and a covered tray. She wears an embroidered deep purple sleeveless robe over a vibrant green gown. Leon stands and gives her a deep head nod that makes her laugh.

"None of that. Please sit back down."

Leon follows her instructions as she brings the covered gold tray to my desk and uncovers its delicious contents.

There are two golden teacups and a short milk pot, and matching it all, is a teapot with little emerald leaves on its base. Next to the teacups is a small tray of creamy dark chocolate truffles with crushed golden shortbread on top. Pouring the tea into a cup, she adds in a generous splash of the milk and brings it, along with the truffles, over to me. "How are you feeling, my dewling?"

"Better now, thank you." I hold up the cup in gratitude before taking a sip of the sweet almond tea with its nutty notes layered with honey and a hint of caramel.

"Good." She gives me an affectionate pat on the top of my head as she always did when I was a dewling. "I'll come check on you later and see what you would like for dinner if you cannot make it down to the dining chamber, all right?"

Her motherly concern has always been such a gift in my life. "Thank you, Ny."

Nyvenah gives Leon and me another bright smile before leaving.

Leon waits 'til he hears the front doors close before giving me a puzzled expression, but I only give him a smile as I sip on my delightful tea, watching him with amusement as he thinks of how to phrase the question I know he is finding a polite way of asking.

He takes a moment before speaking. "Why is the Realm Keeper of Ellova personally bringing you tea and chocolate in a palace overflowing with helpful attendants?"

"Cause I'm not feeling well and she loves me, hence the tea and chocolate." I give him an innocent smile.

Setting the teacup down and picking up the plate, I choose the biggest piece of chocolate and plop it into my mouth. It melts on my tongue, and a happy moan escapes my lips at the rich, bitter flavor of the cocoa.

I offer him a truffle. "No chocolate in Adreania compares to the taste of Ellova's candy." And I eat another one.

He only watches my tongue dart across my lips as I lick away the chocolate there.

"And she was made aware of your monthly bleeding because?"

I give in to end his confusion. "I'm on shyrell. It is what we call resting during bleeding. Magic is passed down through birth. Since any fae bleeding typically displays the possibility of fertility to carry on the magical bloodline, it is a sacred tradition for the heads of the family to bring tea and sweets. It is like a little thank-you for the suffering to one day continue the family's magic in a way. Bleeding is treated with great care and rest here, and I am, unfortunately, more mortal than fae in this regard so I suffer five or six times a year instead of only once, but it only lasts two or three days."

His eyes soften at that. "And Nyvenah treats you like her own."

I only nod and close my eyes, savoring the chocolate flavor.

"Are you having cramps now?"

Nodding again, I feel him shift from the bed, and I peek one eye open as he stands above me.

"I'll be right back, then." He leaves the room and returns a minute later with his worn leather medical satchel. "I have something that will help. That is, if you would allow my touch." He holds up a crystal vial of a soft pink oil.

"Of course, Leon." Before I can stop myself, "Always" slips out.

His relief is immediate, as if he expected me to say no. "I would need access to your stomach to massage it in."

A flutter of tension builds low in my gut at his words. It is on the tip of my tongue to say that I possess the ability to place the oil on myself, but I'm hungry for his touch, *greedy* for it, and I need to make things right between us. "All right."

He moves onto the bed. "I will need to get close."

I pull back the blanket and spread my thighs wide to give him space. He pauses for a moment, looking at my exposed skin as if surprised by the invitation of the intimate position. He slowly kneels in front of me, between my thighs, and I drape my legs over his knees. The wrap covers my breast, and I pull the light pants lower, exposing more of the round softness of my stomach as he pours the oil into one hand.

He holds eye contact, staring down at me, his green eyes lit with such hunger as he rubs his hands together to heat the oil. His fingers are light touches, and they start low on my hips and work their way up, moving in soft circles, pushing the oil into my skin. I close my eyes as the scent hits me.

It smells like him.

Bright strawberries and woodsy herbs.

His hand movements are bordering on sexual, not the massage of a skillful but indifferent healer, but the hands of a lover. He knows exactly where to apply pressure over the pain but is gentle when he moves around my hips and waist.

I moan freely as the pressured circles dissolve the pain, the dull ache of the cramps fading away every second his hands are on me.

"Turn over. Let me massage your back." It's a soft demand, and for a moment I debate which I want more, his hands on me again or to kiss him. I cannot stand another moment without his lips on mine, so I grab the front of his tunic and pull him down over me.

His lips open to me greedily, his tongue sweeping in. I moan into his commanding kiss. Leon's hands circle around my waist; my back bows as he pulls me up towards him. We stay like that for a long time, locked in a tight embrace but never going beyond soft kisses. He kisses me until I pull away with a small gasp, needing air. His lips move down my neck to show the skin there attention with gentle sucks.

"Leon," I breathe, and he moans into my neck at the sound.

"I know, Strawberries, I know."

The dull ache in my lower back demands his healing touch, and he lets me go so I can flip over. I hate the clothes we wear, the separation it brings. I want us skin to skin.

Leon rolls down my pants even lower to just above my backside and leans forward to place a lingering kiss between my shoulder blades, undoing the tie around my breasts so my back is fully exposed. He gets more oil and moves up and down my back, switching between blissful pressures. Starting at the top near my shoulders, he makes loops and swirls, going side to side. He presses low to my backside before working his way up, just to repeat the caress. I giggle into the silk pillow as he does it two more times, each of his playful touches getting a little lower.

The scent of him is so strong I can almost taste it. The warmth of his palms, the deep strokes, the gentle caresses, relieves the ache in my back and head. The press of his hands softens until he is drawing lazy swirls on my back with his fingers, which draws me towards sleep.

It is truly divine.

I can sense the smile on his lips as he kisses my cheek. "Get some sleep." I expect him to leave, but he re-ties my top and lies down with me.

I curl into his side, and he pulls me close before he gently places the blanket over us.

CHAPTER 39

I've recovered from my bleeding and Nueena and I are in the command room with her parents and Lillian, taking a rare break from the makeshift apothecary.

Tavien, Leon, and I work from sunup 'til sundown on the elixir, stopping only for meals or coronation planning. Leon and I have avoided speaking about the events at Quartzridge. I catch him staring at times, but he always looks away when I notice.

I'm weaker and weaker every day, the magic taking its toll on me, but I do my best to hide it from them, not wishing them to worry.

Plans for the coronation are strewn about with the estimate of food that will need to be traded, and the amount of palace attendants needed. The late-afternoon sun brings a glaze of gold to the room.

Kaylena runs into the room, the doors slamming behind her, rattling her family's portrait.

"Delly, can you take me to the chocolate shop? Everyone is busy with the crown party." She sends a pout in her mother's direction for emphasis.

"As long as your mother says it's fine, I would love to go to the shops." We both look at Nyvenah with the same hopeful expression.

Nyvenah just chuckles as she puts down the quill she was writing with. "You may go. Bring me back some of those chocolates with the buttercream inside. Take a guard with you." We've never needed a guard for a simple shopping excursion before, and my surprise must show on my face because she adds, "We're so close to the coronation, I don't wish to take any chances."

"Of course."

Lillian leaves and returns with Everett, who is carrying the leather-bound book I lent him a while ago. He hands it to me with a lopsided grin. "Here, I wanted to make sure I got this back to you. I heard some chocolate was in order?"

"Everett!" Kaylena shouts with delight, racing over to him.

"Hello, Kaylena! Are you ready for some chocolate?"

"Yes! Yes! Delly, let's go!" She bounces around before taking his hand and pulling him out the doors.

He looks back at me with a playful expression. "Come on, Delly!"

Everett's carefree attitude and kind disposition make him cheerful company on the short walk out of the palace and into the bustling city center. The Lavencia market around us is rich with the scent of perfumes and oils from the perfumeries' open windows, mingling with the rare spices and roasting meats from street vendors. We pass shops selling delicate candles, custom stationery, and specialty foods, moving out of the way of the lively crowds teeming from one business to the next.

"Della, are we in danger?" Kaylena asks.

"No, no. Sometimes a little extra protection can go a long way," I say, trying to sound like she has nothing to worry about. Nyvenah requesting a guard means we are no closer to discovering who the traitor is.

"Can I wear your dagger?" she asks Everett eagerly. "Then I can protect myself!"

"You may, but you cannot take the dagger out unless you are in danger, and you can only wear it until we get back to the palace. Deal?" He holds out his hand to shake her small one.

"Deal!" she squeals.

I laugh at this, and Everett slips off a thin belt that holds one of his daggers in its sheath and puts it over her shoulder.

She puffs out her chest with pride, holding on to the belt as we walk. She drags us over to a flower shop and stops to smell the bouquets on display in front of the frosted windows.

"Sorry you're on babysitting duty," I tell him as he leans down to smell the lavender bundles.

"That's quite all right. Anything is better than listening to Kole harp on how you rejected him," he says, his eyes sliding to mine with a playful glance.

"Ah, he told you about that, did he?" I mirror his mirth.

"Oh, yes, he may be grumpy about it 'til the next coronation."

"Good! His ego needed it."

Everett laughs. "That it did; that it did."

"I've made it increasingly clear I have no interest in him."

"That only adds to the allure, I'm afraid."

I roll my eyes. "It really shouldn't."

"I've repeatedly told him to leave you be, but if it happens again, let me know. I will shove him into the harbor and make him swim to shore. It's not as if he could complain to Lillian about it."

The mental image is a delightful one. "I would appreciate that. How's your family? Is your mother excited for the coronation?"

"Oh, you know her. Obsessed with nature, as always. She's definitely looking forward to the coronation, though. We all agree Nueena will make for an excellent ruler of Ellova. Even when we were dewlings, she was a natural leader. Remember when our teacher fell ill unexpectedly and no one from the Ink Court sent another scholar to teach for the day? Nueena just took over the lessons without a second thought." We both laugh at the memory.

With the coronation so close, every shop seems busier than expected. Hiliyah's display windows are full of new fabrics to entice customers, lush velvets and shining silks, and she has a line wrapping around the corner.

We can smell the chocolatier before it even comes into view.

Everett holds the door open for me and a bouncing Kaylena. The three of us are greeted with the gratifying scent of roasting cocoa beans. The chocolate confections sit behind long countertops covered with arching glass, and the shelves have everything from tall chocolate liqueur bottles to chocolate-dipped candied fruits.

Kaylena rushes to the sweet treats, her face pressed to the glass, gazing at the rows and rows of luxurious truffles dusted with a thick layer of cocoa powder.

Everett lifts up Kaylena and asks for Nyvenah's buttercreams. "Should we get some for your sister too?"

"Yeah!" Kaylena scrunches up her nose, leaning against me. "She likes the salty ones."

I laugh and order Nueena a few of the buttery caramel pieces with salt from the Elbasan Sea and some smooth hazelnut truffles for Tavien. Leon seems to love how overly sweet everything tastes here, and I find the perfect one for him among the decadent selections: a milky chocolate with a creamy brown sugar center.

Rich like all the fae food, and sweet like him.

We leave with our trades and head back to the palace.

Everett holds out his bag. "Here, have some. I know they are your favorite."

I peek inside and reach for the dark chocolate kneaded with crushed walnuts. "You remembered!"

"Of course, they are my favorite too."

I eat a few more pieces and lick the rich and velvety texture off my fingers as Everett escorts us back to the palace.

He looks back and forth, surveying the crowd, before his hand goes to his sword. I pick up speed, tightening my hand in Kaylena's, and turn to attempt to find where he is looking but he quickly spins around. I desperately search the crowd, but I see nothing suspicious or out of place. No one is paying us any mind as they walk from shop to shop.

Kaylena looks from me to Everett, who has drawn his sword, and eagerly asks, "Can I take out my dagger now?"

"No, no, Everett is just being careful," I say, still scanning around us. I feel nothing, no eyes on us, and no sensation of being followed.

Everett makes a whistling nose and two guards from the Court of Swords appear. "Take them back to the palace," he orders before he dashes off into the crowd. The new guards take their positions on each side of us. They keep their swords tucked in their sheath but continue to assess for some invisible danger.

My stomach is in knots by the time we arrive at the palace steps. "I need the commander *now*," I tell the first honeyguard I see, who dashes back inside.

Lillian must have been nearby. She comes racing towards us, Nyvenah on her heels. "What's wrong? What happened?" Lillian frantically looks over Kaylena, and then at me for injuries.

Nyvenah picks Kaylena up, showering her with kisses. Before I can answer, Kaylena shouts, "Everett's back!"

Lillian, Nyvenah, and I spin to find him stalking towards us. "There was a hooded figure following us. I tried to follow but they escaped," Everett explains angrily.

"Where?" Lillian demands, sending honeyguards to search for whoever was foolish enough to attempt to harm us, and he tells her everything.

"Thank you, Everett." Nyvenah opens one arm to me, and I join Kaylena in their embrace. "No one leaves here without multiple honeyguards from now on."

"Della, are you all right?" Everett asks, placing his hand on my upper arm. "I'm going to come check on you later tonight, all right?" I nod and he gives me a sad smile.

Once Kaylena is taken upstairs with Nyvenah and Everett escorts Lillian back to the market, I go in search of Leon. Light crystals keep me company during the journey to the royal gardens. Once my heart has stopped racing, it is a pleasant walk. The sun has set, and now the stars shine above me, a slightly sweet evening breeze in the air.

Through the foliage, Leon's lone form is visible as he works. He checks a plant's leaves and writes something down in his book before moving to the next one and taking more notes on its progression. A bird with blue wings sits on a branch near him, but it takes flight when I get closer.

I want to tell him what has happened, but I also know how he will react.

Leon's shoulders are tight, and exhaustion is evident in his body, yet he continues to document, unwaveringly, assisting with the creation of the elixir. When he finishes, he walks towards the small flowing water basin, rolling up his sleeves, revealing the tight muscles in his forearms while he washes his hands of the day's soil.

I stand there, staring at his arms, my mouth dry, desire snaking through my body. A memory flashes of those arms flexing as he moves his fingers inside me beneath the flowing spring.

There's been tension between us since he soothed my pain away last week. We have not brought up what happened on the beach or the kiss I gave him on my bed. Every night this week he has worked late with Tavien, slipping into his own bed, away from me. I have spent the midnight hours torn between calling out for him and leaving him be, knowing this is all for the best. Even if it feels like I'm ripping my own heart out in doing so. It's been days of longing glances, polite conversations, and this aching physical distance that gnaws at me.

I hate it.

He notices me watching him, half-hidden in the dark of the archway.

"Come here. I want to show you something," he says, walking over to where he has been taking notes.

Since I've known him, he's spoken of finding a cure, spending countless hours seeking an end to the suffering of the Adreanians. How many bedsides was he called to only for them to pass away before him? How many white sheets did he pull over faces while families wept around him? Leon is a selfless man, pouring all his energy into helping the mortals, desiring nothing in return. It warms my heart, and as we stand before each other in the garden, I am overwhelmed at the sight of him.

New vines twist around his ankles, and Leon looks down at the plant attack taking place at his feet. He laughs. "I think the strawberries are happy to see me."

Deep red strawberries bloom out along the vines and Leon reaches down to remove one before biting into it. He closes his eyes and lets out a contented sigh.

"Are you not sick of that traitorous fruit yet?" I mean the words, but they hold no bite.

He turns to face me and steps even closer to me. "Never." His voice is low, unwavering. "How could I ever be sick of them? They are the sweetest reminder, tangible proof, that you feel for me what I feel for you."

Emboldened by the darkness and the selflessness of his heart, I can no longer bear to keep my hands to myself. I wrap my arms around his neck, knowing I may regret it but unable to deny myself of this touch. He makes a startled noise and drops the half-eaten fruit on the ground, hauling me to him, his hands sliding on my hips, wrapping around me.

"I need you. Kiss me. Touch me," I beg.

I will not hold back from him a moment longer. I need all of him, desperate for him to fully consume me. For the fire between us to burn away the fear of losing him.

"Always." His voice is just as husky as my broken plea, and he kisses me with all the lust and longing that has been building within us for so long.

CHAPTER 40

*A*ll those longing glances and sweet touches.

All those nights I slept in a cold bed and dreamt he was near.

All those times I told myself it was better to stay away.

Under the stars, our shadows are lined with moonlight, our mouths moving together, and, unlike our first kiss at the spring, this one is unhurried, our lips exploring each other with slow, delicate brushes. He takes his time moving down my neck until he finds a spot that makes me moan, sucking gently and focusing there until I squirm. My fingers are in his hair, desperate to keep him near. He is content with the soft kisses, but I am not. I move my hand to the front of the impressive bulge that has grown between us, rubbing him over the fabric of his breeches.

He stops his exploration of my throat to kiss my forehead. "Izadella, we do not have to." His voice is kind, yet slightly strangled.

"Stop speaking."

He does stop talking, but he also stops my hands from their inspection of his body, holding my wrists tightly to my sides as he leans down so we are at eye level. "That is not how this works, Strawberries. You can tell me what you want, or we stop this, and I will return to showing you the detailed flower analysis I completed. I will not have you leave here with regrets."

"I could never regret you!" A tidal wave of longing crests between us. "*Please*, I'm desperate for you. This is agony, Leon."

His eyes soften, and he releases my wrists. "I know."

I start to tremble. "Touch me?" I ask with a whimper.

That is all it takes. His lips return to mine as we tell each other how we feel with touch and taste, his kiss transforming from slow and teasing to rough and demanding.

I love it.

I love *him*.

I meet Leon's hunger with my own. One moment we are kissing, and the next I'm pulling at him, desperate for more of him. My attempt to push him down is unsuccessful, and he laughs at my efforts in the curve of my neck. He takes off the cloak he's wearing, drapes it on the ground between the planters, and lowers me to the soft fabric, positioning himself above me.

Beneath the flowers, the air is full of healing floral notes and Leon's scent. More strawberry bushes bloom around me, small white buds bringing forth plump, red berries.

Leon moves slowly down my body. I pull up my gown and he lets out a small laugh at the sight of my dagger strapped to my thigh. He carefully avoids the weapon and holster when he slides the lace undergarment off me, which he pockets with a smile. Now that my thighs are open to the night air, he spreads them wide before he trails soft, unhurried kisses down them.

"Izadella, can I taste you, truly taste you?" He stares at my exposed center, waiting for my response.

I nod frantically.

But that is apparently not enough since he continues waiting, his eyes sliding to my face with one eyebrow raised.

"Yes, yes, Ellova's grave, yes!"

When he finally settles between me, my legs over his shoulders, he unleashes himself to devour me. His lick up my cunt is swift and consuming until he reaches my aching clit, going back down to my center to dip his tongue into me, teasing but deliberately avoiding exactly where I need him. The infuriating man.

I moan my displeasure and drop my hips, desperate for his tongue to follow, only for him to pull away from me.

"You will not come 'til I have had my fill, and I'm just getting started."

He slips his full tongue back inside me and pumps his head back and forth for a moment of friction before he finally brings his mouth to my clit and slips two fingers into me. His tongue explores me, devours me, first long and slow, and then frantic and feral.

A starving man at his own personal feast.

"Please, Leon, you need to go faster. Please, please, please," I pant, gasping for air as the pleasure he is giving drives me closer to the edge.

Leon's thumb swirls on my clit while two fingers roughly pump into me, stretching, building a new pressure. "Do you know how long I've waited to taste you like this, open before me, ready to be worshiped? It's been *agony*, knowing how honeyed you are between your thighs while you slept in the next room without me."

I beg and plead and whimper at his confession.

His reply to my begging is the press of his tongue to my clit, drawing rough, magnificent circles around it, sinking into the desperate nerves there over and over again while I moan, the sound echoing off the high garden walls. Just when I am about to go over the edge, he slows, his tongue moving down. He pulls his hand away and uses his thumb to move rapidly over my clit, his tongue circling my center that his fingers have stretched, dipping inside. I am panting, desperate to finish, and groaning his name. He must know what I want because his touch returns to their home inside me, and he moves the two digits in and out with leisurely pumps, driving deep. He slides his tongue up, pulls my clit into his mouth, and hums while he sucks.

Leon breathes into my center in a ragged breath, running his nose over the inside of my thighs, and growls into me, "This dripping cunt is mine, Izadella, only ever mine." His teeth sink into the soft flesh, not deep but enough that I scream, his fingers still rocking inside me.

"Yes, yes, yours. Only yours!" I wish to weep at his claiming words.

"No one else will ever know your taste, your touch. I will cut out their tongues if anyone else *dares* to taste you."

He moves his curved fingers in time with his circling, and his tongue returns to its blissful assault on my senses. Each pump of his hand presses inside me as he licks and sucks with ferocious intent.

Leon speeds up his hand to a steady rhythm while his tongue moves in endless circles, my moans guiding him to the perfect spot.

"Yes! Just. Like. That." Each word pauses with a gasp.

My orgasm crashes into me, sending my back bending towards the stars as the pleasure explodes through me like a lightning strike. My hips jerk, overwhelmed with sensation. He groans with satisfaction; his tongue slows but he continues to lick and tease my overstimulated center as if he found paradise between my legs. Elation ripples through me.

After one last, long swipe of his tongue, he finally raises his head, and we stare at each other. He chuckles, his lips wet, and he grabs the thickest, ripest strawberry off the bush next to us. Leon looks at it with a playful smile, spreads me wide with two fingers, and slowly slides the plump fruit through the mess we made between my thighs, circling my overly sensitive bud once before bringing the glistening fruit to his lips.

He chews with his eyes closed and moans in pleasure at the taste. "The sweetest delicacy I've ever had."

As I watch him savor the glazed fruit, arousal pours into me, burning like white fire into my blood. I *need* him. Every part of me needs him. Inside me, on me, skin to skin. I reach up, grab him by the collar, and crash his lips into mine. His devouring kiss tastes like sweet summer strawberries and my own essence. I lick and suck his lower lip until I'm boneless with satisfaction and he's tearing himself away from me.

Faster than I have ever seen him move before, he rips the dagger out of its sheath on my thigh.

"I need this for a moment, love," he says, and I yelp as he grabs the fabric of the gown bunched around my waist and roughly pulls it down before his arm wraps around my waist. He stands, taking me with him, and shoves me behind him as dark figures approach us.

The three unmistakably male figures have black fabric covering their faces. One laughs mercilessly at the sight of Leon standing in front of me with only my dagger.

"Step away from her and she will not be subjected to the view of your head being removed from your body," he says to Leon.

"No," Leon snarls at them, "but she may watch *your* death if she wishes."

The other two males' fists erupt in crimson flames, and they launch fireballs at Leon. Leon shoves me out of the way but isn't quick enough to save himself as well; the fire burns the fabric away as he grunts in pain.

The magic rises within me, ready to defend, but then an iron net is thrown over me. Like a candle being blown out, the iron nullifies the magic within me.

"Watch it! We need her alive!" the third figure yells at the first.

The fire lands in the planter growing the anafaea flowers, incinerating the precious plants we need for the elixir, before spreading outward into the gardens. One of the males is sending more and more fireballs.

"NO!" My scream for the ignited flora turns into a scream of terror for myself as one of the firefae grabs both of my arms from behind to drag me away. His armor clicks, and rage boils within me when my call to my metal-wielding goes unanswered, the crown's magic just wisps of fog.

He shouts next to my ear, "I got her—"

Leon's arm flies past my face, lodging my dagger in the male's eye socket. The attacker's shriek of pain turns my stomach, but his grip loosens enough for me to struggle away. Blood from his injury soaks my hair and streaks down one side of my attacker's face in waves as he launches forward, half-blinded, at Leon, but another impact quickly takes out his other eye. Leon shoves him to the ground and rips my dagger out of the dead fae's skull.

The other firefae attack from behind, and one drives his blade towards Leon. It slices into Leon's arm as he shields me again, and the other attacker rips me away from Leon by my hair. Leon's attacker turns back to my lover, and Leon's enraged face is the last thing I see before he is knocked unconscious.

No, no, no, no.

I love him.

I haven't told him yet.

He cannot die!

The net pulls taut and I am hurled to the ground. The other firefae drags me away while I fight to return to Leon, my nails breaking as I claw the dirt to get closer. "LEON! NO, *PLEASE!* LEON!"

Della's Strawberry Whipped Cream Tart
By Gabriela Leon @HappyGabyCooking

Shortbread Tart Shell:
6 inch tart pan with a removable bottom
1 cup of all-purpose flour
1/4 cup confectioners' sugar
1/4 teaspoon kosher salt
1/2 cup unsalted butter
1/2 teaspoon vanilla extract

Whipped Cream:
Hand or stand-mixer
1 ¼ cups of heavy cream (preferably cold)
4 tablespoons of powdered sugar
1 tablespoon of vanilla extract

Tart Topping:
1 pint of fresh strawberries

Optional: Two tablespoons of strawberry or apricot jelly

- Begin by making the shortbread tart crust. Preheat your oven to 350°F.
- Into a large bowl add in the flour, powdered sugar, and salt. Whisk them together until they are evenly distributed and set aside.
- Into a small pan over medium-low heat or in a small bowl in the microwave, melt the butter. Once the butter is melted, add the vanilla extract and stir together.
- Pour the butter mixture into the bowl with flour and stir together. This will create a very moist looking mound of dough.
- Into your tart pan, press the dough into an even layer in the bottom and up the sides of the tart pan. If you do not have a pan with a removable bottom, you can use a regular round pan but apply parchment paper first to

avoid sticking. Prick the bottom of the crust with a fork a few times to create ventilation holes for the pastry.

- Once the pan is ready, place the tart pan on a baking sheet and bake for 15 to 20 minutes or until the crust is golden brown. Let the tart shell cool completely before beginning to assemble the tart.
- Into a large bowl pour in the cold heavy cream, begin to mix using a stand or hand mixer until soft peaks have formed (about 3 minutes). Then add in the powdered sugar and vanilla extract. Continue whisking until stiff peaks are formed. At this point, taste the whipped cream to ensure that it is sweet enough to your liking. If needed, add in one more tablespoon of powdered sugar at a time until your desired sweetness is met but avoid overmixing.
- Prepare the toppings. Into a large bowl add in the strawberries you want to use and wash them thoroughly. Pat them dry with a towel or paper towels. Cut off the top of the strawberries and cut them in half lengthwise. Repeat this step with all of the strawberries and set aside.
- Into the tart shell, add in the whipped cream until there is an even layer that fills the shell.
- Place a strawberry half in the center of the tart, then arrange the rest of the strawberries into partially overlapping rings around it until all of the whipped cream is covered.
- Optional: Warm the jelly in the microwave in increments of 10 to 15 seconds until it is slightly runny. If needed, add in a teaspoon of warm water. Using a brush, layer a small coating of jelly over the strawberries and let set for five minutes.
- Serve and enjoy!

ACKNOWLEDGMENTS

To my parents who always let me be completely myself, even when that self was weird. I know it wasn't easy to have a neurodivergent child with too much personality and lots of stories to tell, but you raised me with love, kindness, and respect that was always free and never needed to be earned. Thanks for letting me draw on the walls and being so chill about me failing *all* of my math classes.

And to my mom, thanks for letting me turn your clean, minimalist dining room into a disastrous ADHD makeshift office space that drove you absolutely up a wall for years but let me be there anyway so I could write this.

To my sister-in-law and brother, who were so supportive and adamant about wanting to read this.

Thank you to everyone who read, posted, shared, reviewed, recommended, and commented. I could not have done this without you! Thank you for making this dream come true!

To my epic team! My rock stars! The best group of ladies a writer could ask for. I could not have done this without them!

First and foremost, Sierra, for being such an amazing friend and holding my hand during this whole process. Thank you for believing in this story on the days when I did not. For all the times you let me know it was gonna be okay, and for guiding me every single step of the way. For the late-night Zoom calls you spent helping me with this book, and for the writing advice, endless TikToks, and for being my first author friend.

Ash, who let me bounce ideas off her, was subjected to my never-ending chaotic voice memos. You remembered my own plot points when I forgot them. Thank you for the Smutty Sunday movie nights when I needed an escape. For all the things you spell-checked, and for being a great early draft proofreader and friend. They say don't meet up with strangers on the internet, but you always were a little rebel.

Mary, who asked the best questions, gave great story advice, and was so funny. I'm forever grateful for the time you put into *Ellova*. Sorry my characters did so much smiling.

My editor, Ivy, my literary goddess, my comma connoisseur, thank you for fixing the *thousands* of spelling errors, missing commas, and grammar issues. Who knew Google had a suggestion limit? You truly saved my dyslexic ass!

Genevieve, the ultimate hype woman. Your line comments made me laugh and your encouragement made me cry. I'm so glad we found each other.

Sandra, for your beautiful covers that brought my vision to life!

Hina, for her honest and helpful feedback on the early draft.

Gaby, for her fantastic strawberry tart recipe!

Jade, for wonderful feedback back when this was a 170k standalone.

My sensitivity readers:

Alexia, who will always have a very special place in my heart as you were the first person to read *Crown of Ellova* who didn't actually know me and still loved it. Your comments were hilarious; Tavien is all yours.

Stephanie, thank you so much for your insightful and beautiful feedback on this book.

Blair, for your wonderful feedback on Reyna, sign language, and insights on Deaf culture.

My killer beta reader team. Thank you! Thank you! Thank you! I will forever be grateful for your efforts to help this book shine!

Erin: Thank you for being so enthusiastic about this book! Your input was incredibly helpful!

Taylor: For your passionate feedback and fantastic insights I never would have seen myself.

Delani: I loved walking this debut author journey with you!

Justine: Thank you for loving my characters so much! If I could make Leon real, you could totally have him.

My writing community!

My writing groups, *Late Night Writes & Late Night Writes: San Diego*—Tehya, Mary, Taylor, Nicole C., Delani, Kristen, Genevieve, Bri, Fallon, Danielle, Sarena, Erika, Sierra, Brittney, Annie, Ashley, Nicole Y., and all the other members for joining me in my writing journey night after night. I started LNW with nothing but a Zoom account and a dream of building a writing community, and I'm so glad I found all of you!

Callie Dahl, Fallon English, and L.L. Graves for their friendship in this wild author world.

All my amazing fellow writers in the 2024 debuts and writer's sprint Discord/Slack groups. For all the support, suggestions, endless writing sprints, and community I found there. Y'all rock!

To my biggest cheerleaders—

Dannie, who was the first person to love this book, its very first fan, when it was nothing more than a few incredibly misspelled chapters and a dream. You never got tired of hearing about it and listened to me talk for two hours straight about it on that cold December night in 2021 over drinks. You loved this book from the start. Thank you.

To Hillary, the inspiration for Hiliyah, sliding into your DMs on Twitter was one of the best decisions. You cheered loudest and loved my characters like I did. A part of my heart will always be in Brazil with you.

Chelsea, the inspiration for Lillian, your epically fierce loyalty over the years has truly been a gift. Decades of friendship is not enough; let's plan for forever.

Jess, our souls just "clicked." Thanks for all the laughs. I love you to pieces.

To my favorite power couple—Nicole, *Crown of Ellova* was already dedicated to you but there are not enough words to express how much you mean to me. Your constant encouragement, loyalty, and sisterhood are the truest treasures in my life. Chris, I adore you. Thanks for reading *CoE* early, and for all the drinks you've made me while we watched rom-coms together and bonded over happy endings.

Linda, Lisa, Kimya, and Jamie—this book was born in quarantine. Thanks for making lockdown so much better.

And Linda, who kept my head above water in those early weeks when the world was ending. For doorstep pizza and happy hour baskets filled with pupusas and palomas. For the countless hours of work over video chat so I could body double. You were the lighthouse in my sea of despair that first month of covid. A part of Davion will live forever in Tavien.

Kayla and Britt, who came into my life when I needed them most.

Lindsay, my Prongs, for a beautiful friendship and childhood steeped in magic. Thanks for answering all those medical questions that I was too afraid to Google for this book.

To Scarlett, Malisa, Elliott, Hilary, and Nicole, thank you for over twenty years of friendship.

I couldn't write a book about friendship without mentioning my first friend, Lua. Wherever you are in the world, I hope you are safe and happy.

To all the members of the Book Slut Society of San Diego. I adore you sluts!

Smutty Brunch book club! Thanks for all the book talk over espresso martinis, eggs benedict, and sausage talk over sausages.

Joanne Crigamire, thank you for all the advice and support and for being such a great shoulder to cry on about being a writer with ADHD.

Liliver, who can't read this because she is a grouchy little cat and probably wouldn't read this book even if she had the ability to read. (She has more of a dark thriller vibe.) Thanks for the countless hours you slept at my side while I wrote.

Paru Tea shop and Lani—for all the matcha drinks while I wrote and for creating a place for creativity and community to bloom.

To all the authors that have inspired me over the years, especially Patricia C. Wrede, Holly Black, and Mary E. Pearson.

Rae Carson for her book *The Girl of Fire and Thorns*. The first book I read after many years of not reading and during the worst month of my life in 2020. Alone, terrified at the state of the world, and too sad to get out of bed, I put on the audiobook read by Jennifer Ikeda with a desperate desire to escape the dumpster fire that was reality.

It changed the *entire* trajectory of my life.

Thank you. Everything, absolutely *everything*, in my life after April 2020 I owe to you. The fantastic lifelong writer and reader friends, the renewed love of reading, this whole amazing bookish community, some of my best friends, and seeing Taylor Swift on night six in LA.

It cannot be overstated how much goodness was added into my life by reading that book. It lit the fires of a long-dead dream to write a novel. Rae, I truly cannot express how thankful I am for you and your book. Listening to the first chapter, my eyes burning from days of crying over a covid world, opened a door to this creative, passionate, and joyful life I'm blessed to live now.

Last, to my right hip and wrist for their sacrifice to this book.

<u>*Biography & Social Media*</u>

Sienna Harlow is a neurodivergent writer and digital artist from Southern California. She loves writing about fierce friendships, heroes with hearts of gold, and whimsical world-building.

As a storyteller with dyslexia, she is eternally grateful for spell check and compassionate editors.

When she is not daydreaming about romantasy, she runs two book clubs, a weekly writing group, and enjoys sending her friends an alarming amount of TikToks and voice memos.

Find Sienna all over the internet.
Instagram: @SiennaHarlowAuthor
TikTok:@SiennaHarlowAuthor
Twitter:@Sienna_Harlow
Substack: @SiennaHarlow
Patreon: SiennaHarlow

9 798999 168300 5